To Judy
Happy Reading!

Makeovers

Rex John

1

Kneeling, and without touching the form still huddled on the ground in front of him, he removed the protective cap from the syringe and slid it into his pocket. Following standard procedure, he then jammed the needle through the blanket-covered leg nearest to him. There was an immediate, tense jerk of the leg accompanied by a low, guttural noise -- then stillness. He waited, silently counting to ten, knowing the drug would have its intended effect before he even got to three.

Only moments earlier, Carson Kirkpatrick was talking to himself -- debating, really -- on whether he was more of a doctor or a teacher.

A teacher, he reasoned, instills new ideas and helps his students adopt new ways of thinking, and an excellent teacher can actually change the course of a student's life.

Even a stupid one.

On the other hand, a doctor can heal. A doctor can cut a patient open to extract the very thing that made him sick in the first place.

Even one who deserves to die.

As he pondered the question, he noticed that it had begun snowing again -- but only intermittently. The flickering street lamp at the far end of the alley gave the impression that the storm was being switched on and off every few seconds. When the light flickered on, big wide flakes were brightly visible in the reflected light of the high-pressure sodium bulb. But when it fizzled off, it left him kneeling in the dark. A flush of anger caused the muscles in his neck to contract. He squeezed his eyes tightly shut.

Carson was easily annoyed, although most who knew him would never guess as much. He subscribed to his father's philosophy that one must appear to be, at all times, "unflappable."

He smiled at the memory of his father's use of the word "unflappable." The old man was gone now, but his strongly held notions of what was right and wrong, acceptable and unacceptable, lived on.

Boy, do they.

The lamp fluttered again, this time causing him to clinch his jaw.

He caught his reflection in the rearview mirror and noticed that all of his features seemed set in anger. This was not acceptable; it was too telling. Studying his face, he wondered: was this something his father had done? He couldn't remember. But now that he was aware of it, he would simply stop doing it. He was, if anything, self-disciplined.

Discipline. That's what people need. Self-discipline is best, but if people can't discipline themselves then perhaps they need someone to do it for them.

Maybe he wasn't a doctor or a teacher. Maybe he was just a prison warden.

2

He looked over his shoulder to the flickering light. What kind of city would allow its street lamps to fall into such disrepair?

He realized now why he disliked coming downtown: it was too unkempt. He wished he didn't need to come at all, even though his only trips occurred when it was time to enroll a new student -- or patient, depending on whether he was a teacher or a doctor. Regardless, it was time to complete the task at hand.

The only question was, who was this new student -- or patient -- or prisoner?

The street lamp suddenly popped a last time before going completely dark. For a second, he thought about dialing 3-1-1, the city's "maintenance hot line." He smiled at the stupidity of the idea. *Yeah, right.* He would be taking no chances of anyone connecting him – or his cell phone – to Denver, Colorado on this particular night. He could imagine the headline: *World's Richest Man Apprehended in Denver Alley.*

He picked up his cell phone and touched it anyway, causing it to illuminate: 3:41 a.m. Only six minutes earlier he had been sitting in his van on the street at the end of the alley. He had noticed the *Denver Post* truck idling its motor against the curb in the next block, hazard lights blinking. He knew the driver was in a self-created staging area, waiting for three other trucks to line up behind him before all four proceeded another six blocks to the loading dock. On previous days he noticed the drivers would often get out of their trucks, engines running, and congregate on the sidewalk to swap lies and smoke cigarettes, their sophomoric laughter echoing up and down the deserted streets. He knew this morning's snowfall kept them in their trucks longer than usual, which was fine. Even so, the paper started coming off the presses at the prescribed time – 3:30 – and by now the first trucks would be loaded and rolling away from the dock.

To pass the time, he wondered what today's edition would hold. Mostly he ignored the local papers, not really caring if City Council wanted to increase the fees for parking meters or tighten the leash laws. He typically read the *Post* quickly, pausing only to shake his head at the occasional headline so poorly written that one was left wondering what the story could possibly contain. He preferred the *New York Times* and had read it from cover-to-cover for as long as he could remember. Even though he rarely agreed with the *Times'* liberal viewpoint, at least the stories were well-written. In contrast, these days his preferred source of news and stimulating thought was *Today's Conservative* -- although nobody would make the mistake of calling the stories "well-written." But at least they didn't mince words on what was wrong with the world: sick, stupid people.

Carson continued to kneel beside the still figure. He had located him under a large pile of cardboard and newspapers, stopping the van to stare at the blanket of trash to see if he could detect movement underneath. A mangled piece of cardboard with the words *This Side Up* printed in red ink seemed to provide the most cover. Toward the bottom of the panel, in the same red ink, was the well-known eco symbol and the request *Please Recycle*.

Exactly. Just what I've come to do.

Glancing around again, Carson noted that all was quiet, almost pretty. At least half an inch of snow had fallen in the past thirty minutes.

He withdrew a small camera from his parka. He wondered how good a photo would be with a backdrop of snowflakes. It was snowing hard now. Ordinarily he would have used the digicam, but he knew that would be hopeless because of the lighting. He took aim and pushed the button. The flash was blinding, but the lump under the cardboard remained still. He looked at the mini-screen on the back of the camera and determined that one could, indeed, see the outline of a body under the trash piled on top of it. It would be a nice souvenir for the student someday: a candid shot to accompany the first entry into his permanent record.

Hmmm. I said 'student.' I guess that's my answer. I'm not a doctor, I'm a teacher.

He re-pocketed the camera. He gently pulled the cardboard away and stood it neatly against the wall to await the city sanitation truck when it made its rounds a few hours later.

Only a haphazard blanket of newspapers remained. He stared at the pile trying to spot any movement, noticing, idly, yesterday's headline: *Body Of Missing Person Found in Park*.

An old Nike shoe stuck out at the edge of the paper. As he began removing pieces of the newspaper, one at a time, he folded them along their original creases. He didn't hurry, and he kept one eye on the form beginning to emerge as the papers were lifted. The body was pulled into a fetal position, an old dirty stocking hat pulled low as a defense against the cold. The figure was wrapped in an old Army blanket, which he simply left in place. He noticed a discarded McDonald's bag in the corner, filled with what he assumed were remnants of dinner – no doubt donated by some do-gooder in lieu of cash, or scrounged out of the dumpster behind the McDonald's down on 15th Street. He left the bag where it was. As he lifted and folded the last piece of newspaper, he watched for movement, even the smallest, most subtle movement. But the body was still.

He considered what to do next. Experience had taught him to be cautious, because it wasn't at all uncommon to be surprised with a knife or broken bottle brandished as a weapon. He hadn't yet encountered a gun, but with the proliferation of weaponry on the streets today, he knew it was just a matter of time.

He stood staring at the form at his feet. The Methohexital had obviously done the job. It had been his "enrollment inducer" from the beginning. Early on, he knew nothing about pharmacology, so he'd gone to the library to look up "Mickey Finn," an expression he'd heard while watching the film *The Maltese Falcon* with his grandmother. From there he learned about Flunitrazepam, Temazepam, Midazolam and finally Rohypnol, which would soon become popularized as the "date rape drug." He eventually found his way to Methohexital, but at first he couldn't think of where or how he could get some.

The solution came in the form of an addle-brained doctor who made a pass at him in a public men's room. The guy had no idea who Carson was, but as Carson pressed the guy's face into the filthy tile floor and threatened to kill him, he'd begged for his life, saying, "Please...don't kill me...I'm a doctor!" The guy didn't see Carson's faint smile at the inane remark, wondering if he possibly thought that being a doctor somehow justified allowing him to live. But he eased up on him and, after making it clear that there would be no sexual activity, he realized he'd found a source for the drug he needed.

MAKEOVERS - REX JOHN

3

The figure remained still. Satisfied that there was no longer any chance of surprise, Carson stepped backward to open the back doors of the van and grabbed the end of the lightweight gurney inside. Quickly tearing the velcro straps apart, he slid the gurney out and watched the wheels expand downward to touch the snow.

Pushing the gurney to the side of the now unconscious form, he lowered it to ground level. He tucked the blanket tightly around the figure before lifting it, with little effort, onto the gurney.

He realized he'd been unconsciously holding his breath. He knew from past experience that some of the students were pretty ripe at this point, and on at least one occasion the stench threatened to overwhelm him. Forced finally to breathe, he was pleased to note that there was no smell. *That's good. I guess you don't sweat much when it's this cold.*

Moving quickly, he shoved the gurney through the snow to the back of the van. Allowing the built-in hydraulics to raise the stretcher up to waist level, he easily pushed it inside, re-fastened the velcro straps and quickly shut the doors.

Can't hurt you now, Buddy.

MAKEOVERS - REX JOHN

4

The black van, now covered with snow, inched toward the end of the alley, windshield wipers trying valiantly to keep up with the snow, which was now falling hard and heavy. Carson pulled slowly onto 17th Street, even though there wasn't a car in sight. He knew the snow plows would arrive any minute now, blustering their way down the street, but leaving an even bigger mess in their wake. He continued down 17th to Broadway, where he made a full stop at the red light before proceeding cautiously, very cautiously, onto Broadway. This would not be a good night to be pulled over for a so-called "California stop." Besides, he thought, a California stop doesn't mean slowing down anymore; it means speeding up. That reminded him to check his own speed, which was exactly 30 miles an hour.

At 8th Avenue he turned west, toward the mountains, eventually merging onto the 6th Avenue Freeway, which carried him ten miles to the I-70 on-ramp. From there he knew he would have another two hours of driving, maybe twice that in this weather. If he was correct, he should arrive at his front gate no later than 8 o'clock, which was good, since his housekeeper didn't arrive until 8:30, and she might be even later this morning because of the weather.

He didn't like driving, but it was a good time to gather his thoughts and mentally work on his lesson plans. Now that he had decided he was a teacher and not a doctor, he would need to keep up with his lesson plans.

The school mission statement was straight-forward: first, remind each student that the world is in bad shape and getting worse by the minute. Second, if they want to change the world, they must imagine drawing a three foot circle on the ground and then stepping inside that circle. "Now," he would intone at this point in the lesson, "we will begin the process of changing what's inside the circle."

The problem is, most of his students didn't care that the world was such a mess, and they certainly didn't see themselves as part of the problem – nor did plan to do anything about it. As far as changing what was inside the circle, well, he knew his students were more concerned about getting the hell away from him than changing what was inside the circle. So, that was his job, and with few exceptions he'd done it well – as his graduates would surely attest if they knew who he was or how to reach him.

He wrinkled his brow as he processed this one flaw in the otherwise brilliant success of the school: there could never be a class reunion. The students didn't even know him, much less each other. So, once they graduated he never saw them again. He made sure of that.

He adjusted the rearview mirror so he could keep an eye on the blanket-covered figure in the back, although he knew from experience there was no need. They never woke up.

5

Mark Boston
Three Months Earlier

My name is Mark Boston, and I'm an alcoholic.
I've never said those words in a group, nor have I ever been to an AA meeting. That's too bad, too. I might have saved myself a lot of grief. The problem is, there aren't a lot of AA meetings for junior high kids, and that's when my drinking first got out of hand.

I am also an author – yes, I am "that" Mark Boston. My book "Exquisite Rain" has been number one on the *New York Times* bestseller list for 18 consecutive weeks with no sign of letting up. Not bad for a first-time author, and I will admit that it has blown me away, changing my life like no other event. Well, maybe like no other event, except one.

I like to tell people there isn't a 12-step group for recovering authors, but there probably should be. But that's just me, being a smart-ass. I love what I do and, based on the weekly sales report that my publisher just e-mailed me, I'm pretty damn good at it.

Now that you know I'm "that" Mark Boston, you probably also know about my kidnapping story, since right after I wrote "Exquisite Rain," *People* magazine ran a cover story telling everything anybody ever wanted to know about me, and then some. They used a lot of ink on the kidnapping – or at least what I could remember about it at the time of the interview. I had specifically asked the reporter not to write about the kidnapping, and she promised she wouldn't – saying she just needed to know about it for "background." Of course she printed everything I'd told her, and some I didn't. What a fool I was. The worst thing is, I did what I was specifically asked not to do: reveal what happened to me. And I did it to an audience of over three million readers!

Since then, folks who have read that story ask me all the time who my kidnapper was. I wish I knew, but I don't. Not everybody believes me when I say that, however. When a certain well-known author was asked what he thought of my work, he used the occasion to refer to my "alleged" kidnapping – as though I'd made the whole thing up! Don't I wish.

Actually, that's not quite true. I mean, no, I didn't make it up, but I'm not entirely unhappy that it happened. The honest to God truth is, I'm glad it happened. I would not be where I am today if I hadn't been kidnapped, and I only hope that came through to Sir in the *People* story.

That's the name of my kidnapper: Sir. It's the only name he gave me, and it's the only way I addressed him for the entire time I was held in captivity -- except for the first time I met him, of course. I think I called him "asshole" then, but I learned very quickly not to do that.

I'd be surprised if Sir read the article about me, because *People* magazine is probably a bit down-market for him. If he did read it, though, I'll bet he was livid, and I don't blame him. It's not at all what we agreed on just before he released me. He asked me if I could keep what he did to me private – "just between the two of us" – and of course I said I would. I remember that day vividly. I had no idea that my time at the School of Life was coming to an end, and I certainly didn't want it to. I thought Sir and I were just having a conversation – one of the lively, interesting and intellectual discussions we had every day. That conversation, like all of the others, was full of hypotheticals, "What would you do if..." and "How would you feel when..." – that sort of thing. So, when he said, "What about when I release you, Mark? Will you run to the police or the newspapers first?" I assumed it was just another hypothetical lead-in to an in-depth discussion about the social ills which, in his words, "plague our society."

It never occurred to me such a thing would ever happen, that I would be released. I had long since given up hope of ever returning to my old life, so I was momentarily taken aback. Frankly, I didn't want to go anywhere. We had a good life, Sir and I, if you can call our strange existence a "life." My food was prepared and served to me, my laundry was done for me and all I did all day was lie around watching movies and reading books -- oh, and talking to Sir. It frightened me to think about what might happen to me when it ended.

But I considered his question carefully – he had taught me to think before responding. "Well," I began. "I really don't think much about leaving this place, and I really don't want to. But if ever you throw me out..." I added the last part to amuse him, but it didn't seem to have the intended effect, so I continued. "If ever you throw me out, I don't plan on telling anyone."

"You promise?"

That got my attention, because I could tell from his voice this wasn't hypothetical. He was dead serious. "Yes, I promise," I said, never imagining I'd have a chance to make good on my promise the very next day.

Looking back, I am absolutely certain I didn't promise just so he would let me go. I honestly never thought I would be released, and I never wanted to be. Of course now that almost five years have lapsed since my graduation, I realize he did the right thing – letting me go, I mean. Otherwise, why put me through all that?

6

Once the *People* story came out, I was deluged with requests for additional interviews, but I wasn't having it. "Fool me once," Sir used to say, "shame on you. Fool me twice, shame on me." I hated that cliche, but it certainly fit this occasion. I'd been fooled by a dishonest reporter once; I wasn't about to let it happen again. I'm proud to say I have never given an interview since the *People* incident, much to my editors' chagrin. I did write a critical letter to the editors of *People*, however, complaining that the reporter had been unprofessional and inaccurate, etc., which they dutifully printed – along with their own insistence that they stood by their reporter. "Never get in a pissing match with a man who buys his ink by the barrel," Sir had taught me in his Communication Skills class. But it was a lesson I'd already learned in high school when I got riled up at some anti-pot editorial they ran in the local rag. I wrote a snotty letter to the editor which was actually printed -- right beside another, even more critical op-ed on the subject. I figured out pretty quick that I could never win -- unless I bought the damn newspaper, which wasn't about to happen.

What I learned then, and never forgot, was that the media will always have the last word, so don't bother trying to argue your point with them. So I didn't write the letter to *People* expecting a retraction or an apology or anything like that. I wrote it with the simple hope that if Sir read the original story he would also read my letter disavowing it – and maybe forgive me for breaking my promise.

After the magazine came out, I actually wondered if he would kidnap me again, and possibly punish me for not keeping my word. I was completely paranoid for a while, because even though my only experience with Sir had been positive, who knew what he was capable of when he was crossed? I spent a fair amount of time looking over my shoulder, but it turned out it wasn't Sir I should have been worried about. My former fiancée, who also read the article, came looking for me about the same time, and by that point she had actually blossomed into a total whack-job. She started sending me threatening notes and leaving weird messages at the hotels I stayed at on my book tour. Finally my publisher hired a bodyguard, or "security service" as they called it -- or so I learned when I noticed they deducted the fees for it on my royalties statement.

But Sir never came looking for me, so now I've decided to start looking for him.

7

So, just in case you're one of the people who *didn't* read about what happened to me in the *People* story, here it is again – this time "on the record."

I was kidnapped off a park bench – as best I recall – in Denver, Colorado, about five years ago. The reason I don't know for sure is that I was completely wasted for the better part of a month to the point that I'm really not sure where I was. Denver is the last place I remember being, so that's where I've concluded that it must have happened.

A month or so earlier, I was about to graduate from the Yale School of Law, but I ran away instead. It wasn't exactly like Tom Sawyer or Huck Finn tying a bandana full of stuff to the end of a stick, but that's not that far from what happened, either. I wrote a couple of letters: one to my roommate, one to my folks, and one to my fiancee, and packed up only the barest of necessities in my backpack before hitting the road. Oh, I should probably mention that my "barest necessities" included a big bottle of Grey Goose. Boy, I loved the Goose back then!

At the time I self-righteously thought I was taking the high road – no pun intended, since I also smoked a lot of pot – but the alternative I'd seriously considered was suicide. By running away instead of killing myself, I thought I was doing the right thing. I know – strange reasoning, but that's the way I thought back then.

I just didn't have the balls to kill myself. I'm not a religious person, but when it comes right down to it, I don't want to piss God off – just in case he really exists. So, I guess I decided to do the next best thing: to kill myself the slow way – by alcohol poisoning – which is exactly how they described what happened to my drinking buddy Stacy back in tenth grade. By the time I got to law school, I had built Stacy into a martyr in my own mind. In my warped thinking, Stacy was lucky; he got out early.

I was thinking about Stacy the day I walked down the steps of the Sterling Law Building and never looked back. What I wasn't thinking about was how I had gotten to the place where I wanted to kill myself. That would come later – and it would be Sir who would help me figure it out.

8

Yale was a great school, and the fact that I dropped out shouldn't be construed as a judgment on them. I just couldn't go on hiding my little problem – my love affair with alcohol – and when I finally realized that I'd completely lost all self-control, I decided not to go on with the charade. I guess I had a vision of how it would end.

Running away certainly wasn't complicated, and I tried to cut down the melodrama in the letters I left behind. That was fairly easy, since I didn't really have a lot of feelings for any of the recipients. To my mom and stepdad I apologized, even though I was just paying lip service. Neither one of them meant anything to me. My mom was a bitch and my stepdad was an idiot, and I really didn't owe them anything, since they'd never done anything for me. If it hadn't been for the trust fund my grandmother left me, I wouldn't have been able to go to college, and certainly not Yale. I only wrote to the "parental units" as I've taken to referring to them, because I knew when they made their obligatory Sunday afternoon phone call, they might wonder why I no longer answered.

I also wrote a longer letter to my roommate Sean, telling him he could have all the shit I left behind. Some of it I knew he'd be glad to get. He'd told me previously that he always had the hots for Cookie, my fiancee, so I told him he could have her, too. Good luck with *that*.

Honestly, I never figured out what came over me when I asked Cookie to marry me. I didn't even like her, much less love her. All I can figure out is that I was obviously drunk when I asked her, since I was drunk when I did anything back then. So, to Cookie I wrote that I was really sorry, and that she was a great person, etc. No sense in sending her into therapy, although God knows she could use some. A more self-righteous bitch I've never known in my life. Good in the sack, though...just not what I need.

I left all three letters, with Sean's on top, on his bed – with strict instructions not to mail the others until at least a day after he got back from his ski trip to Vermont.

It never occurred to me he would arrive back a day early.

9

After walking off campus without so much as a backward glance, it didn't take me long to discover that hitching rides on the interstate isn't my style. I never picked up any of the losers who stood out their with their thumbs extended, so why should anybody pick me up? I didn't even bother trying. I took the city bus through New Haven, Fair Haven and all the other Havens until I finally got to the end of the line in East Haven. The driver pulled over to the curb and said, "This is it, Buddy." I hadn't noticed that the bus was empty and the driver was about to drive it through a chain-link gate marked "buses only." I nodded to the driver, hoisted my pack onto my back and climbed down the back steps of the bus. I knew the bus driver was watching me, so I walked with purpose toward the end of the block and around the corner before putting the pack down on the curb and trying to think of what to do.

I sort of remember my line of thinking as I sat there. *It's not too late to change your mind, stupid. They don't even know you're gone yet. You could get back, destroy the letters and get to the library in time to...what? Pull another all-nighter? Sit there staring at words that no longer made any sense, held any interest? No thanks.*

I walked about six miles before arriving at a truck stop on I-95 – the name everybody in Connecticut referred to this highway, even though the hotshot local politicians insisted on calling it "The Governor John Davis Lodge Turnpike." Pretentious bastards. I made my way to the counter, put my pack on the floor and ordered a cup of coffee. I wanted a drink, but alcohol was conspicuously missing from the menu. Hmmm. What's going on here? You'd think they were trying to discourage truck drivers from drinking and driving. Novel idea, I thought to myself. *There's no point in getting drunk 'til you get out of town, asshole.* As I sipped my coffee, I waited to see what would happen, who I might meet. At that point I was still confident enough to believe someone would eventually offer me a ride. After all, I was still clean from the shower I took early in the day, and my clothes were reasonably clean. As it turned out, I was right. It didn't take long before a trucker struck up a conversation.

"Where you headed, kid?"

"Not sure yet. Just need some adventure, I guess." Flashing the perfect teeth and opening the big blues wide always worked, and today was no exception.

Before the trucker could respond, a big-busted waitress with a mop of bleached blonde hair swept down on us and began re-filling our coffee cups.

"Why, thank you Gretchen," the trucker said, obviously flirting with the fast-moving figure. (Funny how I still remember her name after all these years. Not sure why that is.)

"You betcha, honey." Then, in a conspiratorial tone directed at me, "You listen to this one, honey. Si here won't give you any bad advice." I looked at "Si," which I took to be short for Simon, and gave a half-smile.

He better not give me any fuckin' advice, lady. I don't need advice. I need a ride.

Gretchen disappeared as fast as she'd arrived, and the trucker returned to our conversation. "Not running from the law, are ya?"

"Nope."

"Girlfriend dump ya?"

None of your fuckin' business. Trying to think of a response that wouldn't cost me a ride, I simply stared at my coffee cup. The guy mistook my silence for acquiescene, and apparently took pity, because he said, "I'll take you as far as Omaha. I ain't queer, and you better not be, either. And you can't sleep the whole time, y'hear? I need somebody to keep me awake, not put me to sleep. Deal?"

I nodded, picked up my pack and followed the guy to the 18-wheeler parked on the far side of the parking lot. On the hood was a shiny bulldog and the word MACK. *So this is what a Mack truck looks like. Big fuckin' deal.*

Makeovers - Rex John

10

Picking up Mark Boston would be the last time Simon Hecht – "Si" to his friends – would ever drive his company-owned Mack truck.

The 58 year-old husband and father of two had only been driving big rigs for a year, having graduated from a three-week class in truck driving at National Big Rig School in Bangor, Maine. Part of the eight grand tuition to BRS included "job placement," so Si was offered a job working for the Bangor Department of Sanitation which, with only one look from his wife Judy, he decided to turn down.

He finally landed the job with Global Moving the old fashioned way: searching the newspaper want ads. Better to move people's furniture than their trash cans, he'd thought at the time, but now he realized the sanitation job would have at least kept him at home.

Until now, he never ignored the phrase repeated at every single driver's meeting: *Global doesn't pick up hitchhikers*.

He was about to find out why.

As they walked across the parking lot, Si tried to catch a good look at the kid without staring at him. He knew Judy would ask for all sorts of details when they talked later on the phone. The kid looked OK; Judy would say he was good looking, he was pretty sure. He looked to be about six foot two or three, blond hair cut in what she would call an "east coast haircut," and his light-weight frame certainly wouldn't be a threat to Si's 280 "mass o' muscle," as she liked to describe him. Catching another sideways glance at the kid walking next to him, sporting that ridiculous looking backpack, Simon wondered what the kid was running from. *Can't have been on the road too long; he's too clean. Can't be too broke; he's got twenty grand worth of orthodontia in that pretty mouth.*

Walking beside him, Mark wondered what he was getting himself into. The guy was too fuckin' friendly. Obnoxious Maine accent. *He says he's not gay, but I'll bet they all say that. But I'm not giving him a blow-job, so I hope that's not where this is heading. Omaha! Omaha? Omaha-ha-ha-ha. Well, at least nobody will think to look for me there. New York City, yeah. Florida, maybe. San Francisco, definitely. But, Omaha? Never.*

The two men sat in silence for most of the first day. The big rig skirted New York City on the Jersey Turnpike, and just as Si was navigating the cloverleaf onto I-80, Mark opened his mouth, as if to speak. The older man caught the movement and said, "Yeah? You want to say something, kid?"

"No...not really," came the reply. But, in fact, there was plenty Mark wanted to say, not the least of which was "What have I done? Stop this truck! I need to go back; maybe I can still turn this situation around." But he sat in silence, staring out the window.

Selfish brat. He's gettin' a free ride and he can't be bothered to provide some good company? I even told him I needed him to stay awake and talk to me! But even as Si fumed silently, he could see that the kid was struggling with something. He would wait him out, let him talk when he was ready.

It was time for his morning break. Si knew better than to look for an old fashioned rest stop -- a place where a guy could jump down, take a leak in some smelly bathroom and be back on the road in minutes. Those mini-parks that once dotted the landscape along I-80 had been long closed, so Si had no choice but to pull the rig into a so-called "service plaza," a football field sized parking lot surrounding one or more buildings housing a cafe, rest rooms, car wash and mini-mart.

Still silent, Mark followed Si into the men's room but headed for a urinal as far from Si as possible. *Well, that's a good sign,* Si thought.

After a cup of coffee, sipped in silence, Si said, "OK, let's head out." But, before he could grab the check, Mark did so as he mumbled "'least I can do."

Well, at least he ain't a schnor. Si smiled as he remembered the Yiddish word his grandmother had taught him. "Simon," she would say. "Don't ever be a schnor. With a schnor, it's always take, take, take, and never give. That isn't right. Don't be cheap! Nobody likes a cheapsakate!"

The two stopped for lunch a few hours later, and it, too, was eaten in silence. As they sat waiting for the waitress to bring the check, the younger man once again headed to the men's room. "Be right back," he said as he exited the booth.

Ten minutes later, Mark returned and, as Si recalled later, he was a whole new kid. Would not shut up. He told Si about his childhood, his girlfriend, his roommate and law school. The conversation started at the table but continued to the truck and for most of the afternoon.

The transition, while welcome, caught Si off-guard. He couldn't figure out how somebody could be so completely shut down one moment and talk your ear of the next. He ventured a guess. "You been drinkin' kid?" he asked.

"Maybe. What of it?"

"Well, it's just that you didn't say a word for 400 miles and now you won't shut up."

"Yeah, well, I'm not driving, so why not?"

Si didn't have an answer. He'd seen the ravages of alcohol on his own family and he didn't want any part of it. Tempted to lecture the kid on the dangers of booze, he bit his tongue instead. *Let the kid talk. Might do him good. Besides, he ain't your problem.*

The two chatted amiably the rest of the ten-hour day, at which time Si announced that they would be stopping at a motel for the night.

"A motel?" Mark asked. "I thought you guys slept in your truck in some parking lot."

"Yeah, I've done that a few too many times. I need a decent bed. Don't worry, we'll get a room with twin beds." He smiled as he delivered the line and Mark smiled in return, now convinced that the older guy wasn't trying to perv on him.

At 5 o'clock the next morning, Si shook the kid and said, "Let's go." And, after a quick breakfast in the motel coffee shop, they headed for the truck.

11

Mark had no way of knowing that even as he and Si were climbing into the big rig, his roommate Sean was unlocking the door to their apartment back in New Haven. Sean took a spill on the slopes in Vermont, twisting both his ankle and his pride, so he headed home. He spotted the letters on his bed the moment he opened the door and, ignoring Mark's request that he wait until Monday to mail them, called Cookie and told her she better come over because "I think something's happened to Mark."

Cookie seemed to arrive at the apartment room before Sean hung up the phone and stood by helplessly (Cookie would describe it as "stupidly" when she later recounted the event to her mother) as she fell to pieces. But, just as quickly as she fell apart, she pulled herself back together and called her folks. After filling them in – and reading Mark's sappy note aloud to them over the phone – she left Sean standing there, wondering how the hell he was supposed to get through his Constitutional Law class without Mark's help.

So much for giving Cookie to Sean. It appeared she wasn't interested.

It didn't hurt that Cookie's Dad had a buddy who was the Deputy Director of the Connecticut State Patrol. Within three hours after Cookie left the apartment, an APB was issued for his arrest. Cookie's

Dad had to make something up about Mark's stealing Cookie's Rolex before the Deputy Director, an old frat brother, would issue the bulletin, but he'd be goddamned if this smart ass kid would walk out on his daughter.

The next morning, CSP Patrolman Everett Donohue walked into the I-95 diner at three o'clock to have his usual: scrambled eggs, crisp bacon and well-buttered whole wheat toast – when he decided to flip through the stack of paperwork he'd been handed when he started his shift at 11 p.m. the previous evening. Mark's photo, furnished by Cookie, was centered prominently on the APB, and happened to be on top of the pile when Gretchen, now exhausted from working 16 hours straight because *that bitch Pam didn't show up again*, noticed it was the same kid she'd served only yesterday.

"I know that kid," she told Donohue. "He was sitting right where you are, not twenty-four hours ago."

Donohue asked all the proper questions and, after determining Mark Boston left the diner with Global driver Simon something-or-other, he called it in. Global had over 200 drivers, but only one Simon, so the area supervisor had him on the phone within minutes.

"Hecht!" the supervisor began. "You pick up some kid two days ago in New Branford?"

After admitting that he had, Simon Hecht was ordered to remain in Davenport, Iowa – by now he had dropped his load in Omaha and was headed back to his home state of Maine – and an Iowa State Trooper was dispatched to interview him.

"No way that kid stole anything, I can tell you for sure," Simon told the officer. "I know people, and that kid ain't no thief."

Simon told the trooper he had picked the kid up outside New Haven, Connecticut, and yes, he told the kid he would take him as far as Omaha. No, the kid didn't tell him where he was headed, but Simon seemed to recall that he talked about dropping in on a friend in Tulsa. "That's all I can remember. He didn't talk much."

It really was all Simon could remember, since he did most of the talking. *That kid was so quiet!* Truth is, Simon could hardly remember anything about that trip. For example, he completely forgot that even though he'd told the trooper he'd taken the kid to Omaha, they actually parted ways in Des Moines when they stopped for more coffee. *Oh, and he's not going by Mark Boston. He told me his name was Cary Evans.*

When Simon finally remembered these two important details, he started searching his motel room for the business card the trooper had given him so he could call and fill him in. But, before he even located the card, he received another knock on the door of his EconoLodge room. This time it was the head of Global's Iowa Dispatch Center, with Simon's final check and a bus ticket back to Bangor, Maine.

Global doesn't pick up hitchhikers.

Makeovers - Rex John

12

I liked my new name. Looking back, I don't even know why I changed it. Probably because at some subconscious level I was so sick of who I was I thought that a new name would make me a new person. Maybe I wanted to make sure nobody found me. I honestly don't know. That's not how it works, of course, but I gave it a try and for that brief period of time I actually grew to like being Cary Evans.

I had a hunch the minute we got in the truck the big trucker dude would ask what my name was, and that's exactly what he did.

Moments earlier I came up with the name Cary Evans so quickly it surprised even me. Cary Garnett was head boy back at Morey Junior High School and Tom Evans was my best friend during the same period of my life, so I just combined the two names and, presto, I was now Cary Evans. What's weird is, I hadn't thought of Cary or Tom for at least ten years and yet their names were both on the tip of my tongue. It makes you wonder about all this subconscious shit you hear about. Well, I'd be thinking about Cary and Tom all the time now. Like every time somebody called me Cary Evans.

That was a long-ass trip, and that Si guy would not shut up. He told me so much about his wife Judy I felt like I'd known her all my life. Turns out he loved reading science fiction books, so of course he quickly became "Sci-Fi-Si" to me.

While Sci Fi Si was talking non-stop, I'd amuse myself by thinking up names and recipes for new drinks using the names of towns we were passing through or names on highway exit signs. A Manhattan, with sweet vermouth and bourbon – became a "Dubuque," in honor of Dubuque, Iowa. A Singapore Sling – with gin, cherry brandy, pineapple juice, lime juice, Cointreau, benedictine, and grenadine – became "Sioux City Sling," and a good old-fashioned Sex on the Beach (peach Schnapps, vodka, cranberry and orange juice) became "Sex in Bureau Junction." You get the idea. Each time I'd think of one, I'd imagine going to the liquor cabinet I'd had back in New Haven, take the necessary ingredients off the shelf, find the proper glass, plop a few ice cubes in, measure, pour, and sit down and start sipping. When I'd finished one, I'd have another, and another, until I couldn't hear Sci Fi Si guy's voice anymore. I swear, even though I was only getting drunk in my imagination, I started slurring my words – whenever I got a word in edgewise, that is.

I wasn't the only one. Si started slurring his words, too, and I realized the poor guy was so tired he couldn't keep his eyes open. All of a sudden I had a premonition that he would fall completely asleep, and since I was drunk by this time (at least in my imagination) and couldn't drive, the huge truck would eventually slam into the concrete abutment of an overpass, killing us both on impact. I broke out in a sweat.

I may have wanted to die, but I didn't want to die in a fiery ball of some stranger's crappy furniture hurtled at my spine at fifty-five miles an hour while I was sitting there, helpless, completely drunk. OK, it was only "pretend drunk," but it felt enough like the real thing that I decided I'd get out of that death trap the first chance I got.

My chance came on day number two after ten solid hours on the road. We pulled into a truck stop just out of Des Moines, Iowa because I said I had to take a piss and Si Fi Si said maybe he could use a cup of coffee. I'll say! *Give this man a quadruple vente espresso, please!*

I went into the coffee shop with him – no bar in sight – and while we were sitting there pounding back coffee, I pretended I'd just noticed the big map of the U.S. hanging on the wall next to us and said, "You know, Si, I see we're directly above Tulsa right now, and I just remembered I have a buddy there I think I'd like to look up." He seemed to be buying it, so I continued. "So, you know, man, I think I'll head down there from here and see if I can find him." That, of course, would be a neat trick because he didn't exist any more than Cary Evans did.

I wouldn't swear to it, but the big dude actually looked like he might cry at this point. Either he was so fucking tired he was overreacting to everything, or maybe he'd started thinking I'd just stay with him from now on, becoming his little road buddy or something, listening to him blather on while we drove back and forth across the United States. Well, that wasn't about to happen, so he'd just have to mourn his loss – me. I smiled as I thought maybe I should send him a photo of myself so he could put it up on his visor, next to the photo of Judy. What a little shit I'd become. When I smiled, he assumed I was smiling at him, so he pulled me into a big bear hug and said, "Whatever you want, Cary. You just take care of yourself, you hear?"

Now it was my turn to fight back tears, since no man had hugged me since before my dad died and, well, never mind. I turned quickly, picked up my backpack and headed out the door. I knew Si was still watching me, so I walked quickly across the parking lot like I knew where the hell I was going, aiming at what I hoped was the big interchange we'd passed a few miles earlier – where I'd supposedly start hitching south.

But I wasn't going south; I was still going west – at least to Omaha, since by now I'd managed to wrap my head around the idea. But first I was going to find a goddamned bar.

13

It didn't take long. Just as I was approaching the place where I-35 drops down from I-80, which would take me down to Kansas City and ultimately to Tulsa if I were really going there, I noticed the tell-tale blinking orange neon lights of a bar about half a mile down a side street. At first I couldn't make out the three words in the name on the sign, but as it blinked off and on, I imagined it said "Get...Drunk...Here.   Get...Drunk...Here. Get...Drunk...Here." *OK, Baby, I hear 'ya. I'm on my way!*

As I got closer, I could see that the three words actually read "Woe...B...Gone."

Oh yeah? We'll see about that. If there was such a thing as truth in advertising, that sign, at least for me, would have read, "Your woes are just beginning."

The parking lot was jammed, which was a good sign. Maybe I could get drunk *and* laid. In that order.

It turned out that the Woe-B-Gone was, and probably still is, Des Moines' destination bar for the "problem drinkers" of Drake University. We had 'em at Yale, too, and I'd gotten so I could spot them pretty easily. Takes one to know one, as they say. They always laugh too hard, talk too loud and drink 'til they throw up. In other words, my kind of people!

Safely located on the other side of town from campus, the "Woe-B," as everybody called it, attracted kids who weren't able or willing to abide by Drake's strict policies on alcohol consumption. Kids like Jonah Rosen and Eldon Duncan, two Phi Delts I met within two minutes after I walked in the door and who each appeared, as I imagined their university records would say, to have "serious problems with alcohol consumption."

Jonah and Eldon were pounding them down at the rate of about one every ten minutes, as far as I could tell. When I sat down beside them the barely noticed them at first. But after I noticed Eldon's Phi Delt t-shirt, amiable guy that I am, I said, "Hey! A fellow Phi-Delt! Buy you a beer?"

Eldon looked me over quickly, realized he'd never seen me before, took one look at the backpack and said, "Huh?"

I realized Eldon must have been on that stool for awhile. Finally processing what I said, he asked, "What's with the backpack? You live here?"

"No man, I just got into town and I need a drink!" I said, sounding a little desperate, even to me.

"You really a Phi Delt?" he slurred.

"Sure am, man! Pledge class of 89' at good ole' Yale."

"Well then!" Eldon exclaimed. "There's no fuckin' way you're buyin' us a beer! We'll buy *you* a beer! Isn't that right, Jonah," he said, turning to the guy on his right, who had been taking in the whole conversation.

"Damn straight, man," Jonah agreed.

And then, as if by magic – my favorite kind of magic – a beer appeared in front of me – the first of many I would see that night. Eldon nodded his thanks at the bartender, who was obviously familiar to him, and turned to me and said, "Whadsup?"

"Nothin' up, dude. Just passin' through town."

"In this fuckin' weather?" This was actually the first time I'd thought about the weather, since Connecticut's interminable winter had simply turned into Pennsylvania's interminable weather, which had turned into Ohio's interminable weather, and so on, 'til I'd gotten to Des Moines. Besides, my grandfather kept up a running commentary on the weather my entire life – yesterday's temp, tomorrow's expected temp, wind velocity, humidity, etc. – to the point that sometime in high school I'd vowed I'd never allow myself to become *that* kind of old guy.

"What weather?" I said.

"Are you fuckin' kiddin' me? This is another goddamned fucking blizzard, man. That's all we ever have around here. They're gettin' ready to shut the interstate, you mark my word. You ain't goin' nowhere tonight, buddy." Then, looking me over again, he extended his hand as though he's just seen me, said, "Hey man. I'm Eldon...and this here's Jonah The Whale Rosen."

"Cary Evans," I said, and shook hands with both guys. I wondered where the hell Jonah The Whale got his nickname, since there wasn't a clue he was or ever had been heavyset.

We sat there for I don't know how long, because I didn't have a clue as to the time when I first walked in, but I'm guessing it was about five hours earlier when all of a sudden the bartender called out "Last call!"

I knew I'd met my soulmates when we all three put our hands up at the same time and said, "Bring me another!" and then, laughing at how fuckin' predictable we were, and looking at each other as we yelled it, we added, "And make it a double!"

The hilarity stopped abruptly twenty minutes later when they turned the florescent lights on in the filthy bar, and we all almost fell off our barstools from the blinding flash of lights.

Somehow we managed to make it to the parking lot, and with Jonah's arm draped around my shoulder I couldn't tell who was holding who up.

"Now what?" Eldon said, as he wrapped his arm around my waist from the other side. "I turned to look at him and, noticing the big smile on his face, said, "What! This is where you kiss me, right?"

Well, their arms came off me pretty fast at that remark but, noticing the wicked smile on my face, they both figured out pretty quickly that I was kidding and more laughter ensued. Before I knew what happened – I think I must have blacked out at some point – the three of us were standing in front of a giant snowbank on the side of the building, dicks in hand, trying to write our names in the snow.

"Whadsup with that?" Jonah asked, spotting my backpack. "You just come from class or somethin'?"

"Dude!" Eldon said. "It's fuckin two o'clock! What fuckin' class do you think he has at 2 o'clock?"

Chastised, Jonah acted thoughtful before responding, "Shit! I have lots of 2 o'clock classes! They're just at the other two o'clock!" More laughter.

Eldon was still transfixed by my backpack, and seemed determined to get to the bottom of why I had a backpack, in this parking lot, at the particular time of day. He was like a TSA agent in the security line at the airport.

"Are you on the road, man? Are you *hitchin'*?" The way he emphasized the word "hitchin'" momentarily made me wonder if he thought that was a good thing, or a bad thing.

"You got it, man."

"No way! Well, you won't get a ride at this hour, dude. Where you stayin?"

"Hadn't thought about..."

Before he could finish his sentence, Jonah, anticipating his answer interrupted to say, "C'mon, dude. You can stay at the house tonight. We'll have another drink there!"

I'll never know why, but at this point I allowed myself to be pushed into the backseat of Eldon's sporty BMW – "is this where you fuck me, man?" – more laughter, and then we were somehow back at the Phi Delta Theta house, faster than the magic school bus.

None of the three of us remembered the trip the next day. Hell, we barely remembered our names, especially me, who more than once started to introduce myself to the other guys in the house. The problem was, I'd forgotten that I'd changed my name from Mark to Cary until I was half-way through it, so I heard myself say "Ma...Cary," except that it came out like "Mary."

"Mary!" one guy said. "That's your name? *Mary?*"

"I didn't say Mary, you dickwad. I said *Cary,*" even though Mary is exactly what I said.

"You did not, man. You said Mary," the guy said and I was just about to pop him when Eldon stumbled down the stairs and plopped down next to me on the sofa where I'd just spent the night.

"Hey, Cary," he managed to utter, which seemed to convince the other guy that maybe I'd been telling the truth. We were in the rec room of the house, located down a narrow set of steps off the kitchen and carpeted with the filthiest and ugliest plaid carpeting I'd ever seen. In fact, as I looked around, and especially at the sofa I'd just spent the night on, I realized the whole place was filthy. Perfect, I thought. Home sweet home.

Jonah came into the middle of the inane name conversation and said, "Whadya say your name was again, man?"

"Cary, goddamn it! We went over this twenty times last night, Whale!"

"Oh yeah. Cary. Cary. That's right, Cary the hitcher from...sorry, dude, where'd you say you were from?"

"Doesn't matter, man...I gotta take a piss...where's the..."

"Over there, man...next to the bar..."

After relieving myself, I returned to the sofa where Eldon and the Whale were sitting, side-by-side, eyes half-closed and obviously feeling just like I did.

"Hey man, thanks for the hospitality..." I said.

"S'o.k., man. Now what?"

"Not sure. Back to the highway, I guess. I think I'll go to Denver."

"No way, man! Really? Me and Jonah were talking about a road trip to Colorado this weekend to ski! Why don't you come with us?"

"Jonah and I," I corrected.

"Huh?" he said.

"Jonah and I. You said 'me and Jonah' but if you take away Jonah, you'd be saying 'me was talking...'" He just stared at me like I was speaking a goddamned foreign language. Whatever. What can I say: my grandmother was a stickler for good grammar – clearly a wasted skill with these two. Finally, I answered his question. "I don't know, man...".

"Yeah, man! You gotta do it! You can crash here 'til Friday and we'll leave then. That's it, man. That's what we're gonna do!"

And with that, my travel plans changed from Omaha to Denver.

14

The next week was a blur. We spent every day at the Woe-B and every night partying at the house, excepting a few hours of sleep here and there and the occasional class one or both guys might decide to attend.

Just a month earlier I had admitted to Cookie that I might have a "slight drinking problem," when she asked me why I was drunk at nine o'clock in the morning. We'd talked about it at length, deciding finally that I should "do something about it."

I smiled at the thought of what she might think about this new set of developments. *Well, babe, how do you like this? This is what I'm doin' about it!*

I really didn't give a shit what she thought. This was the new me, and besides, she was a bitch.

On Friday, seriously hung-over from the night before, the three of us piled into the beemer and headed to Breckenridge, Colorado for what was supposed to be three days of skiing and boarding. Jonah and I were boarders – he loaned me some of his gear – while Eldon used old-fashioned skis.

The drive took slightly over twelve hours with occasional pauses to "hang it over the side of the road."

We had a ball. Before any of us knew what happened, three days turned into four, and then a week, and then two weeks. Finally, at three weeks, Eldon's dad, who had been monitoring the activity on Eldon's credit cards, called to find out what the hell was going on.

Jonah and I went out on the balcony and passed a bottle of Jack Daniels back and forth while Eldon stood screaming into the phone at his dad. Jonah lit up a cigarette, and it completely shocked me because I'd never seen him smoke.

"You know, dude, they've done some studies," I said, deciding to give him shit.

"Oh, yeah, man? What kind of studies?" he said, taking a drag.

"On smoking, man. They think it might be bad for your health."

He looked at me like I was nuts and realized that I was just giving him a hard time. "You don't say. Well, maybe I'll think about quitting."

"Yeah, you do that man," I said, and before he knew what was happening, I reached over and jerked the cigarette out of his mouth and threw it over the balcony into a snowbank below. "Now's as good a time as any."

"What the fuck!"

He was getting ready to rant, so I just grabbed the bottle out of his hand and took a big swig before handing it back to him, "There you go, man."

Mission accomplished. I'd distracted him enough so he'd already forgotten the cigarette and had gone back to the bottle like a goddamned baby – or a monkey and a shiny object.

"So, Eldon's old man controls the cash, huh? I asked, finally taking note that somebody must be paying for our so-called lifestyle over the past three weeks, and it sure as hell wasn't me.

"Oh, man. You have no idea," he said, contented again. "The guy is seriously loaded. Owns banks, real estate, and other shit I forget about. He owns most of Chicago, man. Seriously."

Eldon apparently worked it out with his dad, because as soon as he hung up he called room service and ordered $600 worth of food and alcohol which the three of us consumed well into the night. But the next day, Eldon announced that it was time to get back to school, where he would eventually discover that his dad had made arrangements for him to continue on academic probation while Jonah would discover, to his great surprise, that he had been suspended. I didn't have anything to worry about, since I'd taken care of my own "school problem" by simply dropping out – long before ever arriving in Des Moines.

They dropped me off in Denver on their way back to Iowa, because I told them I had relatives who lived there, and because I don't think they would have let me out of the car otherwise. I liked Colorado and decided I didn't want to go back to Des Moines with them. Case closed. They wrote their names and addresses down on little scraps of paper they found in the glove box, and they made me swear I'd keep in touch. I meant to, too. But...well, I can just hear my grandmother saying, "The road to you-know-where is paved with good intentions, Mark." I'm truly sorry to say I haven't been in touch with them since.

I used my last twenty dollars to buy a bottle of 80-proof, which I slowly consumed while sitting in Civic Center Park, watching the sun go down over the bell tower. I was vaguely aware that if I didn't do something, sleeping on park benches was about to become my new life. I didn't think about it too much, though, because it wasn't long before I passed out.

If I had awakened on that park bench the next morning, I probably would have discovered my pack was gone – stolen, I would assume, by any of the number of punks that prey on the homeless. I probably wouldn't have cared though, since it didn't have anything in it I wanted anymore anyway. My Grey Goose miniatures were long gone. My Connecticut driver's license, as it turns out, was in the pocket of my jeans, so it was the only thing I owned that wasn't stolen.

I've often wondered what would have happened to me if I really had made it through the night on that bench. I had plenty of money, thanks to the trust Grandmother left me, but it had certain "conditions" -- such as the requirement to complete my college degree *and* graduate school, and to do that I'd have to go back to a life I'd found unbearable. Going back would be worse, because I'd have to admit what a fuck-up I'd been. But, how could I live without money? Would I have to start panhandling to score cash for my next bottle? Would I have to embark upon a life of crime? Would I have tried to reach Eldon and Jonah or tried to find my way back to Des Moines? Obviously, I'll never know, because I didn't wake up on that park bench. I woke up in a place I'd never seen before.

And somebody was cutting my pants off.

15

Glancing at the digital radio as the black van turned off the main highway onto the service road, Carson noticed that it was 7:45 a.m. *Perfect.* He mentally started working out the schedule backward from 8:30 when his housekeeper was supposed to arrive. He'd have fifteen minutes to take a shower and change his clothes, which would take him back to 8:15. Twenty minutes to empty the van, strip this guy, give him another injection and put him in the classroom. That brought him back to 7:55. That meant he had about ten minutes more of driving, which brought him back to exactly where they were right now: 7:45.

Perfect.

At precisely 7:44, the van pulled up to the big solid privacy gates. They were double panels, twelve feet high and constructed of solid steel, but veneered with a beautiful dark mahogany with raised panels so they wouldn't make the place look like such a fortress. They were coated with several coats of polyurethane each Fall to protect them from the weather. *They really are quite lovely.*

He noticed with satisfaction that the county had already plowed the road up leading up to the gates, where the heated driveway took over. He punched in his access code and the gates began to roll into the side pockets built into each fence. The fence itself was twelve-feet tall and constructed out of cannon-ball sized stones removed from various Colorado riverbeds. A single alarm system trip wire had been strung across the top of the fence around the entire perimeter of the property, but it had long ago been disconnected from the system because various winged wildlife seemed to think it had been placed there as a perch for them. It now crackled with electricity. Now, birds who carelessly sat on the wire where it wrapped around the small ceramic insulators on the pillars every twenty feet or so created a ground, instantly electrocuting them. It was not unusual for his gardener to gather several little bird carcasses from the flower beds each week.

He watched in his side view mirrors to make sure the gates had closed behind him and, once assured that they had, the van quickly negotiated the long driveway curving to the back of the property. As he approached, he reached up to the sun visor and felt around for the garage door opener, pushing it as he drove. The big garage door opened slowly and, as he sat idling waiting for it to open, he marveled once again at the pristine condition of his garage.

One could eat off this floor, he thought as he eased the van into place. Turning the ignition to "off," he once again pushed the button on the visor and ensured that the door had completely returned to its closed position before he exited the van.

Moving quickly, he retrieved a hospital gurney from against the wall where he'd placed it before leaving last night, and rolled it over to the back of the van. Opening the right rear door slowly, and only about two inches, he stood feet apart, shoulder against the door as he cautiously peeked around the door into the back of the van. Nobody had ever surprised him by bursting out unexpectedly like a damn Jack in the Box, but he wasn't about to let it happen, either.

Convinced the figure was still sleeping soundly and, in fact, had not moved at all, he flung both doors open wide. After rolling the gurney to the end of the van and using the foot pedal to lower it to the exact height of the floor of the van, he reached in and grabbed the guy's feet, pulling him – and the Army green blanket in which he was wrapped – face down onto the gurney. He reached under the gurney and found each of three heavy leather straps that he proceeded to buckle across the guy's back, mid-section and legs. He returned to the front of the van where he retrieved the little silk pouch where he had another three syringes loaded and ready to go. The syringe he'd already used had been returned to its proper place and was now empty.

He withdrew another syringe and after holding it upright and tapping it to release any air bubbles, shoved it through the blanket and into the upper leg beneath. There was an imperceptible twitch and he realized he could probably leave the guy here in the garage, stretched out on the gurney, until after he returned from breakfast. But no, he decided, that wasn't correct procedure and besides, the garage wasn't soundproofed, whereas the classroom was. Nobody ever woke up in the garage, but there was always a first time and he didn't want anybody to hear any screams that might occur if they did.

He rolled the gurney through the big double doors on the side of the garage and into a wide, well-lit hallway lined with framed photographs. From there it was only another fifty feet of shiny corridor until he reached the security door leading to the classroom. He high-five'd the clear glass panel next to each door which quickly read his biometric palm print before the door quietly swung open.

Once inside the classroom, he gave the gurney a slight shove toward the middle of the room and, doing a quick visual inventory to make sure everything was ready, withdrew, the door closing silently behind him. He ducked into the control room and, punching three lighted buttons in a row, turned on the cameras and monitors before hitting a button which plunged the classroom into darkness. He looked at the image on the monitors to ensure that the infra-red cameras were properly focused. Assured that they were, he noted the position of the figure on the gurney before preparing to leave.

Out of habit he pushed the button on the microphone and said, "I'll be right back, buddy. Gotta get some breakfast."

As the light went out, the figure on the gurney moved slightly, causing the blanket to expose the tips of the fingers on his left hand.

He stopped mid-turn and stared at the monitor for a few moments. It was highly unusual for anyone to move at this point. Assured it probably was a muscle spasm and nothing more, he headed to the door of his study. Everything was fine; everything was as it should be.

16

I never got a clear picture of the guy who was cutting through my pants. He wore a blue cloth or paper mask covering his nose and mouth – the kind surgeons wear, or those Japanese people you see in photos, pushing their way into the subway.

As soon as I realized somebody messing with my pants, I tried to pull away, but nothing would move. I also tried to open my eyes, but when I got one of them about half-open, the guy who was messing with me stopped doing what he was doing and said, "Oh. Awake, huh? Well, I guess we'll have to take care of that." Or at least I think that's what he said, but I wouldn't swear to it, because it was hard to hear him and impossible to read his lips through that mask. With that, I was out again.

17

This time when I woke up, it was with a start. I wanted to be awake. I had to be awake. And then, by God, I was awake – bolting upright on what appeared to be a steel shelf. All I know was my back hurt like hell, but I didn't know if it was from the park bench or the steel bunk on which I now found myself. There wasn't a pillow and I remember thinking vaguely that my neck hurt, probably from the way I'd been sleeping. I swung my feet to the floor and noticed I was barefoot. I was also wearing gym shorts, a soft grey cotton or flannel fabric with an elastic waist. I wasn't wearing a shirt, and I felt a slight chill.

The lights above me were recessed can lights, and there were ten of them about 20 feet above my head. Jesus, they were bright. I remember mumbling *turn the fuckin' lights off!*

In response, a booming voice which appeared to emanate from a hidden public address system somewhere said, "too bright for you?"

I looked around, but not quickly, because some damn monkey must have been pounding cymbals in my head. I wondered where the voice had come from. I looked for speakers up on the wall or ceiling, but I never saw them.

As my eyes began to focus, I took in the rest of the space. The floor appeared to be constructed of little stainless steel tiles, about three inches square, the material from which a lot of kitchen sinks are made. These seemed to alternate, in checkerboard fashion, with miniature hardwood tiles, also about three inches square. As my bare feet touched the floor, I was aware the steel squares were cold, while the wood seemed warm. It was a strange juxtaposition. The walls were also stainless steel, but they weren't shiny, but dull. I couldn't see myself in them. I wasn't sure where I was, but it was pretty obvious I wouldn't be digging my way out.

The floors looked like they could be easily mopped if somebody were to, say, throw up on them, which I promptly did.

I was on the floor when I woke up this time. I assumed I'd hit my head when I blacked out, and I knew I vomited because I still had that taste in my mouth. But if I did, it had been cleaned up because the floor was clean and dry, and so was I.

Plus, I was now wearing a loose-fitting t-shirt, blue, with no words or design on it. I was still barefoot, and I could feel that strange sensation of cold and warm between the steel tiles and the wood tiles. I wondered briefly if I was inside of some sort of oversized storage container or, worse yet, a refrigerator or cold storage locker. I shuddered at the thought.

I remained on the floor, afraid to get up. From my vantage point I continued to take in my surroundings. I noticed there were no windows in the room – the only light came from the bright lights in the high ceiling. The steel shelf extended about two and a half feet from the wall and was about as wide as a bunk bed. You couldn't even call it a bed, really, but I had obviously been asleep on it, and there wasn't anything that looked like a bed in the room, so I declared it a bed. There was a toilet in the corner of the room, stainless steel, with a stainless steel sink next to it. A pipe hung down from the ceiling in the corner with what appeared to be a shower head on the end, but there were no handles or controls, and I didn't see how it could be a shower until I noticed a drain in the floor beneath it, so obviously it was.

The only furniture in the room was a desk and chair, also stainless steel, but they both seemed to be bolted to the floor.

I noticed that the wall to my left consisted of what appeared to be four doors, although none of them had hinges, which were obviously on the other side.

One of the doors wasn't a door as much as it was a cabinet, roughly four-feet square and located about waist-high above the floor. The others doors were normal-sized, although one of them was double-wide. They were all constructed of gray steel.

The cabinet and two of the full-size doors had small metal pulls imbedded where a knob might otherwise have been. These pulls looked like they were designed to be opened by three of four fingers curled into the small opening. As I focused on the doors, I wondered where they would take me -- assuming I could open them, of course. The doors had numbers painted on them: 1, 2, 3, and 4. The wider door had no pull, but it did have a glass panel about the size of a paperback book inset into the wall next to it. I decided it must be some kind of security system.

I either saw or imagined a very faint line of light under the door marked number one, and I wondered if it might lead outdoors.

On the wall adjacent to the wall of doors, all by itself, is what looked to be a large flat-screen television, only it wasn't *on* the wall so much as it was in it, covered by what looked like a thick piece of plexiglass or something, attached from the other side so there weren't any screws or other hardware that I could see: just a big thick piece of plastic with a television behind it. I knew it was a television because it emitted a bluish light.

I was sitting there staring at it when suddenly an image appeared on the screen.

"I see you've found me."

It was a man, head and shoulders only, wearing a coat and tie – the tie was red, I think – and he had blue eyes and blond hair. He just sat there and it looked like he was looking right at me.

Oh, and did I mention he was a *cartoon*? It wasn't a real person. It was *drawn* person, a kind of caricature. It was a good drawing, really, as real as the Andy Warhol Campbell's Soup Can. When the drawing talked, the mouth moved exactly as you would expect it to – in synchronization with the words he was saying.

"I said, I see you've found me, *Mark*."

I just stared at the screen, since I have a policy about not talking to the television and certainly not talking to cartoon characters.

"That's OK. Take your time," he said.

If this was a jail cell, it was the strangest one I'd ever seen, not that I'd seen many. Whatever it was, I wasn't about to sit there watching cartoons – even if they did appear to be talking to me. I needed a drink. I got up and walked across the cold steel floor to the set of doors with pulls in them. The first one, with the number "1" painted on it and the one with the faint strip of light beneath it, was apparently locked from the other side, and didn't budge. I tried the second door – number "2" – and it opened right up.

It was a closet.

It was only about eight inches deep, and had no rod, hangers or anything else, but other than the fact that it was so shallow, it was like any other closet. I studied the inside closely. It was completely empty. I couldn't be sure, but I wondered if the back wall of the closet opened up somehow. I pushed on it, but there wasn't any give, so I stepped back and pushed the door shut. I moved on and looked at the last big door, the double-wide, which had a big "4" painted on it. It didn't have a handle or hinges. There was no way to open it, so I banged on it.

Behind me, I heard the cartoon guy say, "It's locked."

No shit. I glanced warily in the direction of the TV to find that he was still sitting there on the screen, acting like he could see me.

I ignored him and moved down the wall to the half door – the one that looked like oversized cupboard door – and wondered what would be inside. It had a large 3 painted on it. I put my fingers in the inset and pulled. It opened right up. It was probably about a foot deep. Not big enough to hold a person, but big enough to build some shelves and store some booze. I must suggest that to whoever lives here, I thought.

The cupboard wasn't empty. I found myself face-to-face with a banana and a bottle of water. Evian.

What the...

"I thought you might be hungry," the cartoon character on the TV said. "You better eat it so you can get your strength up."

"With a banana?" I asked incredulously, and immediately wanted to bite my tongue for acknowledging the cartoon character.

"Yes, I'm afraid that's it for now," he said. "Unfortunately, you may be facing some, um, tough times ahead, depending on the extent of your dependance on alcohol."

"Yeah, about that..." I said, deciding I might as well play along. "I could really use a drink right now. Do you suppose you could work that out? And then I think I'd better be going..."

I was standing right in front of the screen now, talking to this cartoon character like he was a real person. He smiled at me indulgently, as one might look at an imbecile.

"Yes, I'm sure you would."

And with that, the screen went blank.

18

The figure on the gurney would be safe, he knew, because those leather straps had been tested on more than one occasion. He made his way down his "hall of fame," filled with before and after photos of his students – photos that he alone would ever see.

Unlocking and locking doors as he went, he made his way into the main part of the house where he finally emerged into the front hall. Crossing the hall, he skirted past a round burled mahogany table, which featured a Waterford crystal chandelier hung over a Baccarat crystal vase. Usually the vase was filled with French tulips, delivered fresh every Tuesday and Friday by overnight delivery from a flowers-by-mail place in Holland. Today the vase sat empty. He would have to ask Greta about that.

He moved quickly toward the dining room, entering through double pocket doors which had been left open. He found his place setting at the far end of the table, as it always was. It consisted of a crisply ironed linen place mat, centered exactly one-half inch from the edge of the highly polished Duncan Fife table. A Limoges service plate was centered on the placemat, flanked by flatware from Tiffany & Company. A bowl of fresh daffodils sat in the middle of the table. A silver pot of coffee sat just to the right of the upper right hand corner of the placemat, but his own cup of coffee had already been poured and sat, steaming, to the right of his plate. A *New York Times*, folded once in half was on the table in front of him, but he knew it was yesterday's edition, since the *Times* was not delivered locally.

Breakfast was unusually good. Greta apologized repeatedly for being late, but he assured her it was OK, that he knew the roads were bad because of the snow. That explained the missing tulips in the entry foyer; they were probably still in their shipping container in the kitchen, and she simply hadn't had a chance to place them yet. She still seemed worried about being late, even after he assured her she needn't be. She was too valuable to him, and he needed her. Besides, she knew too much, and if she ever stopped to put all the pieces together, she might know way too much.

A small glass of apple juice, placed on a small linen cocktail napkin, sat in the middle of his plate and after he drank it in two large gulps, Greta whisked the glass away and replaced it with a plate with steam rising from it. This was good, since he liked his food hot.

She had made his favorite breakfast: Belgian waffle with melted butter, maple syrup and a side plate with four pieces of crisp bacon. Greta had been with him for only a couple of years now, but he must remember to give her another raise – although he knew from past experience she would insist she didn't deserve it. When she first replied to his want ad in the *Chaffee County Times*, he took one look at her and figured she would never work out, but he decided he would give her a two week tryout.

How wrong his first impression had been! Greta was everything he needed and wanted: a fastidious housekeeper and a terrific cook who went so far as to plant and maintain a vegetable garden in the small space on the south of the house, just off the kitchen. She was a little nosy for his tastes, but perhaps that was to be expected – because he, in turn, was a little mysterious.

He watched her out of the corner of his eye and wondered what she would look like without that circle braid on top of her head. In the time she had been with him, he had never seen her with her hair down, literally and certainly not figuratively. She was all business, German through and through, although as he looked at her now, he realized she was actually a good looking woman. She had a nice, healthy tan and rosy cheeks which he guessed she might have gotten from pinching them or, on a day like this, from the cold weather. He knew they weren't red from make-up, because she didn't use any.

The braid was all that still existed from the German *fräulein* look she'd had when he first found her. During her first year with him, she wore traditional German clothing, which consisted of alternating red and blue pinafores with white frilly blouses underneath. Bizarre, even in this somewhat eclectic Colorado mountain community. "They are 'dirndl,'" she explained. "Native dress in Deutschland." He had smiled indulgently at the time, but every time he saw her, he half expected her to break into a polka. After she'd been with him for two weeks and he had decided she was just what he'd been looking for, he decided it was time to confront the issue of that get-up.

"Greta," he explained kindly, "I think I would prefer that you wear something a bit more professional and less, um, *deutsch*." She was clearly put off by this suggestion, and even though she appeared in a white blouse and navy blue skirt the next day and every day since, she barely spoke to him for over a week afterward.

He didn't care, and eventually she seemed to forgive him and returned to her old self – minus the *dirndl*.

Yes, Greta was worth her weight in gold, other than the fact that she was so damned *nosy*.

19

Greta had heard him enter the dining room, as he did every morning he was in residence and not on one of his many "business" trips. He took his place at the head of the big table. She always greeted him with a big smile and a cheery "Good Morning!" or, if she was feeling a bit feisty, "Guten Morgen!"

She never addressed him by name, even though he invited her early on to call him by his first name. She knew he didn't mean it, so she simply called him "Mister" or "Sir."

She served him breakfast and busied herself with other things in the kitchen as he ate. The laundry was unusually light this week, and it appeared that his brother must not have worn any clothes this week; or if he did, he didn't get them dirty. Very strange, indeed.

Ah, the mysterious brother. As Greta loaded the washing machine she recalled the day she almost lost her job – all because of that damn brother.

Mister had told her, the day she applied for the job, that he had a brother who lived in a separate wing of the house; he was emotionally "handicapped" and got enormously upset when exposed to anyone other than his brother. She was never, ever to go to that part of the house – Mister would do all the cleaning in the brother's room himself – and all Greta had to do was prepare his meals and do his laundry. Mister would do everything else. *Gott im Himmel; she didn't even know the brother's name! "Scooter?" What kind of name is that? Not a real name, certainly.*

During the first few weeks of her employment, she decided she should eventually meet and befriend this mystery brother, whether Mister wanted her to or not. After all, didn't she have a special needs cousin herself? And hadn't she taken care of that sweet girl until she was old enough to go into a special training school in Munich? But when she suggested this plan to Mister one morning at breakfast, he told her in no uncertain terms that it would never happen, and she was never to bring it up again.

She never did, but that didn't stop her from wanting to simply *see* the brother – perhaps smile at him and hand him one of the shortbread cookies he seemed to like so much. If she happened to be outside the back of the house, maybe he would see her and come to the window or something. So, when Mister drove away from the house one day, Greta waited an hour to be sure he wouldn't come back for something. Satisfied that he would be gone for awhile, she took a plate of cookies, walked out the front door and all the way around the big house to where she knew his quarters must be located. It was quite an adventure, since there was no walkway or even a path on that side of the house.

She negotiated the large stones filling the strip between the house and the lawn, occasionally peering in a window to get her bearings, based on what she knew of the house inside. But when she got toward the back of the house, she discovered there were no more windows, only a solid wall of the large white building blocks that had been used to construct the house. She was mystified as to why there weren't any windows – *Wouldn't the brother enjoy seeing the magnificent view from atop this mountain? Why in the world would Mister deprive his brother of some outside air once in awhile – or at least another person to look at?*

When she came to the three-car garage, she knew she had gone beyond where the brother's rooms must be located, so she simply stood in the driveway, holding the plate of cookies and looking backward to where she'd just come from – nonplussed that she had failed in her mission. Finally she re-traced her steps, cookies in hand, back to the kitchen, where she placed the plate of cookies on the counter before sitting down, defeated.

Mister returned shortly thereafter, and he was furious.

"Greta," he said. "I thought I very specifically instructed you not to bother my brother *under any circumstances*."

Greta's cheeks instantly turned crimson. "Honestly, I didn't, Sir. I...I...I just wondered what he looked like...but I never saw him, Sir, honest!"

Seeing how upset she was, he softened his tone slightly. "I believe you, Greta. But you are not to disobey my instructions regarding my brother again, or I shall have to dismiss you." And then, as though he read her mind as she wondered, *But how did you know?* he said, "By now I should think you would have noticed that this house is under video surveillance *at all times*." She couldn't help glancing at the camera in the corner of the room in which they sat and thought to herself, *Of course. He taped me.*

MAKEOVERS - REX JOHN

20

He taped everything. The moment Greta had stepped around the corner of the house, a motion-detector in his security system triggered an alert to his iPhone.

He was, at the time, sitting in a Starbucks in nearby Salida reading the *Wall Street Journal*. Although his attorneys had already notified him, he wanted to read for himself that there was a major play under way for his family's firm. He already had more money than he could count, much less use, so the fact that the sale would vault him into the stratosphere of the rich and famous meant nothing to him. His father may have felt "bums" might as well die if they didn't work, but Carson felt certain they could be saved -- one person at a time. One hopeless person at a time. And, God knows, he was doing his part.

The buzzing of his phone annoyed him, as did every phone call, e-mail and tweet. He was tempted to let it go to voice mail until he glanced down and saw that the screen was flashing "Security Intrusion." Even at that, he almost turned the phone off without a second thought since this was the time of year when an occasional deer would somehow manage to vault the fence before eventually being chased out the front gate by his handyman.

But just to be sure that it was, in fact, an errant deer, he pushed a few buttons on his phone until the screen filled with an image taken by camera number 6, located on the south side of the house. He was horrified at the image that filled the screen. It wasn't a deer at all.

It was his new housekeeper. Greta.

He watched, fascinated, as the woman -- dressed incongruously in a German folk costume and carrying a plate of cookies – walked gingerly atop the large bed of river rocks used as ground cover between the house and the vast expanse of lawn. He made a mental note to speak to her about a uniform to replace the get-up she now wore.

Don't do it Greta. Don't you dare do what I think you're going to do. Don't do it if you want to live.

He continued to watch even as he began slipping on his jacket. He was at least twenty minutes from home, even at top speed. Who knows what she could do in that length of time?

The image switched to camera 7 as Greta continued her trek.

Oh Greta. Why can't you mind your own business, you silly, stubborn woman. What a nosy, hardheaded German you are!

The image switched again, this time to number 8. He sat back down and smiled slightly, realizing that it didn't really matter what she saw, because there wasn't anything to see. There were no windows on that side of the house, save for the large picture window in his study, and it was coated with a film that prevented sunlight – or prying eyes – from piercing its shiny reflective shield. Besides, he thought, even if she could see into that room, all she would see that might interest her further would be the door into the control room, and that would be tightly shut.

He now watched, entranced, as Greta came all the way to the garage, and then around the corner. Camera 9 picked up the image, now a full frontal view, of the puzzled look on Greta's face as she apparently processed the fact that there was nothing to see.

He breathed a sigh of relief, knowing she had walked right past the section of the house that, from the outside, looked like all the other exterior walls, but which actually concealed a large courtyard – the "playground," as he referred to it – where good students were sometimes allowed to go relax after a hard day of studies. If she could fly – and who would put it past her, the witch – well, he didn't want to think about that.

But he couldn't stop thinking about it, even as he watched her retrace her steps toward the front of the house, her body language betraying her defeat. What if Harry had been in the playground? And what if he had thrown one of his screaming fits? Would she have been able to hear it? Probably. He frowned at the notion before dismissing it as impossible. Harry would *never* be allowed to use the playground, so nobody would ever hear him, including Greta.

Harry Lythgott had been enrolled in the school a few weeks earlier and, as was so often the case during those first days, things were not going well. Boy, could he scream. This guy had been into everything: booze, pot, heroin. Detox was miserable for both of them, which was why Carson had escaped to Starbucks.

Almost as bad as the drug and alcohol problems was Harry's weight. He was easily 75 pounds overweight, and Carson remembered thinking twice about his selection as he loaded him into the back of the "school bus." He managed, with some difficulty, to roll him in, but on the way back to the compound he'd made a quick and simple decision: this guy was going to lose weight if it killed him.

Greta was told that "Scooter," the name Mister had given his imaginary brother – in honor of the cocker spaniel he'd had growing up – had been thriving under her fabulous German cooking, and would she please follow a strict diet for him, beginning immediately. She had made a feeble attempt to do so, but as each guest tray appeared on the hall table outside the door of the study, he sighed and proceeded to walk directly to his private bathroom and flush half of whatever was on the plate down the toilet before placing the remainder in the cupboard for Harry.

But, Harry wasn't buying it. If he wasn't writhing in pain on the floor with various withdrawal symptoms, he was whining about the fact that he was "starving." Most of his cries were ignored – courtesy of a mute button on the console – but as Greta walked unwittingly past the portion of the wall which screened the courtyard and the classroom beyond, Carson held his breath as he wondered if she would somehow be able to hear the screaming.

Apparently the soundproofing on that section of the house worked, because he noted that she didn't break stride as she walked along the wall of the courtyard.

He snapped the phone off and sat there, enraged that she had disobeyed his instructions. He had to get control of himself. *I can't ask my students to control their anger if I don't control mine.*

Satisfied that he had calmed down, he neatly folded his Wall Street Journal and left it on the table before him before rising slowly and casually walking out of the coffee shop to his car in the parking lot.

On the way home he decided all he would do is simply speak to her. She would be embarrassed and apologetic – and probably furious with herself for not realizing that in a house where every inch was under constant video surveillance, she hadn't thought to look for exterior cameras. He had little doubt that it would ever happen again.

But unbeknownst to Carson, Greta's curiosity was far from being satiated. She was as hungry for more information about "Scooter" as Harry was for something more to eat.

MAKEOVERS - REX JOHN

21

It took me a couple of weeks to get used to the cartoon figure on the screen – and to talking to a television screen, for that matter. But eventually I adjusted and it ceased to annoy me. But, oh what an experience those first few weeks were!

I didn't get that drink, of course. In fact, the last bit of alcohol that ever passed my lips from that day to this was on that park bench in downtown Denver. I won't deny that I still crave it from time to time, but nothing like I did during those first few days in the "classroom."

But Sir knew what he was doing. He knew I was well on my way to completely ruining my life when he found me and helped me see the light. "Mark," he would say, even after I'd tried to convince him repeatedly that my name was Cary Evans, "Mark, that was the *old you*. We're in the process of making a *new you,* and even though it isn't easy I think you'll be pleased when we're finished."

He was right, of course, and if I find him – and I hope I will – I will tell him again how grateful I am for everything he did for me, even though some of his methods were, shall we say, *shocking*.

22

Carson Kirkpatrick was only nine years old when he discovered the power of electricity. He had, in direct disobedience to his mother's instructions, climbed up the aluminum ladder to help Morris, the family chauffeur, attach Christmas lights to the big wreath hanging on the front door. After the lights were woven in and out of the evergreen boughs, Carson inserted the plug into the end of the extension cord, not realizing that one of the prongs didn't go into the proper hole but, rather, touched the aluminum ladder on which he stood.

The resulting shock threw him from the ladder, breaking the circuit and no doubt saving his life. For years afterward, the boy wouldn't even turn on a light switch, so fearful was he that he would be electrocuted. Then while he was watching the 60's television show *Mr. Wizard* he learned that electricity, when used properly, was not inherently dangerous.

Not that the students who passed through Carson's steel-lined "classroom" would necessarily agree.

MAKEOVERS - REX JOHN

23

Fresh from his reprimand of Greta, Carson was in no mood to put up with Harry's curses and screaming.

He sat back down at the console, flipped the audio switch for the classroom and was immediately assaulted with Harry's screaming gibberish. He switched the audio off and sat in silence, watching fat, naked Harry flailing about the classroom, his mouth twisted in fury as he spewed curses toward the television screen where he had last seen "Sir."

Snapping the control room microphone and video switches on simultaneously, Carson knew that his altered image, now digitized into cartoon form, along with his distorted voice, would once again fill the classroom. He switched the classroom audio on briefly and noted that Harry's shouting subsided only for a moment after he noticed that the "man" was back on the screen. He finally had an audience again, but this only seemed to energize his tirade.

Turning the volume up several notches, Carson leaned into the microphone and said, in a low, firm voice, "I thought we talked about this type of behavior, Harry."

"Yeah, well *fuck you!*" came the reply.

That did it. It was time for Harry to learn that shocking language could have shocking results.

The last words Harry would remember of that particular conversation were, "Watch your language, young man." With that, Carson depressed a large red button on the console that delivered anywhere from 20 to 1100 volts of electricity into the metal floor, bed, table and chair of the classroom. Fortunately for Harry, the regulator on the switch had been set at only 50 volts, but it still brought Harry to his knees, and then to the floor, in profound pain, as the current coursed through his body. The shock only lasted a moment, but in addition to Harry's newly frizzed hair, he had just learned a powerful lesson. Sir didn't like the word *fuck*.

24

As he watched Harry, he would have sworn he saw a plume of smoke rise from his ears. He smiled, since he knew that was only wishful thinking. But at least Harry would know better than to use the "F-word" again; or if he didn't, he soon would.

Carson didn't like profanity and rarely used it himself. As he once explained to one of his more cooperative students, using profanity just shows ignorance – a lack of vocabulary. That particular student had tried to argue the point, and in the interest of fairness Carson pretended to listen attentively.

"Really, they're just words, Sir. Don't you agree? And frankly, if someone is angry, isn't it better for them to swear as opposed to, say, performing an act of violence?"

"Well, if those are your only two choices, of course," Carson replied. "But those are never the only choices."

"Oh?" the student responded, unaware that he would never win this argument no matter what he said.

"No, of course not. He could, for example, learn to control his emotions. Only foolish, low-class people resort to violence and displays of anger. Sensible people learn at an early age to control their feelings." Carson was sure about this, since it was precisely what he had done in his own life.

The student wasn't giving up. "Oh, please. Are you going to tell me, Sir, that you've never had an emotional response to something – a feeling you couldn't control?"

"No, never," Carson replied.

"Really?" the student said, obviously unconvinced. "So you've never been upset? You've never hit your thumb with a hammer and said, 'Oh darn' or something? Because, it's really not the actual word "fuck" that bothers you, is it? Isn't it the emotion behind the word?"

"No," Carson said firmly. "I have not. And, for the record, it is not just the emotion behind the word that annoys me. The word itself annoys me – and, by the way, I suggest you not use the word again in my presence, even by way of illustration."

Carson watched carefully for a reaction from the student, his hand poised above the red button to drive home his point if necessary. But the student acquiesced and the matter was dropped.

Carson's beliefs about profanity were not subject to debate. As far as he was concerned, people should not be allowed to use that kind of language anywhere, anytime, and the courts were fully within their rights to slap down those who did. It may be a free country, but it doesn't have to be free when it comes to the way people talk.

And that was that.

25

Sir had *interesting* teaching methods, that's for sure. That first week was a nightmare for me.

I finally ate the banana and drank the water, of course. Drinking the water was my first mistake, because it was obviously doctored with something that put me to sleep again. I learned over time that there was no way to tell where the knockout drops would show up; I was taking my chances any time I ate or drank anything. And from what I could figure out, each time I fell asleep, somebody – Sir, I assume – came in and gave me an injection that caused me to lose consciousness for hours. While I was out is when things were done to me – not bad things, I hope, but who knows? For example, pretty early on I woke up with a new haircut. I couldn't see that it was cut – there wasn't a polished surface anywhere in that room, even with all that steel, but I sure as hell could feel that it had been cut.

The room changed while I was knocked out, too. One time – and I'm pretty sure I'd been there for three or four weeks at that point – a keyboard appeared in the surface of the desk. I'd noticed a keyboard-shaped indentation in the desk early on, but when I got on my hands and knees and looked at it from underneath, I saw that it was a compartment with a keyhole. Then lo and behold, one day I woke up and there was a keyboard, obviously having been flipped into place from the bottom, like the old Singer Sewing Machine cabinet my grandmother used to have. A new TV monitor, in addition to the one across the room, appeared in the wall directly above the keyboard, but it too was installed behind plexiglass so I couldn't touch it.

I'll never forget that morning when I saw the computer keyboard and screen for the first time. (I say it was morning, but for all I know it was nine o'clock at night. I had no concept of time until the last month or so.) Noticing it I said aloud, without thinking, "Oh good, guess I can surf some porn now." I was just kidding, sort of, although I'm sure if it had been available I would have given it a shot. But Sir was not amused at my wisecrack and said, "I don't find that funny, Mark."

Inexplicably, I started to cry. Somehow I knew I had just earned myself a jolt of electricity; it would leave me crying and shaking like a leaf for the next few hours, and I didn't want it to happen.

I can't even describe the first time I got shocked, but I knew I never wanted it to happen again. And yet it did – over and over and over – until my nerves were so frayed that I tried not to do anything even remotely upsetting to Sir. I knew he controlled the switch that caused the walls, desk, chair and bed to come alive in an instant, sending a jolt of who knows how many volts through my body and making my hair literally stand on end. It makes my nerves jump to this day, just remembering it.

I didn't like it, to say the least.

But it didn't come this time. My muscles tensed up, and I'm sure I closed my eyes as hard as I could to brace myself for the pain, but it never came. I had already said, as quickly as I could, "I'm sorry, Sir!" Perhaps that saved my ass this time. Or maybe he never planned to do it anyway. Either way, I sat there tensed up for a minute or two before he said, "You won't be receiving any correction this time, Mark" – that's what he called it, *correction* – "so you can relax." Actually, if I'm not mistaken, I never received correction again. God knows, I tried to be a very, very good boy at all times.

After I relaxed for a few minutes, Sir appeared on the screen again. "Mark, since you brought up the subject of 'porn,' I can't help but notice that you don't seem to be, um, taking care of *those* needs." And then, after another brief pause, "You can, you know." This was the weirdest conversation we ever had, and the only one during which I thought he might be as uncomfortable as I was. Clearly, sex wasn't a part of the school's curriculum.

"Uh...," I said, not really knowing how to go on. The truth is, I did need to crank out a load, and even though my mind had been kept plenty busy on other things, I could feel in my nuts that I needed to get off. But I also knew I was under twenty-four hour surveillance, and I guess I hadn't been horny enough to give him a show.

"Would you like some porn?" he asked. "And if you're worried about my watching, I have better things to do, so all you need to do is let me know you need some privacy and I'll give you an hour by yourself."

"Well, um, yeah, I guess that would be nice," I said.

"What, the porn or the privacy?"

"Well, both really, I guess, Sir, if that's OK."

"Fine.   So, what's your preference in porn, straight or gay?"

I was flabbergasted. I'd always had girlfriends and was even well on my way to marrying Cookie before I ran away. How dare he not see how obviously hetero I was.

But by now I knew better than to show any displeasure about anything Sir did – or, for that matter, to express any personal wishes or preferences of any kind, unless I was specifically invited to do so. He had asked, so I decided to answer. "Either one will be fine, Sir."

The next thing I knew, the ceiling lights dimmed by half, and I was treated to two dudes going at it on the screen above the computer.

I didn't care. I was in prison, so maybe I should have a prison sex life.

26

Carson had been so busy thinking about Harry – one of the few students to ever "drop out" of the School of Life – that he completely forgot he had a new student to process.

Taking one last sip of the hazelnut coffee Greta had poured for him on her last trip from the kitchen, he blotted his mouth, folded his napkin and placed it neatly next to his plate. His knife and fork were now in the proper position on his now empty plate ("eleven o'clock to two o'clock") as he quietly slid his chair away from the table. Once again he had a flash of Harry. He was reminded of the first time he had placed a linen napkin on Harry's food tray behind Door #3. Harry's predictable reaction was, "What the fuck is this for?" That earned him 50 volts, and Carson smiled faintly at the memory. *I'll bet my utility bill went up considerably during Harry's semester with me. I should ask the accountants.* Harry never did learn how to properly use a napkin, often wadding it up and dropping it in the middle of his soiled plate! What a pity.

"Thank you, Greta," he called out, even as he was moving swiftly toward the door. There was no way his new pupil could be awake yet, but just to be sure, he glanced at the gold Piaget his father had left him. *At least two more hours.*

Making his way through the entry foyer and to the door under the stairs, he placed his palm on the pad which was almost invisible on the wallpaper which covered the wall. Instantly, a door swung inward, opening into the hallway toward his study. Even Greta had access to this hallway, which she needed in order to pick up the laundry and deliver the food for his "brother." Carson had been throwing away all the food left on the trays for the last week since, until last night, he hadn't had a student in residence. He always thought of this time off as "spring break," even though this last interlude, for example, had occurred during the dead of winter. He suspected he would need to continue discarding the food for a day or so, since he was fairly certain the new student wouldn't be in any condition to eat soon. They never were.

Rounding the corner of the hallway leading to his study, he noted that last night's dinner tray with its empty plates remained on the console, right where he'd left it after depositing its contents down the toilet the night before. He placed his palm on the electronic palm reader next to the door and slipped through the opening even as the door was still moving. He was now in his study.

Carson loved his study. In addition to the priceless books – many inherited from his father – which lined the floor-to-ceiling shelves on two walls, he loved the thick, hand-tied Persian Rug beneath his feet. The rug had originally been commissioned by the Maharaja of Baroda and was acquired, some say under suspicious circumstances, by Carson's great-great grandfather in the late 19th century. Carson had been told to insure it for $4 million, making it the most expensive single object he owned – excluding his art collection, of course – but, sadly, the rug was a piece few people would ever see because of its location in his private study.

Almost as valuable as the rug was his Louis XVI kingwood desk which sat directly under a beautiful leaded glass window which framed beautiful Mount Princeton. At 14,197 feet, Mount Princeton was not Colorado's tallest peak, but he had climbed it, along with several other peaks when he first moved to the state, hoping to become a member of the elite group of mountaineers who could claim they had climbed all 54 of Colorado's "Fourteeners." After completing a handful of the grueling hikes, he decided he would rather devote his excess energy to his "project." Still, he loved gazing at Mt. Princeton, knowing that at any moment the sun and shadows playing on the peak could create a completely different panorama than he might have seen only an hour earlier.

But for some reason, Mt. Princeton upset him this morning. His brow furrowed as he remembered that it was the beauty of this mountain that caused him to make one of the few missteps he had ever made in the presence of a student. He had grown quite fond of Mark Boston during the last few weeks of his semester, and the two men spent a great deal of time talking like old friends. Never mind that they only spoke when Carson wanted to, and then only via the animated figure that appeared on Mark's screen. Mark had adapted to Carson's image and no longer begged him to reveal his identity which, of course, he would never be stupid enough to do.

But on the morning in question, they had exchanged greetings and pleasantries as Mark sat eating from the breakfast tray before him. Mark asked if it was a nice day. Without thinking, Carson said, "Yes, and Princeton is especially beautiful this morning." No sooner were the words out of his mouth than he realized he had given away his location.

He was prepared to shock the knowledge right out of Mark's head if he had seemed the least bit interested in what he had just heard, but Mark was deeply involved with the Belgian waffle before him and didn't register the incidental comment at all. If Mark's face had been in direct view of a camera at that moment, Carson would have noticed that the corner of his mouth turned up slightly as he made a mental note to remember what he had just heard.

So, I'm in Princeton! But how the hell did Sir get me all the way back to New Jersey from Denver?

27

As Carson walked across the room to his desk, he remembered the worst breach of his own elaborate security precautions – involving the same student, ironically – and the mere memory of it caused him to sit down in order to control his breathing.

One of the school's security procedures had to do with the delivery of food to students. Carson understood from the beginning that he must never reveal his own identity. Even though his intentions were benevolent, and even though his students would surely be grateful for his intervention in their lives when they finally graduated, he didn't want one of them trying to put together a "reunion" or something equally insipid down the road. Nor did he want the authorities knocking at his door with talk of "kidnapping."

So before Carson ever opened his school, he created a long list of security precautions which had evolved into the strict procedures he now followed each and every day.

Except for that one time.

When Carson determined that it was mealtime for a student, which could be three times a day or only twice a week, depending on behavioral changes, the student's food was placed in the food cupboard, Door #3. Initially, this was done on paper plates (even though the food certainly did not come from the kitchen that way), accompanied by a plastic spoon or, in the case of Harry, no utensils whatsoever. As the students moved incrementally through the curriculum, they graduated to Wedgewood china and sterling silver flatware – although never a knife, of course, for the same reason the airlines no longer allowed knives on board. On the off chance that a student would ever break free, which was extremely unlikely, he didn't want them armed. After the food was in place inside the cabinet, Carson released the lock, permitting the student to open the door from the other side and retrieve his food. Students never knew for sure when they would eat, if ever, so Carson had plenty of time to lock the steel security door on his side of the cabinet before returning to the console and directing the student to get his food. The system worked flawlessly – except once.

Carson's breathing became more rapid as he remembered it. Why couldn't he just let it go? Once again, he recapitulated the events of the evening.

Dinner had looked especially good. Mark had become trustworthy enough to eat with real china and silver, and his food was served on the same silver tray which Greta had delivered to the table outside Carson's study. Tonight it was salmon, served with a light lemon sauce, new potatoes and fresh green beans that Greta's husband – who worked as his handyman – had picked in the garden. The tray also bore a small Caesar salad and a ramekin of crème brûlée.

Mark couldn't wait. It had been a long day, filled with discussions about everything from foreign affairs to domestic politics – with travel and religion thrown in for good measure. He was starved and ready to eat. He was hoping for some of Sir's delicious Veal Schnitzel, and he felt impatient. Without thinking, he went to the cupboard to see if the food had been delivered yet – even though he had been told never to open any doors without permission.

Unbeknownst to Mark, Carson had just placed the tray inside the cupboard at the exact same moment when Mark opened the door on his side to retrieve it. The two men froze: Carson, because he was totally unprepared to see Mark standing before him, *looking directly into his face,* and Mark because he was finally seeing the face of another human being – the man who was, most likely, the real-life version of his cartoon captor.

Carson was so startled that if he hadn't already just set the tray inside the cupboard, he would have dropped it on the floor. For a split second, the two men stood, not speaking, frozen in place. Carson finally regained his composure and slammed the steel door in Mark's face, leaving his student standing there, slack-jawed, and staring at the metal panel and the now trivial dinner tray in front of it.

Carson stood on the other side as he frantically tried to decide what to do. Mark had come too far, and he had done too well, to throw him away at this point. Besides he wasn't sure there was enough electricity to erase this particular memory from Mark's mind. Moving hurriedly to the console and attaching his headset, Carson switched on the classroom monitors and watched as Mark slowly removed the tray from the cabinet and placed it on his table. He didn't look up at any of the cameras focused on him, opting instead to simply be seated, slowly unfolding his napkin and placing it on his lap.

Carson cleared his throat, twice, before turning on his microphone and his animated image. "Hello, Mark," he said, trying to sound as nonchalant as possible. "How are you this evening? My, that looks like a good meal, doesn't it? Somebody in the school cafeteria must like you." *Damn. Don't sound so guilty!*

"I hear you saw one of the cafeteria workers when he delivered your food. Ha, ha! I guess you really scared him..."

Yeah, right. Keep talking, Sir. I know that was you, and you know I know it.

Mark looked up at the camera and said simply, "I won't tell, Sir."

There was quiet for several seconds as both men stared at each other's electronic image.

"Well, that's very nice of you, Mark, but I'm sure Manuel doesn't mind that you saw him. It's me I don't want you to see! Now, go ahead and enjoy your dinner." With that, Carson flipped off his microphone, and the screen at which Mark was staring went blank.

Carson sat there, trembling, for an hour or so, until he noticed that Mark had returned his tray to the cabinet and gone to bed, his back to the camera.

Maybe he believes me. Maybe he really does think that was Manuel.

But he didn't.

28

Finding people, my private investigator tells me, isn't all that hard. "It just takes time," she says.

Yes, time that is charged at $500 an hour, plus expenses. No wonder it takes so much time.

Actually, I shouldn't be so hard on this chick...I mean *woman*. (Sir taught me better, and he would not have been amused to hear me refer to a lady as a "chick." God, no! So, I stand corrected. I shouldn't be so hard on this *woman*.)

The fact is, she came highly recommended as someone who has been solving complicated cases since the 1970's. My friend Marco, who recommended her, says he knew her when she "didn't even have a cell phone." To Marco, that is the equivalent of living in a log cabin, because he has every electronic device ever invented. But, according to him, Kinsey – that's her name – was forever plugging dimes into pay phones and going to the library to do her research using microfiche readers. This must have been pre-Google, I guess. What hooked me was Marco's assertion that she always solves her cases. *Always*. That's what I needed to hear.

Besides, I like her as a person. She's been married at least once – twice I think – but she seems hopelessly single now. Not that she couldn't get a man. On the contrary, she is one of the most attractive women

I've ever met. She doesn't even seem to mind that I'm a lowly author, and she didn't turn her nose up when I told her. "I hear writing can be a lucrative business," she said.

The only problem is, Kinsey is in California, and I'm here, in New York. We make it work, though, with periodic updates from her (always by phone, since she's still stuck in the 80's and doesn't use e-mail) and an occasional call from me when I happen to remember anything about Sir that may be helpful to her. I'm getting ready to make one of those calls now, to ask her about Princeton. I just recalled a conversation in which Sir said something about "Princeton looking so beautiful" one morning, even though I know he didn't mean to, because he would never have let me know where I was. I suspect Kinsey will assume, as I did, that Carson had been referring to Princeton, New Jersey, but I just Googled "Princeton" and found that there is also a Princeton, Massachusetts, North Carolina, West Virginia, Kentucky, and Minnesota! I doubt this will be helpful information to her, but I'll make the call anyway and hope she can do something with it.

I hired Kinsey right after the *People* article appeared, and so far I've paid her over $50,000 in fees and expenses. The money doesn't matter to me, or I should say it won't if she locates Sir. I still think that if anybody can do it, this chick can.

I mean *woman*.

29

After recovering his composure from his unplanned trip down memory lane, Carson decided he really must start processing the new student, or at least re-inject him, before he had a chance to wake up.

He had learned that it was much easier to get them to take that first shower after he'd taken away all their clothes. All he had to do was promise them new clothes as soon as they had cleaned up. Cutting their clothes off (and burning them) while they were unconscious was the most efficient way to get the job done. That would be his next task.

He moved to the control room, in front of the console, to check the video feed. The guy was still draped in his old Army blanket, but had apparently worked one hand out from under the blanket and the restraining straps. *That's odd. And what is it that looks so strange about his hand?*

Carson continued into the hallway which circled three sides of the classroom, giving him access to the false backs of the door and cupboard through which he provided things to his students, including their food. The last door, which wasn't a cupboard opening but a true door, led to the exterior courtyard, with its twenty-foot high stone wall. Carson referred to the time spent in this area as "recess," but the students weren't allowed even to know of the existence of the courtyard until they had earned it.

When they did earn it, it was rewarding to see their reaction to seeing it. For some of them, it was the first time they'd seen blue sky or sunlight for several months. Carson had designed this area himself and had made it especially beautiful with trees, bushes, and flowers. A Brown-Jordan recliner chair was situated in the center, on a brick terrace surrounded by closely clipped grass. Sometimes, when his students were doing their "homework" indoors in the classroom, Carson would slip into the courtyard himself, through his own private entrance, and sit in the sun for a few minutes.

When the student was using the area, Carson was there too, in the form of his anime figure on a flat panel television built into the wall, just beneath the roofline. The entire area was under surveillance at all times, via a swivel-camera mounted under the eaves above the monitor. Each student eventually earned the right to enjoy this area, of course, since school wouldn't come to an end until they had – fat Harry being the notable exception.

So far, none of the students had tried to escape over the courtyard wall, which would have been quite a climb for even the most athletic; but just to be sure, Carson had placed a bare electrical wire along the entire perimeter. He turned it on only when he gave them access to the outside door, but he tested it from time to time by simply leaving it on and waiting for a bird to land. That usually didn't take long – he might throw some bread crumbs on the top of the wall to speed up the process – and it was only a matter of minutes before he would see a bird land and light up like a Christmas ornament, making a sound like a very big bug zapper. The bird would then fall to the ground, and Carson would place it in a trash bag so as not to arouse suspicion from Manuel when he tidied up the flower beds on the other side of the wall.

Just inside the hallway, beside Door # 4, he paused again and took a deep breath. He wasn't frightened, exactly, since it was virtually impossible for a new student to (a) be awake or (b) get himself free of the gurney straps. Still, one couldn't be too cautious, so he paused in the hallway and took a moment to fill a fresh syringe with Methohexital.

He took another deep breath, stalling. Processing new students was his least favorite part, since all of them were filthy. He didn't know which was worse: the terrible bad breath they all seemed to have, or the thick matted hair which more often than not was filled with lice and/or other assorted creatures. He almost always shaved their heads that first day, and once again his memory turned to fat Harry whose thick, Rastafarian braids had broken not only a pair of kitchen shears but his barber clippers as well! Few school memories were more pleasurable than that of seeing the look of horror that came over Harry's face when he regained consciousness and realized he was bald as a billiard ball. He couldn't see himself – there were no mirrors in the classroom – but he seemed to immediately sense that his hair was gone and quickly put his hands on his head. He screamed and sputtered and ranted and raved, but it served him right. Barber clippers weren't cheap.

OK, you've put this off long enough. Let's see what we've got here. And with that, he placed his palm

on the electronic pad and watched as the classroom door
swung open.

30

Good. He's still out. I can only wonder what nightmare caused him to wriggle his arm free, but I'm sure I'll meet his demons in the weeks ahead.

He unbuckled the thick leather straps first, allowing them to drop over the edge of the gurney, each making a loud clang as it came into contact with the floor.

As he began peeling off the Army blanket his eyes caught what it was he had noticed fleetingly on the console screen. *This guy's wearing fingernail polish!*

True, it was badly chipped and a goth black color, and it looked ridiculous on his short, raggedly finger nails, *but this ought to be an interesting story. Finger nail polish! On a guy!*

As he peeled the Army blanket off the unconscious figure before him, he immediately realized his mistake.

What the...?!

Not only was this guy wearing fingernail polish, but he was wearing eye shadow as well. And his hair was long, but had been pulled back into a bun. The dress he was wearing was almost floor length, one of those pioneer type get-ups the women of yesteryear wore as they drove their covered wagons across the prairie. The shoes were odd, too: black lace-ups, about six inches above the heel and looking suspiciously like men's work boots, except smaller.

Carson stared, trying to imagine why a man would be dressed like this. Finally, he was able to process the image before him, and he reeled backwards as though the body before him had suddenly come to life.

This had never happened before.

He was about to process his first female student.

31

He eased the woman into a semi upright position, straightening out her legs and arms, then placing her legs side by side and folding her arms across her chest. He allowed her to sink back into a prone position. She was sleeping soundly, and her breathing so shallow that for a moment he wondered if he'd killed her. This was the point at which he usually removed the new student's clothing, and also when he got his first glimpse at what he had to work with.

With fat Harry, it had been a particularly unpleasant sight: in addition to the filthy hair on his head, his back was covered with a blanket of hair that could easily have been made into a throw rug. His triple chins were encrusted with saliva, and even though he was completely knocked out, he snored so loudly that Carson would have sworn the floor was rumbling. Worst of all, of course, were the tattoos. The blue tear drops tattooed on his left cheek, from his eye down to his chin, made him look like someone had splattered blueberry juice all over his face. A spider web extended out from each elbow, and a naked woman reclined in a seductive pose on his upper right arm. A huge native American tribal chief filled the space on his chest, a spider web circled his belly button, and his right calf sported the words "Born to Kill." His left calf said "Claudine" –

both written in huge cursive print. He was a sight to behold.

Carson's reaction to the discovery that Harry was covered in ink was intense, to say the least. He felt like a child at Christmas who had expected one thing and got something entirely different. His disappointment was profound enough that he briefly considered wrapping Harry back up, putting him on the gurney and returning him to the doorway in which he'd found him. Dedication to the "cause" won out, however. *If I can't salvage this fat blub, who can?*

But the tattoos had to go – and did.

But there was a big difference between Harry and the young woman now lying before him. Gazing at her unconscious figure, he scanned her body for tattoos. He couldn't tell for sure, since she was still fully clothed, but there were none exposed. At least he might not have to deal with that.

32

The YAG-CL 1000 Laser Tattoo Removal System was manufactured in Canada and, because of its weight, delivered only by surface freight. Carson hadn't bothered to tell Greta to expect the delivery and, as luck would have it, the truck showed up at the front gate on a day when he was in Poncha Springs, sitting in Starbucks. He'd left Harry quivering in pain after a particularly strong dose of "correction," and he needed to get away while he calmed down.

Greta left the delivery man cooling his heels outside the gate as she called Carson on his cell phone.

"Mr. Kirkpatrick, there is a gentleman here with a large crate for you."

"Oh yes, Greta. Well, please ask him to wait for me in the driveway in front of the garage doors until I get there to sign for it. I'll be less than twenty minutes..."

"I could sign for it if you wish, Mr. Kirkpatrick."

"No!...I mean, that won't be necessary Greta. I'll be there shortly." And with that, Carson ended the call and headed home. Greta was left staring at the now dead telephone receiver in her hand.

Why, I never. What is so special about this big wooden box that I can't even sign for it? It looks like an air-conditioning unit...but that wouldn't make any sense.

We already have air conditioning and I can't remember ever needing to turn it on. An outdoor sculpture, perhaps? There were already a couple of large pieces of art in the yard, enormous Henry Moore bronzes which, according to Mr. Kirkpatrick, "cost a fortune." She remembered the delivery of the last sculpture – it was in a huge wooden crate but clearly visible through the slats. Whatever was in this crate, it was packed securely and completely hidden from view.

She walked around it as the delivery man stood by, smoking a cigarette. She considered telling him that Mr. Kirkpatrick didn't allow smoking on the premises – inside or outside – but decided to let her boss deal with that issue himself, as she knew he would.

She searched for a shipping tag as the driver looked on. There wasn't one, so she concluded it must be on the clipboard the man had left on the seat of his truck.

The only markings on the crate were "YAG CL-1000," which was no help whatsoever. What in the world could "YAG CL-1000" refer to? *I'll ask Manuel. Maybe he will know.*

Carson pulled up in his Lexus SUV just as the delivery man was about to lower the back gate of his truck and begin off-loading. He'd decided he couldn't wait all day for this owner of the house to arrive no matter what the German woman wanted.

Carson exited the car and said, "Hold on there, please."

"Excuse me?"

"Hold on, please. I'd like you to put it inside the garage, down at the third bay."

"Mister, I can't do that."

At this point, Carson noticed the spent cigarette butt which had been ground into the brick pattern of the driveway. He glared at the man, then the cigarette butt, then back at the man. Without another word, the man bent down, picked up the butt, opened the door of his truck and placed it in the ashtray. *Ah, yes, we all know the power of that look,* Greta thought to herself.

Returning to the discussion at hand, Carson picked up where he'd left off. "Yes, well, I'm telling you to move it down there and to put it in the garage instead of leaving it out here in the driveway."

After a quick assessment of the luxurious and finely appointed yard around him, the driver realized this might be an opportunity to make an extra twenty. "It'll cost you."

Carson gave him a withering look. "That's not a problem. Just do it."

Carson watched as the man lowered the gate of his truck and then jumped on to maneuver an oversized motorized forklift onto the gate before lowering it back to the surface of the driveway. After moving its fork into position beneath the pallet, he lifted the crate and drove it down to the third garage door, which Carson had already opened. He directed him into the third bay of the garage – the one where Carson's Lexus was usually parked – and lowered the cargo gently to the polished concrete surface of the garage. He withdrew the fork and aimed the lift back toward the rear of his delivery truck.

"Hold on there."

Under his breath, "Shit." And then, to Carson, "What now, Mister?"

"How much for the fork lift?"

"What?"

"How much for your fork lift," he repeated, as if addressing a slow-witted child.

"Are you kidding, Mister? This thing ain't for sale..."

"I'll give you five-thousand dollars. Cash."

"What? Look Mister, this thing ain't mine; it belongs to my employer, and it ain't for sale."

"Ten thousand, then. You may tell your employer that somebody must have stolen it while you were at lunch this afternoon. Ten thousand. Cash."

That's all it took. The delivery man shrugged as Carson entered the house through the garage and retrieved a stack of bills from the safe in his study. The delivery man was now $10,000 richer, Carson had a new fork lift, and the delivery company would file a police report later that day asserting that somebody had stolen a practically new fork lift from their truck while it was parked in front of a Denny's restaurant in Colorado Springs.

Carson wasn't much on driving. If his mother's driver Morris' hadn't been such a perv, he would probably have kept him on after his parents' accident. But Carson had learned to drive by then, thanks to the Porsche 911 his father had given him for his sixteenth birthday, and now he was used to it. Still, a forklift? How did this damned thing work?

He figured it out and, by luck, he had almost one-eighth of an inch to spare as he drove his new laser tattoo removal equipment into the large hallway just off the garage. Later, after he'd put Harry to sleep, he would drive it on into the classroom.

Tattoo removal was about to begin.

33

Carson didn't like tattoo removal. He didn't like the buzzing sound from the YAG CL-1000, he didn't like the flashing laser light, and he especially didn't like the smell of flesh burning.

Still, it had to be done. What type of person could expect to get ahead in life when their skin was covered with colored doodles? What message does that send to a prospective employer, for example?

When students came to Carson tattooed, their marks were removed whether they liked it or not. That was one of the free services of the school, and besides, it was a rule. Not everybody wanted them removed, or *would* have wanted them removed, had they been asked, and most complained of the pain when they woke up – but by the time the scabs fell off, they fully understood how foolish it had been to get them in the first place. Carson saw to that. *("Next time you feel like being artistic, get a piece of paper and some colored pencils.")*

The pain associated with removal usually wasn't an issue, because the students were put to sleep beforehand. None of them was told in advance what was going to happen; Carson preferred to surprise them when they awakened the next day, often with intense residual pain and always with major scabbing.

Fat Harry, for example, was not pleased when he awakened one morning to discover that "Claudine" had gone missing from his left calf. He didn't realize that all the tattoos had been removed from his back as well.

"What the fuck have you done to me! Who the fuck do you think you are! You have no right to remove my tattoo! I liked that tattoo!"

Calmly, Carson replied, "No you didn't. How could you? And I've told you about using the word 'fuck,' Harry."

"Fuck you anyway!"

He had been given fair warning, so Carson didn't flinch as he gave him a 50-watt jolt to jog his memory, once again. Carson didn't see himself as a sadistic person, but it did give him a strange pleasure to watch Harry's eyes jump around before rolling back into his head. But even after that, when he came around he continued to rant about the removal of his tattoo so much that Carson decided to be a bit more forceful with his next *learning experience*.

Wednesday's tattoo removal began as usual, with two tablespoons of Benzodiazepines mixed into Harry's morning orange juice. Carson actually preferred to use Rohypnol – commonly referred to as "roofies" – the date-rape drug, but he'd had trouble finding any lately after a scandal involving their use on the campus of the University of Durango appeared in the media. As soon as Harry had fallen asleep, Carson elected not to inject him with the Methohexital to take him fully out, as he normally would, but instead strapped him securely onto the gurney, donned a surgical gown, gloves, and, for effect, a rubber mask from the motion picture

"Halloween II." Then he sat down and read a book, waiting until Harry woke up.

When he was sure Harry was fully awake, Carson moved into his line of vision and, to Harry's horror, began removing the remaining tattoos, all located on his chest, arms, and shins. He did so painstakingly, one at a time – fourteen of them – as Harry screamed his head off. *Too bad, really. Some of these are deep.* One, in fact, required incising, not unlike removing paint speckles with a razor blade. There was considerable blood which Carson swabbed with cotton squares dipped in rubbing alcohol. Harry seemed to like that pain least of all, judging from his screams. At some point during the all-day procedure, when Carson had heard enough screaming and tearful pleas, he simply bent down and removed the shoe and sock from his own right foot. Wadding the sock into a ball, he stuck it in Harry's mouth. Harry's eyes opened wide in terror, but at least Carson was able to finish in relative quiet.

As he finished erasing the last of the fourteen tattoos with the laser needle of the YAG CL-1000, he stood back and looked through his mask into Harry's eyes, which were red and full of tears. Leaning in, he whispered into his ear, "Try to remember next time, Harry. We don't like the word 'fuck.'"

Unfortunately, Carson's words were wasted, as Harry was beginning to lose consciousness. Taking no chances, Carson walked to the steel table and picked up the syringe of Methohexital he had prepared and slowly injected it into the now unconscious figure. After tidying up, he loosened the gurney straps and wheeled the gurney back to the steel shelf-bed across the room. After locking the wheels in place, he simply rolled Harry back onto the shelf where he would awaken in about four hours, somewhat groggy and in terrible, lingering pain, but completely free of tattoos.

34

Frowning, he looked at his watch and wondered how long he had been standing next to the gurney, staring at the young woman, but daydreaming about Harry. What an odd juxtaposition. Why, he wondered, did he spend so much time obsessing about fat Harry? Why couldn't he just let him go? Yes, Harry was a failure, a big one. But nobody is successful all the time, are they?

He smiled at his own question. *He was*.

Except for Harry, he thought, the frown returning.

But now he had another opportunity to salvage a life, to reclaim one of society's rejects. The new student before him held promise. Who knows what she may turn out to be? There was no question that eventually she would learn everything she needed to be a successful human being. It would be a painful process – it always was – but eventually she would thank him. They all did.

Focusing on the body before him, he felt the color rise in his cheeks as he realized he must disrobe this new student, just as he had all those who preceded her. He had stripped women before, of course, if you count Sharon Spencer. Sharon had cornered him on the terrace of the country club one hot summer day and insisted he give her a ride home, even though the

Spencer estate wasn't even three blocks from the club. Once they got there, they ended up in Sharon's room, and one thing led to another until the two of them were lying spent, side-by-side on Sharon's big canopied bed. It had been Carson's first time, although he wasn't about to tell Sharon that, and frankly, he hadn't liked it that much. But, Sharon went on and on about how much she enjoyed it, so he must have done something right. Still, the whole thing was far too messy for his taste.

Now, looking at this new student, he wondered if, given the chance, he would try sex again. *Probably not. I doubt that it's any less messy these days.*

Slowly, he unbuttoned the top of her homely little dress. The gingham-looking dress looked incongruous with the black nail polish and heavy eye makeup. *Don't worry dear, we'll teach you some fashion basics. Oh yes, we'll teach you that and so much more.*

There were six more buttons down the front of the cotton dress, not including one that had been replaced with a safety pin. The dress had a built-in fabric belt, which he loosened. He opened the two flaps of the dress, as one would a book, and looked at the cheap bra and panties beneath. Gathering his courage, he reached for the kitchen shears and snipped the bra at the mid-point in front and sliced the panties at the side. As he lifted the bra from her small breasts, a rumpled twenty-dollar bill and a photograph fluttered to the floor. Retrieving them, he slipped the dollar bill in the pocket of his slacks – she wouldn't need any money here, that's for sure – and examined the small photo more closely.

It was a picture of a newborn, taken in a hospital by the name of Casper General, which he took to be Casper, Wyoming. He knew this because the baby was lying in a hospital bassinet with a placard attached at the foot. The placard, held in place by a plastic frame, had the words "Lewis girl," followed by the date – August 28, 1968 at 12:32 p.m., the height, 20 1/4 inches, and the weight, 7 pounds, 1 ounce. He tucked the photo in his shirt pocket.

He removed her shoes and socks, dropping them into the trash bag he had brought for that purpose. He gently lifted the girl a foot off the gurney, extracted the dress, bra and panties, and deposited them into the bag as well. Her disrobing complete, he stood back and looked her over.

She looked young, too young to throw her life away on drugs and booze. Carson stepped forward again and looked for any signs of a crack or heroin habit. Finding none, he decided her drug of choice must be alcohol, and he breathed a short sigh of relief. Drug detox could be complicated and oh-so-messy. He didn't like the screaming and carrying-on. Alcohol wasn't easy, but by comparison it certainly was. After a few days without it, no matter how addicted they were, they began to settle down.

He also noted, with relief, that he had been correct: there were no tattoos to be removed.

He looked at her hair and, lifting her head gently, loosened the bun and let the dirty tresses fall free onto the surface of the gurney. It was a mousy brown color and showed no sign of highlights or bleach. Turning her head toward him, he saw something he had somehow missed until now: a purple birthmark, no bigger than a half-dollar, right in the middle of her left cheek. He bent in to study it. It was shaped somewhat like the state of Florida, and looked like it had been rubber-stamped on her otherwise flawless skin. His mind flashed to photos he had once seen of Soviet former president Mikhail Gorbachev. Everybody commented on the mark on his forehead. This was the same thing, except a different shape in a different place on an beautiful young woman instead of a balding middle-aged man. It was exceedingly unattractive on an otherwise attractive young woman.

It would have to be removed.

35

I won't lie to you. Adjusting to Sir's classroom was hard. Real hard. At first, I wished he had left me on that bench – and left me *alone*.

In time, though, I knew it was the best thing that ever happened to me. He taught me things about myself I never knew. He made me think about stuff I'd never considered. And, by God, he helped me stop drinking once and for all.

I know there were other students before me. In fact, he told me so. Sometimes he even mentioned their names – not their full names, of course, but their first names. He talked a lot about some guy named "Harry," and I got the distinct impression that Sir didn't like the guy. I asked him once what became of Harry, but he wouldn't tell me.

"It wasn't my greatest accomplishment. Let's just leave it at that," he said.

I think Harry must have had tattoos, because early on Sir said to me, "At least you're nothing like Harry, Mark. You don't have tattoos. You don't know how lucky you are."

I stupidly replied, "Oh, do you have tattoos you don't like?"

With that, Sir laughed. He didn't laugh easily or often, but I liked to hear it when he did. It always made me laugh when he did. In fact, toward the end, before Sir released me, I spent a lot of time trying to make him laugh, and I'd say I succeeded about half the time. When I got up my nerve to ask him once why it seemed so hard for him to laugh, he told me it was because his childhood hadn't been that funny.

I think I was his favorite. I have no way of knowing this, but I think we had things in common: for example, I think his family might have been wealthy. Not that mine was, mind you, except for my grandmother. My grandmother was very, *very* rich, according to my mother. But she and my mother were barely on speaking terms for as long as I can remember, and my visits to her were usually by myself. She would send her driver or, on rare occasions, she would come with him to pick me up. I have an early memory of waiting on our front porch for her to arrive. Mom had told me at breakfast that I would be spending a few days with my grandmother and that I was to take a bath and put on "decent clothes." She came into my room while I was getting dressed and gave me a navy blue duffle bag that had the words *Boston National Bank* stenciled on the side and gave me a little lecture about *minding my manners* because "manners are very important to your grandmother." It's funny how I can remember things like that little blue bag, which happened at least twenty years ago, but I can't remember what I ate for breakfast this morning. I carried that bag everywhere after that, so proud of the fact that our family obviously owned a bank. When I once said something about that to my grandmother, she laughed and said, "Wherever did you get that idea, Mark? Because our last name happens to be Boston? You do realize, I assume, that there is also a city named Boston and that, I should think, is where the Boston National Bank is located. You sweet boy. We're not involved in anything as tawdry as banking, darling. We're in oil."

I flushed with embarrassment: not because I'd made a mistake, but because we were involved in the oil business – or, as Grandmother humorously referred to it, the "all bidness."

In any case, Sir and my grandmother were *very* much alike in that they both insisted that things should be done in a "certain way." I also think he liked it that I'd obviously had "good training."

When he quizzed me at length one day about my childhood, which I rarely talked about, I told him about a visit with my grandmother that I have never been able to get out of my mind.

I was four or five years old and had been sent to spend the weekend with Grandmother. (I was permitted to call her "Nana" when we were alone together.) When her driver brought me home again Sunday night, I found mother crying, and my dad was gone. I approached her warily. Mom and I were never very close, but my dad and I were "best buddies," as he used to say. As an only child, it means a lot to have a dad you're close to, and boy, were we close.

I asked where he was, and Mom said, "He's gone Mark."

"What do you mean 'he's gone'? Gone where?"

"We're getting divorced, Mark. He's moved out. You will visit him every other weekend. Now go get ready for bed."

As I said, Mom and I were never close, but after that night I can barely remember speaking to her again.

It wasn't a year later, when I was waiting for Dad to pick me up for our weekend together, that Mom came into the living room and sat me down and said, "Mark, your Dad won't be coming to pick you up today..."

I interrupted. "Yes, he will. He said he would. This is his weekend to have me."

She ignored me and was silent for a moment. I noticed that she had been crying, so I said, "Why? Why isn't he coming?"

"Because your Dad died this morning, Mark." And with that, she grabbed me and pulled me close to her and buried her face in my hair, sobbing. I was having none of it. I pushed back and slipped from her embrace.

"No!" I shouted. "He is not! You're lying!" But even as I screamed the words, somehow I knew they were true, and I was as sad as I can ever remember being.

I don't know why I wasn't allowed to attend my Dad's funeral. I was six years old, so I could probably have handled it, but I wasn't allowed to go. One of Nana's maids was sent to babysit me while everyone else rode off in the back seats of two big black cars. The day after, grandmother's own car pulled up and she made one of her rare appearances inside our house. She and mother talked quietly in the kitchen and I overheard Mom say, "I haven't told him yet, *Mother*." The way she spit out the word *mother* was full of so much venom it made me cringe, even though my own tone of voice wasn't much different.

"Mark, come in here a moment, please," Grandmother said, which caused me to jump. I went in the kitchen and approached her slowly. Pulling me toward her, she said, "How would you like to come live with me for awhile? You already have a room at my house, and we'll get you a bicycle and send you to the Randolph School in the village. Wouldn't you like that?"

I don't know whether or not she thought she needed to talk me into it, but she didn't. I was ready to go in a heartbeat, and I welcomed a chance to get away from my mother.

Truth is, Mom had been mean to me – physically abusive, that is – and I was scared to death of her. Grandmother, on the other hand, as strict as she was about manners, was very kind to me. I never needed to worry about getting away from her, as I did my mother during her frequent outbursts of rage. Answering Grandmother's question, I said, "Would I!" and ran off to get my things. Charley, her driver, was waiting on the front porch, and he took my suitcase as soon as we stepped out the door. I was half way to the car before Grandmother called to me and said, "Mark, come back here and say good-bye to your mother, please."

I did as I was told, but the hug we gave each other was for Grandmother's sake. Neither one of us meant it.

36

I liked living with Grandmother. I had some chores, of course, but mostly everything was done for me. I really liked her driver, Charley. I could tell he was a nice guy, but Grandmother didn't encourage me to get close to the "help," as she called them. "You must be respectful, Mark, but don't forget they are not here to be your friends. They are here to serve you." That conversation took place in the backseat of Grandmother's Lincoln Continental with a glass partition between the front and back seats and two little footrests that folded up out of the floor just behind the front seat. The window between the front and back was down at the time, and as soon as Grandmother said, "They are here to serve you," I saw Charley give us a look in the rearview mirror. She noticed it, too, and without saying a word, simply pushed a button in her armrest to raise the window to its closed position. It was the only time I can recall when Grandmother embarrassed me.

I lived with Grandmother for eight years, from the second to ninth grade, and I loved it. I especially loved the Randolph School, where I had lots of friends. I was taken to visit Mother every few months, but the visits were never planned in advance and certainly never looked forward to. I would hear the phone ring, and shortly thereafter Ellie, Nana's maid, would come find us and announce, "It's Miss Boston, Ma'am." I would detect a slight grimace and Grandmother would leave the room to take the call. When she came back into the room, she would simply announce, "Your mother wants to see you tomorrow, Mark. Would you be ready to go at eight o'clock, please? Charley will drive you."

My visits with my mother were always strained and awkward. She rarely spoke to me, and I remember that we watched a lot of television which, of course, was discouraged at Grandmother's house. *Intelligent people don't waste time watching television, Mark. They read books!* Sir repeated those exact same words to me one day during class, and it made me smile as I remembered my dear Nana.

Mother also drank a lot when I visited and, I suppose, when I didn't. In one of my first visits with her, she asked if I would like a "sip" of her drink – I couldn't have been more than eight years old – and, to avoid another disagreement, I took one.

I really liked it.

Over time, that became the only reason I could stand to visit my mother – I knew she would offer me sips of her drinks and, eventually, allowed me to have my own. Looking back on it, I was probably a full-fledged alcoholic by the time I was ten, but of course that was something I kept hidden from Grandmother, who had a very well-stocked bar, even though she didn't drink herself. Well-stocked until I got into it, that is.

That bar almost got me in big trouble. Emma, the cook, was responsible for ordering food and liquor for the house, and since Grandmother gave big parties, it wasn't unusual for the truck from Kreck's Liquors to pull up to the service entrance on a weekly basis. I had just filled the water bottle for my bike with vodka one day when Emma popped around the corner and hissed, "I *knew* it was you! What in the world are you doing, Mister Mark! Your grandmother would have a fit if she knew you was drinkin' like that! Now cut it out!"

"OK," I said. But I didn't. Not by a long shot. And Emma never said another word about it. But, as I told Sir, *I knew that she knew, and she knew that I knew she knew. You know?* When I said that, it made him laugh.

37

I was in ninth grade, bored and possibly a little drunk when I went out riding my bike in Grandmother's neighborhood: lots of winding, tree-lined streets with big walls and gates protecting them. I had just come back into our circle drive when Mother pulled into the driveway in her old Chevy Caprice. At first I didn't believe it was her, because I had never seen her at Grandmother's house before. There was a strange man in the passenger seat. I rode up to her car and asked, rather rudely, "What are you doing here?" At the same time, I recall wishing she had a drink in her hand, as she usually did when I was with her, but she didn't. She was cold sober. "Never mind. Where is your Grandmother?"

"In the house of course." I looked across her to the guy who, when we made eye contact, said, "Hi, Mark!" like we were old friends. I'd never seen him before, so I ignored him.

Mother said, "Mind your manners," but by this time she was on her way into the house, through the side door into the kitchen. I watched her go, turned and looked at the strange man again, who sat right where she'd left him, and I prepared to pedal away. He said, "So, whatcha doin', Mark?" I just looked at him, since it seemed pretty obvious what I was doing, and rode off down the driveway.

It couldn't have been more than ten minutes before Ellie came scurrying out of the house and waved frantically at me down in the driveway, signaling me to come up to the house. I did, but I took my sweet time, and I could tell she was agitated when I finally pedaled up to her. "Your Grandmother wants to see you *right now*. She's in the drawing room."

I left my bike where it was, went in through the kitchen door and grabbed two chocolate chip cookies off the counter as I walked by, earning a scowl from Emma. I went through the kitchen into the butler's pantry and on into the dining room. From there I walked through the big double doors into the entry way, crossed it, and over to the sliding doors into the drawing room. I knocked as I'd been taught to do and waited until I heard Grandmother say, "Enter."

Grandmother was seated at a big desk in an alcove at the far end of the room, at least fifty feet away. Mother was standing just inside the door. I glanced at Mother and went immediately to Grandmother's side.

"Dear, I'm afraid I have some news you may find unpleasant," she began. "But I shall expect you to behave properly, with no emotional outburst. Do you understand me?"

"Yes, Grandmother," I replied, a bit puzzled by the request, since I couldn't recall ever having an "emotional outburst" and knew that such a thing would never be tolerated.

"Your mother has come for you," she continued. "She has some good news, indeed. She has met and married a very nice gentleman who has never had children of his own, and he should like to be your new father. You will be leaving me to go live with them."

With those last words, her voice caught and I saw that she was about to cry.

I don't really remember what happened after that, but I'm pretty sure it involved an emotional outburst.

38

Dave, as I was instructed to call him, was my new stepdad. He was ten years older than my mother and also liked to drink. They built a new house out in the suburbs, nice but certainly not as posh as Grandmother's. I had my own room, which I stayed in virtually every minute that I was home, avoiding both of them as much as possible. I had my own television and extension phone – although I didn't use it much because I knew one of them was sure to be listening in.

Mother turned out to be even meaner than I remembered, and it wasn't any time at all before she and Dave began having serious problems. I would sometimes awaken in the middle of the night to hear them shouting at one another, wishing I were back in the oh-so-civilized world of my grandmother.

Dave, who initially made a big production about wanting to be "friends," turned out to be almost as mean as Mother, and he frequently referred to me as an asshole.

Maybe I was. I was drinking pretty heavily now, even though the liquor cabinet was kept under lock and key. I knew where the key was hidden and I made good use of it. Mother once said, "You better lay off the booze, Mark. That's what killed your dad, you know." If anything, I drank even more after that.

Charley, Grandmother's driver, still picked me up on occasion to go visit Grandmother, but only for lunch or dinner – never overnight. "You've spent enough time with the old lady," Mother said. "Your home is here now."

Indeed, the "old lady" was becoming older, and even though her house was the first place I went when Mother bought me a car for my seventeenth birthday, my visits became more and more infrequent as her aging became more apparent – and painful – for me to watch. I am ashamed to admit that I had all but abandoned her completely by the time she died, at 92, while I was a senior in high school. Mother, Dave and I went to the funeral, which was a big affair at St. Elizabeth's Episcopal Church where she and I had attended church every Sunday when I lived with her. Mother didn't cry at the funeral, and I hated her for it. I was inconsolable.

Grandmother left me a ton of money in a trust, and although I wouldn't find out about it until years later, my mother and Dave did everything they could legally to try to break the trust and take it. They didn't succeed, thankfully, which is how I managed to get a Yale education.

Of course I almost threw all that away, and would have too, if Sir hadn't rescued me off that park bench.

39

Carson took one last look around the classroom to make sure nothing had been missed. He had moved the girl from the gurney to the steel shelf and was half tempted to bring in a mattress and pillow to make it more comfortable – something he'd never done with any of the male students. He thought better of it, though, since he didn't know what she would do or how she would react to her new surroundings. He did make one concession, though, something he never would have considered for his other students: he dressed her in an oversized t-shirt and gym shorts. He decided it wouldn't be "seemly" for her to realize he could see her walking around naked, even though he obviously had – and would.

He withdrew from the classroom, noting that the steel door had closed with a whoosh behind him and that the double electric deadbolts had clicked into place.

Seated at the control console, he put his headset on and checked one of the monitors above him which showed exactly what the students were seeing on the monitor in the classroom. He gave a small smile as he remembered his trip to Japan to buy the equipment and software in front of him. Mr. Yakamoto, sales director of *Tokyo Anime*, had listened patiently as Carson outlined his requirements.

"I would like your talented artists to create an anime representation of me," he explained. "I don't want it to be too overdone – you can skip the oversized eyes and eyelashes – and I would like the mouth of the new figure to move when my mouth moves and its eyes to open and close when mine do. Is that possible?"

"Oh yes!" Mr. Yakamoto exclaimed. "So easy! Have ready for you today!" And with that, Carson was escorted onto a sound stage where a host of young assistants scurried around to make him comfortable. He was seated in a leather swivel chair in front of a large, electric blue background, and little sensors with protruding wires were glued all over his face. These, in turn, were plugged into a computer a few feet away, at which sat an attractive young woman named Kiko. Kiko wore a headset, and Carson could see his image, wires and all, on the screen before her.

A TelePrompTer was attached to the large television camera in front of him, and after the director had called "Quiet!" he was asked to simply read a long list of words as they scrolled before him.

The words were mostly nonsensical, just various English words that required different movements of the face. *Persnickety. Oblong. Butter. Elephant.* Word after word, which he had been told to read "with great pleasure, please."

The word list morphed into paragraphs of text, including several nursery rhymes and children's poems. *Peter Piper picked a peck of pickled peppers*, he read over and over before a new phrase appeared.

The entire exercise took less than an hour, but Carson was exhausted afterward and had his driver return him directly to The Imperial, where he proceeded to take a three-hour nap. By six o'clock that evening, a package was delivered to him, containing several computer disks and an invoice for ten thousand dollars – the amount Mr. Yakamoto had quoted when he said he was willing to pay rush charges, expecting that it would shorten his wait time from a couple of months to a couple of days. He never imagined it would take less than a day.

He went across the living room of his suite and popped a DVD into the large screen TV. He couldn't help but smile as his avatar appeared before him. *Carson Sai,* was his new name, according to the label on the disk. It didn't look anything like him – it was, after all, a cartoon figure – but its mouth moved in exact synchronization with the words he was hearing on the soundtrack. The software altered the character's voice as well as its wardrobe. When Carson was home again, his own computer would "learn" even more movements of Carson's mouth so, as he spoke, the character would mimic perfectly what Carson was saying.

Fascinating. Excellent.

MAKEOVERS - REX JOHN

40

The girl slept. Carson watched her for a long while, running questions through his mind. This was the exciting part. He felt like a kid on Christmas morning, unable to wait to see what was in his package. What were her addictions? He had already examined her for tell-tale needle tracks, including on the heels of her feet, where many addicts who still functioned in the mainstream tried to hide the evidence. As far as he could tell, there weren't any marks indicating that she was a user of heroin – or worse. That didn't eliminate other drugs, of course. He'd enrolled more than one student who had a crack cocaine addiction, which required a special small-bowl pipe and a flame. Others were addicted to pharmaceuticals, everything from valium to morphine. And of course they all smoked pot, insisting that it was harmless and seemingly unaware of its connection to the next drug they would eventually try in order to "relax." Carson didn't buy it. He didn't have any patience for drug or alcohol abuse, and he took care of those addictions right at the start, using what some would say was an unorthodox methodology: complete and immediate withdrawal. *Cold Turkey.*

But, oh the screaming, vomiting, fainting and other histrionics!

The problem was, once the patient was fully awake, it was impossible to re-sedate them, except orally, through their food. So, if they wouldn't or couldn't eat – which many of them couldn't – he had no way of knocking them out and administering a compassionate dose of pain-killer. So, they suffered. *Well, maybe they should have thought about the consequences before deciding to try drugs. It's not like they weren't warned of the dangers of drug abuse!*

Thinking about drugs and the effect they'd had on society upset him. He tried to put the subject out of his mind, turning his attention to the sleeping figure on the gurney. Where was she from? What was her childhood like? Were her parents alive? Were they looking for her, worried sick about a daughter they loved and cared about? Or was she a product of a broken home, thrown out on the street to fend for herself at a young age?

She appeared to be in her mid to late twenties. She should have finished college by now and become a productive citizen. Had she enrolled and dropped out for lack of funds? Or had she simply walked away?

And what about the bizarre nail polish? What was that about? And that *dress!* That was one of the biggest pieces of the puzzle, and Carson tried to imagine what type of girl would actually walk around in such a get up. Was she the product of some hippie commune, raised by sixties parents without the benefit of being able to keep abreast of current styles? Whatever the reason, clothes would be the easiest thing to fix. The dress had already been taken from her, and by tomorrow it would be nothing but ashes in the fireplace in his study. Her new wardrobe would be much more fashionable, that was a given.

As he pondered her appearance, he glanced at his own anime image in the monitor above his head. What would *she* think as she looked at him? Would she think he was cute? Sophisticated? Urbane? *Would she learn to like him?*

He didn't realize he'd fallen asleep until he woke up with a jolt and found her face taking up almost the entire screen before him. He jumped back, even as she withdrew a few inches but continued to stare at the image on the screen before her.

She thinks she's watching television. She doesn't realize I can see her.

He quietly engaged his microphone. Softly and as gently as he could, he said, "Hello?"

She didn't reply, but tilted her head slightly, continuing to stare at the screen.

He tried again. "Hello...?" And then, sounding a bit like a parent playing a game with a pre-schooler, added, "I can see you..."

Her brow wrinkled, and she turned her head slightly as if looking to see if anyone else was there to verify this apparition on the screen before her. As she did, he noticed a detail he had missed before: her ears showed no signs of ever having been pierced. That in itself was rarity these days. Even his male students frequently arrived with one, two, or half a dozen ear rings dotting their ears, or at least sporting the scars where they had been before being removed – or ripped out in a fight – and sold or pawned to finance a habit. But this girl didn't have any. Why?

He waited a moment as she turned back to the screen. With a tone of embarrassment in her voice, as though anyone who heard or saw her would think she was crazy for talking to a television, she said, tentatively and in slightly more than a whisper, "Hello...?"

41

"Hello," he said again, trying to sound friendly and non-threatening. And then, "What's your name?" He grimaced inwardly as soon as he uttered those words. *I sound like I'm addressing an addled child.*

She cocked her head slightly, still unsure what was going on. Finally, she whispered, "Janet..."

Now he could establish two way communication, since she appeared to catch on that the cartoon image before her could actually hear and understand what she was saying and, better yet, respond to her.

He had gone through a similar adjustment period with previous students, but usually the student was more belligerent, threatening. Harry, for example, had raised his fist to the screen and said, "I don't give a shit who you are. I will fuckin' kill you, man! Do you hear me? When I get out of here, I don't care how long it takes, I will track you down and kill you!"

Carson smiled at the memory of how Harry's tone changed over the months, although in the end he still had to admit that Harry was his first and only failure. And what a spectacular failure it was.

"Well, Janet, I'm pleased to meet you. I'm sure we will be good friends by the time we're finished."

"Where am I?" she asked, looking around the steel room nervously.

"You are in a special classroom, Janet. I call it my 'Classroom of Life,' and you have been chosen as my only student."

She frowned. "Are you going to rape me?"

"What!" He was at once surprised and offended by the question. "Of course not! You will be perfectly safe and well cared for as long as you are a student here."

And then, quietly, "You're going to kill me, aren't you?"

Again, he was nonplussed. "No! I am not going to kill you. I told you, you will be safe and well cared for as long as you are here."

She looked skeptical. What was it about this girl that made him feel defensive? His hands were moist, and he felt flush. *What is this? What is happening here? Get a grip, Carson.*

Whatever it was, it was too late to change it. The teacher, Carson realized, was about to become a student, too.

His eyes – or rather those of his screen avatar – looked deeply into the beautiful eyes before him. *Who is this lovely creature? What have I done?*

They sat there for several moments, each staring intently at the video image before them. Janet was the first to speak again. She asked the question they all eventually asked: "Why me?"

42

If I have one regret, it is that I have such a bad memory. I used to tease Grandmother about her bad memory, and while she always laughed, I could tell it really troubled her that she forgot that she had already told me whatever story it was she was telling me again, as I so rudely pointed out. I know now that it embarrassed her, and I feel badly that I wasn't more sensitive – especially now that I realize I seem to have been afflicted with the same problem.

For a writer, it is time-consuming to have a bad memory. I've found that I must keep a list of all my characters' names next to my computer – and, believe me, I consult it all the time.

So there are lots of things I've forgotten but, to be honest, I don't care about most of them. In fact, I'd say there are very few things I truly wish I could remember. But at the top of my list would be the three brief glimpses I got of Sir's physical appearance.

If I could remember more about his facial features, it would give Kinsey, my private investigator, a lot more to go on. She told me early on that she worked closely with a police artist who could draw anyone or anything from a verbal description. That's how they get those pencil drawings of the dead people they find out in the woods. Apparently they don't have photo shoots, with the corpse sitting up smiling at the portrait artist. Sometimes they don't have much more than a skull or jawbone. The whole thing sounds pretty gruesome to me, but I still wish I could remember enough to describe Sir to an artist who could create a drawing we could use to search for him.

I only vaguely recall that first morning when I half-awoke to the feeling of having my pants cut off. As I already mentioned, I was in a stupor and barely aware of what was going on. I say it was "morning," but for all I know it could have been in the middle of the night.

Sir, if that's who it was, and I'm pretty sure it was, was wearing a surgical mask, so of course I didn't get a good look at him before I was put under again. I do remember that his hair was black or dark brown, with a little gray along the temples, but that's all.

The second time, only long enough to blink, the cartoon character of Sir which always appeared on the screen in front of me all of a sudden became a real person. It was brief, like the clicking of a camera shutter, and then it became the cartoon character again. For a moment, I couldn't believe it had even happened. Of course, the cartoon character showed pure terror when he came back on the screen, apparently realizing that the wrong button had been pushed. Still, it allowed me a short glimpse of the "man behind the curtain."

But it was such a brief glimpse, I can barely believe it even happened. *I wonder if Kinsey knows a hypnotist who could put me under and then quiz me about what I saw. I'll ask her.*

The real face morphed so quickly back into the cartoon image that my mind seemed to merge the two back into one. I remember the eyes, but only because they weren't much different from the cartoon eyes. They were dark and the eyelids kind of heavy, droopy even, like someone who was about to fall asleep. But that's it. That's all I can remember from that electronic hiccup on the screen.

My third and final look at Sir – if that's who it was – was a few seconds longer, although equally difficult to remember because of the surprise involved. I opened the food cupboard too soon, and there, standing before me, was Sir – even though he tried to pretend it was "Manuel," someone he referred to as one of the "school's cafeteria workers."

It was both exhilarating and terrifying to see a real person standing there – the first human being I had seen in many weeks – and I believe it was Sir himself.

But no sooner had it happened than I became scared to death *because* it had happened. I actually wondered if Sir would now decide he had no choice but to kill me, since I had seen his face. No surgical mask, no anime figure. It was a real person; the real Sir.

Clearly, he didn't want to be known. That's why I didn't press him when he said that I had only seen a "cafeteria worker." Perhaps if I went along, pretending I believed him, he wouldn't see the need to eliminate me.

Apparently it worked, because here I am.

In the back of my mind, though, I have to consider the possibility that he – Sir – may have been telling the truth. Maybe it wasn't him. Maybe it *was* a so-called cafeteria worker. Clearly, he had other people working for him, because there were days we would be working together non-stop on my "lessons," when all of a sudden Sir would call a break, and within minutes a fabulous lunch or dinner would appear in the cupboard.

The lapse between the time when he called the break and the time the food appeared certainly wasn't enough time for him to prepare it, so, he obviously had at least one other person working for him.

But – and trust me, I've gone over this so many times my head aches – if he did have other "accomplices," why did I never see *them* on screen? Why were all my contacts with Sir alone? And why, in God's name, would these people, whoever they were, allow him to keep me a prisoner for all those months without contacting the authorities? Obviously, they were in on it.

That makes me smile. Imagine – a group of people who want nothing more than to take down-and-outers like me and remake them into their own image. Sounds a bit like a religious cult. Hell, it sounds just like most of the churches I've attended or read about.

43

Greta could not get over the embarrassment of being caught trying to get a glimpse of Mr. Kirkpatrick's poor brother – who, as far as she could tell, spent his whole life in confinement.

Nor could she get over her curiosity. Who was this man? How old was he? What was wrong with him? What did he look like? And why, oh why, was her boss so determined that she never see him?

These were the questions she mulled over day after day as she prepared plate after plate of delicious food for "Mister Scooter," delivering the trays faithfully, as Mr. Kirkpatrick had ordered, to the console table outside his study. If she couldn't meet the brother, smile at him, and possibly give him a big hug, the least she could do was to ensure that he was well fed. And judging by the fact that every plate on every tray came back completely clean, he must like the menu.

Back in Düsseldorf, Greta's mother was known for her cooking, and after hearing so many compliments from friends over the years, she and her husband talked often about opening a small restaurant. Greta was only a year old at the time, and less than a year later, her mother had another baby, also a girl. "We could run the restaurant right here, out of our own living room," she dreamed aloud. "The girls would work with us. Everybody would come. You'll see."

Dietrich, Greta's father, was slight in stature and certainly no match for his ample and headstrong wife. He had learned long ago that it was easiest to simply go along to get along. "Yes, that would be wonderful," he assured her. Their plans were well underway when the brash young leader of the National Socialists party changed everything. The restaurant was shelved when Dietrich was called into active service, and Helga was sent to cook for none other than the Kommandant at the Dachau Camp, just outside Munich. Greta and her sister, five and six years old at the time, were cared for by their grandmother in the nearby mountain village of Oberaudorf, two hours south of Dachau, and less than a mile from the Austrian border.

Helga hated working for the Nazis and knew they *ver up to no gut*, but she was never permitted to go anywhere in the camp beyond the Kommandant's kitchen. She tried to question the ever-changing "helpers" who were brought from the camp to assist her in the kitchen, but the look in their eyes told her they didn't like or trust her. For the rest of her life she would be met with skepticism when she insisted she hadn't known what was going on, but the truth was, she never had.

At the end of the war she found herself a widow, learning that Dietrich had been killed by the Russians as they stormed Berlin. Helga joined her mother and her two daughters in Oberaudorf, where the girls had a relatively happy childhood – filled with games and long walks into the surrounding mountains. Mount Sudelfeld was Greta's favorite, and by the time she turned ten years old she was considered an accomplished hiker and skier.

When one of Helga's cousins wrote from America to encourage her to bring the girls and join him, she didn't hesitate. The three, along with Helga's elderly mother, made their way to a German community located in Fredericksburg, Texas. It was here that Helga was finally able to realize her dream.

When the girls were just starting junior high, she opened a tiny restaurant which she named the Old Heidelberg – simply because she had visited the town of Heidelberg as a little girl and liked it.

The specialties of the Old Heidelberg were Schlachtplatte, Veal Schnitzel, and the best red cabbage "this side of Berlin." Greta and her sister worked in the kitchen after school and on weekends, and they continued to do so for more than twenty years before Greta met and fell in love with Manuel Martinez.

By this time, Helga had made some money and decided it was time to sell the restaurant and retire, freeing Greta and her new husband to move from Texas to the mountain town of Salida, Colorado, where Manuel had been offered a job as a mechanic in an auto repair shop.

Three days after closing on the sale of the Old Heidelberg, Helga was crossing the street in downtown Fredericksburg when a teenager ran a red light and hit her, knocking her "half-way down the block," according to one witness. She died at the scene, leaving her daughters bereft, but also financially comfortable. Greta and Manuel came back from Colorado for the funeral, but stayed only one night. Her sister married Dieter

Rosencranz shortly thereafter and followed Greta to Colorado, settling in the capital city of Denver.

Greta knew her mother's recipes well, and they quickly became the signature items of her menus. She was most proud of her baking, offering delicious rhubarb pie (with a bowl of vanilla ice cream on the side), apple pie, apple strudel, and, of course, her famous German chocolate cake. Mr. Kirkpatrick obviously loved her cooking, although he rarely offered any comments, and it was obvious that Mister Scooter liked it as well.

Based on what she found in the laundry hamper, Mister Scooter did have strange habits, though. For weeks at a time he would wear nothing but gym shorts and t-shirts, with no socks or underwear. Greta came to this conclusion after she had been on the job only a short time. Each Monday she would go through the laundry hamper in Mr. Kirkpatrick's dressing room: throwing everything on the floor to make piles of whites and darks, and also separating what she knew to be Mr. Kirkpatrick's and what must be, by subtraction, Mister Scooter's. "Quite a difference in the size of those piles, let me tell you," she often said to her husband.

But then, after weeks of nothing but gym shorts and t-shirts, all of a sudden nice dress shirts and slacks would appear. Beautiful things, including Jhane Barnes, Gucci, Tom Ford, Polo, and even Armani – things Greta had to send to the dry cleaners. She didn't always recognize the names on the designer labels, but she could tell they were expensive. But just as quickly as the beautiful clothing appeared, it would disappear again, and the laundry hamper would contain nothing more than gym shorts and t-shirts again. *Is bizarre!* she would tell Manuel.

The ever-changing composition of the laundry made Greta even more determined to find out what was going on. She just didn't know how she would do it. She spent too much time worrying about it, or so Manuel said, until one day when she paid a visit to her hairdresser in Poncha Springs. That day her cut, wash and set sent her mind veering in an entirely different direction.

44

"God may love us, but he expects us to live our lives in a way that honors him!" shouted the Reverend John McCallister – "Pastor Jack" to his friends. "That means," he continued, "no drugs, no alcohol, no cigarettes, and *no tattoos!*"

Well, that's a new one, Greta thought. *I'd love to see where it says that in the Bible.* But she had grown bored with this sermon, and, truth be told, with her regular attendance at the Second Baptist Church of Poncha Springs. She had heard so many variations of the "do not do" list she'd lost count. And the list seemed to be growing longer all the time – especially since her boss had made his big contribution to the church building fund. Mr. Kirkpatrick had plenty of opinions – God knows she'd heard most of them by now – but apparently now Pastor Jack had become his mouthpiece.

The whole thing bored her. She leaned over and whispered to Janice Moser, sitting next to her, "I'm thinking of cutting my hair."

Janice was shocked, and opened her mouth and eyes wide to show her surprise. But to herself Janice thought, *it's about time. That bun is so yesterday.* She whispered, "Really? Why?" and then she added, "When?" – hoping Greta wouldn't chicken out.

"I'm not sure," Greta whispered back. Maybe this week. I don't think Mr. Kirkpatrick likes it."

I'm not surprised, Janice thought.

"I'm going to call Maggie tomorrow," Greta said, sitting back in her seat and allowing her mind to rejoin the sermon now in progress.

As promised, Greta phoned Margaret Cordone – "Maggie" – first thing Monday morning. Maggie was the only decent hairdresser in Poncha Springs, and every woman within a thirty-mile radius went to her. Her shop was painted a sickly pink color, with turquoise and cream linoleum tiles arranged in a checkerboard pattern. Although Maggie was the only hairdresser, four sinks lined one wall, each a different shade of pink. Maggie considered the effect *chic* – or, "chick," as she pronounced it – much to the consternation of the high school French teacher. The effect may have been "chick" to Maggie, but first time visitors usually reacted by dropping their jaws.

Photos of Maggie's nephews and nieces, along with photos of her customers' kids and grandkids, circled the mirror above each sink. Four large-helmet dryers stood guard against the back wall, the gold naugahyde covered lounge chairs positioned beneath them offering a comfortable nest for the wet-headed women who perched there.

Maggie kept a variety of magazines on the various mis-matched Formica coffee- and end-tables. Most of them had been contributed by patrons who had stripped them of their mailing labels – presumably so future readers wouldn't be able to see, for example, that Mabel Thornton subscribed to *The National Inquirer*. All the magazines were showing the wear and tear of being passed back and forth among patrons for the twelve years Maggie had been in business, and Greta reminded herself to bring her own reading material next time. Still, she expected to end up under one of the dryers today, so she needed something – anything – to read.

She picked through the stack and located a *Reader's Digest* that was identifiable only because of its distinctive size, since it was missing its cover and back page. Disgusted, she tossed it aside and settled on a three year old copy of *People* magazine instead. The cover featured an attractive man, who couldn't have been more than thirty years old, hunched over an Apple laptop computer, looking as if he'd been surprised by the photographer. He was wearing a blue blazer and white shirt, both open at the collar. He had dark, unruly hair, but plenty of it. His dark eyes and engaging smile attracted Greta at once. She didn't recognize the man as a movie or television star, but since she rarely went to movies or watched television, this wasn't surprising. The teaser headline next to the photo said, "First Time Author Mark Boston - The next Hemingway?"

Greta had never heard of Mark Boston, but she liked Ernest Hemingway's work, having read a German translation of *The Old Man and The Sea* when she was in Junior High. So, she carried the magazine with her to the first chair where Maggie stood waiting, tucking it under the burgundy-colored plastic cape that Maggie draped over her for the shampoo.

When Maggie sat her back up in the chair and began toweling her wet head, Greta withdrew the magazine from under the cape and tried to locate the article about this "new Hemingway." One thing she liked about Maggie was that she didn't talk to you unless you instigated it, and today Greta didn't feel like talking. She buried her face in the magazine.

As she flipped the pages, she glanced only briefly at the titles of the other stories as they flashed by, including the latest on Brad and Angelina, and something about a new dog in the White House. She had almost given it up when another large photo of the same man on the cover jumped out at her. This time he was dressed in a blue-checked shirt – *exactly like Mr. Kirkpatrick's*.

She began reading and was fully engrossed in the story before she even realized that Maggie had proceeded to cut over fourteen inches from her long hair.

"Well, there goes at least five pounds of hair," Maggie sang, but Greta was busy concentrating on translating the English words into German, quietly moving her lips as she did, so that she wasn't aware of what Maggie had said.

The story told of the remarkable transformation of bestselling author Mark Boston, whose book *Exquisite Rain* was breaking all kinds of sales records. Mr. Boston, she learned, had dropped out of Yale University during his last year of law school and ended up homeless, broke and frequently drunk. Miraculously, he was kidnapped from a park bench by an unknown captor who proceeded not to harm or torture him in any way, but to help him reclaim his life. From that, he had returned to society and gone on to become a best selling author. It was an inspirational story, and Greta found herself vacillating between tears and laughter several times as she read it.

Maggie, meanwhile, wondered what Greta was reading that was so fascinating, but she was grateful that the German woman hadn't yet noticed that she was, by comparison to the way she looked when she arrived, practically bald headed – or so she would say later, as she stormed out of the shop, vowing never to return again. But, for now, the German terror, as she was often referred to around town, was happily preoccupied as Maggie shaped her new coiffure, added a few highlights, and applied a perm before rolling it into large curlers. She stopped to admire her handiwork. It was no accident that she was chosen as "Curl Queen" so many years ago at the Centennial School of Beauty in Denver.

Greta continued reading. In a large shaded sidebar on the last page of the article, she noticed that the reporter had written what amounted to a separate story entitled "An Author Finds Purpose at a mysterious 'School of Life'."

The sidebar recounted how Mr. Boston's captor, whom he only saw fleetingly, kept him sequestered in an all-steel room as he force-fed him movies and "video lessons devised to teach him how to cope with life." He never learned where he was being held and wasn't told in advance before he was released. He simply woke up one morning on yet another park bench, this time in a Brooks Brother's suit with more than $50,000 cash in his pocket. *Incredible!* Greta thought as she read, and the dryer under which she now sat became increasingly hot.

Reading on, Greta learned that Mr. Boston's captor was very kind to him, providing excellent German cuisine, including Veal Schnitzel and the "best red cabbage" he'd ever tasted!

The article went on to say that he was initially kept in gym shorts and t-shirts, but gradually the wardrobe was upgraded to designer-label men's wear.

But Greta had stopped reading. She went back and re-read the words *best red cabbage he'd ever tasted. Oh, yeah? Well, this Mark Boston should eat my red cabbage if he wants the best red cabbage ever!*

It would be some time before she would discover that he already had.

45

For an author, I think I have an exceptionally poor memory. I compensate for this flaw by keeping copious notes of anything and everything, which seems to help. I still forget a lot of things, but I will never forget those first few days in Sir's so-called "Classroom of Life."

Once I figured out that I was enclosed in a steel room, with no way of escape, I panicked.

"Uh, Mister..." I said, addressing the little guy on the screen. That alone is a vivid memory. I call him a cartoon, but in reality he wasn't really a cartoon in the sense that Mickey Mouse or Homer Simpson are 'cartoons.' Rather, he was like one of those Japanese "anime" creations. Everything was human – no big mouse ears – but it was clearly a drawing, and not a photograph. He was always dressed in a coat and tie – the rest of him was hidden under his little desk, so for all I know he was sitting there in his underwear!

If anything was exaggerated, it was the size of his eyes – but only slightly. From the two flashes I got of the real human being – once on the screen (which couldn't have lasted more than a mili-second) and once when I opened Door #3 and saw him standing there, I know the cartoon character was pretty close to the real thing. Except for the eyes. The cartoon had big eyes, not huge but bigger than normal size eyes, and the real guy had eyes that were not big as they were *scary*.

One thing is sure, though. Both sets of eyes, the cartoon and the real guy, were expressive in a way I had never seen anybody else's eyes be. When he didn't like something, his brow would furrow and his big eyes would zero in to little more than pinpoints. This look would frequently precede "correction," so I grew to fear that look more than any other.

His mouth was normal. Lips that weren't too thick or thin. He didn't smile much, though, and later on during my "stay" I made it my goal to try to make him smile. For all I knew at the time, I would be there for the rest of my life, so why not make the best of it? Besides, by that time, the steel cell had been transformed into a very livable space, as various pieces of furniture and furnishings appeared while I was asleep. I will say that even at my Grandmother's house, which was luxurious by most standards, I never slept on bed linens as nice as those I eventually "earned" at the School of Life. Ultra soft Pratesi sheets and pillow slips. Scandia Down feather pillows – two of them – with another two encased in crisp white linen cases. And the duvet! It was feather filled, and in all my life I'd never slept under anything like it. All of this appeared one morning, and I woke up inside this bed made up with all these expensive linens. That alone was a neat trick. Either Sir was exceedingly strong to be able to move my dead weight around the room as he performed this little transformation, or he had someone helping him.

Finally, the mattress which appeared at the same time as the bed linen was a Tempurpedic. I'd never heard of that brand, but after sleeping on it for the first time, I looked for a tag. I'd never slept on anything more comfortable – and certainly not any park bench!

I didn't find a tag, unfortunately. I looked again on "laundry day," when Sir informed me it was time to change my bed. I did a thorough inspection of everything as I removed it and placed it inside Door # 3 as I had been instructed. Fresh new linen was already waiting for me there, and I simply changed the bed, as I'd been told. But, other than the manufacturer's tags – the word "Pratesi" subtly stitched onto a small linen tab at the bottom of the sheets – there wasn't anything to identify the source of anything.

I'll let you guess the first thing I bought with my book advance. It wasn't a new car or a new house – it was the exact same mattress and linen I'd had when I was locked up.

Anyway, back to that first day, when I first realized I was a prisoner, I said, "Uh, Mister..." and he said, "Sir."

"What?" I said.

"Sir, Mark. That is what I wish to be called: Sir."

I stared blankly. "Sir? Really? *Sir?*" I said sarcastically.

He stopped me before I could say another word.

"All right. I can see it's time for you to learn your first lesson in what happens when you address me rudely or, as you've just done, sarcastically."

"Oh, yeah, *Mister* cartoon *Sir?* And how do you propose to do *that?* Are you going to jump out of your little TV and *box my ears?*"

It happened without further warning. I felt the most intense pain I'd ever felt, and it coursed through me like *electricity*, which is exactly what it was. I have no idea how much it was, but if you've ever been shocked when you screwed in a lightbulb or turned off a switch with wet hands, I'll tell you this was about a million times worse. It hurt like fucking hell. I felt like my fingertips and toes were on fire. My hair felt like it was flying off my head. My lips and tongue burned, and my ass, on which I'd obviously landed with a thud, now throbbed.

"What the fucking hell?" I yelled, and those were the last words I have ever yelled at anyone from that day to this. I got it again, instantly, only this time it was even more intense than before.

To this day, I truly wonder at the fact that I am still alive.

46

I learn quickly. I had just experienced Sir's favorite method of "correction," – twice, no less – and I resolved never to again. But electricity wasn't all he used. He had other teaching methods, such as when he accused me of being "deliberately thickheaded" during a movie quiz – I'll tell you about those in a minute – and even though I swore I wasn't trying to be obtuse, he waited until I was in the shower, completely soaped up, shampoo on my hair, before turning the water to the coldest temperature I'd ever felt in my life. Piercing, ice-cube cold. I couldn't just step out from under the flow, since I was covered with soap and shampoo, so I had to finish under needle-like jets of ice cold water, whimpering all the time like a little girl. "Please, Sir, please, Sir, please, Sir," I said. "I'm sorry, I'm sorry, I'm sorry." But he never restored the hot water and by the time I finished and wrapped myself in the fluffy white Ralph Lauren towel I'd found in the cupboard an hour earlier, I was shaking like a leaf. I guess I should be grateful he didn't use scalding hot water to make the same point.

If I had any modesty after (almost) making it through law school, and a lifetime of locker rooms before and after whatever sport I happened to be playing, I certainly lost it in Sir's "classroom." I knew he was watching me every moment, and at first I snuggled into the corner toilet to pee, hoping there wasn't a camera that could pick up my image as I did. I recall wondering, once, if he was taping me in the shower or maybe when I masturbated so he could sell it on some sicko porn site. Maybe I was on a live webcam, with old pervs paying to see my every move.

For some reason this actually turned me on, and I quickly got to the place where I was actually performing for the cameras during times that, at any other time of my life, would have been private and intimate. I'd make a big show of bending over and spreading my cheeks as I soaped up my ass, and spent far too much time washing my dick and balls, staring lasciviously at the camera until Sir finally said, from his screen across the room, "I don't know who you think is watching you, Mark, but stop it." I stopped, but I thought to myself, *well, you obviously are*.

Now that I've resumed my "old" life – and my old standards of modesty– I realize that it would have been out of character for Sir to violate my privacy, and I'm reasonably sure he never paid any attention to me while I was showering or jerking off. Still, back then, I wondered.

The shower itself consisted of nothing but a shower head hanging from the ceiling. There were no controls, no soap dish, and no towel bar – at least not during the early days of my "visit." I could never predict when shower day would be – it certainly wasn't every day, at least not until my wardrobe was upgraded, at which time I guess showering did finally become an every day occurrence.

On the morning when I was expected to take a shower, Sir would wake me with his usual cheerful greeting – this, after the lights were turned on full blast in an instant, blinding notification that a new day had begun. "Good morning, Mark!" the little cartoon Sir would sing out. "Time to rise and shine!" On more than one occasion, he would actually sing, "Get up, get up, get out of bed! Get up, get up, get up you sleep head!" It's one of the many weird things that he did that made me smile even as I wondered in the back of my mind who this nut was.

I didn't waste any time hitting the floor when it was time to get up, worried that if I did the blanket might suddenly turn into an *electric* blanket, if you catch my drift. I'd shuffle over to the stainless steel toilet in the corner and do my business, and then move over to the screen to await further instructions.

"Today is shower day," he might announce. "You will find everything you need behind Door # 3." I moved quickly, since I learned to do what I was told without delay. There I found a towel and, at least in the early days, three styrofoam cups filled variously with liquid soap, shampoo, and conditioner – just enough for that day's shower. Later on, I would receive my own supply of these items, in the original bottles, which I was allowed to keep on the floor in the corner of the shower. One morning I woke up to find that a towel bar had miraculously been installed during the night. After that, I was given permission to simply indicate every time I wanted to take a shower, which I did almost every day.

It wasn't all that bad, and I quickly adjusted to the routine as well as the complete lack of privacy. I would occasionally wonder about the "other" students and how they reacted, but Sir didn't encourage questions of that sort, so I stopped asking. Once he volunteered that another student had "problems" with personal hygiene, so he simply opened up what I had assumed were fire sprinklers – the kind you see in the ceilings of office buildings – and flooded the entire room for about an hour. Sir laughed when he told me this story, and I think I did, too, but I was secretly glad it hadn't been a teaching technique he'd used on me. God help anybody who would receive one of Sir's "corrective" electrical shocks when they were wet!

47

Janet considered her options. She had already determined there was no obvious means of escape. She hadn't tried the series of cupboards and doors that took up most of one wall, but she assumed they were secured from the other side. Locked tight. Now she wondered if she could get the puppet master who was behind the little cartoon figure on the screen to eventually identify himself. Even if he offered something as innocuous as his first name, it might be the wedge she would need to draw him out, to find out his vulnerabilities.

Quietly, as she stared absentmindedly at the screen, she reviewed her cover story. *She had been chosen to be one of eight wives of the prophet Elias Joseph Hatch, but she had run away from the Church of Yesterday, Today, and Tomorrow, located on a 100-acre piece of land just outside of Lemon, Utah. She managed to hitch a ride to Denver, where she landed without a dime to her name. A big black guy named Rodney offered to take her in, but it quickly became apparent that he was a pimp and expected her to turn tricks for him. She was in the process of running away from Rodney when...*

What the hell *had* happened?

The last thing she remembered – before this nut job must have injected her with something and brought her to this tin box – was that her partner, Lieutenant Detective Joel Goldstein, had shouted from the next doorway that he would "watch her back" if she wanted to catch some shut eye. The dick had obviously fallen asleep himself! And, boy, could he sleep. She knew from experience that if that's what happened, he would have slept like a dead man through whatever happened. She smiled inwardly at what she knew would happen to him when he had to tell their boss. Joel Goldstein had gotten by with entirely too much shit as far as she was concerned. He deserved every reprimand he would get when he finally had to report that his partner had simply disappeared from the face of the earth.

But the question remained: how did she plan to get out of here?

The stake-out had been routine enough. The Denver Police Department had been deluged with missing person calls after the body of that teenager turned up in Daniels Park, on the south side of town. That, coupled with a *New York Times* story about runaways from some jack-Mormon group in Utah turning up as prostitutes, sent the higher ups into a tizzy. The *Denver Post* printed numerous outraged letters to the editor asking what the police were doing about all the disappearances and finally ran its own editorial calling for the resignation of the chief himself! Well, *that* wouldn't happen; Janet knew that much for sure.

Finally, in a department meeting, it was decided that Janet and Joel would team up undercover to see what they could find out from living on the street for a few days. Neither one of them liked the assignment – it was cold as shit outside – but they would do their job and collect their pay, just as they'd always done.

Now Janet was pissed because she realized she'd left her gun in an old McDonald's take-out bag in the corner of the doorway where she had been sleeping. Her kidnapper had obviously missed it, which was just as well, since possession of a gun would have made it difficult to maintain her cover story. *Asshole.* For a moment she felt a wave of panic. *What if some kid finds it?* But then she thought, "What kid? How many kids play in the alleys downtown?" Besides, she knew all the resources of the DPD would be called into play to try to find her – and when Joel went to relieve her from her post in the doorway, he would find her gun and know that something was amiss. *Or would he?*

The cartoon perv was still staring at her. He hadn't answered her question, so she decided to ask it again. Mustering her little girl voice again and trying to appear as vulnerable as possible, she repeated, "Why me, Mister?"

The cartoon figure opened its mouth as if to speak, and then shut it just as quickly. Then it opened its mouth again and said, "Well, I guess it's just because you're special, Janet."

Oh God. He really is nuts.

MAKEOVERS - REX JOHN

48

It is said that love is a distraction, but not all distractions are necessarily good, as Carson would soon learn.

A confessed "news junkie," he knew he was behaving oddly when he stopped reading the newspapers and turned off Fox News in his study. Clearly, he was preoccupied. His thinking was muddled. He needed time. He needed time to be quiet and think. *He needed time to watch Janet.*

But his self-imposed isolation had its price. The banner headline on this next day's *Denver Post* screamed "Female Cop Kidnapped," and the long story that followed, featuring a large photo of Lt. Detective Janet Musgrave, would have changed things dramatically. Even the *New York Times* ran a story, although smaller and without a photo, in their national news section. But Carson wouldn't see those headlines, and the television in his study, which was almost always on, would remain silent for the next several weeks.

Even Greta sensed that something was amiss, that her boss was obviously brooding about something. When she intended to say something about that "poor female cop who was kidnapped," she remained silent instead, allowing him to simply sit at the breakfast table, staring out the window. The newspapers were thrown into the recycling bin, un-read.

Janet, meanwhile, wasn't sure how to proceed. *Should I tell him I'm a cop and threaten him with...with what? I'm locked in a friggin' cell, for chrissakes. What am I going to do, use my laser vision to cut through the steel wall?*

And what's with these steel walls, anyway? Was she inside a big truck or one of those shipping containers they place on cargo ships? Was she above ground or beneath it? The fact that there was a toilet and plumbing coming out of the ceiling suggested that she wasn't in a vehicle, but she couldn't be sure. She hadn't felt any movement, so she was fairly certain she wasn't in transit.

She listened for noises, but her cell was completely soundproof. As he sat staring at her, his funny big cartoon eyes seldom blinking, she turned and walked slowly around the room. The ceiling was at least twenty feet high, but it was made of large acoustical tiles with recessed can lights and fire sprinklers sticking out. Because of its height, even if she could unscrew the desk and chair from the floor and somehow stack them on her bed, they still wouldn't be tall enough for her to climb to the top. But what about those closet doors? If she could jimmy one of those open, she might be able to use it as a swing out stepladder...but how? She looked carefully at the edges of the doors. Not a hinge in sight, and even the handles were recessed into the door, with nothing protruding into the room that she might step on. *This guy's good. He ought to be designing prisons for the Department of Corrections.*

She walked over to the toilet, and as soon as she looked at it, she realized she needed to use it. She glanced back at the screen, where, as if by cue, the figure before her came to life.

"I won't look," the character said.

Yeah, right. Playing the coquette, she said, "Promise?"

"Yes, of course. I promise."

Right, you perv. You've already seen me naked. I guess I shouldn't worry too much about your watching me take a piss.

She lowered her gym shorts, noticing that she had no underwear of any kind, and sat down on the stool. A fourth of a roll of toilet paper sat on the floor at her feet, and she picked it up and neatly tore off a few sheets. She knew he was watching her.

She blotted daintily, as her mother had taught her, but when she got up and turned around to flush, she found there was no handle.

"Um..." she said, trying not to sound pissed off.

Once again, the figure on the screen became animated. "Oh! All finished?" he asked.

Like you didn't know that.

"Yes, but I don't know how to..." she began, looking helplessly at the toilet.

"Oh, I take care of that from back here," he said, and with that the toilet flushed.

Hope you enjoy it, asshole.

She smiled demurely at the figure on the screen and returned to the steel bed and sat down. There was nothing more she could do but wait to see what was next.

MAKEOVERS - REX JOHN

49

Greta was troubled. Mr. Kirkpatrick didn't seem himself. She couldn't quite put her finger on it, but a major change had come over him during the past two weeks. Shortly after he stopped reading the newspapers, the FedEx and UPS trucks started making almost daily stops. Some of the packages were addressed to Ms. C. Kirkpatrick, which she thought was amusing the first time she saw it. But when others arrived addressed to "Ms." instead of "Mr." she began to wonder if Mr. Kirkpatrick had somehow gotten married and just forgot to mention it to her! She thought briefly about asking him, but decided against it the next time he glared at her for no apparent reason. She signed for the packages, as were her standing instructions, but it wasn't unusual for her to shake each package vigorously to try to guess what was inside.

Clothing, she concluded. They weren't heavy enough to be books. She knew from previous experience that the books came fast and furious most of the time, but not now. Each package was light as a feather.

But if he is buying clothes, why? He has the biggest wardrobe of any man I've ever met. What could he possibly need?

She was right, of course. As soon as Janet arrived, Carson realized he had some new skills to learn himself. Using the computer in his study, he took his first foray into the mystical world of women's clothing, shopping for hours on the websites of the only stores he could remember his mother using: Neiman Marcus, Saks Fifth Avenue, Bloomingdales, and Talbots.

At first it was daunting, but Janet had helpfully provided her sizes– grateful, he supposed, that she wouldn't have to wander around anymore in gym shorts and no underwear!

Janet, on the other hand, wasn't looking for a new wardrobe. Her uniforms and a few old pairs of comfortable jeans were all she ever wore, anyway. But each time a new package appeared, all shipping tags removed, she showed a proper mix of wonder and gratitude, and immediately modeled her new outfit for the little cartoon man on the screen.

"Why are you so nice to me?" she once asked the crazy man who insisted she address him as "Sir."

He almost sounded shy when he said, "Well, you're my guest, and I promised I would take care of you."

Yeah, "guest." Now that's rich, she thought, but once again she simply smiled sweetly into the camera.

Somewhat emboldened by what appeared to be a genuine smile from this woman who completely mystified him, Carson decided to use the opportunity to ask her, once again, for more information about her past.

"I don't like to talk about that," she had said repeatedly, as he tried to coax information out of her.

The first time she refused to give him a straight answer about who she was and where she came from, he had to restrain himself from administering immediate "correction". *Why? I've never allowed any of the others to be coy with me; why am I allowing this young woman to get by with such behavior?* His mind turned to Harry, as it did so often when he was faced with a behavioral problem with a student. Harry certainly learned how to give a straight, polite answer – although it took him a couple of months and God knows how much electricity.

50

Spring has finally come to Manhattan, and the air is alive with the sounds and smells of the season. I live on Central Park West, so I try to take a break from writing at least once a day for a stroll through the park, usually ending up at the Starbucks at 68th and Columbus. If I've chosen to bring my laptop, I continue writing there; otherwise I simply sit and people watch for as long as it takes me to work my way through a Venti, non-fat, no-foam latte. I sometimes flirt with Amy, one of the employees, but we both know it's just that: me messing around. She flirts right back, and once in awhile we exchange bits of personal information to make it feel like a real friendship, which of course it's not. She's looking for a "real" job, as she puts it, and has a background in human resources as I recall. I find myself wishing I could help her somehow.

I do some of my best thinking in public places, and I can sit for hours before I realize I've been so lost in thought that I've lost track of time.

I did the same thing in Sir's classroom. I've tried to figure out how long I was there, and I think it might have been as long as six months or as short as four. I was so drunk when he snatched me off that bench that, for all I know, I may have only been there for a month.

Then, because of the absence of any windows, I couldn't tell you if twenty-four hours was really three days, or vice versa. It helped when I began earning "recess" privileges – at least when I went into that beautiful courtyard I could tell if it was day or night. Even so, my internal clock never quite re-set itself after being denied natural light for so long, and to this day I still find myself falling asleep in the middle of the day, like some narcoleptic, only to jolt wide awake at 3 a.m., eager to start my day! Black-out drapes solved some of the problem, but I didn't have those when I first got out.

That is another day I will never forget. I am still dumbfounded about how I found my sorry ass back on a park bench, probably the same one from which I'd been snatched. True, I was in a lot better shape, there's no denying that.

My wardrobe had certainly changed. When Sir found me, I was probably wearing jeans and an old sweatshirt, since that's pretty much what I wore every day. But when I was released, I was wearing a gray, worsted wool suit with a Hermes tie in a subtle purple pattern. The starch in my white shirt was so heavy it had barely wrinkled after who-knows-how-long I'd been conked out on that bench. I had on well-polished, black Allen-Edmonds and over-the-calf black cotton socks – the perfect thickness, which is to say thin. I have never been able to find the same socks anywhere else, so that's another reason to try to find Sir – to ask him where he got those great socks!

I felt my hair, which had been newly cut and surprisingly in-place, as far as I could tell. I had a white, linen handkerchief in my breast pocket which I withdrew and used to wipe the saliva from my chin. Then I sat there for several minutes trying to remember what had happened.

I concluded that Sir must have been planning to let me go on that particular day all along, because he had asked me just the day before if, when he released me, I would go to the police or newspapers first. Frankly, I'd never thought about it, because I'd long since given up on the notion of ever being released. But I answered his question, and promised I wouldn't go to either one. He appeared skeptical, and we didn't discuss it further.

And then, there I was – dressed like a normal businessman, sitting on a park bench in the middle of the morning trying to figure out how the hell I got there and trying desperately to remember what Sir had said to me. I don't think he even told me goodbye, and that kind of bothered me. No, it bothered me a lot. I had grown to like him – a phenomenon I've since heard described as "Stockholm Syndrome," named after some people who were held captive for six days during a bank robbery in Sweden. When they got out, everybody was amazed that they defended their captors. And that's exactly how I feel about Sir. I know what he did in kidnapping me – and others, as best I can tell – is wrong, but if he hadn't, I'd probably be dead. He literally saved my life. What's not to like about that?

On the day he released me, I sat on that bench for a few minutes but finally gave up trying to remember what was said or done to forewarn me that I was about to be let go. I couldn't. It's as though my mind had been wiped clean. So, I replaced the handkerchief in my breast pocket and started going though the other pockets for clues. In my inside right breast pocket I found a letter, addressed simply to "Mark," in what I assume is

Sir's handwriting. I tore it open, hoping it would solve this latest mystery. But unlike the envelope, which was handwritten, the inside was typewritten:

Dear Mark,

I can only imagine how surprised you are, since I gave you no forewarning that today would be graduation day. I'm sure you will understand why I don't tell my students in advance. Remember how, in school, everyone stopped paying attention during the last few weeks before summer break? Well, we couldn't have that, could we!

I would like to tell you how proud I am of you. After the initial shock (pardon the pun) of coming to my school, you settled in nicely and worked hard. Together, we discovered how your mother and stepfather's unkindness hurt you and how you allowed that hurt to almost destroy you. We also talked about the love and kindness shown by your grandmother, and how you abandoned her when she probably needed you most. But now that you've forgiven yourself, and hopefully the others who have mistreated you, perhaps you will be able to restart your life from the point where I first discovered you on this bench. You've had a major course adjustment, and I truly think you'll be fine.

You would have no way of knowing this, but I determined early on that we could skip many chapters in our school curriculum, because somewhere along the way you seemed to learn what many young men and women never learn: to take responsibility for the conduct of your life. For that, you should be truly grateful. (For example, did you know that many of my students must be taught to put their linen napkin on their lap when they eat, and not to wad it up and throw it in the middle of their plate when they finish?) But because you came to me knowing so many of the basics of good manners, you have graduated somewhat earlier than most.

You have talked of a writing career, and I hope you will pursue that. I read everything you wrote after the computer was placed in the classroom, and I must say, it's very good. Keep it up.

I've provided a little something to help you get restarted, which you will find, if you have not done so already, in your other inside breast pocket. I suggest you use it judiciously until you get back on your feet.

You have promised that you will not notify the authorities, and I take you at your word. The last thing I need is someone trying to track me down. Regrettably, that must also include you. Please do not make an effort to find me.

All good wishes to you, Mark. I have every confidence in your future.

Your friend,
"Sir"

His name was written in the same perfect penmanship as appeared on the envelope, and had obviously been done with a fountain pen – probably a Mont Blanc similar to the one he allowed me to use during our last weeks together. In fact, I found that very pen in my front shirt pocket – and I treasure it to this day.

In my left breast pocket I found the packet of money, bills so crisp I actually wondered for a moment if they were counterfeit (later the bank would assure me they weren't.) In total, I found ten of them. Five of them were twenties (or "Yuppie Food Stamps," as we used to refer to them, since people my age typically get them out of the ATM before going out to dinner).

I looked at the other five bills and knew they *had* to be counterfeit. They looked like regular ten dollar bills – same color, same size – although the familiar face of Alexander Hamilton had been replaced with another old guy, but the name under this one was "Salmon Chase, Secretary of the Treasury." Following the "10" were three zeros. Sir had given me five *ten-thousand dollar bills*, for a grand total of $50,100!

I glanced at the guy sitting on another bench about fifty yards away, reading his newspaper. I wondered what he would think if I told him I'd been lying there asleep with fifty grand in my pocket!

As much as I doubted those ten thousand dollar bills were real, it didn't seem like Sir to give me fake money. But, still....

There was only one way to find out. I would take them to a bank.

51

I never had a bank account in Denver, but I was downtown, so I knew it couldn't be too hard to find a bank. I stood up, a little shaky on my feet for a few seconds, and headed down Colfax Avenue toward the biggest buildings. I turned onto 14th Street at the next intersection, walking purposefully, remembering that Sir had taught me that the way I sat and stood and moved gave people clues about my self-confidence and even my energy level.

I eventually made my way to 17th Street, which seemed to lack any retail storefronts, but no shortage of...*banks!* I went inside the first one I came to and walked up to the teller window, trying to look like I did it every day.

A heavyset woman with bleached blond hair looked up and greeted me. "Yes, Sir?" It sounded strange for someone to call me "Sir" when that term belonged, at least in my mind, to only one person: the *real* Sir.

It was the first human interaction I'd had for months, and I felt my hands immediately start to perspire.

"I'd...I'd...like to open an account!" I finally managed to stammer.

"Oh. Yes, Sir," she said, pointing, "Miss Jenkins in new accounts should be able to assist you with that."

I turned and looked at Miss Jenkins, who was now staring right at me, and looked back at the teller and said, "thank you."

When I arrived at Miss Jenkins' desk, I saw from the name plate that her first name was Darlene. She invited me to have a seat.

"Yes, Sir? How can I help you?"

There it was again. Somebody calling me *Sir*. "Well, I'd like to open an account I think."

I "think"??? You mean you don't know, you putz? Honestly! Pull yourself together!

"Yes. Yes, I'd like to open a new account."

"Very well, then," Darlene said, eyeing me somewhat suspiciously even as she effortlessly withdrew a small set of forms from her desk drawer. The stammering had obviously not escaped her notice. "We'll just be needing a little information..."

Oh shit. I'd forgotten how to open a bank account – they'd need I.D.! Acting as though I had absent-mindedly misplaced my wallet, I started patting my pants pockets and found – a wallet! I withdrew it, and both Darlene and I got our first look at it.

It, too, was Hermes, and it was all I could do to keep from pulling it up to my nose to smell the leather. I decided Darlene might think it a little weird if I started sniffing a wallet I'd just pulled out of my back pocket, so I restrained myself. Curious, I opened it up to see what surprise Sir would have for me now.

I wasn't disappointed. I found another thousand dollars, this time in crisp hundred dollar bills, but I left these in place, hoping Darlene had noticed them, and looked into the other compartments. In one of them I found what Sir had known I would need: my own Connecticut Driver's License, with a photo that had been taken on my birthday a year ago but which, thankfully, didn't look anything like me. I handed it to Darlene, who seemed to agree with me after looking at the photo, looking at me, and looking at the photo again. Finally, she said, "Do you have anything else?"

"Um, no, actually, I don't. You see, my old wallet was stolen, and I just happened to have my driver's license in a different pocket."

"I see," she said sympathetically, obviously having heard the same story before. "Well, let's see what we can do."

I could tell that she was sizing me up, probably trying to decided if I was casing the bank to come back and rob it later. By this time she had stood up, papers in hand, and was apparently preparing to consult a colleague on the other side of the room. As she stepped away from her desk, she said, "How much will you be depositing in your new account, Mister...?" With that, she looked down at my driver's license which she still held, and then looked at me again, as if testing me.

"Boston. Mark Boston. Oh, um, I'll deposit $50,000."

This seemed to please her, and I realized later she probably was accustomed to the schlubs who walk in off the street with a hundred bucks to try to get checks and a Visa card. Larger depositors, I would learn in the years ahead, have "private bankers" who would never sit at some desk in the middle of the first floor lobby.

Darlene marched off to see if the bank could stoop so low as to accept fifty grand from the likes of me.

Apparently they could, as she came back pretty quickly, with a big smile on her face.

I thought we'd gotten through the worst of it, but that's before I pulled the five ten-thousand dollar bills out of my pocket.

By this time Darlene had begun a deposit slip for my new account and was waiting for me to ante up. "OK, Mr. Boston, we're ready for whatever checks you wish to deposit..." she said, holding out her hand expectantly.

"Oh. Well, actually, I have *cash.*"

"No problem," she said, smiling. Smiling, that is, until she saw the bills. The smile faded quickly.

"What's this?"

"That's my deposit. Fifty thousand dollars, as I said."

She took the bills I proffered and examined them closely. "Are these for real?" she asked, skeptically.

"I certainly hope so!" I said, chuckling, although I thought to myself, *We'll see, won't we?*

"Well, excuse me again, please." This time her manner was a little less friendly.

A minute later, I heard her heels clicking on the marble and turned to see her approaching, this time accompanied by a bald man about sixty years old.

"Mr. Boston, this is Mr. Abernathy, our Senior Vice President."

Abernathy held out his hand to shake, which I did.

"Now, Mr. Boston, could you tell me about these bills, please. Where did you get them?"

"Excuse me?"

"Well, these bills are, as you notice, of an unusually large denomination. In fact, I've never seen a $10,000 bill myself, and I've been in banking for 40 years."

"Is that so?" I said, trying not to be a smart ass. "Well, I hope they're real – my grandmother gave them to me."

"Oh, they're real. I just verified them with our head vault cashier. But they haven't been printed in this country since 1934, and they are withdrawn from circulation whenever they get back to the Federal Reserve. It's quite unusual to see one – much less five."

"I see," I said, trying to remember what I had just told him about where I'd gotten them. "Well, as I said, my grandmother gave them to me, and for all I know she may have had them since 1934!"

Abernathy stared at me as he processed this information, and lacking any real reason to refuse my request to deposit them, finally after a pause said, "Fine! Miss Jenkins, allow me to initial the deposit slip and you may continue opening Mr. Boston's account." Then beaming in my direction, he added, "Welcome to Denver National, Mr. Boston. Please call on me personally whenever I may be of personal assistance."

"I'll do that," I mumbled, not looking at him and turning to follow Miss Jenkins – Darlene – who was well on her way back to her desk.

Once I had my new bank account plus another eleven hundred still in my pocket, I was ready to tackle my new life. I felt exhilarated in a way I'd never felt before.

What do I do first? Let's see. I guess finding somewhere to live would be nice. I kind of felt I'd outgrown my park bench.

But, boy, I'd sure love a drink first.

52

It didn't take long for me to re-adapt to normal living, whatever the hell that is. With my temporary checks in hand, I walked the streets of Capitol Hill until I found a handsome old building. As luck would have it, there was a sign out front that said: "Available Furn 1BR Inquire Within." I did, and the landlady and I hit it off immediately. She showed me the apartment, on the third (top) floor, with a big double window in the living room looking out through the branches of a large oak tree. The branches were close enough, and looked strong enough, that I wondered if I could climb up and in to my apartment. Its leaves were just beginning to take on autumn color. I realized it would be especially pretty in a couple of weeks, and with a desk strategically placed in front of the window, it might provide good atmosphere for my new career as a writer.

The landlady, about sixty years old with a heavy German accent, introduced herself as "Frau Rosencranz." I discovered when I signed the rental agreement that her first name was Gertrude. How German is that?

Mrs. Rosencranz asked very few questions, which was fine with me, since I'd just spent several weeks of my life doing little more than answering one question after another. She did recite a list of rules that mostly had to do with wild parties and heavy drinking – neither of which I planned to do.

Since it was a pre-war building, the ceilings were high, with crown molding circling the room about a foot from the top of the walls, which were painted a warm yellow, or tan, depending on the time of the day. At least they weren't stainless steel.

There was good natural light streaming in, but the windows were painted shut. That's OK, I figured, I would find a way to pry them open for fresh air. The bedroom had an old-fashioned window air conditioner which, as it turned out, was a good background noise machine – assuming you like the sound of a jet airplane engine while you sleep, that is.

The bed was a double with a decent mattress, a nice surprise. In addition to the bed, the bedroom had only a dresser and a chair. Spartan, but after learning to live in what amounted to a cell, it really didn't matter that much. It stayed that way for the entire time I lived there.

The bathroom was small, with a slanted ceiling following the angle of the roof. I had to stoop a bit when I took a shower, but that wasn't a big deal. It would be nice to take a shower without having someone watch me.

The kitchen was little more than a stove, refrigerator and sink. No dishwasher, and no garbage disposal, which surprised me. "Um, where does the garbage go?"

"Where you tink it go!" she demanded. "Downstairs in da trash room!" Some time later, when I would try to imitate Mrs. Rosencranz' German accent, one of my buddies told me I made her sound like she was Swedish instead of German. Impressions never were my thing, but one thing is sure: her voice could be harsh and all business, but I had a hunch she was all bluster.

"Oh. Fine. OK."

My tone seemed to soften hers a bit, since she apparently decided I wasn't going to refuse the apartment because it didn't have a garbage disposal or dishwasher. I wasn't about to. I loved it.

As if to test my resolve one last time, she said, "No elevator."

"Not a problem," I said.

"You have car?"

"Not yet."

"Job?"

"Not yet." That earned a frown, but only a brief pause.

"Girlfriend?"

I grinned. She answered for me, "Ja, ja. I know. 'Not yet.'"

The rent was $600 a month. I wrote her one of my temporary checks for three months – $1,800 – on the spot, which surprised and pleased her. She had me sign a short rental agreement and handed me two keys, one for the building entrance and one for my apartment. After she left, I plopped down on the bed and just stared out the bedroom window until I could see the sun was about to go down. I fell asleep, and when I first woke up I was completely disoriented. I had fallen asleep in my steel room not 24 hours ago, so in my mind, that's where I thought I would be when I woke up. I instinctively looked toward the wall where the television screen had been in the classroom. It wasn't there, of course, and neither was the little cartoon image of Sir, staring at me.

I lay still for a few minutes, enjoying the darkness, since it, too, was strange to me. Finally, I got up and moved back into the living room and then into the kitchen. I opened the refrigerator and all the cupboards, wondering how far away I was from a 7-Eleven or grocery store. I was hungry.

As if on cue, there was a knock on the door. When I opened it, there was Mrs. Rosencranz standing with a tray.

"Hungry." It wasn't a question, but a statement which by its tone and simplicity defied me to argue.

"I sure am," I said, smiling broadly and stepping aside so she could come in.

When I looked at what was on the tray, I felt my knees go weak. It was a plate of veal schnitzel, with a large portion of red cabbage to the side. A big piece of German chocolate cake, and a glass of milk rounded out the tray. I stared at the food, hardly able to comprehend what I was seeing. It was arranged on the plate exactly as it was when it appeared in the food cupboard of Sir's classroom. It was Sir's cooking. It had to be. I'd recognize it anywhere.

I sat down abruptly, knowing I would faint if I didn't.

"What? You don't like *Deutsch* cooking?"

I looked at her feebly, fearful of the answer I might receive to my question.

I whispered, "He's here, isn't he?"

53

Mrs. Rosencranz stood there staring at me. "Who!" she demanded.

"Sir. He's here, isn't he? Where am I?"

At this, Mrs. Rozencranz looked at me suspiciously, wondering, I suppose, if I was on drugs. Or drunk. Or both. She was obviously beginning to wonder if she'd rented her apartment to a nut.

"Who is das 'Sir'? Das ist no 'Sir' here. Vat are you talking about? Das ist veal schnitzel. Meine mutter teach my sister and me to make dis all zee time from time we vas little fraulein in Germany."

I could see that she was sincere. This was a cosmic joke of some kind. By pure coincidence I had been served an exact replica of a meal I'd eaten at least a half dozen times, most recently about three days ago. (It was delicious each time, but to be honest, the last time Sir left it for me, I had grown a little tired of it. I'm sure he thought he was pleasing me, because the first time I had it, I couldn't rave about it enough.)

My stomach wasn't in the mood to complain, however. I was hungry, and this was food. I sat down and began eating. It was just as I remembered it: delicious.

I could tell Mrs. Rozencranz was still mystified by my strange reaction to her kind deed. I kept talking until I finally convinced her that I was simply groggy from my nap and that I frequently didn't make any sense when I first woke up, *blah, blah, blah*. I think she bought it, because she finally smiled slightly and said, "Ja. OK. *Mahlzeit*."

Mahlzeit. I remembered that word from high school German. *Mealtime*. In other words, dinner was served. And with that, she walked out.

When I finished eating, I rinsed the dishes off and left them in the sink, since I didn't have dish detergent. I decided I'd better explore the neighborhood a bit, if only to scope out where I could buy groceries – and soap.

As I walked quietly past Mrs. Rozencranz' first floor apartment, I could hear the television blaring away *in German*! I would learn later that she subscribed to a German satellite channel, and it would be a sound I could expect to hear every time I walked in or out of the building.

54

As I walked down the sidewalk, I didn't have a clue as to where I was going, so I was surprised to find myself after a couple blocks in front of a big 24-hour grocery store with a big sign declaring it to be King Soopers. A few weeks later I would discover that other people in the neighborhood referred to this particular store as "Queen" Soopers because of its heavily gay customer base. That was OK with me, as long as I could get some cereal and milk – my "go-to" foods for when I'm hungry and don't know what I want to eat.

I also bought a toothbrush, toothpaste, toilet paper, soap (dish detergent and bath) and paper towels. I was overdressed for this time of night – it was almost nine o'clock – but I didn't have anything else to wear. I got a few stares, which seemed ironic, coming from people who had multi-colored hair, dozens of piercings, and wearing everything from caftans to what looked like a negligee. I didn't care; I just wanted to get back to my new apartment before I forgot where it was!

I wisely asked the clerk if she would accept my check, but because it wasn't pre-printed with my name, and because my driver's license was out of state, of course the answer was "Sorry, no." I paid cash, something I found I would always have to do until I received my printed checks (and eventually a credit card) in the mail a week later. I probably still have those temporary checks somewhere.

I managed to find my new apartment again and was back on my bed by 10 p.m. I say "on" it, because I didn't have sheets, blankets, or even a pillow case. That reminded me of the first week or two in the classroom, when I had to sleep on that steel shelf that Sir kept referring to as my "bed." When he asked one morning if I'd slept comfortably, I must not have responded correctly, because he said, "Oh, would you prefer a park bench?"

The next morning I got up and brushed my teeth, ate some cereal right out of the box (I forgot to buy a bowl or spoon) and drank half the container of milk directly from the carton. (No glass, either.) When I'd finished "breakfast," I put my suit back on and headed out the door.

I remembered seeing a department store when I'd found the bank the day before, and I didn't have any trouble finding it again. I still had plenty of cash, so I decided to stock up. In the men's department, I bought two pairs of jeans, a half dozen t-shirts, underwear, socks, a sweater and a pair of sneakers. Rather than carry the three big bags around the store, I told the young clerk I had some other shopping to do in the store and asked if I could leave my purchases with him until I was ready to go home. He seemed more than happy to oblige and even gave me a little wink, which seemed a bit strange.

I went to housewares next, and bought a set of sheets, two pillows, a blanket and a couple of towels. I also bought two dinner plates, two bowls, and two place settings of stainless steel silverware. I had noticed the exact pattern of silverware which always appeared on my tray in the classroom – when I was allowed silverware, that is – but when I saw that they were sterling silver and cost over four-hundred dollars a place-setting, I decided I could make-do with stainless steel. Looking back, I'm sorry I didn't get the sterling silver. I like the weight and feel of the "real thing." Apparently I was planning to entertain, because I also bought some place mats and linen napkins. That alone showed Sir's influence, because before he made me over I only used paper towels as napkins (if anything) and now it would never occur to me to use anything other than linen.

I also bought a coffee maker and a toaster oven and, at the last moment, a mini-microwave that was less than a hundred bucks. After everything was rung up, I realized there was no way I could carry it, along with my menswear purchases, by myself. I explained my predicament to the clerk in housewares, a nice woman in her mid-thirties with oversized glasses and a bouffant hairstyle, and asked if there was somebody who could help me out.

"That depends, sir. Where are you parked?"

"Oh. I don't have a car; I guess I'll need to call a cab."

"I'm happy to do that for you sir, why don't you go gather your menswear purchases, and I'll get a stock boy to bring these things and meet you at the 15th Street entrance. I'll tell the taxi to pick you up there."

As the cab pulled away from the curb, I noticed an Apple Computer store next door and realized I had another important purchase to make.

Back at the apartment, I told the cabbie, whose name was Fayad, that I'd give him twenty bucks if he would help me lug all my stuff upstairs, which he readily agreed to do. It took us three trips – the entire trunk and most of the back seat were full – but when it was all inside, I breathed a sigh of relief and then stripped off my suit and put my jeans on. Sir might not approve of the clothing change, but I felt out of place in anything but jeans the whole time I lived in Denver. Now, in New York, I'm back to wearing suits much of the time – just to blend in, I guess.

But back in Denver, in my new jeans, I was me again, or at least the new me.

55

Janet felt like she was in a brightly lit cave. Even though the lights in her cell shone twenty-four hours a day, she felt an internal darkness descend over her like a blanket. She had inspected every inch of the steel room, checking each smooth rivet in the steel to see if even one of them could be pried loose. She pulled on the recessed handles of doors 1 and 2 until she thought they would pop off in her hand, but they didn't budge. She no longer cared if the cartoon character was watching her from his television screen; her police training had kicked back in and she needed to know her environment, to find out if there was a way of escape.

There wasn't.

She closely examined the thick plexiglass panel covering the television screen and determined that it was fastened from the other side, but she couldn't tell where or how. In frustration she banged her fist on the screen, causing the little cartoon character to jump back, surprised. *Well, at least I know he's watching me. Always watching me.* But he said nothing, as she continued exploring the space.

But even as a deep sense of despair was beginning to envelop Janet, in another part of the house Greta was exhilarated by the new theories she was developing about Mr. Kirkpatrick's brother, Mr. Scooter.

Obviously, he had shamed the family by becoming a transvestite. What other explanation could their possibly be for the bra and panties that suddenly showed up in Mr. Kirkpatrick's laundry basket? Greta frowned. No wonder the poor boy was kept under lock and key. The Kirkpatricks were among the richest and most powerful families in the world. The last thing they needed was a scandal like *that*. Greta dutifully washed and dried the garments and placed them on top of the pile of clean laundry in Mr. Kirkpatrick's bedroom. *Let's see how he explains this!*

Carson was mortified when he realized he'd let some of Janet's *personal items* slip into the regular laundry, instead of being hand-washed, as he had been doing until now. *Who knows what the nosy German frau will think.* But, uncharacteristically, he didn't give it another thought. He had more important things to worry about.

Janet began dribbling out parts of her cover story, to try to buy time. She told about the terrible beatings she had received at the hands of the Prophet Elias, and finally managed to spit out the story of how she fell under the spell of Rodney, her pimp. As these details emerged, they were accompanied by oceans of tears, which were not lost on poor Carson, who more than once had to switch to showing a still photo of himself on Janet's screen while he wept privately at the heartbreaking story he'd just heard.

Although the details of the Prophet Elias and her so-called marriage at age eleven were contrived as part of her cover story and embellished even as she told it, and even though she'd never met a pimp called Rodney, the actual facts about her personal life were, in her view, every bit as depressing.

She hated the police force. Oh, she loved cops – she just didn't want to be one anymore. In the twelve years she'd worked for the Denver Police Department, she had never received a promotion. All of her performance reviews were "exemplary" or "above average." Her command officers – and there had been a new one almost every year she'd been on the force – were unanimous in their praise of her work. But any raises she received were perfunctory, mostly the same cost-of-living increases every other officer got. She suspected that much of it had to do with the fact that she was a woman; the DPD was still a "good old boys club," but of course she couldn't prove that. But she hated the politics of police work, the constant kissing up to the brass just to get what she should have gotten automatically.

Plus, she was sick of street work. She knew by the time she finished the police academy that it was going to be a grimy job, and she thought she could handle it. And she did, dammit. But now she was sick of it. She longed to quit, and move as far away from Denver as she could.

She had a boyfriend, but that relationship wasn't going anywhere, either. He was on the force too – did she know anybody who wasn't? Troy was a nice enough guy, but he had no ambition, no *ummph,* as her father would put it. He lived in a one-bedroom apartment on Cap Hill with a crazy German woman as his landlady. She used to spend the night with him once in awhile, but between the nosy German landlady and the mess of his apartment, she'd stopped that a year ago. If they spent the night together now, it was always at her place. But they didn't even do that much anymore.

So, while Janet was recounting the sad but made-up tales from her childhood to the little cartoon figure on the screen, she was really thinking about her miserable real-life situation. If she ever got out of here, and she was seriously wondering if she ever would, she resolved to quit her job and move to Mexico. Troy could come with her if he wanted to, but she knew he wouldn't. She would start over, withdrawing every cent she'd put into the city employee's retirement fund and living on it until it ran out. She didn't know what she would do after that, and she didn't care.

She'd practiced her cover story so much that she could actually tell it without even thinking about the words as they came out of her mouth. That's what she was doing now, her mind on a completely different track while her voice droned on about how miserable her childhood was – even though in reality, she'd had a pretty good childhood.

She was now at the part of her story where the little delinquents with whom she attended school teased her about her "ugly face." She could see that the cartoon figure on the screen was eating this stuff up.

What she did not see was Carson's new resolve that he would not let her leave this place until he had removed that "ugly birthmark" and restored her face to its natural and complete beauty. The little terrorists who gave her so much grief growing up were, sadly, correct. That birthmark *was* ugly, and it must go. He would personally see to it that nobody ever made fun of this beautiful girl again! He would surgically remove that scar himself. Never mind that he had never attended medical school and certainly didn't know anything about cosmetic surgery. *How hard can it be? I can learn.*

What he did not realize is that *naevus flammeus*, or "port wine stain," is not removed surgically. If he'd bothered to research it, he would have discovered that many such scars are easily removed by *laser* – the very laser, in fact, that he'd used to remove Harry's tattoos.

MAKEOVERS - REX JOHN

56

I see we're back to books again, Greta thought, as she signed for a heavy package from Amazon – addressed, appropriately this time, to *Mr.* Carson Kirkpatrick.

When Carson withdrew from his study to eat lunch and bring one back for his "brother," he noticed the box on the hall table. Reversing his steps, he brought it to his desk and could not resist opening it.

One of the three books he wanted was on back order, but he took the other two out and examined them carefully. *Key Notes on Plastic Surgery,* by Adrian M. Richards, was divided into ten chapters, including separate ones for each body region, plus chapters on burns, microsurgery and aesthetic surgery. Perfect. The foreword was written by Dr. Ian Jackson, who was described on the book jacket as "one of the foremost plastic surgeons in the world." He looked at the packing slip and noted that the book regularly sold for $75.95, but Amazon sold it to him for $64.56. Such a deal!

The second book was *Plastic Surgery: Clinical Problem Solving*, by Peter Taub and R. Michael Koch. A note on the inside jacket cover described the book as a way to "learn how to manage commonly encountered problems in plastic and reconstructive surgery with this unique case-based approach"; and the note continued,

"Covering head, neck, trunk, extremities, and cosmetic concerns, this sourcebook uses numerous visual clinical scenarios to illustrate essential plastic and reconstructive surgical principles. Each chapter is organized by a well-illustrated case, followed by algorithms that take you through effective management strategies and clinically relevant information. The result is an ideal resource for oral board preparation and a valuable primer for students, residents, and attending physicians from diverse specialties." The book also boasted that "Full-color clinical photos add emphasis to must-know points throughout each case."

Another good choice and, thanks to Amazon, a savings of $9.95.

Carson was hungry, but he couldn't resist flipping through the books. Could he do this? He didn't have any medical instruments, but he could obviously buy some on-line. And what about anesthetic? He had a hunch that an injection of Methohexital might not be enough. He would probably need to order whatever equipment anesthesiologists use in the average hospital surgery. He was relatively sure that the classroom itself could be adequately sterilized, since the only time the outside air was allowed in was during the last few weeks of each student's stay, when they were allowed in and out of the courtyard at various times of the day. How many germs could they possibly track in?

Opening the top middle drawer of his desk, he withdrew a yellow legal pad. Removing the cap from his Mont Blanc, he wrote, *anesthetic, scalpel and other stuff* – then he crossed out "stuff" and wrote *surgical implements*. He frowned when he realized he'd just done what he lectures all of his students to avoid: the use of sloppy language. *Precise use of the English language will set you apart from the average dolt who can't put a proper sentence together.* He forbade the use of slang in the classroom – words such as "whatever" and "dude" were met with disdain, and repeated violations always earned *correction*.

He thought for a moment and the questions started coming. What if there were surgical complications? He was nothing if not organized and methodical, so he began making a list of questions as he thought of them. *Is blood used in all surgeries? Where do I get it? What happens if I botch the removal? What then? Total failure? Define. Death???*

The last possibility troubled him.

He absolutely did not want Janet to die. Should he even do this? Or should he release her and give her enough money to have the surgery done by a competent surgeon in a real hospital? No, she probably wouldn't do it. If she's had that birthmark this long, she probably doesn't even notice it any more. But it's hideous, and it keeps her from being the beautiful young woman she could be. I have an opportunity to help her. How can I pass that up?

Flipping through the *"Key Notes"* book again, he looked out the window and made up his mind.

This book looks pretty complete. How hard can performing cosmetic surgery be?

57

After I settled into my new apartment, the weeks raced by, and I'm sure it had something to do with my newly acquired knowledge of day and night. In the classroom, there weren't any windows, so I had to trust Sir to tell me when it was time to get up and when it was time to go to bed. But now I had a southern exposure, with a big window facing the tree in the side yard, which provided a never-ending kaleidoscope of light and color on my living room walls.

It's not quite true that I never saw sunlight while I attended Sir's School of Life. I didn't for a very long time, but that finally changed when he gave me permission to open Door #1. What a day!

Sir had just quizzed me on three movies I'd watched in a row: *Good Will Hunting*, *My Life as a House* and *Ordinary People*. He was big on movies and considered them "powerful teaching tools." Some of them were pretty obscure, but I could always depend on them to have a powerful moral lesson. Needless to say, *Beavis and Butthead* movies were not shown.

I'd already seen *Ordinary People*, but the other two were new to me and they had their desired effect. As the final credits rolled, I could feel the swell of tears forming behind my eyes. I sat there, on the edge of my bed, elbows on my knees, head between my hands, and sobbed.

I cried until I felt I had no more tears.

Things I hadn't ever thought about – or hadn't for a long time – came rushing into my head in a torrent. I felt the shame of my Dad's suicide. Why hadn't he loved me enough to stick around – for me, if for no other reason? And I felt the shame of abandoning my grandmother. I'd loved her dearly, so how could I just walk away from her? What was wrong with me?

When I finally regained my composure, I dried my eyes and saw that Sir – that is, his cartoon equivalent – was staring me, as always. There were times he sat in exactly the same position for hours, unblinking, and it took me a while to realize it was a "still shot" – designed, I suspect, to remind me that he could be watching me if he wanted to. But this wasn't the still shot; this was the animated version of Sir himself. He looked at me kindly, big eyes seeming to blink back tears of his own. Finally he spoke.

"Tough movies, huh?"

"Yes, Sir. They were."

"Well, let's get started."

For the next two or three hours we analyzed each of the three movies, scene by scene, character by character. Each plot line was dissected and reassembled. Each conflict between characters was deconstructed. Different endings were considered. Apparently I answered all of Sir's questions correctly, because just as I was feeling some fatigue, he said, "You look tired, Mark. You look like you could use some fresh air."

I smiled at his little joke, since we both knew it had been weeks, if not months, since I'd breathed "fresh" air, or experienced any other connection to the real world. I was kept so busy most of the time I didn't think about it much, and once the new bed and bed linens arrived, along with other little goodies I earned, I had enough of the creature comforts to enable me to settle into an easy routine. My former life began to fade completely. There were moments, of course, that I wondered about my roommate Sean, and even my mom and stepdad. But Cookie never entered my mind. She didn't even enter my porn fantasies, and I probably couldn't have conjured up an image of her even if I tried.

Sir cleared his throat.

"I'm sorry, Sir. I think I was daydreaming. What was it you said?"

"I said, Mark, that you look like you could use some fresh air."

Frankly, I didn't know how to respond to that. Was he fucking with me? Was he trying to remind me that I was a prisoner? I stared at him.

"Why don't you give Door #1 a try, Mark? I don't think you've tried to open it since your first day, have you?"

I was dumbfounded. It never occurred to me to try again to open any of the locked doors after that first day.

As if reading my mind, Sir said, "This might be a lesson to you, Mark. Just because a door won't open the first time doesn't mean you shouldn't keep trying."

"Yes, Sir," I said, sounding tentative and unsure. Finally I realized he was waiting for me to try to open the door again. But I sensed that when I did, whatever happened as a result would change things. Was I being released from captivity, like a parakeet being allowed to fly free from its cage? And if I was going to be allowed outside, should I try to run away, to escape for good? I didn't know what would change, or how, but I knew that because my environment had been static for so long, just opening the door was bound to change everything I'd come to know as my reality.

Worse, I knew that if the door didn't open, if he was just fucking with me, I would never forgive him.

I walked over and placed my hand in the metal pull. I tugged forcefully, which turned out to be unnecessary, because it swung open easily.

I had to shade my eyes.

The sun was shining brightly, glaring really, directly into my eyes. I stepped out into a courtyard, square in shape, measuring about thirty or forty feet along each wall. There was another door at a right angle from the one I had just come through, but it was obviously controlled on the other side, because it had no visible knob or lock.

There was a small brick paved area, and a slightly larger grassy area, and the grass had been freshly mowed. A redwood chaise lounge sat in the middle of the brick pad. It looked like a little park.

A clump of three aspen trees stood in one corner, their leaves a brilliant green against their white trunks. They were about 20 feet high, just a few feet higher than the white stone wall which surrounded the space. The perimeter of the space was lined with carefully groomed bushes of varying heights, interspersed with a variety of wild flowers. I glanced over my shoulder at Sir, whose image remained on the screen on the other side of the classroom, but I think it was the still shot, since it didn't move. Above me, on the wall above the door, was an outdoor speaker, situated next to a camera. Through the speaker, I heard Sir's voice: "Go ahead, Mark, make yourself at home."

I looked into the camera and smiled, even as tears flooded my eyes.

"Thank you."

MAKEOVERS - REX JOHN

58

I'd been daydreaming again – not an uncommon occurrence since being released. Even though I loved remembering that magical day I was first allowed into the courtyard, today I needed to focus. I tried to gather my thoughts, which had been triggered, I suppose, by the beautiful tree outside my window.

The day after the cabbie helped me schlep all my new stuff to my room, I walked back downtown and relocated the Apple Store I had seen the day before. A nice looking kid with a scrubbed face asked if he could help me. I told him I needed a computer and asked what he would recommend.

"Desk top or laptop?"

"Laptop, I think."

"Cool. Let me show you our new models."

The kid's name was Chip, and he obviously knew his stuff. He was also easy to talk to, and I found myself wondering if I should ask him if he wanted to get together for a drink after work, but I thought better of it when I realized how lame it would sound. Besides, I reminded myself, I don't drink. In retrospect, I realize that this may have been one of the most dramatic changes that occurred as a result of my time in Sir's School of Life. For at least a year before I dropped out of law school, I had become increasingly anti-social.

My girlfriend and roommate were pretty much the extent of my social orbit -- and I wasn't that crazy about either of them. I was borderline rude with Si the Sci-Fi Guy during most of our trip west and even during the brief time I was with the Phi Delts in Des Moines and skiing in Breckenridge I pretty much kept to myself. Oh, I laughed and screwed around enough so that people wouldn't get on my case, but the truth is, I didn't like people and I didn't want to be around them. The fact that I had thought about connecting with this clerk at the Apple Store should have tipped me off that I was a completely different person.

I chose a MacBook Air because the thing was light as a feather and, well, it just looked cool.

I needed a printer, too, which Chip chose for me, without even bothering to talk me into it. "What the hell," I said, "let me get an iPhone, too." He walked me across the store to the iPhones and walked me through the differences between the various models.

"You know you'll have to call AT&T to activate this," he told me. "AT&T sucks, but they're your only choice, I'm afraid."

"Got it," I said.

I rounded out my selections with a cool canvas messenger bag, and together we headed for the check stand at the front of the store. In true Apple style and fashion, there wasn't anything as crass as a cash register but, rather, three desk top computers lined up like they might be at the library. Chip rang up my purchase and gave me the total: $3,294.90.

I stared at him. "Shit," I finally said. "You know what, Dude, I forgot to stop at the bank on my way over here." His face showed that he was unamused.

I knew better than to try to get him to take a blank check with no information printed on it, and I wouldn't get my debit card for a couple of weeks, according to what Abernathy at the bank had told me.

"Listen," I said, talking too fast. "How about if you just hold this stuff for fifteen minutes? I'll run to the bank, it's just down the street, and I'll be right back. OK?"

Like I have a choice, I could almost hear him think.

"Really, dude. I promise. I'll be right back."

Chip gave me a feeble smile as I dashed out the door.

As promised, I was back in less than fifteen minutes, and I could see that Chip was relieved, even though he tried to play it cool. Darlene Jenkins at the bank remembered me and initialed the check I had written for cash in the amount of five thousand dollars.

Chip was right where I'd left him, so I withdrew the bills from my pocket and counted them out on the counter. He printed out a receipt and handed it to me.

When I saw the pile of boxes and bags he'd stacked up on the counter I realized I couldn't possibly carry them by myself. I said, "Hey, Chip, could you do me one more favor? Could you call me a cab?" He did, and then helped me move the stack of packages to the curb, not two blocks from where I'd stood yesterday, where we both stood waiting until the cab pulled up.

I couldn't believe it. The driver was Fayad.

Makeovers - Rex John

59

Janet was becoming morose. Carson still hadn't allowed himself to administer "correction" – *yet* – but he began to wonder if that would help her, shock her back into reality, so to speak.

He decided against it. He came as close as setting the voltage control – to as low a setting as he'd ever dialed – and even put his hand on the red button, but he just couldn't bring himself to push it.

The girl hadn't taken a shower for several days, and she had resumed wearing the gym shorts and t-shirt, sans underwear, while her new garments lay on the steel table. She slept interminably. When he spoke to her, she ignored him. He'd put an antidepressant in two of Greta's dishes – including her famous German chocolate cake – the day before, but they still sat untouched, inside the food cupboard, even though he'd reminded her that there was a "surprise" waiting for her behind Door #3. On the same try he'd also put enough Benzodiazepine in a glass of milk to knock her out quickly, at which time he planned to sweep in, administer an injection, and give her a shower himself. He would also remove the gym shorts and t-shirt from the classroom once and for all, giving her no choice but to wear the new clothes he'd purchased for her.

But Janet wasn't having it. She didn't care if she ever got out of the steel room. She would die here, for all she knew. And that would be fine. This had been a good experience in that it gave her time to assess her life, and it came up short. Way short. She hated her job and would never go back to it. Troy was an idiot and a slob, and she knew he would never commit, so that was over, too. Her parents, whom she loved dearly, had died within four months of each other a year earlier; with no brothers and sisters, what did she have to live for?

Besides, as grim as the steel cell was, at least it gave her peace. She was relieved that this nut hadn't raped her or worse, but she knew he was always watching her and that was bad enough. She would just sleep. Maybe when she woke up, she'd find it had all been a dream.

Greta, meanwhile, was beside herself. Mr. Scooter's tray hadn't come back from yesterday – she'd checked the hall table at least a dozen times today; it remained empty, and Mr. Kirkpatrick's study door remained tightly closed. What was going on? She briefly considered asking Mr. Kirkpatrick at breakfast if something was troubling him, but the look she received when she said, "Excuse me, Sir..." told her not to add another word. He hadn't asked what she wanted to say, and she didn't say another word, so the words "excuse me Sir" were left hanging in the air like smoke in a stuffy room.

The newspapers, which Greta dutifully placed on the breakfast table as she had been trained to do, remained unread until one morning she decided to "forget" to place them on the table, just to see what her boss would do. He didn't say a word, and that was the last time she put them out. When she drove into the compound each morning, she picked them up just outside the gate and dropped them into the recycling bin outside the kitchen door.

She briefly considered another trip around the side of the house to try, once again, to look in the windows in that wing of the sprawling house. Too risky, she decided. Thanks to the ubiquitous security cameras, he knew what she was doing even when he wasn't at home.

Still mulling over her dilemma, she arrived at the Poncha Springs Library one evening after work to return a book before it became overdue. She elected not to use the drop box in front of the library, but to go inside and select another book.

As she was walking toward the fiction section of the small library, she ran into Asner Johnson, the teenage son of her friend Peggy who attended the same church Greta and Manuel attended. Asner, who was seated at one of the five new computers the county library association had just installed, seemed to be watching for her as she walked toward him. He hit a key to quickly change whatever it was he had been looking at as Greta approached, and Greta thought to herself, *Girlie pictures, I'll bet. Boys!*

As if to reassure her that he wasn't up to no good, even though Greta knew he was, he sung out, "Hi, Mrs. Martinez!" Greta smiled politely and walked toward him. "Hello, Asner. What are you working on?"

"Oh, I was just playing with Google maps," he replied. *Lying through his teeth,* Greta thought.

"Look," Asner continued. "You can even see Mr. Kirkpatrick's big house in satellite view." Asner liked Mrs. Martinez, even though he'd heard his parents on more than one occasion make fun of her name. "Martinez?" his Dad said one day, "Oh yes, that's an old German name isn't it?" His mother, ever ready to banter back and forth with her husband said, "Now, you behave yourself, or I won't make you my special Taco Schnitzel tonight!" They both laughed hilariously at their own lame humor, but Asner just sat staring at the two of them wondering whether – hoping, even – that he was adopted.

Everybody always wants to see Mr. Kirkpatrick's house, don't they, Greta thought to herself. But you never will, folks. It's more tightly guarded than the *Deutsche Bank.*

She thought back to the first time she drove up to Carson's big gate, got out of the car and tried to peer inside. But the driveway made a right turn shortly after one entered the grounds, effectively blocking a view of more than fifty feet or so inside.

She was about to politely walk on, leaving Asner free to return to whatever he had really been looking at, when she glanced at the screen he was trying to show her. There was the house, all right, surrounded by its beautifully landscaped grounds and perched on the side of a mountain in a way that gave a stunning unobstructed view of Mt. Princeton across the valley. She could easily make out the front gate and the driveway winding down to the house and around the side to the attached garage. Even though the house had only one level, it had a large mansard roof, with assorted peaks and gables, making it even higher than it already was. She couldn't resist taking a closer look. Who knew you could do something like this?

She continued to stare at the screen because something didn't make sense. There appeared to be a opening in the roof on the south side of the house, where it looked like a section had simply blown off.

"Das ist very interesting, Asner," she said. "Is possible to make larger?"

"Sure, Mrs. Martinez. You just do this..." and then, with a few key strokes, Greta found herself flying from the sky, toward the roof of the house, at supersonic speed, causing her to step back from the computer.

"Oh!" she exclaimed. And then, leaning in again, "Ja, like dat." What she saw jolted her. There, along the south side of the house, was a wall that looked like it was simply a roofless extension of the walls on either side of it. She remembered this section from her fact-finding mission to look for Mister Scooter. She wondered then why there weren't any windows in such a long expanse of wall, and now she knew why. There, in plain view from the air, she could see easily what was on the other side of that wall: a *park*. She could clearly see trees, bushes, and even flowers. It appeared in the photo that there was a lawn chair of some sort in which a man was reclining. She couldn't make out the features of the man, or even if it was a man, but she could tell it wasn't Mr. Kirkpatrick.

So! Ist that the transvestite, I wonder? Ist dat Mister Scooter?

MAKEOVERS - REX JOHN

60

As soon as I had my new Mac out of the box I powered it up and sat down to write. I wasn't sure what I would write, but I knew that's what I wanted to do.

Looking back, I'm not sure why I went to law school. Maybe because my dad did, maybe because my high school advisor recommended it; I honestly don't remember. There are worse things, I guess, but I pretty much hated every day of it, and I have a feeling I would have hated actually being a lawyer even more.

That, combined with the fact that I was a drunk and a pot head, cast a thick pall over my future. I was an idiot to run away, an idiot to drop out of law school in my last year, and an idiot to hitchhike across the country. But I'm glad I did all three. Otherwise, I wouldn't have ended up on that park bench, and I wouldn't have ended up being chosen to attend Sir's School of Life. *That's* where I really got my education; that's where I found myself.

Now I want to find him. I want to thank Sir – not only for the gift of fifty grand, although God knows, that helped me get a good start – but for choosing *me*. I'm certainly not the only guy to spend the night on a park bench, so why me? I have all kinds of questions to ask him.

And I will admit that I'd like to know for sure that the guy on the other side of the food cupboard was really him.

Finding the proverbial needle in a haystack might be easier, though. I don't know if Sir has any other "students" out here – alumni, I guess you'd call them. I have a hunch there are, and I can't help but wonder if some of them wouldn't like to find him, too – to thank him, just as I want to do.

I started writing the day I brought my computer back to the apartment. At first, I just wrote crap – short stories, stuff like that. I also took a couple of evening classes at the University of Denver, through their continuing education program, and that really turned me on. Eleanor was an attractive young woman who taught one of my classes (and who freely admitted that she was a lesbian). I liked her a lot, and she provided just the support and encouragement I needed.

"This is the best story I've ever received, Mark," she said one night after class. "I want you to send it to an agent-friend of mine in New York." I did, and, well that, as they say, is the rest of the story.

In my little Capitol Hill apartment in Denver, I'd get up early in the morning – sometimes as early as 3 a.m. – make myself a pot of coffee, and sit down to write. I would write, literally all day long, stopping only to go to the bathroom and get a bite to eat when my stomach started growling. Mrs. Rosencranz continued to bring me trays of food at dinner time at least two or three times a week, and to this day I marvel that, without exception, every single dish was an exact duplicate of the meals Sir fixed for me. I obsessed about that for the longest time, wondering about the odds of that happening, but I finally gave it up trying to figure it out – since Sir sounded much more like a Brit than a German. Besides, I couldn't think of a way to ask Mrs. Rosencranz if she knew somebody named "Sir," who lived "somewhere" – I didn't know where – and how he might have gotten hold of all her recipes.

But, when I allow myself to think about it, it still bugs me.

I wrote *Exquisite Rain* in a little over three months. By that time, Eleanor's agent-friend had become very interested in my writing, so by the time I finished it all I had to do was ship it to him.

Sometimes when I write, I plug in a set of mini-speakers that Chip sold me on one of my subsequent visits to the Apple Store and crank up the iTunes.

Chip and I actually did become friends, and I even listed him on the acknowledgements page of my book as "my buddy and computer guru, Chip," which he said was "awesome."

The first song I bought on line was "Hey Good Lookin'" by Hank Williams, Sr. Now, if you'd told me at anytime in my life before I met Sir that I would someday listen to, much less *like*, any form of country music, I'd have told you you're nuts. My tastes changed, though, along with everything else, thanks to Sir.

The story of how I grew to like Country-Western, or C/W as we true aficionados call it, is an excellent example of how Sir caused me to grow and learn.

We'd been getting along pretty well. I hadn't had any recent doses of "correction," and I think my hair finally stopped standing on end. I'd already earned a couple of creature comforts, but if I screwed up on anything, I'd awaken the next morning to find that they'd disappeared during the night, and I'd have to earn them all over again.

We were talking one day about the movie he'd just had me watch – *The Legend of Bagger Vance*, I think it was – and I said something about really liking the soundtrack.

"Oh, do you like music, Mark?" Sir asked me.

"Oh, sure. I used to always have it on at..." I stopped, uncertain of how to finish the sentence. I didn't allow myself to think about "home" that often, not because it was so wonderful and I wanted to go back, but because it reminded me that, no matter what I wanted to believe, the truth is I was a kidnap victim and my freedom had been taken from me. That, in turn, would generate a thought process that took me places I didn't want to go – like, would I actually die in this steel room? Would Sir get crazier than he already was sometimes? Besides, I probably didn't want to think too much about "home" because I felt so much guilt about the way I'd left – and especially about how I'd treated my grandmother.

"Yes, Mark? What is it you were saying?"

"Oh, nothing, Sir. Just that, yeah, I like music."

"That's great. What kind of music do you like?"

"Oh, I don't know. Rock, mostly. Pop, too. Jazz...some rap. Actually, pretty much anything except country."

As soon as the word "country" was out of my mouth I wanted to bite my tongue off. I knew, somehow, that my answer would come to haunt me, and less than two hours later, it did.

We had moved on from discussing the movie to a book he had left on my food tray one day with a sticky note saying "Read this." I did, and now he wanted to discuss it. It was what they call a "motivational book," full of platitudes and supposedly good advice on how to become a better person. As with so many books in that genre, it tended to be somewhat simplistic, offering advice like "If you feel bad, just smile and you will start to feel better." That kind of bullshit.

"I notice you've been reading the book I gave you. Have you finished it?" he asked.

"Yes, Sir, I have."

"And? What did you think of it?"

Here's where I made my first mistake. Sir didn't really want to know *if* I liked it. He wanted to know that I *did* like it. If I liked it, he was more than happy to hear me tell him how much. But if I didn't like it, well, I'd be better off just re-reading it until I did. That's how it worked with him. If he gave it to you, you better like it, period. But I didn't know that back then. I foolishly said, "Well, Sir, I thought it sucked." And then, just to make sure I'd dug a hole I could never climb out of, I added, "It's probably one of the dumbest books I ever read."

There was silence for a moment, until he finally said, his tone flat and cold, "Well. OK, then. Perhaps we've worked enough today. Would you like to listen to some music?"

Like a dope, I said, "Sure."

Then, for the next twenty-four hours, without pause, except ever-so-briefly when Sir's voice would override the music to say, "Lunch is served" – or whatever meal it happened to be, I got to listen to music.

One song.

Over and over and over and over and over and over and over again.

I found out later that the name of the song I was forced to listen to, like a thousand times, was *"Be Careful of Stones That You Throw"* in the distinctive voice of Hank Williams, Sr.

> *"A tongue can accuse and carry bad news*
> *The seeds of distrust, it will sow*
> *But unless you've made no mistakes in your life*
> *Be careful of stones that you throw..."*

I got the message. From that day on, it's amazing how much I liked every single movie and book Sir sent my way. Even more curious, I now listen to the occasional C/W tune – and like it.

I also smile when I feel bad and, sure enough, I usually start to feel better. Go figure.

61

So. I was all set: new apartment, computer, printer, tunes, German cook at my disposal.

I had been alone, essentially, for the past several months. My only "friend," if you can call him that, was a little animated character who could shock the shit out of me with the push of a button, and now even he was gone. I hadn't had any "flesh and blood" contact until a few days ago when I staggered from my park bench back into real life. I should be ecstatic. I was slowly gaining the freedom to do whatever I damn well pleased.

So, why was I so lonely? One night, while "taking care of personal business," I briefly thought of calling Cookie. How desperate is that? I quickly came to my senses when I remembered that I didn't even *like* Cookie. The urge quickly passed. Besides, I didn't want Cookie. I wanted Sir. Sir listened to me. He cared what happened to me. He taught me stuff. Sir was the parent I never had. Shit. Was this a man crush? A so-called "bromance"? I didn't want him romantically, and certainly not sexually, but I really missed him. How lame is that?

Clearly, I needed a friend.

That's when Troy showed up. Troy lived across the hall from me, and just when I'd begun to wonder if Mrs. Rosencranz and I were the only two people in the building, I opened my door one day and there was Troy, standing in front of his own doorway.

Troy was about six feet tall, same as me, and he had dark brown hair that was sort of wavy, but not curly, and in the style of what you might expect a surfer to wear – a little long, a week or two past time to get it cut. He had a bit of a stubble, probably from skipping shaving that morning, just as I had. He had a good smile, good teeth, and a dimple in his chin, sort of like the actor Kirk Douglas, only not quite as pronounced. He was dressed in jeans and a T-shirt, just as I was. He was wearing sneakers. He looked like an overgrown college kid.

He turned toward me when he heard my door open. "Hey, man."

"Hey."

That would have probably comprised our entire conversation for a year or two if I'd done what straight guys usually do in those awkward social situations. Your voice drops an octave to make sure your first impression isn't ambiguous, that is, leaving no doubt that you are 100% hetero. The "hey man" is always accompanied by the obligatory head-snap – an almost imperceptible tilt upward of the chin with a slight squinting of the eyes, as if to say, "I'm not somebody to fuck with, dude."

We both did it during that microsecond while Troy was fumbling to unlock his door, and if I'd pussied-out a second longer, I would have lost him.

"Um..."

"Yeah?" he said.

My mind was scrambling to think of something intelligent to say. As usual, it failed me.

"Whadsup?"

It is to Troy's credit that he figured out in an instant that, (a) I wasn't coming on to him; and, (b) I was trying to start a conversation. I would learn much later that he was actually wondering at the moment if I was mildly addled. By now his key was in the door, but he left it there and turned toward me, extending his hand. I took it, shook it.

"You just moved in, didn't you?"

"Yeah, I said, relieved that he didn't rush into his apartment and slam the door in my face. "Just a couple of days ago."

"Cool." And then, his eyes doing a quick once-over, he apparently decided he could risk it, he added, "Want a beer?"

"Hell, yeah," I said, temporarily forgetting I was an alcoholic and no longer drank beer.

"Great. Come on in."

He unlocked the door and flung it open for me to go first. "After you."

His place was OK, basically the same as mine, only reversed and with a view of the city skyline as well as the mountains. He certainly had more furniture than me, mostly guy stuff, including a supersize black leather sofa aimed at a big screen TV. I guess I knew where I'd be on game day.

"Have a seat. I'll get the beer."

My memory had returned by then. "Um...do you mind if I start light – maybe with just a glass of water?" I figured we might as well get the alcoholic thing out in the open right off the bat, so he could figure out if he could deal with somebody who doesn't drink.

But I didn't even need to tell him; the questions came fast and furious. "What's up with that? You drink at all?"

"Not any more."

"You're not a Mormon?"

"What? Oh. No, I'm not a Mormon."

"A born again?"

"Nope," I said, wondering how long this would go on.

"Ah. An alkie, huh?"

He said it with a smile, so I didn't take offense. "Yeah, something like that."

"Well, that's OK," he said. "As long as it's not some religious thing. I can't deal with that shit."

"No worries. I gave religion up for lent."

Head snap, big grin. "Cool. Alright, then. How about a soda?"

"Perfect."

He brought out two sodas – guess he didn't want to try his luck. Some people are like that. When they find out you don't drink, they won't either, maybe because they're worried that they're drinking too much themselves, or maybe because they're afraid I'll punch 'em out and steal their drink. Who knows. He didn't drink that day, but, by God, he drank plenty in the months ahead. He also powered up the bong on a daily basis and, while I certainly have no right to criticize anyone for being a drunk or a pothead, I will admit that it occasionally got tiresome.

You can imagine how surprised I was to find out several weeks later that he was a cop – as was his girlfriend. I asked him one day if the Denver Police Department didn't have routine drug tests.

"Nah," he said. "Only when you first get hired and, of course, if you're ever in an accident...or have an 'incident.'"

"An 'incident'?"

"You know, like when you shoot someone in the line of duty, stuff like that. They usually test you then."

"Doesn't that worry you?"

"Nah, not really."

I couldn't resist asking. "Why not?"

"Because," he said sheepishly, "I'm the drug testing guy for the department."

This resulted in great hilarity on my part, accompanied by loud guffawing and finger-pointing.

But, to his credit, once Troy found out that I was on the wagon and clean as a whistle, he never tried to get me to drink or smoke pot with him. I think he secretly wanted to quit, but that's a drunk talking. We think anybody who drinks should quit and probably wants to.

All this stuff didn't come out the night of that first hallway meeting, of course. Most of it I learned in the weeks and months ahead. That night we just sat around playing what amounted to "twenty questions." Where are you from? Where'd you go to school? What sports do you follow? How 'bout them Broncos? That kind of thing.

I didn't tell him that I'd spent the past few months in solitary confinement, that I'd been kidnapped. For some reason it embarrassed me, even though I hadn't done anything wrong except fall asleep on the wrong park bench. I think it might have been because I really liked being locked up. I know that sounds crazy, but I liked it that Sir took care of everything – and that he kept me from hurting myself further with booze and drugs. I know that's weird, but once I settled in to his "classroom," I really didn't want to leave. I think that's probably the part I was most embarrassed to tell Troy about: that I had enjoyed being held prisoner. Talk about kinky!

He got another soda for each of us, and at some point I said I needed to use the bathroom. He told me where it was, and I went through his bedroom into the bathroom adjoining it, although in retrospect I wonder why I didn't just go across the hall to my own apartment.

When I came out, I noticed a photo of a very pretty girl on his dresser. It was one of those "glam shots" that so many girls were getting back then, with their hair and make up fixed perfectly and dramatic lighting to make them look like movie stars. She had light brown hair, long, past her shoulders, but all teased up into a big ball of fluff. It looked like she was wearing a ton of make-up, too, like she had zits she was trying to cover up. Still, she had pretty eyes and a big smile showing two rows of gleaming white teeth, shiny like they'd been covered with Vaseline.

Returning to the living room, I said, "Who's the girl?" He had to think for a second and then seemed to figure out that I'd seen the photo on his dresser.

"Oh. That's my girlfriend, Janet." He seemed subdued, like he either wasn't sure that was his girlfriend or he was pissed off at her.

"You live together?" I asked.

"No. She works all the time. I don't see her that much."

I got the feeling he didn't want to talk anymore about her, so I changed the subject.

I didn't want to overstay my welcome, but I really liked hanging out with this guy. I decided to test the waters; to see if he felt the same way. "Well, I guess I should go..."

"Don't do that, man! Let's go get a bite to eat or something."

Perfect. He liked me, too. I know that sounds faggy to say, but with guys friendship is a whole different dance than it is with women. With guys, the fewer words the better. Guys don't want to talk about being friends, they just want to do stuff. Shoot hoops, grab food, go to a game, that sort of thing. I would no more have said, "Hey, man, you want to be friends?" than I would have kissed him. Still, I was glad when he suggested that we not end the evening yet.

"Well, OK," I said. "But I probably should tell Mrs. Rosencranz that I won't be eating in tonight..."

Troy broke out in a big grin. "Ja, vol! Das ist verboten!" And then, "So, you're on the German food train too, huh? I've had the same treatment since I first moved it, and I must say, I love that sauerkraut!"

I wasn't sure if he was talking about the food or Mrs. Rosencranz herself, but I said, "Yeah, her stuff is pretty good."

We stopped by Mrs. Rosencranz' apartment when we got to the first floor and knocked. Troy stood slightly behind me, so when the door first opened, I don't think she saw him. "Herr Mark!" she exclaimed, opening the door wider. "Komm in, komm in!"

"I really can't, Mrs. Rosencranz. I'm going out to dinner tonight with my buddy..." and, as I gestured toward Troy over my shoulder, I realized I didn't even know his name.

"Troy," he offered, laughing as he stepped forward and gave Mrs. Rosencranz a hug. "How ya' doin' Mrs. R?"

"Oh you!" she said, pushing him away teasingly. "What you doing wit Herr Mark! Don't you make him a bad boy like you!"

"Him? 'Herr Mark'? Hey, we're neighbors, so we figured we should be friends!"

Those few words, offered as almost a throw-away line, were music to my ears. I finally had a friend. And now I even knew his name.

62

During the next several months, Troy and I were inseparable. If he wasn't at work, or if we weren't in our respective apartments asleep, we were together. After I'd known him about a week, I finally met Janet when the two of them showed up at my door one afternoon. He said, "Mark, this is my girlfriend Janet."

I got the idea she didn't like being referred to as the "girlfriend," by the look she gave him. "And Janet, this is the guy I've been telling you about, Mark."

She mumbled something like "Nice to meet you," and I stood back waiting for Troy to barge in, as he usually did.

"Let's go in, honey," he said as he apparently nudged her from the back. She spun on her heels and grabbed his arm, like a Karate expert. I honestly thought she was going to fling him to the ground, and I wondered if she did if I would have to stand over him, upraising her arm and declaring her the winner. It was surreal. My mouth must have dropped open, because Troy gave sort of an embarrassed smile even as he stepped away from her and she quickly dropped his arm. I caught the look on her face and all I can say is, if looks could kill, he'd have been lying dead in a pool of blood on my doorstep.

They came in and, since I had only two chairs at my table, they sat there while I parked my ass on the kitchen counter. I gave them some coffee and tried to figure out what the deal was with this crazy woman.

That, in fact, was when I first found out they were both cops. I'd asked Troy a few days earlier what he did for a living and he responded with some smart ass answer like "I'm a pimp" or something equally stupid. I let it slide, because I didn't care what he did. I just liked spending time with him.

So, you could have knocked me over with a feather when I said to Janet, "So, what kind of work do you do?" And she said, "Same as Troy."

"And what is that?" I said, directing the question to Troy, wondering if he would still claim to be a pimp.

He grinned at Janet, then at me. "We're cops."

"No, seriously, dude, what the hell do you do for a living?"

"I'm telling you the truth, Mark. We're cops."

I couldn't get my head around it. "Seriously, man..."

"Goddamn it man, it's true. Janet's in the detective squad and I'm in admin."

"But, what about the..." I stopped, unsure if I should say "dope," wondering if she knew what a pothead he was and, if she didn't, if she would arrest him on the spot.

"Oh, you mean the fact that I smoke a lot of dope?" There was that stupid grin again. "Well, the department doesn't know – although I'm certainly not the only one – and yes, Janet knows, but she's not really keen on the idea." He grinned at her, she glared at him.

A few days later, we had the conversation where he told me that he actually handled the drug testing duties for the department -- something I still find hard to believe.

I didn't like it that Troy smoked so much pot – been there, done that – but I also didn't like this young woman whose every look was critical and judgmental. If I were less of a gentleman, I'd say she was a bitch.

"Cool," is all I could think of to say.

Curiously, given that first impression, in the months ahead I would get to know Janet as well as I did Troy and she began to grow on me. She was attractive: she had long light brown hair which she typically kept pulled back into a ponytail. She had beautiful big brown eyes and perfectly straight teeth, white from what I imagine were frequent bleachings. She wore a bit too much make-up for my taste, but I suspect that may have had more to do with a desire to cover a port wine stain on her left cheek. I didn't notice it for a long time – that's how thick her make-up was – and when I did, it made me sad, because I knew it must embarrass her. It didn't bother me, though. She was a beautiful young woman and this one imperfection didn't do anything to change that.

I say she was a 'young woman,' but, in fact, she was older than she looked. I was shocked when I found out she would be turning thirty in April. I would have sworn she was about 19, and I often gave Troy a hard time about not dating women his own age.

When Janet wasn't working weird hours, the three of us usually walked to a place just a couple of blocks away called "The Parlour." It looked like a dive bar, but according to Troy they had the best burgers in

town.   Sir had taught me the importance of good
nutrition, and eating beef wasn't at the top of the list of
healthy foods; but he also taught me every nuance of
etiquette and good manners – the number one principle
of which was not to do anything to hurt the feelings of
others. So, I decided as we entered The Parlour that I'd
eat a burger and worry about the health implications
some other time. (And I did – about 3 o'clock the next
morning.)

We talked about innocuous stuff. Over time, I
told them parts of my life story – about my grandmother,
my parents, even my dad's death.   I told them I'd
dropped out of law school, but I didn't tell him that it
was arguably the most prestigious law school in the
country, and neither of them asked. That struck me as
odd – especially since Janet was a detective and all – but
the truth is, most people these days are terrible
conversationalists, preferring to talk only about
themselves. I stopped my story after my dropping out,
not offering any details about my cross-country
hitchhike with Sci-Fi Si or my weeks of drunken
debauchery with my Phi Delt buddies. I decided not to
tell them about my kidnapping and make-over, either.

Troy told me about his own upbringing – perfect
parents, enough money to pay the bills, and four
siblings, all girls. Janet did a lot of eye-rolling when
Troy talked, which annoyed the hell out of me, and I
noticed she rarely contributed any information about her
own life.

I liked Troy. I could see that he was intelligent,
which was a real plus. But I also remember thinking that
he seemed a little spoiled, like a kid whose parents did
everything for him and probably solved all his problems.

Much later in our friendship I would tell him what a slacker he was, pointing out that the constant pot smoking had taken a toll on his brain cells. He denied it, said he could stop any time he wanted, that he only smoked to relax, etc. – the usual bullshit that potheads drag out to try to convince themselves that they're not really watching big chunks of their life go up in smoke.

Once in awhile we would even take Mrs. Rosencranz out to the Parlour with us, even though she protested every step of the way. We'd buy her dinner and she turned into a food critic. "Dis food ist awful," she would say, but only after cleaning her plate. "Vat dey need is good German cooking." She was right about that – I'd never had food as good as Mrs. Rosencranz' – except for Sir's cooking, but to me they were the same.

Exactly a year later, I finished the first draft of my book, and thanks to Eleanor, my writing teacher, I already had an agent, so I simply boxed up the draft and shipped it off to him. My own copy was still stored electronically on my computer. My timing couldn't have been better, because even living as modestly as I had been, the money Sir had left in my pocket was dwindling quickly.

Nobody was more surprised than I was when I received a call from Marty a couple of days later – Marty's my agent – telling me he'd gotten the draft, read it, and already had a potential buyer lined up! Troy, Janet and I went to The Parlour that night and celebrated. I came as close as I had since Sir released me to having a glass of the champagne from one of several bottles I would end up buying that night. But I didn't.

Everything began moving at warp speed. Contracts arrived by FedEx for me to sign, and I sent them back by Fedex next-day, as instructed.

Marty soon asked me to come to New York to meet an editor he'd lined up, and then to meet with the prospective publisher. I had to tell Marty I wasn't sure I could afford such a trip, since by this time my money had gotten so low I'd taken a part time job as a waiter at The Parlour. He said not to worry about it, that it was all-expenses paid.

Sure enough, I went to the airport and found that a ticket had been paid for – first-class, no less – and when I arrived, there was a guy in uniform standing at the baggage carousel with a sign with my name on it. He led me to a black Lincoln Town Car and drove me to the Waldorf-Astoria. There was a bottle of Veuve-Cliquot waiting for me in my room, which was still sitting there untouched when I left – along with a $10 tip for the maid.

Marty turned out to be an affable guy in person, and we had good meetings with the editor and publisher. As a first time fiction author, I knew nobody would offer me an advance, but my publisher kind of took me under his wing and said if I signed the contract he would arrange for me to make "draws" against my future earnings. He stressed repeatedly that "this just wasn't done for debut authors," and I believed him. But it also meant I could afford to move to New York, which is where I had decided I wanted to live, since I'd already decided my next book would take place there, and I wanted to absorb the feel of the city.

I signed the contract.

I returned to Denver, and Troy and Janet sounded disappointed when I told them I was moving, and I think they really were sorry to see me go. We'd had lots of fun together during that year, and I ran interference for Troy quite a bit, calming Janet down when she periodically threatened to leave him for good.

I was sorry to leave them, too, because it meant starting all over again, and making new friends was never easy for me, even though Sir had equipped me with excellent social skills.

It's still strange to me that I never quite got around to telling them about my kidnapping. I skirted the issue a couple of times and came close, but I always pulled back at the last minute and never quite got it out. I wonder if at some subconscious level, I was worried that I wouldn't be believed – it sounded far-fetched even to me, and I was there! Or maybe it was because the experience was so life-changing – Sir literally gave me my life back – and I didn't want anybody mocking the process, bizarre as it was. Whatever the reason, I never got around to revealing it, and I don't suppose they ever would have found out if it weren't for the cover photo of me on the cover of *People* magazine. When that appeared on the newsstands, I braced myself for a call, but it never came. I knew they weren't big magazine people, but I thought for sure they might see it on the rack at the grocery store or something. I almost called to ask, but I decided that would be too weird and, as grandmother used to say, "too braggadocio." So they never said anything about it in our phone conversations, and neither did I.

Actually, we talked on the phone so often, it was almost like Troy and I were still living across the hall from each other. I swear, one of us called the other at least once a day if not more often. How gay is that? If Janet was there when I called, he would put her on for a few minutes and she and I would always laugh and talk just like we did when we sat in the Parlour till all hours of the night.

I got the feeling that things were still tense between them, though, and it made me sad because I genuinely liked them both. I hoped they would learn to love each other more – or at least better. I knew they were both needy enough (Troy more than Janet) that I wondered how either one of them could ever live without the other – but I never imagined they were about to find out.

63

Carson was relieved when Janet finally gave in and ate on day number three of her self-imposed fast. But because her stomach had shrunk, the heavy German food didn't sit well and she promptly threw it up.

Carson watched the whole spectacle in the control room, and he silently cursed himself for not realizing that Greta's cooking would not be easily digested by a stomach that had been empty for three days. He picked up the phone pushed the button for the intercom. He dialed 20 for the kitchen, and Greta answered on the first ring. "Ja, Mr. Kirkpatrick?"

He grimaced, having asked repeatedly that Greta use the anglicized "Yes," rather than the Germanic "Ja," even though he knew her continued use of the word was attributable to habit and bad memory, and certainly not in deliberate disobedience to his orders. *Maybe I should wire the kitchen floor for electrical shock. That ought to help her remember.*

Ignoring his own mean streak, he stated the purpose of his call. "Greta, Mr. Scooter has been ill for a few days..." but, before he could finish, she interrupted, as she often did, this time to express her concern.

"Oh, no! Das ist aber schade! Do I call the doktor?"

"No, that won't be necessary. I think he will be fine, but perhaps we should change his diet. Something bland, not spicy, something like pudding and perhaps some soda crackers..."

"Ja, ja, I make now. I bring right away!" And with that, she simply hung up on him. That was another thing he loathed. Bad phone etiquette. One must always begin a phone call with self-identification, followed immediately with a statement of the purpose of the call. The call should be short and to the point, followed by a cordial "good-bye," to signal that the call is over. His students learned this during the module on "everyday living," but of course Greta had never been given the privilege of being a student in the School of Life, so perhaps she simply didn't know any better. He had to admit she was in abundant company. Few people knew how to use the phone properly.

But he planned to change that, one person at a time.

While he waited for Greta to come tromping down the hall with the tray of pudding and soda crackers – he hoped she would think to include a pot of tea – he pulled down the curriculum notebook.

The notebook was three inches thick, and made of fine Italian kid leather, because he detested anything made of plastic. The words "School of Life" were embossed in gold leaf at the bottom right corner of the front cover. He pursed his lips in displeasure as he remembered the reaction of the clerk at Denver's oldest stationery store when he placed his order. "'School of Life'?" she said mockingly. "That's a pretty broad topic for a three inch notebook, isn't it?" He could have slapped her. Instead, he simply arched his eyebrows and glared at her. She got the message, all right, and the sale was concluded without another word.

Inside were four sections, divided by heavy cream-colored card stock dividers with neatly lettered script identifying each section. He passed by "Why nobody likes you," and "What you can do about it," and went directly to "Qualities that set you apart." The last section, the thickest, was labeled, "Functioning in a dysfunctional world."

Each page in the book consisted of a standard-sized 8.5" x 11" piece of 100% cotton paper, 25 pound weight. Carson taught his charges about the fine variations in paper stock and how such things contributed to one's image. The watermarked paper he used, for example, cost almost fifty dollars a ream and was increasingly difficult to find, thanks to the declining tastes of the average American.

His name didn't appear anywhere in the book, just in case it should fall into the wrong hands, but of course his full name was engraved on the stack of gray, monarch-sized personal stationery that sat on the shelf above him. He taught his students early on the difference between genuine engraving and the modern faux engraving called "thermography." The later, of course, was never acceptable.

As he continued to wait for Greta, he flipped idly through the book, remembering some of his former students and how grateful they were for some of the things he taught them. Each completed all of the modules, of course – they couldn't graduate until they did. There were no drop-outs at the School of Life, that's for sure. With one notable exception.

Harry.

Every time Carson remembered Harry, his body tensed and his brow wrinkled. Harry was an abomination. He was the most thick-headed and stubbornly stupid student Carson had ever had. He was, in a word, impossible.

Carson stared at the page open before him. The headline, "Your Stationery Wardrobe" was sub-titled, "The imperceptible differences in distinctive stationery." This was near the end of the course, so Harry never saw it. *It's just as well. He would have been too stupid to understand the differences between Crane's paper and notebook paper, or a Mont Blanc and a Bic.*

But just how far had Harry progressed before he had to...*drop out,* Carson wondered. He flipped to the front of the book. *Did we even finish the chapter on "First Impressions?" No, I don't think we even got that far.*

A sharp rap on the door caused Carson to close the book and return it to the shelf above his desk. He glanced at the door to the control room to ensure that it was closed before opening the door. Greta stood before him with a silver tray. As was her habit, she tried to walk into the room, but Carson, expecting the move, blocked her way. He stood solidly in the doorway as she tried to look over and around him into the study, talking as she did so as though he wouldn't notice what she was doing.

"Ja. Dis should help Mister Scooter feel better. Soup, tapioca pudding and soda crackers. I also bring tea in case he is thirsty."

"Thank you very much, Greta. I was hoping you would bring the tea, and I'm glad to see that you did."

"Shall I see Mister Scooter to ask if I can make him something else, something special?"

"No, that won't be necessary," Carson replied, adding, for what seemed like the thousandth time, "You know how much my brother hates to be around other people."

"Ja..." Greta said despondently, looking beyond Carson one last time. "Ja."

At that, Carson took the tray and pushed the door shut with his foot. Hearing the self-locking mechanism, he placed the tray on the credenza and retrieved the tasteless powder he had ready to mix into Janet's tapioca pudding. It was enough to knock out a 300 pound man – *someone Harry's size* he thought bitterly, and he briefly hoped it wouldn't be too much. After mixing it into the pudding, he placed the small spoon back in the container of Benzodiazepine and locked both in the credenza. He then placed the palm of his hand on the palm reader next to the control room door. The door swung open silently. As he walked through, he thought he heard Greta in the outside hallway picking up the untouched dishes from that morning's breakfast.

Slipping through the control room and into the hallway just beyond, he placed the tray on another hall table as he opened the outer door to the food passage – or Door # 3, as the students knew it. He opened it just a crack to ensure that it was still locked on the other side of the cabinet. Assured that it was, he turned to retrieve the tray, and placed it inside the cabinet. He released the inside lock on the classroom-side door and quickly closed and locked the one on his side.

He then returned to the control room and watched. Janet was still lying still on her bed, but when he re-wound the tape to a time-stop only a few moments earlier, he noted that she had stirred slightly when she heard the sound of the outer food passage door being unlatched. Satisfied that he hadn't missed anything, he resumed watching the young woman in real time.

She has to be weak from lack of food. Eat, girl, eat! Almost as though she had heard him, Janet turned and glanced toward the screen, where Carson's anime figure sat watching her. Carson flipped the switch to activate his microphone.

"Hello, Janet."

She looked at him but didn't respond. With some effort, she swiveled her feet onto the steel floor. Keeping her eyes on the screen, she slowly stood, but immediately became lightheaded and sat down again.

"That's OK, dear. Take it slowly."

She glared at the screen, but said nothing aloud, forcing herself to smile weakly instead. Inwardly, she seethed. *Shut the fuck up you asshole.*

Standing again, she tried to straighten her posture, willing herself not to sit again.

Shaking, she made her way across the room and opened Door # 3. She looked at the tray and immediately smelled the chicken broth. Taking the bowl carefully in her hands, she leaned against the wall and sipped from it. But the weight of the bowl was too heavy in her weakened state, so she returned it to the tray. Propping the door open, she looked at the tapioca pudding, remembering in a flash that her mother had served her the same pudding the day she had her first period. Summoning all her strength, she reached for the bowl of pudding and the spoon sitting on a folded linen napkin next to it. Leaning against the wall, she allowed herself to slide slowly to the floor, pudding and spoon in hand.

She ate.

Shit. More drugs. She detected the faint aftertaste of chemicals – was it valium, she wondered? No matter, she'd already eaten half the bowl and she knew it wouldn't be long till she slept again.

Carson watched as the bowl and spoon slid from her hands onto the steel floor, noisy but intact. He continued to watch for a few minutes before moving swiftly into the classroom hallway. After donning his surgical mask, he placed his palm on the reader, the door to the classroom opened quietly, bumping Janet's head slightly when it made contact with her inert body on the floor. Janet stirred, and Carson stopped in his tracks. Satisfied that she was indeed out, he adjusted his surgical mask and stepped across her. Picking up the bowl, he noticed that she continued to grip her spoon tightly. He pried it loose and placed both the bowl and spoon on the tray.

Grabbing Janet's arm, he swiveled her into a prone position on the floor and straightened her legs. Moving quickly and efficiently, he knelt beside her and placed his left hand behind her neck. Pulling her upright, into a sitting position, he slipped the t-shirt over her head and threw it through the open door into the hallway. Her breasts were now free, and for a moment he stared at them before gently lowering her head to the floor.

Reaching under her, he grasped the elastic waist of the gym shorts and began maneuvering them down her legs, alternating from side to side as he did so. They, too, were thrown into the hallway outside the room.

He sat back on the floor and observed the now naked woman stretched before him. He placed his right hand on the breast nearest him and squeezed softly. He released the breast and slowly moved his flattened hand down the girl's belly and abdomen, stopping only when his fingers moved into the tangle of pubic hair. *This should be trimmed*. He looked at her face and the shallow movement of her chest as she breathed.

He abruptly stood, pulling her hand with him. Dragging her by one arm across the slick steel floor, he dropped her arm onto her chest when they reached the floor of the shower. Exiting the classroom briefly, he walked into the control room and pushed two buttons in quick succession. The first, marked "hose," released a hidden panel in the wall next to the shower in which a fifteen-foot coiled hose hung on a hook. The next, marked "water" sent water into the hose, causing the trigger nozzle at the end to drip. A valve next to the button determined the temperature of the water, and he left it as it was: 100 degrees. Pausing outside the classroom door, which still stood open, he reached into a cupboard and retrieved soap, shampoo, conditioner and a big fluffy towel.

He re-entered the classroom and went to work.

64

As Carson worked on Janet, he recalled the dreaded washings of fat Harry. After he'd finished removing the acres of tattoos which covered Harry's body, he allowed the scars to heal for a few days before instructing him to take a shower. Harry didn't respond with "fuck you," as Carson knew he wanted to, so at least *that* lesson had been learned. As Carson explained to him at the time, you use shocking language, you get shocked; it's that simple.

And he had, quite literally, shocked the words "fuck you" right out of him.

But he also didn't like to take showers, and Carson wasn't sure why. It probably had something to do with the size and weight of the big guy, combined with not wanting "Sir" to see him naked. Who knows. But Carson couldn't have him running around with a week's worth of dirt clinging to his skin, could he?

"It's time for a shower, Harry. Your tattoo scars have healed adequately now, so I doubt you'll have too much pain. I've put shampoo, soap and a towel in cupboard #3 and I'll start the water when you're ready."

He didn't budge. He glared fleetingly at the screen where "Sir" had just delivered these instructions and then lay flat on his bed!

Carson could have shocked him right then, of course. He still hadn't earned a mattress, so the "bed," as it were, was still nothing more than a steel shelf and very much connected to the high-voltage lines that made the room little more than a big electrical outlet.

Carson studied him. What makes this cretin tick? What terrible things had happened to him during his childhood to make him so sullen and withdrawn?

He was mystified. He'd never encountered a student who had been so difficult. In the three months that Harry had been with him, his physical appearance had changed radically. Carson had practically starved him to death, giving him only the smallest quantities of food and an occasional protein shake concoction to administer the Benzodiazepine. Carson was sure Harry knew the drug was in the shake, but he drank it anyway. It was almost as though he wanted to be knocked out; that he liked being unconscious.

Carson continued to study him. He must have lost almost fifty pounds. He still didn't look good and was a long way from being thin, but it was a marked improvement. The gym shorts looked ridiculous on him now, and there were many times that he simply let them slide to the floor and walked around naked! That was clearly unacceptable behavior – students were to be properly dressed at all times – but he had allowed it to slide, realizing he had a much bigger problem on his hands. His head was shaved every few days, when he was out cold, but the stubble grew quickly and Carson had grown tired of the process. He noted that it was now about a half-inch long, giving him the appearance of a short-haired dog. Usually at this point – three months into the program – a student's behavior would have warranted some earned privileges – such as longer hair – but clearly that wasn't the case here. Carson made a note to shave him again the next time he was unconscious.

Perhaps he should try to reason with him. Intuitively Carson knew better, but he decided to try it anyway. Clearing his throat and taking a deep breath, he engaged his microphone.

Harry...

There was no response, and Carson wondered briefly if he was asleep, since his back was turned toward camera #1. Carson flipped on the switch for camera #2 so he could see his face. His eyes were wide open.

"Harry? You know, I've never told a student this before, but I'm going to tell you something that may help you."

He paused, for effect. Harry's eyes still remained open and still.

"You will eventually get out of here. Did you know that? It's true. Once we have...um...finished our work here, you will be a different person. A better person. And you will be better equipped to tackle the world and respond to what life throws at you. As soon as I think you have learned those lessons, you will graduate! That's right – as soon as you learn those lessons, you will be allowed to leave the classroom and resume life on your own.

"Isn't that worth doing your best job now – to hasten that day?

"Harry?

"Harry?"

The hulking figure remained silent...and still. Once again, Carson fleetingly considered administering a corrective shock, but he had noticed recently that while Harry continued to respond physically to the shocks – body twitching, eye-rolling and the like, and his hair, if he still had it, would probably still stand on end – afterward he still wouldn't budge. More than once Carson had wondered if he'd actually killed him, but then, the big lug would turn over, or blink, or move in some other way, proving to Carson that he was still alive.

There were other forms of correction, of course, and Carson had used them all at one time or another. Hot water, cold water – he was pretty sure Harry hated them both, but probably not as much as Carson hated cleaning up the mess afterward. That was tiresome. First, he would need to wait, sometimes days, until Harry ate something with enough Benzodiazepine in it to cause him to fall asleep, at which time Carson would enter the classroom with a large squeegee and begin the tedious process of mopping any water that remained out of the room. And of course, he wouldn't dare shock Harry while everything was sopping wet.

But he didn't feel like opening the water jets today. He wasn't sure what he wanted to do. On impulse, he grabbed one of the hundreds of DVDs from the shelf in the control room, each chosen for their instructive messages – "That's Life", for example, to teach students about the importance of education. "About a Boy," to define true maturity. "The Shawshank Redemption," for loyalty and friendship.

The students reactions were invariably the same to the movies Carson showed. "Rudy" almost always resulted in tears. "Better Off Dead," starring John Cusack made them laugh – but it also made them think, which was the whole idea. And most students became very quiet after watching the classic "Old Yeller," which invariably caused Carson to say to himself *boys and their dogs!*

One thing was certain. Each student was able to answer perfectly the discussion questions that Carson presented at the end of each film. If they didn't, they got to watch it again – and again...and again – until they could.

Carson didn't bother looking at the title on the DVD he popped into the player today. He simply pushed "play," and left the room. It was *Dead Poets Society*, the story of an English teacher who inspires his students to change their lives through poetry and literature.

Harry's face was turned away from the screen, but the soundtrack was perfectly audible.

[Mr. Nolan] *"One hundred years ago, in 1859, 41 boys sat in this room and were asked the same question that greets you at the start of each semester. Gentlemen, what are the four pillars?*

[Boys] *Tradition, honor, discipline, excellence.*

65

Harry didn't make it.

Carson had returned to the control room just as the credits were rolling at the end of *Dead Poets Society* and knew intuitively that something was wrong. Harry hadn't moved from the position he'd been left in an hour and a half earlier. None of the cameras gave a clear view of his face which was turned toward the wall, so Carson did the only thing he knew would get a reaction. He dialed up the electric current flowing to the bed, slowly at first, knowing that it wouldn't take long for Harry to jump up screaming. But he never did. Carson dialed the voltage back down and stared at the lifeless figure on the screen in front of him, absorbing the fact that he now had a dead body on his hands.

And all that tattoo removal for nothing.

Carson couldn't be sure about what happened. Had he starved him to death? He didn't think so; he would be thinner than he was.

Did he shock him one too many times? Probably, but that couldn't be helped, could it?

Were there complications from the tattoo removal; an infection, maybe? Who knows. Again, that couldn't be helped. Nobody should have any tattoos at all, much less a hundred of them.

Regardless, this wasn't a case where he could order an autopsy so, at least for the present, his curiosity about what had caused Harry's demise would not be satiated.

Was he even really dead? As he stood over him, surgical mask in place, loaded syringe at the ready, he poked him with his index finger. He didn't stir and his eyes were still open, which is how Carson first determined that something was seriously wrong. He'd watched him on Camera #2 for at least an hour and his eyes never blinked.

It's not like he could dial 9-1-1 and report an "unresponsive fat male who exhibits signs of being terminally rebellious and difficult."

He shook him. He slapped him. *Wake up, you fat fuck*. Nothing. He turned to leave the classroom. He would go to his study to try to figure out what to do next. But as he reached the door, something stopped him.

66

I was just about to walk into my building from my daily trip to Starbucks, where I like to go to work on my book. I was about half-way through the first chapter, and it had been slow going; in fact, I'd been staring at the same computer screen for at least three days, typing then deleting, typing then deleting. I was sick of it. When I get stuck like that, I tend to waste a lot of time. I people watch, of course – I can come up with some pretty wicked backstories just by letting my imagination run wild as I sit and stare at somebody who isn't doing anything but ordering a Grande Latte.

Just as I was approaching the doorman, my cell rang and I could tell from the ring-tone that it was Troy. I smiled, as I usually did when he called, because he just rambled on about anything and everything – and I knew he would say something to take my mind off my writer's block.

I nodded at the doorman who now stood holding the door open for me, holding up my index finger as if to say "I'll be right back" – and kept on walking. I leaned against the building to take the call, as I knew I'd lose it inside the stainless steel elevator car – its similarity to Sir's "classroom" not lost on me. In fact, every time I got in that damn elevator and watched the doors close, I couldn't help but wonder if I'd ever get out again.

"Hey man," I said into the phone.

Silence.

At first I thought I'd lost the call, but then I heard a murmur, a whimper really, followed by a half-whisper. "Gotta help me, man. Don't know what to do."

It didn't sound like Troy, so I looked at the screen again just to make sure.

"Troy? Is that you? What's going on? What's wrong?"

The response shook me. I couldn't be sure he was crying, exactly, but he could barely talk. His words were painful whispers with frequent pauses as he seemed to gasp for air. "Janet...gone...can't find her...nobody knows..." Then, absolute silence making me wonder if he had hung up.

"Troy!" I strained to hear a response, but got nothing more than labored breathing. My mouth went dry and my palms got sweaty. I stood there, jaw dropped, as I listened to the silent meltdown my friend was having on the other end of the phone. Some lady walked by me on the sidewalk and looked at me like I was a mouth-breather or something, which is exactly as I must have looked. I snapped my mouth shut. I had to get him to respond. I sensed that he was weeping -- but I couldn't be sure. Trying again, I said, "Troy, can you tell me exactly what happened? What are you saying? What's happened to Janet? Try to tell me what's going on."

He did, finally, and then it was my turn to fight back tears and panic. Janet, he told me, had been on an undercover assignment. Something about Mormon women released onto the streets of Denver from some rural Colorado compound and were being forced into sexual slavery. A few of them had turned up dead and all of Denver was up in arms.

Janet and some other cop had been assigned to spend the night in a downtown alley, living in the entrances to a couple of buildings like homeless people, just to see if they could flush out whoever was killing these women. The partner apparently fell asleep in his doorway when he was supposed to be covering Janet while she was on her own sleep break. When he woke up, she and the Army blanket in which she was wrapped were gone, her gun still in an old McDonald's bag a few inches from where she'd been sleeping. This was apparently a major clue, since anybody who knew Janet knew she would never leave her gun behind – especially in a McDonald's bag, where some kid could find it.

The whole town was in an uproar and a massive search was underway. But, as Troy pointed out, the search was all for show because nobody had a clue as to where they should start looking.

It brought back uncomfortable memories. I had disappeared from the streets of Denver myself almost five years ago, but the difference was, I had been a washed-up misfit with nothing to lose – and in dire need of the makeover I got, courtesy of "Sir."

Janet, on the other hand, was a beautiful young woman with a life and a career and everything to live for. Nobody thought she was depressed, including Troy, so it seemed unlikely that she had run away without a word to anyone.

It also seemed highly unlikely that somebody would kidnap her. Why would they? Unless, of course, she had fallen victim to the very scheme she and her partner were trying to uncover. That possibility made me shudder. Janet couldn't have been murdered. I refused to consider the possibility. And, until a body was recovered, I would operate on the assumption that she was very much alive.

"Troy," I said into the phone. "I'll be there this afternoon. I'll go upstairs right now and pack a couple of things and I'll go directly out to the airport and I'll take a cab to your place as soon as I arrive."

He murmured something like "O.K.," so I decided he was cool with the plan. I could tell he was out of it – I hoped he wasn't stoned – but I could tell I wasn't going to get anything more from him, so I released the call and went upstairs. I threw some stuff in a duffle bag and went back out to fetch the elevator, which was still waiting on my floor, just as I'd left it less than five minutes earlier. When I got downstairs I asked the doorman to flag me a cab, and while I waited I started calling airlines to see what was available to Denver in the next couple of hours.

I lucked out – United had a flight that left in an hour and a half, so I booked a ticket. They charged me twenty bucks for the "privilege" of talking to a reservation agent, which pissed me off, but I had the last laugh since I wouldn't need to check a bag and therefore wouldn't be paying their stupid bag check fee. *Assholes*.

On the way to the airport I wondered what I would do when I got there. I also wondered if, by some chance, Janet had been kidnapped in the same way I had been.

I hadn't considered that possibility until now, and as far-fetched as it seemed, now that I'd thought of it, I couldn't think of anything else. What if Sir had chosen Janet as his next "student?" Well, if that had happened, I knew she would at least be in good hands, and safe.

I only hope she likes German cooking.

67

My flight sat on the tarmac at J.F.K. for two hours and fifty-five minutes: just five minutes short of the three-hour rule, after which the airline supposedly gets a big fine for holding passengers involuntarily. The three-hour delay plus the three hours it would take us once we were airborne meant I wouldn't arrive in Denver until close to eight o'clock. By the time I caught a cab and went directly to Troy's place, it would be close to ten. I cursed Denver for building the airport out in the sticks – ostensibly to rescue the folks living around the old neighborhood from noise – and then allowing people to build houses next to the new airport!

Besides, I groused, why the hell would they build an airport out in *bumfuck* and not put in some sort of high-speed rail to access it? I was full-fledged into my rant now, with nobody to listen to it except the woman who was sound-asleep and slobbering in the seat next to me. I smiled when I remembered what Troy used to say when I launched into one of these tirades: "Man, you need to get a blog!"

The flight attendant finally came around with drinks and I was sorely tempted to order a vodka-tonic or a stiff Scotch, but I had been clean and sober for long enough now that I didn't figure a messed up airline flight justified falling off the wagon. So I ordered a Diet Coke and settled back into my seat to read the inflight magazine for the twentieth time. Somehow during the first nineteen readings I had missed the fact that my book was reviewed in this issue and the review wasn't half bad. Then, as icing on the cake, I happened to glance across the aisle and noticed a middle-aged hispanic guy staring at me. I gave him kind of a half-smile in acknowledgement and he broke into a big grin as he held up a copy of my book with my photo as big as life on the back of the dust jacket. I smiled back and nodded and returned to my magazine thinking maybe this wasn't such a bad flight after all.

Mostly I agonized over the fact that Janet was missing, and I wondered what I would do to help Troy find her. If, in fact, she was with "Sir," I wouldn't know where to begin because I didn't know where he was myself! I made a mental note to call Kinsey, my P.I., when we hit the ground, just to see if she'd found out anything new.

As predicted, the flight was three hours late and when we landed everybody started to pull out their cell phones and power-up. I find that annoying – unless it's me doing it, of course – so I kept mine in my pocket. I must not have turned it off before we departed New York, though, because within a few seconds, it began ringing.

"Great minds think together," I mumbled to myself as I took it out and noticed that it was Kinsey's number on caller I.D.

"Hey," I said by way of greeting.

"Hello, Mark," she replied. "Is this a good time to talk?"

"Well, actually, the plane I'm on is taxiing down the runway toward the terminal but everybody and their brother is babbling on their cell phones, so we'll have to see."

At that, the slobbering woman next to me shot me a look, probably because until that moment she probably thought I was eavesdropping on the conversation she was having with someone at the other end of her cell phone.

"Go ahead, though. If we get cut off, I'll call you back when I'm in the terminal."

I settled back in my seat as Kinsey proceeded to bring me up to date on her investigation. I also told her about Janet and explained that I had come to Denver to see if I could be helpful to Troy. Finally, I told her about the weird thought I'd had – that somehow the same person who kidnapped me might be responsible for Janet's disappearance. She didn't seem to think it was that far-fetched, which was a relief, and she promised to see what she could find out from an old buddy of hers who now worked for the Denver Police Department.

We rang off just as the fasten seat belt sign went out and everybody stood up *en masse* and started flinging open the overhead bins. I didn't stand up fast enough, though, and before I knew what happened, a copy of my own book had been thrust into my lap.

"Would you mind autographing this?" the guy from across the aisle asked.

"Not at all," I said, only half meaning it as I reached in my own bag for a Sharpie. "What's your name?"

"Jeff," he said. But then, before I could write, he added, "but please make it out to my wife, Helen. I'll give it to her as a gift."

I smiled, because I get requests like that all the time – people who are too embarrassed to admit that they've just interrupted you to ask that you write their name in a book, so they change their mind at the last minute and say it's for someone else. I glanced around the gentleman to look for his wife, but I didn't see anybody other than the guy who had obviously been in the middle seat. "Your wife not with you?" I asked as I inscribed his book.

"No, she couldn't leave work. I was attending the baptism of a niece in New Jersey, but my wife stayed at home."

"Oh, and where is that?" I asked absentmindedly as I scribbled the inscription he'd requested.

"We live just outside Salida."

I must have had a blank look on my face, because he continued. "In the Rockies west of Denver?"

I gave him a half-smile. I don't like it when people answer a question with a question. He's asking me where his home town is? I didn't say that, of course. I just smiled again, so he continued.

"Yeah, we're right in the middle of the collegiate peaks?" There it was again: another question.

"Uh, huh," I said, handing his book back to him.

"You know, Harvard, Yale, Princeton?"

68

Harry remained on his steel bed for two more days, his glassy eyes staring at Carson every time he glanced at the monitor. The classroom was as cold as the air conditioner would allow, and it ran 24 hours a day. Still, Carson knew it wasn't cold enough to keep a body from decomposing.

As he sat in his study, pondering what to do, he vaguely recalled hearing a story years ago about a man who killed his wife, then cut her up in little pieces and kept her in the family freezer.

No. That wasn't an option. He wasn't about to cut anybody up, much less Fat Harry. He shuddered at the thought.

What a dilemma. How, exactly, does one dispose of a body?

As he sat at his desk sipping the tea Greta had delivered a few moments earlier, he gazed at Mt. Princeton. He briefly wondered if he could somehow manage to take Harry up as far as the road goes and then throw him off the mountain. But Harry was too big and cumbersome to move easily without a gurney, and besides, who knew how long it would be until his body would finally be devoured by the local wildlife. He could be discovered in the meantime, and who knows where the authorities might start looking.

He frowned as he tried to think of other options. He thought about returning him to where he picked him up – was it a bench or a doorway? He'd have to think. Either choice was too risky, though. He worried every time he went into town looking for a new "student." Carting around a body would present a whole new set of problems.

He couldn't bury him in the yard; Manuel knew every square inch of his property and would know immediately if any of the ground cover had been disturbed in any way.

What to do? Well, whatever he was going to do, he knew he better do it quickly. Placing his teacup back on its saucer, he went back into the control room and looked at Harry's face which now seemed more bloated than usual. Curiously, his hair seemed a fraction of an inch longer than it had a day or so ago, and Carson remembered reading somewhere that hair sometimes continues to grow long after death. *Well, I'm not cutting it again. You can have your long hair back, Harry!* He stared at the monitor and pulled his chair back abruptly when he could have sworn Harry winked at him. *That's it. I can't look at you anymore.* Walking quickly down the hall to the storage closet, Carson chose a heavy wool blanket from the shelf and made a mental note to order another so the next student would have it – after earning it, of course.

Returning to the classroom, he placed his palm on the security pad and waited for the door to open. He had been braced for the blast of cold air – he'd used freezing cold air as a corrective measure in the past – but he was not prepared for the stench. Holding his breath, and pulling the gurney into the classroom from the hall behind him, he pushed it to the side of the steel shelf bed. Working quickly, he spread the blanket out on the gurney, its overlapping width falling to the floor on either side. As he reached to roll Harry onto the blanket, he stopped. He couldn't do it.

Suppressing a retch, he walked from the room and went to the control room. He released, then opened the door into the courtyard. Pushing several buttons in succession, and then placing his palm on the control room reader, he watched on the monitor as the door from the classroom opened and remained ajar. *There. Maybe a little fresh air will help.*

He opened another door from the hallway into the garage and walked over to the black van, the "school bus." He opened the driver's side door, and after rummaging around in the side pocket of the door itself, retrieved two latex gloves. He slammed the door and began pulling the gloves on even as he walked back toward the classroom.

I must do this before I lose it. He marched over to Harry and, without hesitation this time, reached across the decomposing body and rolled it onto the blanket-topped gurney. Continuing to work quickly, he pulled the end of the blanket up over Harry's legs, and the head of the blanket up over his head. Reaching down, he took one side panel and wrapped it across the body before whirling the gurney around and repeating the action with the other side of the blanket.

He still didn't know where he would bury him, but he needed to do so immediately. Tonight. In the meantime, he could only hope the classroom wouldn't be ruined by the permanent smell of rotting flesh.

Retracing his steps out of the classroom and into the hallway leading to his study, he happened to notice an unusually large bird with a wide wingspan circling in the sky above the exterior wall of the courtyard. *A vulture!*

Oh no you don't. As he passed the control panel, he flipped on the switch controlling the flow of electricity to the bare cable lying on the top of the wall. *Or, if you do, you'll wish you hadn't.*

69

Carson didn't have much of an appetite at lunch, and Greta commented on the fact that he hadn't eaten much of his goulash.

"You don't like elk, Mr. Kirkpatrick?" she asked.

"Hmmm? Oh, is that what this is? No, I'm sure it's fine, Greta. I'm just not very hungry today." He hated elk and briefly considered telling her, but he decided to spare her feelings, although he wasn't sure why.

"Vel, you should eat. Manuel shot the elk himself and ve have a whole freezer full of it, but..." she stopped, uncertain how her request would be received, ve don't have enough room in our freezer and..."

He waited. Greta was a slow-talker and it wasn't at all unusual for her to stop talking in between words. Her listener would just have to wait. So German. Exasperated, he couldn't wait any longer. "And *what*, Greta?"

"And ve vas vondering if we could use the big freezer in your basement."

Funny how things work out, isn't it? I have a walk-in freezer? Who knew? Well, Harry, I think we may have found you a home – at least temporarily.

He realized that Greta was watching him patiently, awaiting an answer to her question.

"Well, of course you could, Greta, except that freezer has been out-of-order for years. I'm sorry. Do you have any other options?"

"Vel...it's stored at the butcher's freezer in Poncha Springs, right now, but he says he vil need to charge us storage fees if we leave it any longer..."

"Well, I'll tell you what, Greta. This meat is so tasty that I'll make you a deal. I'll pay the butcher's storage fees if you'll just bring some of this to work once in awhile and make me some delicious goulash just like this!"

"Oh, no, Mr. Kirkpatrick...that isn't necessary..."

"I insist, Greta. Now have that butcher send me the bill for a year's worth of storage and I'll take care of it. That's an order."

"Yes, Mr. Kirkpatrick."

That night, a few hours after Greta had gone, Carson found his way to the basement which he hadn't seen since his house was built. To be honest, he'd completely forgotten that he had a basement, much less a walk-in freezer. Noting that the door to the basement lacked a lock of any kind, he made a note to have a palm panel installed, making it a part of the total house security system. But that would have to wait. Tonight, he simply needed to find this freezer he apparently owned.

Passing through two large storage rooms, he finally discovered the big steel door to the freezer, but he saw that it was locked with a heavy padlock.

Returning to his study, he opened the key cabinet in the closet, punching in the code to unlock it.

Inside were row after row of keys, all carefully labeled, so it only took a moment to find one labeled "walk-in freezer." He took the key, put it in his pocket, and went to fetch Harry.

Makeovers - Rex John

70

He continued to watch her. She lay there, breathing softly, freshly scrubbed and clean. How long had he been sitting here, staring at her? This was starting to happen with increasing frequency, these trips down memory lane, filled with thoughts of Harry. And he didn't like it.

Is Harry still in the walk-in? Yes, I suppose he is. How long has it been? Four years? Five? It seems like forever. Let's see. Since Harry there was Claude, the drifter from Idaho...then Stan, the kid from Florida with the terrible stutter...and Mark, his favorite student and now famous author. There was also Sergio, the smart-alec kid from Chicago...and Lon, the slow-talker from San Jose...and now his first female student, dear beautiful Janet...

So many successes. What's one failure? He had a hallway full of before and after photos and only one dead student in the freezer in the basement.

Ah, yes. The freezer. Perhaps he was still haunted by Harry's memory because he hadn't yet put him to rest. Nobody should have to live in a freezer for five years!

He smiled at his unintended witticism. Forcing his mind to return to the task at hand, he patted Janet's hair dry and then tenderly stroked her cheek where only the birthmark detracted from her flawless beauty.

Not to worry, dear. We'll take care of this. It won't be long now.

71

After dressing Janet in a matching slacks and sweater set he'd ordered from Talbot's, he gently returned her to the steel bed.

He allowed his eyes to take in the beauty of her reclining body for a few more minutes.

Who are you, dear girl? What in the world has happened to you to cause you to end up in a downtown doorway? And who has caused this pain so terrible that it shuts you down like this?

Scowling, he stood up and abruptly walked through the door of the classroom, but leaving the door wide open behind him. Walking to the storage room at the end of the hall, he opened the unlocked door and retrieved the Temperpedic mattress he stored here between students. Returning to the steel bed, he dropped the mattress on the floor. Reaching across to place one hand on her shoulder and the other on her hip, he rolled the unconscious girl back onto the gurney. This took little effort, because although she was dead weight, she couldn't have been more than a hundred pounds. Turning from her, he bent down to retrieve the mattress from the floor and center it neatly on the steel bed. Once again, he strolled from the room and back down the hall to the storage room where he now retrieved linens, a light blanket and a down pillow. After making the bed, he rolled the girl back on top of it and, pushing the gurney ahead of him, retreated into the control room, closing the door behind him.

There you are, dear. Perhaps this will cheer you up. Who says I don't treat my students with kindness and compassion?

Now, about Harry....

72

He needed to think. Now that he had wasted so much time thinking about Harry, he couldn't get him out of his mind. What was wrong with him, leaving a dead body in the basement like that? For five years, no less! True, he would surely be frozen solid, but what if Greta had asked Manuel to cut the lock off to the freezer? What then?

He sat down at his desk. He stared out the window across the vast acre of grass that Manuel kept groomed like a golf course fairway. For a moment, the beauty of the scene before him caused him to push Harry from his mind. *What an ideal spot for a swimming pool. I wonder why I've never had one installed.*

As he imagined how nice a brisk swim would feel, and how it would help him clear his head, he also realized he'd come up with a solution for Harry's final resting place. A swimming pool! Or, more precisely, under one. He would have one installed and then, during construction he would find a way to bury Harry below the floor of the pool. He would then be at least ten feet underground with thousands of pounds of concrete and water holding him in place.

He would mention the idea of installing a pool at lunch to prepare Greta for what was about to happen on the property.

73

"That vould be very nice, Mr. Kirkpatrick," Greta said aloud, but inwardly she cringed. *A swimming pool!* She knew that Manuel would be asked to perform the maintenance and he already had too much to do.

She decided to test her luck. "But, who would take care of it?" she asked, trying to sound only mildly curious.

"Manuel, of course."

Just as I thought.

By now Greta had observed that when her employer wanted something, he got it – and quick. So, it didn't surprise her at all when only three hours later the phone rang, signaling a call from the front gate.

"Ja?" she bellowed into the receiver.

A strange man's voice responded. "Sunrise Pool Company...I have an appointment with Mr. Kirkpatrick...?"

"Ja...just a moment, please." She pushed the house phone button as she had been instructed, and her boss answered on the first ring, as he typically did.

"Yes, Greta?"

"A swimming pool company at the gate, Mr. Kirkpatrick."

"Oh, yes. Let them in and show the gentleman to the terrace. I'll join him presently."

As Carson replaced the phone receiver, he thought of the now frozen body asleep in the freezer in his basement.

Hold on, Harry. It won't be long 'til you can warm up again.

74

"Carson Kirkpatrick may be one of the richest people in the world, but that doesn't mean he is automatically moved to the top of the Sunrise waiting list, by God."

James Troll, the owner of Sunrise Swimming Pools, was speaking to his wife on the telephone. Moments earlier he had received a call from the infamous Carson Kirkpatrick, heir to the mammoth Northern Hemisphere Insurance Company fortune. The billionaire said he had a simple request. He would like a swimming pool installed, and he wanted construction to begin immediately.

"Really?" his wife asked cheerfully. "And how long is that list, exactly?" Darlene was well aware that her husband had installed only three swimming pools in the last ten years. On more than one occasion she had questioned his market research, "or lack thereof," when discussing the poor performance of the swimming pool business, which, as she was quick to remind him, was funded with start-up funds from her own father.

"That's not the point, Darlene. The point is, just because he wants it immediately doesn't mean he gets it immediately."

At least not without some negotiation.

James Troll was a man of principles and ethics. He wasn't about to let some billionaire push him around, either. And he knew one thing for sure: construction was *not* going to start tomorrow – Saturday, for God's sake – no matter how much this jerk says he wants to be able to throw a pool party next weekend. *A party? The biggest recluse in the county? I'd like to see who would come! Besides, swimming pools do not get installed in a week, no matter who wants them.*

Abruptly ending his phone call, James got in his truck and headed toward the Kirkpatrick estate. The housekeeper, a German import that everybody in town seemed to know, admitted him by electronically opening the big wooden gates. Parking in the circular drive in front of a large porte cochère, he reached for the doorbell – but stopped when the door opened before him. The housekeeper greeted him politely, and, after exchanging introductions, invited him to "follow her, please."

She ushered him through a large marble entryway into what could only be described as a "great room," flooded with light and featuring a magnificent and unobstructed view of Mt. Princeton. Opening a double French door with some fanfare, she gestured to a flagstone terrace and said, "If you would kindly wait out here, Mr. Troll, Mr. Kirkpatrick will be with you presently. May I get you some coffee?"

"That would be nice, thank you."

"With cream and sugar?"

"Yes, both, please."

"Ja. Very well. Please have a seat." With that, she turned and left, leaving him on the expansive terrace, filled with comfortable looking patio furniture and various planter boxes filled with flowers. He selected a chair at a circular umbrella table and sat. The housekeeper returned moments later, holding a large and heavy looking silver tray. She sat the tray on the table and then busied herself pouring his coffee into an expensive looking china coffee cup from a silver pitcher. She then passed him the cream and sugar from matching silver containers before handing him a silver spoon which she had taken from the top of a folded linen napkin. *Wait 'till my wife hears about this*. He was stirring his coffee when the door opened again and Carson Kirkpatrick appeared.

Before addressing him, he said, "Thank you Greta, that will be all." He could have sworn he saw a slight bow as she said, simply, "Yes, sir," and walked back through the door from which he had just appeared.

After a quick introduction, Carson sat down and got down to business.

"Mr. Troll, I should mention that I am very particular about who is allowed on my property, and when. As you have already observed, all access to the property is controlled electronically, and I should tell you that all of your actions and those of your workmen will be monitored by security cameras at all times."

"Yes, sir, of course."

"Further, the worksite will be secured at night and you and your crew will not be allowed back on the property until the next morning, no matter what the reason – so I would suggest that you are certain you've removed all your belongings and tools before leaving for the day. Is that clear?"

"Yes, sir, of course."

"Now, about my timetable. I apologize that I am giving you such late notice, and you say it is impossible to meet my deadline. However, I am wondering if you might make an exception just this once..."

Troll began vigorously shaking his head "no," even as Carson continued – an irritating display that did not go unnoticed.

"...perhaps if I offered a bonus, say of a hundred thousand dollars...?"

The back and forth swivel of Troll's head changed to an up and down movement mid-swivel.

There are exceptions to every rule, James Troll would tell his wife later, and why wouldn't he make one – especially when one hundred thousand dollars was at stake? That, on top of the exorbitant installation fee he'd quoted at the outset.

The deal struck, construction would indeed begin tomorrow, Saturday, promptly at eight o'clock, which meant he needed to return to his office in Salida now and start making calls to his workers who were working for his lawn care business. To avoid paying taxes, he employed them as sub-contractors and allowed them a certain amount of latitude in setting their hours and days off.

As he sat waiting for the gate to allow him to exit the Kirkpatrick estate, he studied the check in his hand. *This is all gravy. A bonus! For work I haven't even done yet! How does he even know I'll come back and do it?*

He shook his head. The rich are so strange, and the filthy rich are the strangest of all. Putting his truck in gear, he rolled out the gate and watched in his rearview mirror as the big double gates closed behind him.

But I sure do like their money.

75

Greta only worked half-days on Saturday, because she had a standing appointment with Maggie Cordone, her hairdresser, whom she had finally forgiven for "snatching her baldheaded," after everyone she met told her how cute her new hair style was.

So, on Saturdays, Greta would enter the compound promptly at seven o'clock, tidy up as necessary, and prepare a casserole for Mr. Kirkpatrick to pop in the oven for dinner. He told her he preferred to go out for lunch on Sunday, usually driving into the Poncha Springs Country Club or sometimes into Buena Vista to the Central Colorado Club. Greta's friend Lupe, who worked at the PSCC said Mr. Kirkpatrick often took a "to-go" order with him after he finished his own meal, which Greta knew was for his brother, Mr. Scooter.

Greta prepared sandwiches for the two men for Saturday lunch and wrapped them in plastic wrap before placing them in the refrigerator. She then made breakfast and waited for Mr. Kirkpatrick to finish eating so she could clean up the kitchen. She left Mr. Scooter's breakfast tray on the hall table outside Mr. Kirkpatrick's study, as she always did.

But this Saturday was already off to a bad start. She was only half-way through her casserole preparations when the phone rang from the gate. She admitted the pool man and his crew, as she had been instructed, but had to drop everything and go outside to see the gigantic earthmoving equipment as it edged down the driveway toward the west lawn. There was a front loader, a large dump truck and countless men with shovels. Mr. Kirkpatrick would have a fit when he saw that they had taken out a lilac bush on the side of the driveway!

No sooner had she discovered the mangled lilac bush than Mr. Kirkpatrick himself appeared at her side.

"Supervising the workmen, are we, Greta?" he asked, half-smiling.

"Ja! Look what they've done to your bush, Sir," she replied, pointing out the damage.

"Yes, well, I suppose a certain amount of that is to be expected," he said. "Shall we have breakfast?" He had already turned and was walking back toward the house before she could answer, but she scurried toward the kitchen side-door as he headed toward the front.

Later that day she reported to Maggie and two other women who were in various stages of coiffeur that her employer was installing a swimming pool. Maggie seemed dutifully impressed, but the other two women just looked at her without comment. Somewhat chagrined by what she perceived as a lamentable lack of interest in what she considered a big news story, she headed for the table of magazines.

There it was again, the *People* magazine with the handsome author on front. She had meant to buy his book, but forgot to do so.

"Maggie," she said, "would you mind if I purchase this old magazine from you?"

"Sure, darlin'! Just take it; that's an old one anyway!" At that, Greta stuck it in the side pocket of her handbag and resolved to again read the article about the new young author who liked German cooking, and to order the book when she got home.

76

When Greta arrived for work on Monday, she could scarcely believe her eyes. In two short days an enormous hole had appeared in the middle of the west lawn and the large earthmoving equipment was no where to be seen.

She pulled her car around to the area on the east side of the house that Mr. Kirkpatrick had designated as "staff parking." The area contained about fifteen spaces, where she and Manuel always parked, and where the valet parking attendants placed guest vehicles when her boss entertained – which was almost never.

After parking, she walked around the front of the house, strolled around the circle drive and headed over toward the edge of the big new hole in the yard.

It sure is deep! As she stood near the edge – but not too near, because she wondered how stable the dirt embankment was, she gazed back toward the house. *It is a beautiful home, that's for sure.*

As her eyes skirted the west-facing side of the mansion, she once again noticed the cleverly disguised solid stone block wall that appeared to house a room without windows, but which she now knew was a courtyard – an outdoor area which had apparently been built for Mr. Scooter. *Someday I'll see what's in there if I have to climb over the roof!*

Now that's an interesting thought.

She stared at the roof, a mansard-type with charcoal colored slate shingles and noticed how steep it was.

That roof may be steep, but it's certainly no steeper than Mount Sudelfeld! I could probably even make it without my equipment.

She stood there, considering her options until she noticed that Mr. Kirkpatrick had come out on the front porch looking for her. As she strolled toward him, she called out, "You have a big hole, Sir!" *And also a big roof. But I'll bet I can climb it.*

Carson looked toward the hole and then, as though he'd forgotten something, said, "I'll be in momentarily, Greta. Go ahead and start breakfast."

"Yes, Sir," she said, as she watched him re-trace the path she had just taken to the edge of what was obviously meant to be the deep end of the pool. Just as she put her hand on the door she noted that he seemed to be looking toward the garage, and then back at the hole, then to the garage again.

I vunder if he ist now going to add on to the garage, or vhat?

77

As Carson visually tried to compute the distance between the garage door to the edge of the swimming pool, he realized that rolling a gurney over the golf course-like surface of the lawn would be the easy part. Getting Harry up the stairs from the basement would be the greatest challenge, as he imagined a frozen body of over 200 pounds would be tough to maneuver. He would manage, though, even if it required ropes and pulleys.

Once he was on the first floor, he would use the gurney to drag him down the hallways and back to the garage. After he got him to the garage, it appeared to be only about a hundred feet or so to the edge of the pool where he would dump him.

Of course, it wasn't a matter of just putting him in the pool and hoping the concrete people didn't notice there was a body there when they poured the concrete. Digging would obviously be involved. He would need to dig a grave at the bottom of the deep end – avoiding whatever plumbing would be installed for the drain – and he would need to do it before they placed the lattice work steel rebar over the entire floor, to strengthen the concrete.

Let's see. Troll had told him that they would set the forms today – the large plywood panels forming the walls of the pool. There would be two layers, set about a foot apart and held together with steel ties, creating a pocket in which the concrete would be poured. If they worked fast, it was possible that they would have the concrete poured the following day, after which the quik-set concrete would need to cure for a day before they could remove the plywood forms. That's when he would need to dig the hole at the bottom of the hole; after they removed the side wall forms, but before they created the steel lattice work for the concrete floor.

Reviewing the schedule in his head, he decided he would dig Harry's grave tomorrow night – Wednesday, after the grounds were deserted. This afternoon he would need to double-check to make sure the outbuilding where Manuel kept the lawnmower and assorted tools was left unlocked so he could retrieve a pick and shovel. It would be a long night and he dreaded having to dig through the clay dirt, but the grave would need to be deep enough that the workers wouldn't accidentally discover it as they were working.

Fortunately, the weather report was for clear skies and moderate temperatures, so at least he wouldn't have to deal with an accumulation of water in the deep end of the hole.

As he stood at the edge of the pool reviewing the details of his plan, the crew from Sunrise Swimming Pools arrived. He turned to go into the house so the crew supervisor wouldn't be tempted to try to engage him in silly small talk. They needed to get right to work.

Inside, a call from the gate so startled her that it caused Greta to drop the tray she was holding. She had been standing at the window watching her employer stare into the hole for his new swimming pool. After opening the gate, she had returned to clean up the mess which she was doing when Carson entered the room.

"Accident, Greta?" Carson noted that the tray had been dropped over by the window of the dining room overlooking the lawn – far from the kitchen, or even the dining room table on the other side of the room. *Can't control your nosiness, can you, woman? Well, we'll deal with that in due time.*

"Greta, my brother says he is fasting today; so it won't be necessary to prepare his meals," Carson said.

"Fasting, Sir? Vas is fasting?"

"It means he is choosing not to eat, I'm not sure why, but he can stand to lose a few pounds, so we will honor his request."

"Yes, Sir," Greta said, but she didn't like the idea of not eating and she wondered why anybody would voluntarily decide such a thing.

Taking a chance, since Carson had already seated himself and was reaching for his coffee, she added, "Vil Mister Scooter be liking the new swimming pool?"

"I'm sorry?"

"Vil Mister Scooter be liking to swim in the new swimming pool?" she repeated.

"Oh. Yes, I suppose so," he said, not sounding confident. Then, having quickly thought about the implications of the question, he added, "Yes. I'm sure my brother will want to be in the pool all the time."

Carson returned immediately to his breakfast, and Greta knew the conversation was over. But on her way back to the kitchen she couldn't help thinking about what her employer had just said.

Vel, I guess it vil be hard for me not to see him then!

78

"Excuse me," I said, not quite believing what I had just heard. "Did you say '*Mount* Princeton'?"

The well-built Hispanic guy – good-looking, late 40's – looked momentarily nonplussed, obviously expecting to get his book autographed and certainly not expecting an on-going conversation.

"Yeah..." he said, no doubt surprised at my sudden interest. "It's about five miles out of Buena Vista." Then, as an afterthought, "You a climber?"

Of course. I hadn't been taken to the city of Princeton, New Jersey at all! No wonder the three small towns Kinsey checked out all seemed too far from Denver for me to have been taken there without regaining consciousness. Princeton was a mountain, and it was right here in Colorado! That's what Sir must have been talking about when he said "Princeton is looking especially good this morning."

I could hardly wait to phone Kinsey with this news.

Meanwhile, the hispanic guy was still standing across the aisle, waiting for an answer to his question.

"Oh. I'm sorry. You asked if I'm a climber. Um, no...I just didn't realize there was a mountain named Princeton." I sounded like an idiot, and now the guy was looking at me very strangely. I continued: "You say it's near Buena Vista? That's a town, I assume."

By now the guy looked like he might be regretting asking for my autograph. Clearly, I was behaving bizarrely.

"Yeah..." he said tentatively. "It has a couple thousand people...Arkansas River...whitewater rafting...fly-fishing?"

"Oh, really," I said absentmindedly. I was now impatient to get off the plane. My mind was racing. If Sir had taken me up to a town of fewer than 2,000 people, how hard could it be to find him? I could probably just hang around on Main Street until he came by.

At this point my alter-ego kicked in. *Oh yeah? And how do you propose to recognize him? And, more importantly, what do you plan to do when you do? Besides, first things first. You need to help Troy find Janet.*

"Janet?" the guy said, just as I realized I'd been thinking aloud.

"Oh. Yeah. She's just a friend of mine who may have run away." Then, almost as an afterthought, and as we were walking up the jetway to the terminal, "Hey, listen. Nice talking to you. You've been very helpful." With that, I waved and dashed out the door, reaching for my cell phone as I did. The last I knew, I'd left the man standing at the end of the jetway probably wondering if all authors were as nuts as me.

79

I wasn't able to reach Kinsey, but I left a message on her answering machine, which I imagined to be an old-fashioned contraption with a cassette tape and a red blinking light to indicate that a message was waiting. She was as close to a Luddite as anyone I'd ever met.

I proceeded directly to the car rental counters, since I hadn't checked a bag and could therefore skip baggage claim completely. When I got there, I was relieved to see that there were no long lines of people waiting for cars. In fact, many of the counters didn't even seem to be staffed. The cute blonde agent from Enterprise was being all flirty with the agent at the Avis counter, and he looked like he was having a good time, so I walked on by and stopped at the Hertz counter.

As I approached, a middle-aged woman who gave the impression of having just sucked a lemon looked up from the book she'd been reading. I noticed the book wasn't mine, damn it, so I simply waited as she peered at me over her half-glasses. Her eyes were open wide, as if to say, "Yes?" but her lips remained sealed in a half-frown. Since she didn't say anything, I didn't either, and simply stared right back at her as I decided to wait until she at least greeted me.

I have a "thing" about customer service. If Sir taught me anything, it was how to be respectful of others. I contend that when you're in a job in which you must confront the public, showing respect means showing them common courtesy – something as simple as offering to help a customer who walks up to your counter, which clearly was not going to happen here.

Still, I waited. We were in a stare down. The pickle-puss woman staring at me, unblinking, and me, staring right back. Finally, she apparently caught on that I was determined to out-wait her.

"Yes?" she finally said, her voice full of exasperation. I noted that her greeting was not, "Hello, may I help you?" or anything remotely cordial; just the word "Yes" spoken in a tone that was close to out and out hostility.

"Yes, what?" I asked, deciding to be a smart ass.

"Yes, may I help you, *Sir?*"

"Oh," I said, now flashing a big smile, "Yes! I was hoping you'd ask!"

She seemed unamused as she stood, waiting for an answer, so I continued.

"I'd like to rent a car!"

I'd like to say she warmed up to me, but she never did, but mercifully, the transaction was completed quickly. A few minutes later, I was climbing down from the shuttle to the Hertz lot and heading out of the airport on a seemingly endless four-lane road named for a long forgotten former Denver mayor.

I finally merged from the airport access road and was on my way to Capitol Hill and my old apartment building, where I knew I would find Troy waiting for me. I checked my watch and noticed I'd been pretty close to guessing the correct arrival time. I pulled up in front of the building at exactly ten minutes 'till ten.

I parked and locked the car – I was lucky to find a space at that hour – and bounded up the stairs, eager to see my old buddy and, just maybe, to get a taste of Mrs. Rosencranz' German cooking. I'd momentarily put Janet out of my mind.

I rang Troy's buzzer and he buzzed me in without even knowing for sure it was me – something I would ordinarily give him shit about, since he knew better.

Once inside, I headed to the back steps at the far end of the hall and took them two at a time 'till I got to the third floor. I flew out into the hallway where Troy was waiting for me. His eyes were bloodshot and he had a two or three-day stubble. He looked like hell. That didn't stop me from throwing my arms around him, however. Usually, a hug would be far outside his butch cop comfort level, but he not only allowed it but seemed to fall into it. Obviously he was hurting. Finally I said, "Come on, buddy, let's go inside," leading him through the open door into his own apartment.

"Start at the beginning," I said as we sat at opposite ends of his sofa. "Tell me everything you know."

He took a tissue from a half-empty box on the coffee table and blew his nose. I noticed a half-smoked joint in the ashtray and three empty beer bottles lined up on the floor as if they were preparing to march themselves back into the kitchen.

"That's just it. We don't know *anything*. She didn't leave even one clue. Hell, we don't even know if she ran away or was kidnapped."

"Ran away!" I said, realizing immediately that I sounded more intense than the situation called for. I ratcheted back. "Why would she run away, buddy? Were you two having problems?"

"Fuck. You know we always had problems. The usual shit – same as when you were here. I'm a slob. I'm an idiot. I won't commit..." Then, in a much smaller voice, "She thinks I'm a stoner..."

"Hey, you are a stoner, man," I said, trying to add some levity. "But we love you anyway! Besides," I added, "you know Janet loves you and would never 'run away' without letting you know what's going on. Remember, dude, *she's* the level-headed one!"

He half-smiled at that, and then said, "I guess you're right...but then where the hell is she? It's like she's disappeared from the face of the earth. And...and..." his voice had gotten small and frightened.

"And what?"

"And what if they never find her?" At this, he broke down and sobbed. I quickly moved toward his end of the sofa and he collapsed into my arms. I let him cry until he stopped abruptly. "I don't even know where to start looking."

"Well, buddy, maybe I can help you there. I have an idea. It may be far-fetched, but at least it's somewhere to start...."

80

For a split second, Carson panicked as he put his palm on the electronic reader leading down to the basement. He had only used the new lock a few times since having it installed, shortly after he put Harry in the freezer. On those occasions, Greta had asked for access to take the exterminator downstairs. Carson accompanied them, even though Greta insisted she could take care of it, but he wanted to ensure that nobody became too interested in the big walk-in freezer.

The basement was a bit dusty, but surprisingly clean and neat for a place that was completely ignored. Greta said something about the space needing a good cleaning, but Carson didn't respond and she didn't pursue the matter. He saw her eyeing the freezer once, but she didn't say anything. Carson paid the butcher for a year of meat storage every year before his bill even arrived, so Greta would have no need to ask about using the freezer again. All he had to do in exchange was eat her endless elk "surprises."

But maybe that would end now that Harry would be re-locating to his final resting place. First, though, Carson had to get to him – and the electronic lock refused to release. He tensed. What would he do if he couldn't get Harry out of the freezer and into the dirt under the pool? He would have built a swimming pool for nothing!

He tried again...and then burst out laughing. *What an idiot! Of course it won't open. You've got surgical gloves on!* Still chuckling at his own stupidity, he peeled the latex glove from his right hand and tried again. This time, the lock slid open and the door released. He was still smiling as he descended the concrete steps, until he remembered why he had come.

He dug the key for the freezer padlock out of his pants before slipping the glove back on and heading through the basement to the walk-in.

Once inside, there was Harry – still wrapped in the expensive Hudson Bay wool blanket that now served as a shroud. Carson stood silent at the door, the memories of Harry now flooding his memory. He closed the door, without locking it, and returned upstairs. Retracing his steps to his study, and through the control room, glancing at the monitor to see that Janet was still sleeping peacefully, he continued into the garage where he retrieved the gurney.

Maneuvering the gurney through the house and back to the top of the stairs, he wondered how he could possibly get this chunk of frozen meat up the basement stairs. He returned to the garage and found a rope attached to a block and pulley. At the top of the stairs he attached one end of the block and pulley to the outside handle of a door leading to staff parking, which was conveniently located directly across the small mud room at the top of the basement stairs. He secured the block tightly and then walked the rope and second pulley block back through the door, pulling it closed behind him. It didn't close completely, of course, because of the thickness of the rope, but he was satisfied that the outdoor knob would hold and the weight inside would hold the door closed. He set the second block and pulley down at the top of the stairs and turned to collapse the gurney.

The gurney by itself was light, constructed out of aluminum tubing, and in its folded position it was almost completely flat, except for its wheels. Carson had no trouble carrying it to the bottom of the stairs where he shook it out, as one would a collapsed ironing board, and locked it in place. He rolled it across the basement to the door of the walk-in. Reopening the big steel door, he couldn't resist talking to himself, if only to reduce the tension he felt.

Well, Harry, you blew your chance. I left the door wide open, and you could have walked out, but I see you've chosen to stay. It's just as well, it's late Spring and getting pretty warm out, and I doubt you'd like the smell after you thawed out!

Seemingly oblivious that he was talking to himself, Carson pulled the gurney into the freezer and rolled the frozen body onto it. After exiting, he replaced the padlock but made a mental note that when this was over he would tell Greta he'd had the freezer fixed and she could now use it. *As long as she doesn't fill it with elk.*

He pushed the gurney to the bottom of the stairs, where he left the body on the gurney and went to the top, picked up the pulley block and walking back down, reeling out the rope behind him.

He momentarily thought of attaching the rope to Harry's blanketed head, but decided not to when he wondered if, since it was frozen, it might simply pop off.

The last thing he wanted to do was deal with an errant head.

Instead, he decided to wrap the rope several times around Harry's upper torso before tying it in a slip knot. After tying the end of the rope to the round eye on the pulley box, he began to pull.

The gurney rolled, seemingly of its own accord, to the bottom step, where it abruptly stopped. He continued to pull, causing the body to slowly slip from the gurney and onto the floor, where it landed with a thud. At this point, he had to push the gurney out of the way and straighten and upright the body, pushing and pulling until it lay horizontal up the bottom six basement steps. The blanket, which seemed to have adhered itself to the body, was cold to the touch. After ensuring that the body was properly aligned, he picked up the rope and began pulling again. Harry bumped up the stairs, one at a time until reaching the top, where he scooted across the tile floor of the mud room until Carson stopped pulling and followed him up the stairs.

He quickly dismantled the rope and pulley system and closed the outside door securely. With great effort, he managed to wrestle Harry's frozen body onto the gurney, dropping the block and tackle unceremoniously on top of him and then rolled the whole flotilla back through the house to the garage, which would serve as a "staging area," while Carson climbed into the partially finished pool to dig a grave.

Carson had been checking on the progress of the pool periodically through the day, and he noted that a crew of about eight men were charged with moving the heavy plywood forms into place and attaching each one to twisted metal ties protruding from the other side.

These were secured with long rods of steel, creating a sandwich of air between the two walls of plywood into which concrete was then poured. They worked quickly, ascending and descending into the deep end of the pool – which Carson had specified was to be no less than ten feet – on crudely assembled ladders comprised of two parallel two-by-four pieces of lumber joined together by foot long pieces of board nailed every eight inches or so to create the rungs of the ladder. Carson knew from watching them all day that the ladders could easily support the weight of a normal-sized grown man. Thankfully, Harry wouldn't be an issue, since he wouldn't be using the ladder.

Leaving Harry on the gurney in the garage, he returned to the control room and saw that Janet – looking so cute in her new outfit – was still sleeping soundly. Flipping a few switches on the large control panel, he illuminated the entire west yard with high-intensity lights that normally came on only when the system sensed an intrusion. Checking the monitors, he could see that the space was now brightly illuminated, including, he hoped, the bottom of the excavated hole. He once again checked Janet's status on the monitor and then turned the outside monitors off. No sense in creating a video record of his trek across the lawn with a dead body.

Returning to the garage, he opened the trunk of his Lexus and extracted a large pick, steel shovel, and a new pair of work gloves. He'd made the purchases earlier in the day after discovering that Manuel's storage room lacked the items. He told Greta he had errands to run in town, but went to the Home Depot in the more distant town of Gunnison instead, paying cash for his purchases. The trip took over three hours. *When burying a dead body, one cannot be too careful.* He was not amused when the young clerk handling his purchase quipped, "Hmmm. A shovel, a pick and work gloves. Sure you're not burying a body somewhere, buddy?"

It took great restraint to keep his face from registering shock, if not guilt, but Carson managed, instantly flashing a big smile as he said, "No, something much more exciting. I'm digging for treasure!"

The kid nodded silently, a false smile frozen on his face, but later while sneaking a smoke with his work girlfriend, he would recall the encounter saying, "the guy was creepy. I thought I was being a smart ass, but I think I may have been right. You should have seen his face!" By way of response, she took his hand and pushed it between her legs. "Oh, I don't know," she whispered. "Maybe he really knows where to find a treasure. Do you?"

By the time the kid returned to his check stand twenty minutes late from his break, Carson's visit was completely forgotten.

81

I took a deep breath before starting. I don't know why it is so hard for me to talk about my kidnapping and subsequent imprisonment. Maybe because I'm glad it happened? Maybe because of some misplaced loyalty to Sir?

I cleared my throat. Troy just sat there, waiting for me, eyes glassy from the combination of beer and pot.

"Look, man. I don't know why I haven't told you this before, but, um, I was kidnapped once."

There. I'd said it. If Troy processed what I had said, he didn't let on. "Yeah?"

"Yeah," I continued. "In fact, I've sort of been looking for the guy who nabbed me for the past several years, just to *thank him.*"

This was clearly more than Troy could absorb, and he delivered a look that could only be described as bafflement, bewilderment and disbelief all rolled into one. His mouth was open – a bad habit that many stoners seem to acquire, which unfortunately makes them look like mouth breathers. I used to do it too, but it was something Sir cured me of early on.

"Shut your mouth man, you look like an imbecile." Maybe my teaching style wasn't as subtle as Sir's, but at least it didn't involve electricity. Troy's mouth snapped shut and for a moment he looked hurt. I continued.

"I was on a park bench, stoned and drunk out of my mind..."

Troy stared, unblinking.

"...And some guy apparently shot me up with something and dragged my sorry ass to this...um...*room* somewhere...I'm not sure where...where he proceeded to get me off drugs and booze *cold turkey.*" I emphasized the last two words for effect, and I could see it had one.

"He taught me other stuff, too. Good stuff. Stuff about myself, stuff about my childhood, stuff about how to just function in the real world." I paused for effect. "Basically he saved my life, Troy."

"You're fuckin' kidding me. And you never told me this?"

I didn't dare tell him that he might be the only person in America who didn't know it and was obviously not a big *People* magazine fan, because he might wonder why I could tell a reporter, a complete stranger, and somehow not getting around to telling him, my best friend.

"I couldn't, man. Not only did I promise him I wouldn't, but I was kind of embarrassed to admit it...you know, it kind of sounds like I'm claiming to have been abducted by aliens and taken to a distant planet."

I stopped for a moment and wondered why I hadn't considered this possibility myself until now. Then I remembered: because I'm not crazy.

Troy nodded, as though that was explanation enough.

"Anyway," I went on, "I was thinking that maybe, just maybe, this guy might be the guy who nabbed Janet. And, if he is," I said a bit too excitedly, "then at least we know she's safe! I mean, look at me, man: he not only let me go, but he gave me *fifty grand* to help me get started again!"

At 'fifty grand,' Troy perked up. He always had money problems, even though I knew he got a decent salary from the DPD. "You're shittin' me."

"No, man, I'm not. The only problem is, I don't have a clue who this guy is. The only thing I know about him is, he must be rich – a poor person wouldn't be able to give away fifty grand like that – and he must like German cooking, because I got a boat-load of it."

"German cooking?" he asked. "You mean like Mrs. Rosencranz makes us?"

"Exactly. And by that, I mean, *exactly*, man. In fact, it kind of creeped me out when I first tasted one of her dinners: it was identical to a meal I got a lot when I was being held – right down to the way it was presented on the plate! I couldn't believe it, and for awhile I wondered if somehow the guy who kidnapped me had followed me to this apartment building and was downstairs preparing my food. I'm telling you, it freaked me out for the longest time!

"I even asked Mrs. Rosencranz about it and she got all defensive, like, 'Vhat do you mean? Dis is my cooking! My muter gave me and my sister these recipes!'"

At this point, Troy wrinkled up his brow and looked disgusted. "Stop, man. I've told you – your German accent sucks. You sound like a fuckin' Swede, not a German!"

I ignored him and continued. "So, I stopped bugging Mrs. Rosencranz and finally gave up trying to make sense of it. But, I've always wondered how two people who don't even know each other could prepare such identical meals."

"How do you know they don't know each other?"

"What do you mean?"

"Well, you said yourself that Mrs. Rosencranz said she had a sister. How do you know the sister didn't kidnap you?"

"Well, for one thing, because I know it was a man. But you're going down the same path I've been on since I got your call. What if there is some connection between my kidnapping and Janet's? It can't hurt to check it out."

At this point I'm not sure if the look on Troy's face was pensive or if he really was stoned. He sat there for a moment, looking blank, before he finally said, "I suppose there could be a connection, but it sounds pretty far-fetched. I think we should start by talking to Mrs. Rosencranz, maybe find out about this sister of hers."

"Good idea," I said. "She's up early; let's hit her up first thing in the morning. I could use some shut-eye. How 'bout you?"

Troy nodded twice, as though processing my two questions separately: yes, let's talk to Mrs. Rosencranz first thing in the morning, and yes, let's get some sleep.

He insisted that I sleep in his bedroom, saying that he slept on the sofa most of the time anyway. *Yeah, probably because that's where you pass out, stoner.*

He said we needed to change the sheets on his bed and while I said it wasn't necessary, I was kind of glad he insisted, since I've become somewhat picky after Sir turned me on to fine linen.

Fine linen this was not – but at least now it was clean. As we stood on either side of the bed tucking in corners and changing pillowcases, he became unusually quiet – a sure sign that he was getting ready to say something. I waited for it.

Finally, he said, "I have one question about your kidnapping, Mark..."

"Sure..."

"Did he rape you?"

MAKEOVERS - REX JOHN

82

Climbing down the rickety ladder was nothing compared to digging in the clay-heavy dirt at the bottom of the pool. More than once, Carson thought of giving up, but then what would he do with the body? To say nothing of the swimming pool he didn't need, want, or plan to use.

He could only swing the pick for about ten minutes at a time, stopping frequently to mop his brow. His original idea of burying Harry "at least ten feet under," had now given way to a new plan: he would try to get him far enough below the surface that his nose didn't stick out, but that would have to do.

He was almost finished at three o'clock when he was interrupted by an owl that swept down and grabbed a mouse as it scampered across the top edge of the pool. The flapping of the large bird's wings startled him and he dropped his shovel as he felt the bird sweep down across the edge of the newly poured concrete.

He watched the bird as it carried the mouse through the air and, presumably to an unknown hiding place. Not long afterward, he noticed the bird in a large oak tree at the edge of the yard. He sat perched, watching, cocking his head left, then right, until Carson had had enough. "Who made you supervisor?" he shouted. "Huh? Who? Who?" This made Carson laugh, realizing that he was beginning to sound like an owl himself. "Who! Who!" he repeated loudly, trying to imitate the cry of an owl.

The owl simply cocked his head to the other side and continued to stare. Carson tired of being watched and shouted "either grab a goddamned shovel or get the hell out of here!"

No sooner were the words out of his mouth than he sat down and laughed at the absurdity of his situation. *So, this is what it's come to. Talking to large birds in the night.* It also troubled him that he had cursed; it was something he discouraged in his students and something he rarely did himself. *Oh well. Cut yourself some slack. It's not every night that you have to bury a body."*

Harry, meanwhile, remained blissfully unaware on the gurney in the garage, even as Janet had finally awakened in a room not twenty feet away. She began chattering away to the animated Sir on her monitor, who simply stared at her in response.

"Sir?" she asked plaintively.

"Sir?"

"Good morning, Sir," she said sweetly, hoping her positive attitude would garner a response. *If it is morning, she thought. It's not like I can keep track of time in here with no goddamned windows and the constant flow of knock-out drops.*

"Sir? I'm awake..."

Looking down at her new outfit, which surprisingly well, she said, "I like my new clothes. Thank you, Sir." She preferred not to think about Sir seeing her naked.

"Sir?"

"Sir?"

Carson couldn't hear her, as he was at the bottom of a big hole in the dirt of his own backyard. Satisfied that the hole was big enough for Harry, if just barely, Carson threw the shovel and pick to the side and slowly ascended the ladder. Walking across the lawn, he entered the garage door which had been standing open the entire time. *That was stupid, Carson. You might as well have put out a sign: welcome, wild animals. Come feast on this!*

The body lay exactly as he had left it, the gurney shoved up against the far end of the garage wall. Positioning himself at the round lump that indicated where Harry's head was, he pushed it out of the garage and about fifty feet down the driveway before leaving the brick surface and onto the carpet of grass leading down to the edge of the hole. He maneuvered the gurney down to the deep end, but stopped about three feet short of the edge. *No point of dumping the gurney down, too. I don't need the hassle of pulling it back out.*

He locked the wheels in place and, with some effort, since his shoulder now ached from swinging a pick and pushing a shovel, he raised the top end of the gurney and watched Harry slide to the ground. He then unlocked the wheels and pushed the gurney to the side. Walking over to the blanket-wrapped body, he said aloud, "Nice night for a swim, don't you think, Harry? Oops. Not so fast! There's no water in the pool! Ha, ha! Oh well, you won't notice." And with that, he leaned over and rolled the body over the edge into the deep end, where it landed with a thud, just short of the hole Carson had prepared.

Carson descended the ladder again and walked over to the body. The blanket had partially come off the head of the corpse, and Carson was shocked to see Harry's eyes staring back at him. He quickly covered him back up and rolled him into the shallow grave. Working quickly now – the sight of Harry had caused his adrenalin to kick in – he scooped dirt on top of the body and scattered the remaining dirt around the floor of the unfinished pool. When he finished, he walked and stomped the top of the make-shift grave until he was satisfied it looked much the same as the rest of the pool floor. Gathering his pick and shovel, and taking one last look around, he climbed the ladder for the last time, crossed to the waiting gurney on which he stacked the pick and shovel before rolling everything into the garage. He would tidy up tomorrow. Now he just wanted to go to sleep.

As he passed through the control room, the sound of Janet's voice startled him. Wearily, he sat down.

"Sir?" she said.

"Sir?"

"Sir?"

"Sir?"

I wonder how long this has been going on. Donning his headset, he engaged the switch that controlled his microphone and said, "Yes, Janet?"

She jumped back, obviously having given up on the animated figure ever coming to life again.

"Oh! You scared me! I thought you weren't there! I worried that you would never come back!" She began to cry softly.

"No, dear, I would never do that. I just...um...had something else to do and had to step away for awhile."

"Oh."

"Do you like your new clothes, dear? They look nice on you."

Looking down, as though seeing them for the first time, she tried to control her rage at having been left. *"I don't give a fuck about these stupid goddamned clothes, you asshole! I'm wondering if I'd been buried alive in this goddamned steel coffin and you want a little fashion show? Well, fuck you!"*

Aloud, she replied quietly, "Yes, they're very nice."

"Good, dear. I'm glad you like them," he said, and then added, "How are you feeling? Better, I trust."

"Yes...better."

"I'm glad to hear it. I have left a few items for you to snack on until breakfast is served in a few hours, but I'm afraid that I must leave you again for a short while. Please don't worry, though. I'll be back soon enough and we will resume your lessons."

Oh joy.

With that, Carson removed his headset and, noting that the lights in the west yard were still burning brightly, turned them off as well. He turned the cameras back on, secure in the knowledge that the motion detectors would activate the recording equipment if or when anyone entered that part of his property. Locking doors behind him, he wearily made his way to his bedroom where he collapsed onto his bed, fully clothed and completely exhausted.

Promptly at 8 a.m., Greta responded to a call from the entrance to the compound and opened the big gates. Within minutes at least thirty men filled the side yard with various tools and equipment. Greta was

baffled that Carson had not yet appeared for breakfast –
a first if he was in town – and at 9 o'clock she finally
dialed the bedroom extension from the kitchen phone.
This was something she'd never done before and she
was momentarily nonplused when Carson answered, his
voice heavy with sleep. "Yes, Greta?"

"I'm sorry to disturb you, Mr. Kirkpatrick...I
didn't know if you were aware that the pool crew has
arrived."

"Oh. Already? What time is it?"

"It's after nine o'clock, Sir. Will you be having
breakfast this morning?" she asked, eyeing the now cold
eggs and bacon on the tray before her.

"Yes...I'll be down presently. Kindly have my
coffee ready."

Ja, and when haven't I?

"Yes, Sir."

If Carson had been monitoring the activity in the
back yard instead of eating breakfast at 9:30, he might
have observed a series of rapidly occurring events on the
floor of his unfinished swimming pool that would place
his morning coffee much lower on his list of priorities.

83

I assured Troy that no, Sir didn't rape me. I didn't mention the gay porn he had me watch, but I figured that wasn't what he was worried about. He was worried about Janet, and, specifically whether she would be safe; if, in fact, she was even with Sir.

But what if she wasn't? What then? Troy told me that few people understand that in situations where people "disappear" into thin air, with no sign of a struggle, no note, no "nothin'," it is always assumed that they've run away. Adult run-aways are not that uncommon, either. Many of them are men who are sick of their wives for one reason or another, or vice-versa, who just want to start all over again – somewhere else. Women run-aways typically leave with children, and are almost always discovered when the kids are enrolled in a new school. But, Janet didn't have children, so, if in fact she was a "run-away," – which I seriously doubted – it was possible she would never be found.

We had one thing going for us, though. As a police officer, the search would go on much longer – and with far greater intensity – than if she'd been Suzy Housewife taking a hike from her abusive husband.

I wasn't the only one who doubted that Janet would run away. Nobody at the Denver Police Department saw her as a runaway, either, although I had to wonder if they would have necessarily told him the unvarnished truth. He said they didn't know what to think. They had scraped literally every square inch of the doorway where Janet had been asleep and, other than finding her weapon, found absolutely nothing else. By the time her partner had called her disappearance in and half the brass in the department came flying down the alley to ask him "what the fuck?" any tracks in the snow that might have been helpful had long been obliterated. Besides, it had continued to snow that night, and the alley apparently had a fresh couple of inches before the partner ever woke up.

I knew Troy would have been miffed when they questioned him about their relationship, although he knew that an unusually late night at work – with plenty of witnesses – gave him a solid alibi, at least for the time of her actual disappearance. "But what if you had an accomplice?" some smart ass rookie detective had asked him. A couple of his buddies had to restrain him at that point to keep him from shoving the guy's teeth down his throat.

The bottom line was, nobody had a clue. Not the department, not Troy, not Janet's friends and family, nobody. Except maybe...me.

I woke up at about five o'clock – it was seven in New York, and it always takes my body a couple of days to "adjust." I lay there for a few minutes, trying to decide what to do: get up and pee, but risk awakening Troy in the next room, or lie there and wet the bed.

I got up.

He was wide awake and sitting upright. He looked dazed and I briefly wondered if he'd just smoked a joint. I didn't smell anything, so I decided he probably just hadn't slept very well.

"Mornin' Troy."

"Hey."

I knew from past experience not to pursue a full-blown conversation at this point; Troy isn't what is euphemistically referred to as a "morning person," although I've always wondered where these slackers get off blaming their poor social skills – let's call it rudeness, because that's what it is – on the fact that they aren't "morning people." Hell, if you don't want to get up, don't. Stay in bed. But if you do get up, don't inflict your bad attitude and glum demeanor on the rest of us.

Still, it was his house, and I had slept in his bed, so I guess he was well within his rights to act any way he damned well pleased. I was busy thinking about this when he came to, as though he'd had cold water thrown in his face.

"Hey, buddy," he began. "What time do you think old lady Rosencranz gets up?"

I was tempted to give him a little lecture on a few good reasons why he should never refer to any woman as "old lady," not the least of which was it simply wasn't nice. Sir might have been proud of me for delivering such a lecture, but Troy would most likely throw my ass out in the hall. So, instead, I said, "I seem to recall that she's an early riser. Let's go knock on her door."

He was half-way out the door before I stopped him. "Mind if I put on some pants? I don't want to get *Mrs.* Rosencranz all excited." I deliberately emphasized the "Mrs." to try to subtly make the point that he shouldn't refer to her as "Old Lady Rosencranz." I'm sure it went right over his head.

I slipped on my jeans and a second later we were racing down the stairs, just like old times.

84

Mrs. Rosencranz opened the door before we finished knocking. "Guten Tag!" she cried, obviously delighted to see us both together again. She had told us on more than one occasion that she thought we were brothers raised by different parents, whatever the hell that meant. We swept her into our arms, sort of a group hug, and stood there just basking in the sweetness of this wonderful, kind and generous woman. I hadn't realized how much I'd missed her.

"Got any German beer?" Troy asked.

She looked shocked before she realized he was teasing, which he was, with her – at least, most of the time.

"Nein! Coffee only for you, Weisenheimer!"

"Whatever," Troy said, trying to sound normal, but Mrs. Rosencranz and I exchanged looks. We knew he was in terrible pain and was just trying to go through the motions of normalcy for our sakes.

"Sit down then," she said, and we both took chairs at her kitchen table which was covered with a chinz fabric tablecloth like you might find in a German restaurant. She busied herself getting the coffee and some nice German china before joining us at the table. Turning serious, she looked at Troy and said, "Vhat have you heard?"

"Nothin'" Troy said.

"But," I chimed in, trying to sound an upbeat note, "we have a far-fetched idea...and believe it or not, we think you may be able to help us."

"Me? Vhat can I do? Anything!" She looked earnest and heartsick at the same time. She added quietly, "I like Fraulein Janet. I want you to find her...safe."

"Thank you," Troy mumbled.

"You see," I continued, "I had sort of a similar thing happen to me several years ago, Mrs. Rosencranz. In fact, it was right before I met you."

"What ting?"

"Well, I disappeared. I was kidnapped, actually. I was taken somewhere – I never found out where – and was held as...well...as sort of a prisoner...for several months. I was released right before I came here and rented my apartment from you." I realized I was hem-hawing and probably sounded like some goof-ball claiming to have been abducted by aliens. But, if that's what Troy and Mrs. Rosencranz thought, they didn't let on.

Mrs. Rosencranz looked aghast. "Vhat! You never tell me this, Mark! Why? I mean, why you not tell me?"

"Well, I hadn't told anybody, really until I told Troy when I got to town last night. It just didn't seem that important." I still marveled at the fact that *People* magazine, which was supposedly one of the best-selling magazines in the country seemed to escape the attention of virtually everybody I knew.

Besides, I thought, everybody would probably think I was a freak when they found out I was actually glad I'd been kidnapped.

"Really...!" she said, trying to process what I'd told her. I watched her, and then I watched Troy watch her and I couldn't help thinking, "doesn't anybody subscribe to *People* magazine anymore, for chrissakes? You people must be the only people in America who didn't see my mug on the front page!" I didn't say that, of course, and I'd decided long ago that since *People* was a weekly magazine, its shelf life was, well, just a week – which meant it was entirely possible a front page story could completely disappear a week after it ran. If you didn't happen to be in the grocery store that week, it might have been easy to miss it.

I continued. "Yeah, well, I apologize to both of you for not telling you all about my gruesome past, but now you know, and there's something about that experience, Mrs. Rosencranz, that has always bugged me."

"Vhat is it, Mark? Vhat?"

"Well, do you remember the first night I arrived here you brought me one of your famous dinner trays..."

"Ja, ja, of course..."

"Yes, and, well, do you recall the way I reacted at the time?"

She thought for a moment, but then shook her head. "Nein. Not really..."

"Yeah, well, here's the thing. I almost fainted when you brought that food to me. It was exactly like the food I'd been eating while I was held prisoner – right down to the way it was arranged on the plate! And then, every time you would bring me a different lunch or dinner...or even your occasional breakfasts...they were prepared and presented *exactly* as they had been during that time I was held prisoner." The word prisoner stuck on my tongue, because I knew it was likely to be misunderstood. For me, it was a life-changing experience in all the right ways. Still, I knew I was a prisoner, at least by definition and certainly other people would characterize it as such.

Troy interrupted at this point, obviously agitated. "I gotta ask you, man, why didn't you ask her about it then?"

"I did! Of course I did!" And then, turning back toward the diminutive German woman, I said, "You obviously don't remember it, Mrs. Rosencranz, but initially, I was convinced that Sir – that's what I called the guy who kidnapped me – had somehow followed me after he let me go and that he was just messing with my head by making me think I was free. I asked you about it – if he was here, in the building." At this point, I chuckled. "In fact, I wondered at first if maybe he was your husband or something..."

"Nein! My husband died ten years ago."

Processing what I'd said a moment before, Troy said, "That's weird, man."

"I agree! But I really did grill Mrs. Rosencranz pretty thoroughly at the time...I know you don't remember that, Mrs. Rosencranz, but I did."

"Yah, I tink I remember..."

"Well, now I've decided that it may be a clue to Janet's disappearance. It's a long shot, for sure..."

"Vhat is dis 'long shot'?"

"It means it's probably far-fetched." From her reaction, I could tell she didn't understand the words 'far-fetched' anymore than she did 'long shot,' but I pressed on.

"Anyway, I vaguely remember that you said you have a sister back in Germany, but I'm just wondering if or how there could be some connection..."

"Mein sister ist not in Deutschland! Mein sister Greta lives here, in Colorado! Why do you think she lives in Deutschland?"

"Um...I don't know, actually. I guess I just assumed...but to be real honest, I don't remember where I got that idea."

"Nein. Greta and her husband live in the mountains. He is a part-time auto mechanic and handyman and she works as a housekeeper."

Troy and I glanced at each other. "Where, exactly, does she live in the mountains, Mrs. Rosencranz?"

"She lives just outside Salida in a little town called Poncha Springs. First you go to Fairplay, then you turn South and go about 50 miles, and you come to Salida. You go through Salida and go five more miles to Poncha Springs. Then, you..."

"That's great, Mrs. Rosencranz," I said, stopping her mid-sentence. "But do you think you could draw us a map – and maybe give us her exact address?"

"Ja, ja..." she said even as she was fetching a pad and pen. "She has very nice house," she continued. "Very pretty. Big garden and two dogs...German shepherds!" She smiled at this, presumably because it was such a cliche.

"OK..." I said, trying to imagine how I could have possibly ended up in Poncha Springs, Colorado when I'd never even heard of it.

"Greta is mountain climber, too," she added. "She climb Mt. Princeton at least fifty times!"

"Very impressive," Troy said. "She must be in great shape."

"Excuse me," I asked excitedly. "Mount *what?*"

I'd only just discovered the existence of Mount Princeton from the autograph-seeker on the airplane and now here it was again. For a split second I wondered if there was such a thing as fate, or even some mysterious force that was working on my behalf to help me find Sir, and now Janet.

But I quickly dismissed that thought as "unworthy of me," as Sir liked to say. "Fate"? "Mysterious force"? I made a mental note to try to "get a grip."

85

"Do you have my brother's breakfast ready, Greta?"

"Yes, sir, of course."

"Good. I'll take it to him...I'm sure he's feeling somewhat impatient, since I overslept this morning."

Indeed. He may also be impatient at being held prisoner by his own brother, don't you think?

"Yes, sir. I'll get the tray."

After Carson delivered the tray to the pass-through cupboard, he returned to the control room to tell Janet she could eat.

"Did you sleep well, dear?"

"What? Oh," she said, turning toward the beautifully outfitted "bed," which had manifested itself while she'd been unconscious. "Yes, thank you for the mattress and the bedding."

Pretty rich stuff there, Mister. Another clue. You've obviously got money...and you're obviously gay, gay, gay. No straight man I know would ever have such fancy linens, except maybe Mark...

The thought of Mark caused her to emit a small groan.

"What is it, dear?"

"Wha..oh. Nothing...I was just wondering if you will ever let me go..."

"Why, yes, Janet, of course I will. What you will learn about the 'school' in which you are now enrolled is that everybody graduates...eventually."

Having spoken those words, Carson sat, thinking. *With maybe one exception; and let's just say he dropped out prematurely.*

"But," he continued, "we do have some work to do. You see, I'm still not sure why you're here. Since you haven't chosen to share much of who you are, or your, um, background, it is difficult for me to design the right curriculum for you."

Janet had to think about that. She had given this creep her official story – at least twice. She was brought up by a religious cult in Lemon, Utah. She ran away and hitched a ride to Denver. She had been picked up by a pimp named Rodney. She had told the story so much she was beginning to believe it herself. What else could she tell this guy? The truth? That she was an undercover cop for the Denver Police Department and that probably half the city was out looking for her? That she had a boyfriend she'd fallen out of love with and...and...what? She was worried that she might be falling in love with her boyfriend's best friend? What the hell was going on? What made her think about Mark – and now, of all times?

Mark and Troy were like brothers. Nobody but a slut would flirt with her boyfriend's best friend, but she had – on more than one occasion. He'd ignored her, of course, and she had long ago decided he just wasn't interested. Why, then, did he just pop into her head?

She realized the cartoon character on the screen before her was waiting for an answer. She needed to buy some time.

"Well, I sort of have a guy I'm interested in, and, um, I'm not sure if he likes me." *Christ. I sound like I'm in junior high.*

"Oh?" Carson replied, a lump forming inexplicably in his throat. "Why don't you tell me about him?"

"Well, he left Denver and went to New York City to become an author...well, he did become an author...and I only talk to him on the phone now..." *Shit. She was supposed to be poor and living on the street. How the hell could she carry on a long-distance phone relationship?*

Sir didn't seem to pick up on the implausibility of what she'd just said, so she continued. "I mean, sometimes when Troy goes out and leaves me by myself, I'll call Mark – that's his name – just to talk for a few minutes." Then, to try to make her lie sound more convincing, she added, "I almost got caught a couple of times."

Carson struggled to keep listening. Surely she wasn't talking about *his* Mark. Surely there was more than one author in New York City named Mark. But he had to know.

"Janet, what did you say the author's name was?"

"What? Oh. His name is Mark. Mark Boston. Have you heard of him?"

Carson answered too quickly. "No! I was just wondering if it might be a familiar name, that's all. Please go on..."

86

This was unbelievable. Unthinkable. Carson's hands felt cold and clammy. He could feel color fill his face. How could he have managed to kidnap two people who actually knew each other? Mark was the only one of his students who had ever seen his face. If he knew this young woman and found out she was missing, what would keep him from telling the authorities – and maybe describing his appearance in such a way that they would track him down? As much as he tried to live a quiet and obscure life, there was no getting around his background. It's not like his photo hadn't appeared in print over the years. Thanks to the annual stories about the richest people in the world, he was hardly unknown. If the author – and now this young woman – had been paying attention, it would be easy to connect him to his "students."

He must not be caught. He *mustn't*.

The whole thing had suddenly become very distressing. If she knew Mark Boston, he had to have told her about his own experience, so she must know more than she's letting on. Now what was he going to do?

The girl had stopped talking and was staring at the screen. He was shocked at the next words that came out of his mouth.

"Well, Janet, that's all very interesting, but you must be tired from all this. Maybe we should declare 'recess.' You've heard of the 'playground,' I suppose...?"

"I'm sorry, what? Did you say 'playground'? Um, no...I'm sorry. I don't know what you're talking about."

He studied her image on the screen before him. She certainly looked sincere and didn't appear at all to be lying. But if she knew Mark Boston, and if he told her about his own kidnapping, he would surely have told her about the 'playground.' The author loved the courtyard and thanked Carson a thousand times for allowing him access to it. Of *course* he would have mentioned it to her...if he had told her anything at all about his experience.

Now Carson was confused. He couldn't tell if she was being coy or if she really didn't know about the playground.

Janet was confused as well. *This guy really is crazy. "Recess?" "Playground?" What the hell is he talking about, and why in the hell did he think I would have heard about it? It's not like this place is listed in the Michelin Guide.*

She had to know more. "Sir? What is 'recess,' exactly?

Now Carson had done it. First, he had allowed this woman to stay enrolled in the school for almost three weeks without any 'correction.' Then, he gave her bedding long before she earned it, and now he had set her up for recess – also long before she'd earned it. Why the special treatment, he wondered.

Choosing his words carefully, he said, "Well, recess is a reward to students who have been doing well in their studies. And, since you have been forthcoming about your past..." He paused, realizing he didn't believe a word he was saying. After taking a breath, he continued, "...I have decided to allow you a brief recess so you will continue to do the work necessary to help you graduate."

Now Janet was more confused than ever. *Whatever. Like I have a choice.*

"So, if you will give me a moment, I will prepare the playground and then you will be allowed to use it for one hour today. Please wait right there." At this, he rolled his eyes at the foolishness of his own statement, hoping the computer software wouldn't catch the eye movement and transmit it via his image to Janet's monitor.

He needn't have worried. Janet was busy rolling her own eyes. *Right, asshole. I'll wait right here.*

Carson quickly switched the video feed from the classroom camera to the camera located just under the eaves in the courtyard. Everything appeared to be pristine and in good order. But, what was that noise? Turning up the volume on the console, he could now hear it more clearly. He switched the video feed to the camera on the west side of the house, overlooking the yard. Of course! The concrete trucks were there, pouring cement for the floor of the pool. No matter; even if she screamed when she got outdoors, which he sincerely doubted, she couldn't possibly be heard over that racket.

"O.K., Janet. I think we're ready for you. If you will kindly proceed in an orderly fashion through Door # 1, you may have an hour of recess."

'What fresh hell,' Janet wondered, *thinking of a phrase she and Troy often used to elicit laughter.* She walked slowly to Door 1. *Is this what you mean by orderly fashion, asshole? I'd like to see how one could be disorderly in this box!*

Arriving at the door, she pulled it open and gasped.

87

Greta couldn't stand it any more. Her boss was acting weirder than usual. First, the women's clothing. Then he stopped reading the daily newspapers, which he had done every single day for as long as she could remember. Stopped. Overnight. When she stopped putting them on the table, she put them directly into the recycling bin. After a month of that, she simply cancelled them.

Then there was a matter of the new swimming pool. She had never known her boss to show any interest in swimming. He certainly never drove to Poncha Springs to use the big new Olympic pool at the YMCA, because she and Manuel spent enough time there that she would have seen him. Then, out of the blue he talked about a swimming pool and construction started the next day. Why? Why the big hurry?

But the thing that bugged Greta the most was that courtyard on the East side of the house that Asner Johnson had shown her using the library computer. Who knew? Greta didn't, and she wanted to.

For the past few mornings, after she pulled her old reliable Volkswagen into the staff parking area, she got out of the car and stood for several minutes simply staring at the east-side view of the sprawling mansion. She couldn't walk around the house to the west side, where the courtyard was apparently located, because of the cameras and the fact that she couldn't think of a legitimate reason to do so. Her last trip had so incensed her boss she wouldn't dare do it again. So, she stood here, on the opposite side of the house, staring up at the roof as she tried to decide what to do. She simply had to see that courtyard and hopefully get a glimpse of Mr. Kirkpatrick's brother, the elusive Mister Scooter.

The black slate roof, with six chimneys, was imposing. Had it been a taller house, anything more than a single story, it might have looked like a Bavarian castle. The large white sandstone blocks used in place of standard bricks created an imposing facade.

She had always liked the house. The landscaping, thanks to her long-suffering husband, was exquisite. Since it was late Spring, the numerous flower beds which surrounded the house and lined the fence were overflowing with tulips and daffodils – two of her favorite flowers.

The previous night, when she arrived home, she went into the garage and began sorting through the large plastic storage boxes containing her mountain climbing equipment. She found carefully coiled nylon ropes, dozens of cams and carabiners, crampons and quickdraws. But what she really needed was a grappling hook – the kind firemen used on search and rescue missions. Perhaps she could throw that onto the peak of the house and hope that it would hold as she pulled herself up and then let herself down on other side – into that courtyard.

But what if it didn't? And what about the noise the hook would make when it clattered along the slate shingles? Her boss rarely left home anymore, especially with the swimming pool construction in full force. She wouldn't dare undertake such a mission while he was in the house.

She frowned. A grappling hook would never work, even if she had one. A weather vane whirled slowly on top of one of the chimneys. What about using a chimney as support? Yes, that might work, but she knew she would never be able to throw a rope far enough to lasso one. What a dilemma.

"Manuel," she said to her husband as he pulled his pick-up truck into the space next to hers a few minutes later, "what is that wire thing attached to the shingles and coming down from the chimney?"

"That's the lightning cable," he said. "See, there's one attached to a rod on the side of each chimney and the cable comes down over the side of the house and into the ground."

"Oh. I see..."

"Greta...? What are you up to? I told you to leave it alone. You don't want Mr. Kirkpatrick to fire us, do you?"

"No, of course not. But I want to know what's in that courtyard. I just want to see that brother of his with my own eyes. For all we know, he could be holding his brother prisoner!"

"Leave it alone, Greta. Please! It's none of our business."

But she couldn't. She wouldn't. She had to know.

Makeovers - Rex John

88

Mrs. Rosencranz offered to call her sister immediately, but we couldn't decide what we would want her to say. If, by some fluke she did actually work for Sir, or at least knew who he was, we didn't want her tipping our hand.

"Maybe we should just drop in on her," I suggested.

"I don't know boys," Mrs. Rosencranz said. "I only visited her at work once. Her boss is a very rich and powerful man and he told her after I left that she wasn't to have visitors at work. Can you imagine?"

"Well, he may have something to hide," I ventured. "If we drop in unexpectedly, he won't have a chance to object."

She seemed to buy this, but I wasn't sure. What, exactly, would we say when we got there? "Oh hi, we understand you're holding a friend of ours. Could we have her back, please?"

Not only that, but obviously he would recognize me, and would not have forgotten the promise he secured from me: that I would never, under any circumstances, try to find him. Besides, he hadn't really done anything wrong – at least not to me – and I didn't want him to get in trouble.

But, on the other hand, if he was holding Janet, well, that was a different matter. She wasn't some washed-up, drug and alcohol addicted college drop-out well on the way to destruction. I had obviously needed a make-over, but she certainly didn't.

And yet, I reminded myself, if she was undercover – dressed like a homeless person, no less – Sir would have no way of knowing that.

As these thoughts were racing through my head, Troy had gotten down to business and the next thing I knew, he had Mrs. Rosencranz writing down the directions – and drawing a crude map – of how to get to Poncha Springs.

We asked Mrs. Rosencranz not to contact her sister until after we had been to see her, explaining, lamely I thought, that it would be fun to surprise her. She gave us a skeptical look, but nodded. She seemed to grasp that we had a plan and now she -- and her sister -- were part of it. After a quick stop back upstairs to use the bathroom, we grabbed our jackets and headed out the door.

89

It seemed as though her boss never left the house anymore. After taking his brother's breakfast tray with him as he left the dining room, he disappeared for the greater part of the morning. Meanwhile, she watched concrete trucks come and go throughout the morning, depositing their heavy loads before rumbling back up the driveway and out through the gate, which dutifully closed after each departure.

Would she dare climb the roof if he was still in the house? And, if she did, and got caught, would she be fired? Yes, that much was obvious. Worse yet, Manuel would be fired, too, and then what would they do for money? She wasn't about to tap into the money her mother left her, no matter how much Manuel begged.

Pondering her options, she jumped when the house phone rang, and she could see that the call was coming from elsewhere in the house.

"Ja?" she said as she lifted the receiver.

Carson grimaced. She simply refused to learn – and he refused to stop trying to teach her.

"*Yes*," Greta. "Remember? We do not use 'ja' when we mean 'yes.' You aren't in Germany anymore."

"*Yes, Sir*," she responded. Her tone was testy, and he briefly considered calling her on it. But, in the interest of getting on with his day, which was off to a decidedly poor start, he decided to let it pass.

"My brother has just finished eating his breakfast, Greta, so I shall leave the tray outside the door of my study, as usual. But then I am going to spend some time helping him with his therapy and I am not to be disturbed for the next few hours under any circumstances. Is that clear?"

"Ja...I mean, yes. Sir."

"Very well," he said, and the phone went dead in her hand.

If he's going to be busy for the next few hours, now is my chance.

Moving quickly, Greta ducked out the door of the mud room, idly noticing what appeared to be wheel tracks on the brightly polished floor. *What in the world...?* But that would have to wait. She was on a mission.

90

Janet, meanwhile, was undone by the beauty of the courtyard...or was it just the mere fact that it was the first sunlight and blue sky she'd seen for three weeks?

Carson, watching her on the monitor, wasn't surprised by her reaction. They all reacted the same way. He couldn't blame them, really. It really was a stunning tableau...like something out of a romance novel. Today it was especially beautiful as the tulip bulbs Carson had planted with his own hands were in full bloom.

"It's OK, dear," he said, switching to the outdoor sound system. "You may go out."

Janet stepped out of the doorway and immediately spotted the monitor in the corner of the courtyard, under the roof. There was the ubiquitous cartoon figure, staring at her as he did, twenty-four hours a day. She suppressed an urge to roll her eyes.

Gingerly, she stepped onto the brick path in her bare feet. *Some shoes might have been nice with this new get-up, asshole.* Smiling at the camera under the eaves, she said, in a little girl voice, "Brrr! The bricks are kind of cold!"

The cartoon figure frowned and she knew immediately she'd said the wrong thing. *There's something about this guy. I feel like he's going to blow at any minute.* "But it feels good!" she added quickly, even as she headed to a patch of sunlight. There, of course, the bricks were fiery hot, but she knew better than to register her displeasure. No telling what this nut would do; probably make her go back into that steel room.

Heading toward the chaise lounge with the yellow-striped cushion, she made quick mental notes. Using her peripheral vision, she judged the wall to be about twenty feet high – the same as the house to which it appeared to be attached. The house was much taller than a normal one-story house, and yet it was too short for two full stories. The roof was impressive – as tall and peaked as any roof she'd ever seen, and covered with what appeared to be black slate shingles. It was beautiful, although she could only see a small portion of it from where she stood.

On the far side of the area, where the wall was apparently the only thing separating her from freedom, she noted an electric wire plugged into an outlet box under the eaves. The wire seemed to extend the entire length of the stone wall, and didn't appear to be insulated, which meant anyone touching it could easily be electrocuted. *Nice touch, you jerk.*

It was now clear that she had been kept above ground, which was a relief, since she had wondered more than once if she was in an underground bunker of some sort – buried where nobody would ever find her.

Carson watched as she lowered herself into the chaise. He cleared his throat before engaging his microphone. "It's lovely outside today, isn't it dear?"

"Oh yes," she responded quickly and sincerely, as there was no escaping the fact that it was a gorgeous day – and this was a gorgeous place. The only thing that might make it better is if Mark were with her. *Mark! You mean Troy, girl! Why would you even think about Mark? What's wrong with you! At least try to remember the name of your own boyfriend!*

A thunderous noise on the other side of the wall brought her self-incriminations to an abrupt halt and caused her to jump.

"What the hell was that!" she exclaimed, but fortunately for her, Carson had not heard her. He'd heard the explosion, too, and had quickly jumped up to go look into the side yard from the large window in his study.

He was unaware that, as soon as he moved out of range of the computer camera, the internal sensors responsible for capturing and re-interpreting certain points on his face before converting them into the anime figure on Janet's screen simply ceased operating, allowing the camera to focus on the wall behind Carson's chair.

As a result, Janet – who had now settled back into her chaise lounge – was left staring at a television screen containing an image of nothing more than an empty chair with a plain wall in the background. But it was the wall that caught Janet's eye. On it were several framed photographs, somewhat out of focus, but clearly head shots of men – similar to the photos taken for a high school year book. One, in particular, caught her eye.

It was Mark.

MAKEOVERS - REX JOHN

91

Our ride into the mountains is tension-filled, and it's my fault.

It's been so long since I've driven a car – something I never enjoyed all that much anyway – and I've never been good at map reading. So, of course Troy drove and told me to be his wing man, whatever the hell that means. Apparently it involves map reading, because the minute we headed down Sixth Avenue headed West, he tosses the map into my lap. I resist the temptation to throw it out the window, knowing full well how it will mystify me.

And it does. We miss not one, not two, but three exits – requiring us to go countless miles out of our way. Each time this happens, I mumble something like, "Um, I think that might have been our exit," which prompts another outburst from him.

Troy is what I call a progressive swearer. The first time he said, "Oh...? Shit."

The second time, he said, "Fuck!"

The third time, he was clearly angry, and said, "Goddamn it, Mark, can't you even read a map?"

"Well, no, actually. I should think that would be clear by now." I must have looked and sounded pretty goofy, because that caused him to burst out laughing –

and that was music to my ears because it was the first time I'd heard him laugh since I'd arrived back in town.

We'd only been on the road for about an hour when I needed to take a piss. Badly.

"Hey, man," I ventured. "I gotta take a leak."

"Forget it. We don't have time."

"Seriously, man, I really gotta go."

"No."

Now it was my turn to get pissed off, as it were. "Goddamn it, I'm not kidding. Now find a place before I take my dick out and piss all over your car."

That made him laugh, and he immediately pulled onto the first off-ramp we came to, in Georgetown, Colorado. We rolled into a gas station and he stayed in the car while I went in and waited for some pimply-faced seventeen year old to hand me a miniature baseball bat into which a hole was drilled and a chain attached to a key.

"Sinback," the kid said.

"Pardon me? 'Sinback'? I'm sorry, I don't know what that means," I said.

"It's...in...the...back," he responded slowly and loudly, as if talking to a foreigner.

I glared at him like the asshole he was and headed out the same door I'd just entered. Sure enough, there was a door on the back of the building sporting a sign with a little blue figure on it. The door wasn't closed all the way so I could have saved myself the trouble of asking for the key. I went in, looked for a urinal and seeing none, headed into the first of two stalls. I can say, without equivocation, that it was the dirtiest, filthiest, nastiest bathroom I've ever seen. I flushed with my foot and immediately headed toward the door. I didn't want to touch any other surface and would have used a paper towel to open the door, but of course there wasn't one. Don't get me wrong: I usually wash my hands after using the bathroom, but not in a place like this. I remember Troy and I were in some other dirty public restroom once and he headed out without stopping to wash his hands. I was shocked, and said so. "Hey man," he responded, looking around, "my dick is cleaner than any surface in this place!" It made sense at the time and I will admit that I now sometimes walk past a filthy sink myself -- like now for example. Just as I was going out the door, I noticed a tampon machine on the wall. *That's weird.*

Back in the sunlight, there stood Troy, leaning against the building.

He turned and looked at me as I walked out. "What the hell, man?" he said. "D'you have a sex change operation or something?"

"No," I replied, clearly puzzled. "What are you talking about?"

"So, when did you start using the ladies room?"

I turned and looked at the door. Sure enough, the blue figure was the universal symbol for a ladies room: round blue head on top of a blue stick figure wearing a blue dress, and little blue arms with little round blue hands extended to each side.

"Oh," I said, feeling as stupid as I sounded.

Troy howled. "You know, that's not a guy in a little blue kilt, you dumbass!"

I rolled my eyes and said "whatever..." as we headed toward the car.

He kept at me for the next thirty miles or so until I missed the exit to Highway 9, which would take us through Breckenridge and on into Fairplay, where we would change highways once again. We were five miles past our exit when I realized I would have to tell him now, or we would eventually end up in California.

But at least he shut up about the "guy in the kilt."

92

      Greta sat on the lawn, lacing up her sneakers. As she did so, she looked up at the drainpipe she planned to climb. She'd made a quick dash to her car where she left the black pumps she wore as part of her "uniform" and grabbed her sneakers. She thought about bringing her friction boots, but they were still caked with mud from her last climb of Mt. Princeton. She cursed herself for not having cleaned them. But, even though her sneakers weren't intended for mountain -- or roof -- climbing, they shouldn't be too bad on the slick slate surface of the roof. Her plan was to snake up the drainpipe and pull herself over the gutter onto the edge of the steep roof where she would edge on her belly over to the lightning rod cable coming down from the chimney.

      The drainpipe would be a problem. There wasn't a fastener of any kind. *How does this thing stay on the wall?* Bending forward and stepping on as few tulips as possible, she looked behind the drainpipe to find the answer to her own question. Somehow, probably for aesthetic reasons, black steel fasteners came out from the back of the pipe directly into the stones behind it. She would have to shimmy up the pipe as best she could.

"I told you not to do this," Manuel said as he approached from behind. Greta, who hadn't heard him coming, jumped at the sound of his voice.

"You scared me!" she whispered.

"Why are you whispering?" he said. "There's nobody around."

"I don't know..." she replied using her normal speaking voice. "This is just scary."

"Well, I told you..."

"Ja, ja, I know you told me. But I'm going to do it anyway."

"I figured as much. Maybe this will make it easier," he said, gesturing to a twenty-foot ladder he'd left in the grass behind him.

"Bless you," she said.

After hoisting the ladder into position directly under the lightening rod cable, Greta gave him a peck on the cheek and put her foot on the bottom rung.

"Now, go away," she ordered.

She watched as he walked across the lawn toward the far side of the property where several small buildings stood – outbuildings, as Manuel called them, including the work shed where he kept his tools, a storage building for the lawn equipment, and yet another building for the emergency back up generator. The small structures stood partially hidden behind a brace of trees.

As her foot reached for the third rung, she heard the phone ringing in the kitchen. From the coded rings, three short bursts, she could tell it was coming from the front gate.

Oh, go away, whoever you are. It's probably another cement truck. Maybe the boss will think I'm in the rest room and answer it. Please, God, let him answer it and don't let him come looking for me!

The phone continued to ring, but Greta ignored it and continued to climb. But, just as she stepped off the ladder onto the roof, the noise of an explosion coming from the other side of the house almost caused her to lose her grip on the ladder post and slip off the roof.

The phone continued to ring.

MAKEOVERS - REX JOHN

93

Francisco Abeyta and Eduardo Trujillo had been friends forever, or for at least as long as either one of them could remember. Francisco was older by three years, but it was an interesting dynamic that the younger, Eduardo, exhibited a parental-type responsibility for his older friend, skillfully keeping him out of harm's way his entire life. When the Mexican mafioso tried to recruit the boys to shuttle drugs across the border, it was Eduardo who put his foot down when Francisco asked if they should do it.

"Absolutely not," he told his friend. "People get killed doing that stuff all the time, and we have our lives ahead of us. Why would you want to die so early?" The argument went on for days, but Eduardo eventually prevailed. In exchange, though, Francisco insisted the younger boy accompany him north to visit his father's cousin, who lived in Denver.

The short visit turned into a month, then two. Eduardo was concerned that they might be overstaying their visa, but Francisco insisted his father's cousin "knew people," and that everything was "O.K."

One morning, Francisco greeted Eduardo with exciting news. "Papa's cousin talked to the authorities and got permission for us to stay for another year!"

Francisco said. "Do you know what that means? We can get jobs and make lots and lots of money!"

"Are you sure it's legal?" Eduardo asked.

"It is, I promise!" Francisco said.

It wasn't, but the boys believed their father's cousin, and a few days later they stood on the corner of Alameda and Kalamath, just outside downtown Denver where, according to Francisco, "all the gringos come to hire day-laborers."

That's where they stood when James Troll drove up and beckoned them to the window of his truck. Using his broken high school Spanish, he was direct and to the point.

"Boys," he said, "this job is out of town – up in the mountains. I will pay you five dollars an hour and I will see that you have proper documentation. You can sleep in my garage. If you don't like it, I will bring you back to Denver anytime you ask me to."

Eduardo was skeptical, but he could see how much Francisco wanted a job, so he agreed. Besides, he reasoned, we don't want to wear out our welcome with Mr. Abeyta. The boys actually enjoyed the work, and Mr. Troll's wife Darlene was nice to them, delivering two plates of food to the garage almost every night.

This would be their fifth job for Sunrise Swimming Pools, and it was, by far, the biggest house they had ever seen. The first morning they arrived on the job, to shovel dirt and assist the backhoe operator whenever necessary, it was hard not to stare at the mammoth building in front of them.

"Does one person live there by all by himself?" Eduardo asked Francisco.

"That's what Mr. Troll said," he said. "He must have servants, though. Look how big that place is! It's like a castle!"

It was their third day on the job, and they were busily creating a grid of steel re-bar, wiring each junction together with wire, just as Mr. Troll had taught them. They planted small metal pedestals at certain intersections to keep the grid three inches off the dirt floor, enabling it to "float" in the middle of the concrete – which James Troll persisted in calling "mud" – the latest batch of which was scheduled to arrive at eleven o'clock. Other laborers were dismantling the forms from the inside walls, which had been poured the day before, and then hoisting them up to others stationed on the rim. The entire crew had asked among themselves why everything seemed to be happening so quickly. "What's the hurry?" one of the men asked the boss.

"Because the customer wants the pool done by the weekend," Troll replied. "Now get back to work!"

It was in the midst of all this activity that Francisco made his grisly discovery.

He whispered loudly to his friend, who was working about ten feet away. "Eduardo! Come here!"

The younger boy scanned the top edge of the pool to see if Senior James was watching. Satisfied that he wasn't, he crab-crawled over to where Francisco was sitting, ashen white, eyes wide open.

"*Qué?*" he whispered.

"*Mira!* -- Look!" his buddy said, pointing.

There, protruding about an inch out of the dirt, was the tip of a human finger.

"*Mierda!* -- Shit!" Eduardo said, jumping backward. "*Qué es eso?*"

"I don't know! It looks like..." at this, Francisco used his hand to brush a little more dirt from around the protruding digit and a hand, almost black, began to take shape.

"Shit!" he whispered. "There's somebody buried here! Don't cover it up! We need to tell somebody!"

"No!" Francisco said. "Shush! Don't say anything! Don't you know what they'll do? They will call the police! They will ask who made the discovery. Then, when they find out it's us, do you know what will happen? They'll call immigration, amigo! Do you want to go back to Campañas? I certainly don't. So, forget it. It's obviously a gringo. That's what they do up here; they kill each other all the time!"

Eduardo wasn't so sure. He didn't know what to do. He knew Francisco was telling the truth. If the police implicated them in a crime of some sort they might go to jail. At the very least, they would send them back to Mexico. And he knew it would mean he could no longer send money home. That would be a disaster for everybody. So, maybe Francisco was right. Why get involved? He didn't kill whoever was buried here, so why should he make it his problem?

Meeting Francisco's look of panic, he quietly bent over and re-arranged the dirt so the finger was no longer showing. Francisco nodded appreciatively and crawled back to where he had been working. The grid was finished quickly, and the two moved to the shallow end of the pool, gingerly stepping between the squares of re-bar. Gathering their tools, they climbed up the ladder.

As was his custom, James Troll walked slowly around the ground at the rim of the pool, looking closely at the patchwork of steel bar below him. "Uh huh...hmmm...OK..." he said, adding as he completed walking the rim, "OK, men. Good job. *Buen trabajo!* Now let's take a break while we wait for the mud to arrive."

Eduardo and Francisco headed for the big oak tree at the edge of the yard and plopped down in the shade. They continued their conversation in Spanish, but at a low volume, since many of their co-workers were fellow Mexicanos.

Eduardo was conflicted. He had been raised by a devout Catholic grandmother and had learned the difference between right and wrong at an early age. *Nunca se arrepentirá si lo hace lo correcto.* You will never be sorry if you do the right thing, Eduardo. She drilled it into him from the time he was three years old until the day she died. So far, he had always done the right thing. He had never stolen anything and, as far as he remembered, he'd never even told a lie. And now his best friend Francisco was asking him to lie. Should he? They hadn't done anything wrong; why should they be worried? He tried to reason with his friend. "Maybe they won't do anything to us. Maybe they will just thank us for telling them," he said.

Francisco laughed derisively. "Thank us? Stupido!"

Eduardo's didn't like that, but his reply would have to wait, as at that moment the next concrete truck came rolling through the big gates, which hadn't even closed after allowing the previous truck to exit. The two men knew enough to climb back down the ladder and assume positions down inside the pool, shovels in hand, so they could shovel the concrete to where it was needed as it came off the chute.

It was back-breaking work and certainly allowed no time for conversation. But Eduardo was still able to think about the conversation they'd been having as he spread the heavy concrete around the floor of the large pool, and Francisco's one-word insult rang in his ears. Was he being stupid? Would they both be sent back to Mexico? And, was it fair to do that to his best friend? No, he decided. It wasn't. He would keep quiet.

"I won't tell," he shouted as the concrete began its quick journey down the chute from the newly-arrived truck.

"Cómo?" Francisco shot back, holding his hand to his ear to indicate that he hadn't heard.

But he never would hear. The word *cómo* would hang in the air forever, even as both Mexican nationals, ages 23 and 26, were buried under a landslide involving the enormous truck and its cargo of 40,000 pounds of wet concrete.

94

The road from Dillon to Fairplay, Colorado takes slightly less than an hour. Fortunately there weren't any more exits for me to miss, so we moved right along. Troy had gone silent again, and I knew he was worried about what he would do if this ended up being a wild goose chase. I didn't know what to say, because I wondered the same thing. We sat as the scenery whizzed past.

Fairplay is an ugly town, if you can even call it a town. As best I can tell, it is comprised of two gas stations and a motel. There are a couple of other ramshackle buildings, but that's about it. We got on U.S. Highway 285, without incident. It seemed unbelievable that this so-called highway consisted of one lane in each direction. Troy managed to crank it up to about 90 mph for quite a stretch, but we soon found ourselves behind a cement truck and were unable to pass for several minutes. I could tell that Troy's stress level was rising precipitously, and I found myself frantically trying to think of something to say to lighten him up.

Apparently his speed hadn't gone unnoticed, because the silence was soon broken by the sound of a siren directly behind us.

"Fuck," Troy said, as though reading my mind.

He pulled off and did something I'd never seen him do before. He reached in his back pocket for his wallet and flipped it around so his DPD shield was on top.

"Hello, officer," he said in a friendly tone, with no discernible edge in his voice. *Apparently even cops know enough to put on a happy face when you get pulled over.*

The uniformed officer's name was 'Briggs,' according to the shiny chrome name tag attached to his starched blue uniform shirt. But he wasn't in the mood for friendly banter.

"License and registration, please," he said, curtly.

Troy handed him his wallet and I wished I'd had a camera. In a split second the cop – or sheriff's deputy, as it turned out – transformed from being a by-the-book, no-nonsense type of dickhead into Troy's new best friend.

"Oh...! How you doin' pal?" he said to Troy. Bending down further he looked across Troy to me and smiled. "Sir," he said, touching the brim of his hat.

I smiled slightly and did the head snap, but I didn't bother answering.

The two of them chatted back and forth for a few minutes – 'cop talk,' I guess you'd call it – before the deputy connected Troy to the missing female cop from Denver. Apparently they get the *Denver Post* all the way up here in Summit County.

"Hey, aren't you the boyfriend of that cop who disappeared...?"

Troy grimaced. As best I could figure, he had gotten to the place in his thinking where we were simply on our way to pick Janet up and bring her home. Now he was once again confronted with the cold reality that she was missing...and might never be found.

Troy nodded and managed to say, "Yeah, in fact, that's why we're up here. We have a lead we're checking out..."

That was all it took. Cops stick together and this Sheriff's deputy was now face-to-face with someone on a mission to rescue a fellow cop. As any cop will tell you, there is nothing more important when a fellow law enforcement officer is in distress.

"What can I do to help?" he asked.

"Nothin' now, man, but thank you," Troy said.

"Well, here's my card and my cell phone number. Name's Briggs. Gary Briggs. Don't hesitate to call if you need me."

"Will do, man. And...thank you." Troy's voice caught on the last word and I could see that the deputy was moved, too. He returned Troy's I.D. and gave a little salute as he headed back to his car.

We pulled back into traffic, behind yet another cement truck.

Makeovers - Rex John

95

Gazing out the large window of his study, Carson couldn't believe his eyes. His nearly finished swimming pool was now filled with an upside down cement truck. A bevy of laborers were running around, shouting in Spanish, and pointing to the upside down truck.

In the midst of all this, the phone was ringing incessantly. *Pick up the goddamned phone, Greta. Jesus!*

As he watched the chaos before him, he saw that James Troll, the owner of the swimming pool company, was gesturing and talking into his cell phone. The house phone continued to ring. He assumed Greta had chosen this moment to use the ladies room, or perhaps she had heard the loud noise too and was outside at the front of the house, out of Carson's line of vision.

"Yes?" he snapped into the phone as he answered the call, which he now realized was coming from the front gate.

"We're here to see Greta," came the male voice.

Carson didn't permit his employees to entertain their friends at his house. "She's working," he replied. "She isn't permitted visitors while she is at work."

"Oh no!" the voice responded. "It's just that we haven't seen her for so many years and we just wanted to say a quick hello." Then, as if an afterthought, "She used to babysit us back in Germany!"

Carson was about to tell them no again when the ear-splitting sound of a siren came through the handset. It was clear that an emergency vehicle had arrived at the gate, no doubt at the behest of the pool company owner, and the line went dead. Reluctantly, Carson pushed the button which would open the big gates, allowing the ambulance or fire engine onto his property. Greta's visitors were immediately forgotten.

From her vantage point at the peak of the roof, Greta watched in horror at the scene below her. The embankment at the side of the excavation had apparently given away, causing an enormous concrete truck, it's big drum now stilled, to tip and fall upside down into the unfinished pool, ending with its wheels up in the air and at least twenty men of various ages and nationalities running around the yard and pointing into the hole.

As she pondered what she should do, her eyes fell to the courtyard just below her. She could only see the far edge of it from the peak of the roof where she now stood, leaning against a chimney, but she could see enough to know that it was the same space she had observed on Asner's computer at the library. To get to it, she would have to descend the other side of the peaked roof, without the benefit of the lightning rod cable. She had brought a thin nylon rope with her and she wasted no time looping it around the chimney and then herself.

Using her glove-covered hands, she was able to slowly lower herself down to the edge of the roof, where she would have been easily observed if all the commotion beyond the courtyard wasn't demanding everyone's attention. Her eyes quickly scanned the figures in the yard to see if her boss was among them. He wasn't. That could only mean he was inside the house somewhere – probably not far from the fancy security system he used to monitor everything on his property.

Forcing her eyes from the yard and back to the courtyard in the foreground, she finally saw what she had come to see.

96

Carson wasn't in the mood to deal with any of this. Greta, even if she had been in the ladies room, would soon be out and she could direct the emergency personnel. He assumed from all the panic that someone had been injured in the accident, so there would probably be an ambulance and/or other rescue vehicles. Eventually a crane or some kind of large tow truck would need to be called to upright the cement truck now sitting upside down in the bottom of his swimming pool. That wall of the pool would need to be rebuilt.

Shit.

And what about the floor of the pool? Had they poured the concrete floor before or after they decided to dump the cement truck in the pool? Would the floor need to be dug up and re-poured? If so, this had implications beyond having to re-do the pool. Serious implications.

Carson slowly returned to the control room. He would keep an eye on everything from the electronic comfort of the control room, where he wouldn't need to have any direct contact with any of these people.

Taking his seat at the console, he noticed Janet, reclining peacefully on the chaise lounge, seemingly unaware of the drama unfolding a hundred feet from her on the other side of the wall. Her head was turned toward the television screen in the corner of the courtyard, but her right arm was folded across her face. Was she crying, or just trying to shield her eyes from the sun?

Engaging his microphone, he said, "Too bright for you, dear?"

She knew she must respond carefully. She couldn't let on that, until Sir had come back into view she had been staring at a photograph of the man she...well, her friend. She was filled with questions and wanted to scream at the absurd little cartoon on the screen. *How do you know Mark? Why do you have his photo on your wall! Where is he? Does he know I'm here? What the hell is going on!*

She didn't dare blow her cover. She still didn't know where she was or who this person was or why he was holding her captive. She had determined early on that there was no obvious way of escape – certainly not from the steel bunker in which she had been living until today. And now, even though she was outdoors, it seemed to be little more than a prison exercise yard as far as she was concerned. Certainly, the wall itself was unscalable if only because of its sheer height – to say nothing of the bare electric cable stretched across its length. Still, it was much better being outdoors than locked in that windowless room, and she was determined to stay out here as long as possible. She must not panic, and she must not show her hand.

Carson, wondering now if she was asleep, repeated his question, "Too bright for you dear?"

She slowly looked over to the screen in the corner. But, as she did so, she caught movement on the roofline above her.

"No, that's OK," she said, even as she watched a gray haired woman with a rope around her waist gesture wildly, miming that Janet was to remain quiet.

"Some sunglasses might help..." she added, trying to process what was happening and buy time. She continued to stare at the old woman. She was clearly on a mission. Was it to rescue her? Could it possibly be that she was by herself? Had this old woman been sent to singlehandedly rescue her? Why? Why weren't there battalions of police? Why wasn't the roof crawling with a SWAT team? Why no helicopter?

She *was* alone! Worse, there was no ignoring the look of panic on her face. She clearly didn't want her presence on the roof to be known. Once again, she placed an extended index finger in front of her mouth to indicate that Janet wasn't to talk to her.

But it was too late. The camera pivoted rapidly to the left and then up and down, searching for the object of Janet's fascination. But, because of it's placement under the eave of the house, Janet could tell it was unable to see what she saw.

"You appear to be looking at something, dear. What is it?" the animated figure on the screen asked.

Thinking quickly, Janet replied, "Oh, it's the cutest little squirrel up on the roof, Sir...can't you see him?" Once again, the camera panned left and right, up and down.

"I'm afraid I can't, dear."

"Oh, he's so cute. I wish I had something to feed him..."

"Oh no, dear, we don't want to feed the squirrels!" Carson replied. "That would just attract more of them!" He wondered how Janet would react if her little squirrel stepped onto the electric wire running across the outer wall of the courtyard. Probably not very well, he decided, so he flipped the power switch off. No point in frying the first live creature she's seen in a month right before her eyes.

Janet acted dejected. "Oh. Well, it's just so nice to have a little friend." And, then, looking directly at Greta, she announced loudly, "Well, little squirrel, I don't have anything for you to eat today, but will you come visit me tomorrow?" And then, as an after thought, she added, "I wish I could come play with you, but I can't today. You see, I'm sorry, but I can't leave this place. But you can come visit me!" And then, looking directly into the camera, she added defiantly, "You could even bring some of your other little friends who might want to see me! By the way, what's your name? My name is Janet! Be sure to tell all your friends that Janet wants to meet them!"

Greta was initially puzzled by this woman's goofy conversation, and almost answered before it occurred to her that this was all part of the little play they were acting out for the benefit of her boss, whose voice, while altered, was clearly recognizable. This woman – this "Janet" – wanted her to bring help. That much was clear. Nodding at the girl to indicate that she had understood, she finally realized where she had seen her face before.

This was the missing policewoman everybody was looking for.

97

Neither one of us realized how close we were to what I assumed would be Sir's house until we rounded a corner and there they were: two enormous and solid-looking wooden gates attached to a stone wall that must have been a good twelve feet tall. I noted that the wall was constructed of the same type of stones I'd seen in the wall of the "playground" when I was allowed out for "recess."

We'd been talking for the last half hour about how we should present ourselves; about our cover story. Mrs. Rosencranz had told us there were gates and that we would have to be admitted by her sister. She said we should tell her we were "her sister's friends and that she had sent us with a package for her."

"My sister can't stand not knowing everything, so she will let you in just to see what you have brought her!"

We agreed that even though Troy was driving the car and would be closer to the speaker, I would do the talking by leaning over him and shouting if necessary.

But it wasn't necessary, and it wasn't Mrs. Rosencranz' sister. The voice that finally came out of the speaker was a voice I would never forget as long as I lived. It was him. It was Sir.

98

"Yes?" was the only word that came out of the intercom, but it sent chills up my spine. And even though Troy and I had agreed in advance that I would do the talking, I nudged him to indicate that he should respond. He glared at me but leaned out the window and said, "We're here to see Greta."

Sir apparently didn't like visitors, because his response was fast and furious. "She's working," the voice snapped. "She isn't permitted visitors while she is at work."

"Oh no!" Troy said, without missing a beat. "It's just that we haven't seen her for so many years and we just wanted to say a quick hello. She used to babysit us back in Germany!"

If he responded, we didn't hear it, because all of a sudden an enormous fire truck pulled up behind us, lights flashing and siren blaring. In addition to all that racket, the driver laid on the horn and moved forward like he was going to shove us through the gate. We both thought we were pinned in until Troy noticed that the gates were opening. We drove in and headed toward the left while the big truck skirted around us to the right, its siren still going strong.

We pulled into what appeared to be a small parking lot on the side of the house and sat in the car, trying to decide what to do.

"Those things freak me out, man," I said to Troy. "Fire trucks, I mean. I can't get out of their way fast enough."

He smiled a goofy smile. "That's the whole idea, dude. They want you out of their way so they can, you know, get to the fire."

Glancing up at the massive looming facade of the house in front of us, I said, "Do you think this place is on fire?"

"Nah, probably just an accident or something. These days they send the big rigs out on all kinds of calls, probably because the guys at the station get so fuckin' bored out of their minds that they'd happily go get a cat out of a tree just for something to do. Speaking of which," he added, "what are *we* going to do?"

About that time I noticed a ladder off to the side, propped up against the house, just in front of the parking place we'd pulled into. Nodding toward it, I said, "I guess we could always use that ladder to go in one of the windows..."

"Are you nuts?" Troy began, but he quickly stopped when the ladder wiggled and we looked up to see an old woman trying to steady her footing on one of the top rungs.

"What the...it's Mrs. Rosencranz!" I exclaimed, momentarily forgetting that we had just left Mrs. Rosencranz a few hours earlier and it would be somewhat unlikely that she could have transported herself to the top of the roof of this house in that period of time.

"No, dumbass," Troy said. "It's got to be her sister..." But then, as we both sat there slack-jawed as this old woman climbed down the ladder, he added, "...but it sure does look like her. I'll give you that."

She marched up to the car window.

"*Ja?*" she asked, sounding exactly like her sister. "Vhat do you vant?"

"Mrs. Rosencranz sent us!" I blurted out, as though it were a secret password.

Apparently it was, because it worked. Her face softened immediately, and she said, "Gertrude sent you? OK denn, come in da house." With that she was off, but not toward the door of the house, but toward an old Volkswagen parked a few spaces away. "Haf to change shoes," she said over her shoulder as she popped open the passenger side door and sat down. With lightening speed, it seemed to me, she pulled off the sneakers she'd been wearing. I could hardly wait to ask her what she'd been doing on the roof, but she'd already put some sensible looking black shoes on and then, standing, tied on a white apron that seemed to have appeared from nowhere. I stared at her. I could not believe how much she looked like her sister. They could have easily been twins, except I distinctly remembered Mrs. Rosencranz – Gertrude – referring to her *older* sister. In the time it took me to recall that, she was gesturing that we should follow her as she marched toward the side door of the house.

Once inside she ducked around a corner into a big kitchen, and we followed her. She gestured toward a long white table as though we were supposed to sit, so we did. She began pulling coffee cups out of the cupboard, just as I'd seen her sister do many times.

Apparently we were having coffee whether we wanted it or not. *So, she's bossy, just like her sister.*

As she set two cups of coffee down in front of us and turned to fetch cream out of the refrigerator, she said, "Now then, vat can you do for me?"

We both smiled, because it was something her sister said on occasion, and just as Mrs. Rosencranz always did, she caught herself and said, "I mean vhat can I do for you!"

"Well, I'm looking for my girlfriend," Troy began. "And I think she may be here..."

I don't think she really heard him, because she abruptly turned toward me. "It's you! You're the author! You're dat Mark Brown!"

"Um, Boston..." I corrected.

She ignored me. "I read about you in the people!" I took it that "the people" meant the article in *People* magazine.

"Yeah," I said. "That was me."

She turned serious and her mouth turned downward. "I vas very mad at you, though, Mr. Mark Brown! You said you had eaten the best red cabbage in the world, but that's not true! *I* make the best red cabbage in the world!"

"Well, that's the thing, Mrs..." I stopped, because I realized I didn't know her last name. Mrs. Rosencranz had just referred to her as her 'sister Greta,' with no last name. She looked at me for a moment, waiting for me to continue, before she realized I was waiting for her to finish my sentence by supplying her last name.

"Oh. Martinez. Greta Martinez."

"Oh yeah," Troy said half under his breath. "Martinez. Now there's a good German name."

She reacted quickly, but with a smile on her face. She smacked him on the back of the head! "It's my husband's name, *dummkopf*!" Troy half ducked away from her swing, acting like he was wounded. Clearly, these two had hit it off, literally.

"Yes, well," I continued. "Mrs. *Martinez*...and, by the way, my name is Mark *Boston,* not Mark Brown..."

She sat there, staring at me, clearly not hearing – or choosing to understand – what I had just said.

I ventured on. "But, that's just it. I think the red cabbage I was eating may have been yours."

Now she heard me, but the possibility that I had eaten "her" red cabbage when she'd never met me clearly mystified her. "Vhat...?" she said. I took a deep breath as I prepared to launch into my story, and my now certain hunch that I had been held captive in this very house....

But my story would have to wait.

Makeovers - Rex John

99

A uniformed fireman – or paramedic, I'm never sure which is which – burst into the kitchen.

"What the hell!" he raged. "Who, exactly, is in charge of that fucking electric gate?"

Mrs. Martinez jumped up and ran to greet him in the doorway. "I am, Captain!"

I have no idea if the guy was a captain or, if he was, how she could possibly know that, but he didn't correct her. Rather, he got right in her face and yelled, "Well get the goddamned thing open and leave it open! We have one guy dead and another who probably will be in a couple of minutes but I'd like to try, if it isn't too inconvenient," he said, gesturing toward us as though we were simply in the middle of a coffee klatch, "to get him to the fucking hospital!"

Greta had already turned on her heels and headed toward a small control panel and phone above a small desk at the other end of the kitchen. She pushed a few buttons, which I assumed would mean the big gates were now slowly opening.

"Yes, Captain! They're open now and I vill leave them open for as long as you say!"

He didn't respond, but simply turned on his heels and went out the way he'd come in.

Greta was shaken. "A dead man...! But, how? What happened? Who is it?"

The questions weren't addressed to us but merely uttered aloud. We got up from the table and moved toward her, but she was already heading for the front door, in pursuit of the uniformed guy who just took off.

The three of us poured out the big front door onto the porch and into the driveway just in time to see an ambulance roar through the now open gate. It pulled around the side of the house, and we all walked quickly in its wake.

The scene in the swimming pool, if it hadn't been so tragic, might have been funny. A huge concrete mixer – presumably one of those that had been slowing traffic as we drove the one lane road to get here – was virtually upside down in the unfinished pool. The wall nearest us had crumbled, presumably as the truck drove too close to it. The other walls of the pool were still intact and appeared to be finished. My guess is they had been pouring the floor of the pool – the last thing they do, I think, before coating it with a waterproof paint. At least that's what I recall from the installation of the pool at my grandmother's house shortly after I was sent to live with her.

On the far side of the pool stood a half-dozen laborers in various states of grief and agitation. A guy who appeared to be the foreman was standing with a cop who was busy writing on a clip board. As we neared the edge of the pool, another cop stepped forward and said, "That's far enough, folks." But I could see a pair of legs sticking out from under the upside- down drum of the truck, splayed out on the fresh concrete on the floor of the pool. Perversely, my mind recalled the scene in the movie the Wizard of Oz where the bad witch is killed by the falling house, leaving nothing but her legs sticking out. The only thing missing here were the ruby slippers on the end of the two legs. I frowned at my sick humor.

There were several men – and one woman – down in the pool, hovering around the overturned truck. They were all in uniform – firemen or paramedics.

The scene was surreal. In the distance stood the beautiful stone wall that apparently encircled the whole estate, and the expanse of lawn between us and the wall was beautifully groomed, and looked just like a golf course. A handsome brick driveway led back to garages toward the rear of the house, and I found myself wondering how many homes could have been built from those bricks.

As we stood there, watching the scene unfold, an officer approached us from behind and said to me, "Sir, is this your property?"

"What?" I asked, taken aback by the question. "Oh! No, officer. It's not. Actually, I have no idea who owns the place." Then, noticing the puzzlement on his face, I said, as I pointed to Mrs. Martinez, "This woman should be able to tell you what you need to know."

By this time another man had come up to Mrs. Martinez – I mean Greta – and from the way they were talking, I assume this was Mr. Martinez, her husband. The cop went up to them and although I couldn't hear what was being said over the noise all around us, I saw her gesture toward the house several times. I could tell they were all getting ready to go into the house.

Well, Sir, if you're in there, you'd better prepare for visitors!

Almost before I'd finished my thought, the front door opened and Sir himself came out. He began walking toward us like he owned the place – which of course he did.

It was strange to see him again and I had to fight an impulse to – *hug him!* As soon as he moved into my sight, the anime version of him that I had interacted with during my time in his "classroom" morphed into the real Sir. The features were so similar that it was easy to make the transition, and of course I'd had that glimpse of him through the pass-through meal cupboard, as well as an even briefer glimpse when his real image appeared ever so briefly on my screen. Now that he was here in front of me, I could no longer conjure up the cartoon version of him. It was a strange sensation, like how you might feel if Homer Simpson showed up in the flesh.

"Gentlemen," he said as he approached us. And then, almost as an afterthought, he nodded and said, "Greta."

He only glanced at the police officer and Troy before his eyes met mine. "Mark," he said, extending his hand, "It's so good to see you again."

I took his hand in a brief handshake, and I'm sure my mouth was wide open as my brain tried to process the fact that this man – my hero, I guess – was standing before me, acting as though we were old friends.

His manner could only be described as patrician. Here he was, lord of the manor, greeting me as though I was about to have a drink with him on the veranda. Actually, a drink sounded pretty good right now.

"Hello, Sir," was all I could say. Fortunately, the policeman saved me from having to say more.

"Are you the owner of this property, sir?" the cop asked.

"Yes, officer, I am."

Turning to me, as if to call me a big fat liar, the cop said, "I thought you said you didn't know the owner."

"I suspect he meant he didn't realize this was my house, officer. We've met, of course, but he didn't realize I lived here," Sir said.

Clearly skeptical of this explanation, the cop nonetheless continued. "And your name, sir?"

I almost burst out laughing. *Yes! That's his name! "Sir!" You guessed correctly!*

"Carson Kirkpatrick, officer. And this is my housekeeper, Greta Martinez, and her husband, Manuel." And then, turning back toward me, he said, "And I believe you've already met the famous author, Mr. Boston."

There was a hint of sarcasm in his voice when he said "famous," but I still liked hearing him say it. Obviously he did, in fact, know I had become an author...and "famous" at that. I suppressed a smile which faded as I realized what I'd just heard. Carson Kirkpatrick was rumored to be one of, if not "the," richest people in the world. The likelihood that he had kidnapped me and held me prisoner was implausible. I couldn't process it. Still, there was no mistaking that this was the reclusive billionaire in front of me; photos of him were extremely rare, but I'd see his face at least once in a newspaper or magazine, but the photos were old and he looked different now. I stared at him.

Troy, meanwhile, had wandered away from me and was scoping out the place. The officer said something else to Sir, and I used the opportunity to slip away and walk over toward the garage doors where Troy was heading.

As he saw me approach, he turned and walked back toward me.

"What the fuck, man!" he whispered loudly. "Is that him, or not? Is that the guy who kidnapped you – or is that a long lost friend from your past?" He was clearly annoyed, and I didn't blame him. But in my own defense, I was still trying to process everything around me in this weird world in which I now found myself.

"Because," he hissed, "once you've caught up on old times, I wonder if you might get around to asking him *where the fuck he's keeping Janet!*"

At that moment the cop, Greta, Manuel, and Sir all turned to look at us. I could tell they had turned because of Troy's tone of voice, but I doubted they could have heard exactly what he said.

"Shut up, Troy!" I whispered urgently. "She's got to be in this house somewhere, but the cops can't just storm the place, you know. If he doesn't allow us in voluntarily, we'll have to wait while they pull a search warrant. Play it cool, man, and let's see what we can do without putting him on the defensive. Who knows what he'll do if he feels cornered."

"You mean we should just hang out here, pretending we're just sightseeing, while he chats up the cops?" he whispered furiously. "And what," he added, do we do if..."

He stopped mid-sentence and his eyes flooded with tears. "What," he repeated, before stopping and taking a deep breath, "what do we do if she's already dead?"

I looked directly into his eyes. "She's not, Troy. She's not. I know him. He wouldn't hurt anybody." At that, he sort of melted into my arms in a desperate hug. I could see that he was trying not to cry. As I held him for a moment, my eyes focused on a section of the house where there weren't any windows. I knew that wall. I had seen it many times – from the other side.

100

I'm sure she didn't think I noticed. From where Troy and I were standing, at the end of the driveway, near the garage doors, I had a clear line of vision to Sir, the police officer and the man I took to be a guy from the swimming pool company.

Greta, the housekeeper, had been standing with them, but she must have realized her presence wasn't required, because as I watched she turned slowly and began quickly walking toward the front of the house. That alone wouldn't have merited my attention – but when she was about five feet from turning the corner, she broke into a run.

What could possibly be so urgent inside the house, I wondered. Maybe she hears a phone ringing. Still, it bugged me, and once I felt Troy had regained his composure, I said, "Hey. C'mon. Walk with me, but try not to catch Sir's attention."

We moved to the edge of the pool again, as though we were casual observers. A uniformed officer headed toward us, so we angled across the lawn to the corner of the house. I carried on a conversation as we walked, acting as casually as I could, but informing Troy about what I'd just seen -- the housekeeper breaking into a run. I kept my eyes on Sir the whole time we were walking and talking, and once we had passed out of his line of vision we, like Greta, broke into a run.

Dashing around the corner we noted that the huge front door was closed, and presumably locked, so we kept running. We circled the far corner and emerged into the parking lot where we'd left our car. As we approached our parking space, we could see Greta's feet on the top rung of the ladder, just as she stepped onto the roof. Clearly, something on the roof had captured this woman's imagination, and now it had ours, too.

"Does that woman live on the roof, or does she just work up there?" Troy asked. I snorted because, as sarcastic as it was, I had been thinking the same thing.

And what a roof it was. Constructed with heavy looking charcoal-colored slabs of slate, it pitched steeply up to a peak that seemed at least as high as the lower part of the house itself – if not higher. By the time we got to the base of the ladder, we could no longer see her.

"C'mon," Troy said.

"No fuckin' way, man," I said. "I'm afraid of heights. There's no way I'm climbing that ladder."

"Pussy," he said as his foot hit the bottom rung.

"Whatever," I said, following him a little too quickly and bumping my forehead against the heel of his shoe.

"Hey! Keep your nose out of my ass, you dick," he said.

We made it to the top in seconds, and I made a note to myself to sign up for the citizens' police academy before I tried any more quick pursuits. Clearly, I was out of shape for ladder and roof climbing.

When we reached the roof, we had to consider our options. I didn't see how anyone could climb up the pitch of that roof; it was too steep.

Reading my mind, Troy blurted, "What the hell is she, a mountain goat? How'd she do it?"

"Look at that cable," I said, pointing to a thick wire that curved over the gutter and led up to the chimney. I could see a lightning rod attached to one side of the chimney, so I assumed this was the path the electricity would follow into the ground.

"Um..." I said. "I'm not touching that. Electricity freaks me out." I had told Troy about Sir's unorthodox method of "correction," and the electrified steel-lined room in which I had been held, so I expected him to realize why I was afraid.

"What are you talking about?" he said, impatiently. "There's no juice in that cable, numb nuts – unless we have a lightning storm."

I wasn't entirely convinced, but now that I was on the roof I was too gripped by fear to do anything but follow Troy. He grabbed the cable and started crab-crawling up the steep incline toward the chimney. I waited until he had a twenty-foot head start and then followed.

I had my eyes on him as he reached the peak and touched the chimney. "Oh, shit," he said.

101

Greta was proud that she was still a competent climber. She had mounted the roof in record time and, in a way, it was easier than climbing Mount Sudelfeld as a girl. At least you didn't need to worry about rockfall from the climbers above. It didn't hurt that there was a lightning rod ground cable running up the roof. She could pretend it was a top rope anchored by a lead climber.

She had grabbed the perlon rope from the front seat of her car, right where she'd left it when she came down off the roof: when the nice young men drove up and parked at the base of the ladder. Having carried it over her right shoulder, she now uncoiled it neatly before tying it securely around the chimney and then to her waist.

She tested the knots and, convinced they would hold her, turned around, leaned backward, and allowed the rope to control her speed as she stepped quickly down from the peak of the roof to the lower edge, just above the courtyard where she had seen the girl less than an hour before.

She wasn't there.

The chaise lounge in which she'd been resting was in the same place, but the girl was gone. Greta steadied herself at the edge of the roof and considered her options. Obviously, there must be a door into the courtyard below; how else would the girl have entered the courtyard? There weren't any points of entry in the three sides of the wall that she could see, so whatever door the girl used must be directly below her. As she took in the scene, she marveled at the beauty of the flowers, the trees, the bucolic atmosphere of the place. She felt at peace just looking at it. *How could I work in this house all these years and not know about this place?*

She hesitated only a moment before making the decision to lower herself into the courtyard, even though there was no way to know how far she would swing inward under the eave before finding a suitable foothold. Just as she was about to disappear below the roofline, she looked up and saw the two young men perched next to the chimney looking down at her.

"*Scheisse!*" Shit.

102

The cop would not shut up – although it was a toss-up between him and Troll, the owner of the pool company, as to who talked more.

The pool company guy was in full-bore, cover-your-ass mode. He put forth every theory he could think of that would absolve him of responsibility for the cement mixer falling in the pool. "Maybe your ground is unusually soft," he suggested in one particularly inventive excuse.

"My ground is plenty solid," Carson said in return, recalling vividly how, only three days ago, he could barely dig a three-foot deep grave because there was so much hard clay in the soil.

The cop was winding down, and Carson could tell that he was eager to get back to wherever policemen hang out to write whatever report they are required to write every time they find an upside down cement truck in an unfinished swimming pool -- to say nothing of the two workers who were injured in the accident.

But Carson had only one concern at this point. What would they find when they hauled the truck out? It was probably best that the cop not be here.

Troll, the swimming pool guy, pointed up the driveway to an enormous crane which was about to enter the gate, missing each side pillar by mere millimeters.

The cop went to provide guidance. But as Carson turned his head to look, he saw something far more alarming.

Greta, Mark Boston and that other man were all on top of his roof. How the hell they got there was anybody's guess, he thought, but they needed to come down, right now.

"Yes," he said to Troll, not having a clue as to what the man was blathering on about. "Will you excuse me a moment, please?" And with that, he headed toward the front door of his house.

Rounding the corner, he ran into two paramedics whose ambulance was parked with lights flashing at the far side of the driveway. Their dispatcher had ordered them to wait until the cement truck could be moved so they could recover the second man – now also determined to be dead – from beneath it. They were both smoking cigarettes and seemed surprised to see anyone.

"How ya' doin', sir?" one of them asked mindlessly.

"No smoking," Carson said.

"What?" one of them said, his brow furrowing as if for a fight.

Carson walked up to him and stood with his face less than a foot away. "There is no smoking on my property," he replied curtly.

"But we're outdoors, man..."

"You heard me."

Without waiting for an answer, he turned toward the house before adding, over his shoulder, "And don't stomp them out on the ground, either."

He was already inside the house and out of earshot when one of the men said, "What the fuck are we supposed to do with them, you prick? Eat them?"

If Carson had heard him, it is likely he would have answered in the affirmative, even standing over them to ensure compliance. He did *not* like smoking. But unauthorized smokers on his property were the least of his worries right now.

MAKEOVERS - REX JOHN

103

When Greta's feet touched the previously unseen wall of the courtyard, she realized it would be easy enough to slide down her rope the twenty or so feet down to the brick walkway beneath her, so she did. When she touched bottom, she quickly untied the rope from her waist and let it drop to the ground.

Before her were two solid doors which appeared to be steel. One of them was fitted with commercial-type door handle. Next to the other door was a "palm-plate" as her boss called it, just like the ones found at various doorways inside the big house. She knew the palm plates allowed entry exclusively to those whose palm prints matched those in an internal database.

She reached for the door with the handle attached it and turned the handle. She was surprised that she could pull it open so easily.

"Don't let it close!" cried a woman's voice from inside.

Greta stood frozen in place as her eyes tried to adjust from the bright sunlight to the dim lighting of the room before her.

"There's no way to open it if it closes on you," the voice said. Greta assumed it was the girl – the missing policewoman – she had seen in the chaise earlier. Stepping partially into the room, she was careful to stick her left foot into the doorway to keep it open a crack.

"Who are you dear?" Greta asked. "And how long have you been here?"

As Janet approached her, she said, "I'm Janet Gardner, and I've been kidnapped. I am a member of the Denver Police Department and let me tell you something lady, if you've had anything to do with any of this, you're in big trouble."

"Wha..." Greta started to say, but before the word was out of her mouth, someone pulled the door open just enough to release its weight from the edge of her foot. Surprised, she drew her foot in, and the door slammed shut.

"What the fuck!" Janet shouted just as she reached Greta's side. "Why the hell did you close it when I told you not to!" The girl was enraged.

"I didn't, dear," Greta replied coolly. "Someone else did."

104

It was bad enough creeping up that fucking roof; there was no way I was going down the other side – especially since there didn't seem to be another lightning rod cable on that side to provide a handhold.

"Let's just wait here for a minute," Troy said. "The old lady saw us, let's see if she comes back into view."

"Fine with me," I said, embracing the chimney with my arms, which wasn't exactly comfortable but helped calm the shaking in my legs.

"I think she's down there," Troy offered, sitting down at my feet.

"Who? Mrs. Martinez? Of course she is. Where else would she be?" I asked, but then I realized who he meant. "Oh," I added hastily. "You mean Janet. Well, I hope so, man, because that means she's safe and it means we've found her, and it means we can get her the hell out of here."

He nodded, but didn't respond. As we sat there, I took in the courtyard. It hadn't changed since I'd last seen it. Oh, the aspen trees were a bit taller and the flowers a bit more abundant, but other than that, it was exactly as I'd left it. It truly was a beautiful space and under different circumstances I'd love to spend time there again.

I decided to let Troy know why I was now certain we would find Janet.

"Troy," I began. "You know, until now, I wasn't sure we had found the right place. Remember, I never knew where I was. I was drugged when I was brought here and I was drugged when I left. I never saw this house from the outside."

"Yeah, but the guy knew you. He called you by name," he said.

"Oh, it's Sir all right, I know that. But I couldn't be sure until now that this is also where he was keeping me. I assumed it was, but until now I haven't recognized anything specific. But now I'm sure."

"Oh yeah? And how is that?"

I gestured toward the courtyard. "Because I spent a lot of time in that courtyard. He called it the 'playground,' and that's where I was allowed to go for fresh air when I was 'good.' Recess, he called it."

"Jesus, man," he said.

"I know," I said, acknowledging his mystification. "But now that I've seen the courtyard again, I'm sure this is where I was, in a steel-lined room directly next to it. Which also means that's where Janet is...if Sir abducted her, that is."

That's all it took. He was on his feet instantly and, grabbing the nylon rope, he gave it a firm tug. The rope was completely slack, almost causing him to lose his balance. Clearly, it was no longer attached to Greta, who had slid down it.

"C'mon," he said. "We're going down. Watch what I do, and when I get down I'll take the rope off so you can do the same thing. Got that?"

I nodded my head, not wanting to get it at all.

He pulled the rope up until he had the end in his hand. He wrapped it around his waist several times and then took up the slack, looping it over his lower arm so he could feed it out as he descended.

Looking me right in the eye as he started to back down the roof, he said, "Mark. Don't fuck this up. This is important."

I knew at that moment I was about to win my roof climbing merit badge – or die trying.

MAKEOVERS - REX JOHN

105

"Who are you, anyway?" Janet asked Greta, barely able to keep the hostility out of her voice. She believed her when she said she hadn't released the door after being told explicitly not to, but still it was shut, which meant they were both prisoners now.

"I am the housekeeper. I work for Mr. Kirkpatrick," Greta said.

The television monitor on the wall flickered to life. "Not any more you don't," spoke a voice familiar to both women.

They turned to look. Until now, the monitor had been displaying Carson's cartoon-like anime face which, while strangely familiar, didn't register as her boss in Greta's mind. But now it suddenly showed the real thing. Her boss, talking to her through a television set! Janet, who had never seen him in real life, was transfixed.

He continued. "As I've told you repeatedly, Greta, you're too nosy. You should have minded your own business. Now look what you've done. You've interfered in Miss Janet's lessons, and I dare say she's not happy about it."

Both women stood motionless, staring at the image addressing them from the screen. Janet noted that the photo of Mark, which she had observed earlier on the wall behind where Carson was now seated, had been removed.

"As a result," he continued, looking directly at Greta, "you are hereby discharged."

"I...I..." Greta said, before snapping her mouth shut. How was she to respond to this? How could she be discharged if she was locked in what appeared to be a metal-lined room? She had never seen such anger in anyone's eyes. His voice seemed strangely calm, but she could tell he was livid, and it frightened her.

"Ladies," he continued, "I will have to ask you to move away from the door. You are about to have additional company."

Even as he spoke the words, his eyes darted to the monitors before him. That friend of Mark Boston's had rappelled from the roof into the courtyard – only a foot or two from where he had pushed the door shut on Greta, and right into the middle of a large tulip bed. Carson grimaced as he watched the man trample his flowers while he untied the rope from his waist.

Once unroped, Troy coiled the rope and threw it above his head onto the roof he had just descended, signaling Mark that he was to follow. By doing so, he realized he had also effectively ruined his chances of ever climbing up and out, since the roof eave was clearly out of reach. If Mark changed his mind, he was now a prisoner in this little park.

As he considered this, he noticed the movement of a video camera under the eaves. When he moved, it moved, following his movements. *Oh no you don't, motherfucker.* He bent over and retrieved a fair-sized rock from the flower bed. Taking aim, he threw it as hard as he could, scoring a direct hit and knocking the camera free of its mount. Shards of the camera's lens tinkled onto the brick walkway. *There you go, you asshole. Consider yourself blind.*

But Carson didn't notice he'd lost that particular camera. He had already switched the image on his large monitor back to the view of the classroom.

Concurrently, rather than moving away from the door as she had been instructed, Janet took five long steps to the monitor from which Carson spoke to her. She put her face up to the monitor, as if directly in Carson's face, forgetting that the camera which transmitted her image was, in fact, a few inches above the top of the screen.

"Now you listen to me, you crazy fuck!" she shouted. "This has gone on long enough. I am ordering you to release me – us – right this minute!"

This was too much. Was this woman a schizophrenic? A psychopath? Not an hour ago she was perfectly docile. Quiet. Demure. Shy, even. *A perfect lady.* And now...well, now, she was a raving lunatic.

And, how dare she use the word 'fuck' while addressing me!

Carson reached for the red button. It was time to teach her about that word. And, while he was at it, he would teach the German bitch a thing or two about minding her own business.

106

Manuel knew enough to not try to stop his head-strong German wife when she made up her mind to do something. But that didn't stop him from keeping an eye on her.

Now she had disappeared. He tried to think of where he had seen her last. She was up on the roof, then the two strangers arrived, and she took them into the house. Then he saw them all in the side yard where the cement truck had fallen into the swimming pool. And then she disappeared.

Manuel searched through the house, something he would ordinarily never do. His access to the inside was limited to times when Mr. Kirkpatrick or Greta needed him to assist with moving furniture or other heavy lifting. But he had to find his wife, damn it, and he would – even if it meant going where he wasn't supposed to be.

He stopped outside the boss's study. He recognized the door because he had once been asked to move a huge desk from one side of the room to another. It was the only time he'd ever seen his boss do real work, as he struggled and grunted to hold up his end of the desk.

His wife had talked about so many of the doors in the house being locked all the time, so he wasn't surprised to see that the door to the study was locked.

He had already searched most of the house, except for the basement, which was also protected by an electronic lock. He stood at the door of the study and knocked lightly.

He was terrified of his boss, but more so of his wife. She was probably somewhere in the house, waiting – and not very patiently – as he knew from past experience. He had to find her; he had to know that she was safe.

He knocked again and then put his ear against the door to see if he could hear anything.

Silence.

On impulse, he put his palm on the palm pad, the way he had seen his boss do it. Nothing happened.

This is controlled electronically. What would happen if the power were cut?

Moving quickly, Manuel retraced his steps, fairly jogging into the kitchen and out to the mud room. He opened the enormous breaker box panel on the wall just inside the door and reviewed the rows and rows of breakers. Occasionally his wife would summon him to help her locate a breaker that had tripped. She never seemed to grasp that when a breaker popped – indicating a short somewhere in the line – it must be turned completely off before being re-set.

He knew, too, that the house had a back-up power supply in case of power outages. Leaving the breaker box door open, he went out the mud room door and ran across the yard to the tool shed where the back-up generator was located. He knew from watching repairmen test it that the system had large batteries which kicked in seamlessly when there was a power failure while simultaneously powering-up the gasoline generator. A loud buzzer sounded every time this happened and a signal was sent to the alarm company.

Manuel simply reached for the switch and turned the entire system from "Stand-by" to "Off."

Retracing his steps, he had run half way across the yard before he stopped, turned, and ran back to the shed. He would need a flashlight if his plan worked. He retrieved a flashlight hanging above the work bench and tested it. *Good.* He dashed across the yard again and reentered the mud room.

He began switching breakers off as fast as he could. Using both hands, he moved quickly down the two long lines, pushing each switch firmly into the "off" position. As he neared the bottom row, the light above his head extinguished. The exterior door to the mud room was still standing open, however, so there was no need for the flashlight.

He had to test his theory. The basement door, a few feet away, had been fitted with a palm pad a year ago. He noticed that the small red power light was now dark.

Good. Now, if only it will have released the lock...

He reached for the knob and turned it. The door swung open freely, as he had hoped. He stood looking down the stairs. Withdrawing the flashlight from his back pocket, he called down the stairs. "Greta...? Greta, are you down there...?"

Satisfied that she was not in the now darkened basement, he wondered where else could she be. He closed the door quietly and walked quickly toward the front hall.

107

I will admit that I am a wuss when it comes to heights. Standing next to the chimney, hugging it, I wondered what the hell I had gotten myself into. I willed myself to bend over and start reeling in the nylon rope Troy had flung over the eave and back onto the roof. I wanted to do it, but I couldn't.

I was experiencing a panic attack – not an atypical reaction for those who are afflicted with a fear of heights – acrophobia by its proper name. I couldn't move. I couldn't bend over. I couldn't even move my foot – forwards, backwards or sideways. All I could do was hug the chimney. I tightened my grip.

In stressful situations, I suppose everybody resorts to some form of "self-talk." *You can do it, man. Go get 'em! C'mon, get your shit together! Don't be such a pussy!*

I talked, all right – not silently, not quietly, but aloud. Very loud. I was practically shouting to myself: *C'mon you asshole! You can do this! And you can't stand up here when your friend may need you down there! Now! You've got to move! Now!*

I remained frozen. For all I know, I might be there to this day if it hadn't been for the guy who was operating the crane. He had been trying, futilely, to pull the upside down concrete truck out of the pool. Clearly, the weight of the truck was too much for the crane, and now several men stood around on the ground having an animated conversation – probably debating what they should do next.

Even as I tried to calm myself by distraction – watching the scene unfold before me beside the crane – my panic increased. What if nobody noticed me up here? What if I had to stay up here all night? It was almost dusk; this couldn't go on forever. Or could it? Just as I considered screaming like a little girl, the crane operator, who had been sitting in the cab of the crane awaiting further instruction, grew disgusted and bored. Looking around, he spotted me and shouted – "Hey! You all right?"

Obviously he'd seen the look of panic in my face. I was too panicked to respond. I just shook my head vigorously from side to side.

"Stay right there! I'll get some help," he shouted.

Yeah, right. OK, I'll stay right here. Maybe forever.

I saw him yelling at a group of men on the ground who turned and looked up at where I was perched. One of them shook his head disgustedly, as if to say, "Jesus. What next?"

I couldn't imagine what they were plotting, but after seeing them gesture back and forth I decided it couldn't be good.

108

When the lights and the TV monitor in the classroom went out, it was pitch black and dead silent. Finally, Janet spoke.

"Are you still there?" she whispered.

"Ja," Greta responded, also whispering, "Vhat happened?"

"I'm not sure. I guess the power went out. Are you frightened?"

"*Nein*. The nice young men will rescue us."

"Oh, and what nice young men are those?" Janet asked.

"Mister Mark Brown and his friend," Greta said.

"Mark Brown? Who is Mark Brown and why would he rescue us?" Janet asked.

"You know, dat author Mark Brown."

"What!" Janet exclaimed. "Do you mean Mark *Boston?*"

"Ja, ja. Boston. Mark Boston. Da author."

"Really! Mark is here? And do you know the name of the other man?"

"I can't remember. Troy, I think. Ja. They're on the roof."

Considering this, Janet was subdued when she replied. "I don't think so. Troy may be on the roof, but Mark certainly is not. He's terrified of heights."

Greta didn't like being doubted. She wasn't accustomed to people not believing her. She never lied. Never. Why would she lie now?

"Ja. He is," was all she said.

At that moment the door from the courtyard burst open to silhouette Troy, standing in the sunlight. Janet would later describe his stance in the doorway as "looking like Rambo."

"Troy!" Janet said, running into his arms.

He reacted slowly at first, as he tried to understand why Janet had been in a black void. Mark had said the classroom was steel lined, but he didn't say anything about its being pitch dark. A reflection bouncing off the stainless steel floor from the sunlight streaming in behind him caught his eye, and he recalled what Mark had told him about the "correction" he had received by electric shock.

"C'mon. We need to get out of here." Noticing Greta just over Janet's shoulder, he said, "You too, ma'am. Let's go." Both women moved toward the open door which led into the courtyard.

Holding hands, Troy and Janet exited first, but as the housekeeper was about to step into the courtyard, the lights in the classroom snapped back on, and she received a jolt of electricity that propelled her into the air and out the door. She landed with a thud at Janet's feet. The door slammed shut behind her.

"Oh my God!" Janet said. "What happened?"

But Greta didn't respond.

109

Just as he reached out to push the red button and deliver the biggest jolt of electricity he'd ever administered, hoping to teach Janet and Greta a lesson they would never forget, the console went dark, along with all the lights and monitors in the control room. His hand, already in motion, found its target and he felt himself push the button, almost as an involuntary reaction to suddenly being plunged into darkness. He withdrew his hand and waited for the emergency generator to kick in. *It's just as well. That much electricity could have killed them both. Bitches.*

He continued to wait, in the dark, staring at the monitor, which was also dark, willing it to come back on. He couldn't see the women and he couldn't communicate with them. They had to be terrified, as he knew there wasn't a bit of light anywhere in the classroom. *Too bad. Let 'em suffer.*

Why wasn't the back-up power supply working? He and Manuel had tested it not two weeks ago, as part of his ongoing preventive maintenance program.

It's got to be Manuel! He's the only person who knows about the back-up generator...and the only person who knows how to turn it off. Could he have...?

But, even as he was trying to reconstruct what had happened – and how – the lights came back on, and the control panel flickered back to life. Carson sat, just as he had been, staring at the large monitor before him. But, unbelievably, the women who had just filled his screen moments before were nowhere to be seen. They weren't dead; they weren't even there! The classroom was empty. That could only mean...

He quickly pushed the button to switch the monitor to the courtyard camera, but the image didn't appear. Instead, he got only a blank blue screen.

He pushed the button again and again before deciding to run through the other camera feeds. Was the entire system out? No, because he could still see the classroom when he pushed button #1.

As he pushed button after button, images from various vantage points around his property popped into view. The front gate was still open. The camera showing the side yard revealed that the cement truck was still upside down. The front porch was empty. The camera on the opposite side of his property showed that the paramedics were still standing right where he had left them – *and they were still smoking*. The staff parking lot still contained three vehicles: Greta's, with the passenger door wide open; Manuel's; and another car which he assumed belonged to Mark Boston or his friend.

When he pushed button #7, he could see that the door to the outbuilding in which the emergency generator was located was standing wide open, confirming his suspicions that someone had deliberately disabled it. But then what? The power had been off only a minute or two – and then it came back on. Why? If someone had turned it off deliberately, why wouldn't they have left it off?

Whoever had done this was probably still inside the power building and needed to be stopped. He couldn't afford any more power failures, since he knew that failure of both the primary and back-up systems at the same time would cause the security system to malfunction.

It had to be Manuel; he was the only person who knew where to look or what to do. *Damn Mexican!*

Rising from the console, he turned toward the door to his study to exit into the main part of the house. There, in the doorway, was the last person he ever expected to see in his study, much less the control room.

"Manuel!" he sputtered. "You startled me."

"Where is my wife?"

Recovering his composure, he felt his anger rise. "What are you doing in here? Who gave you permission to be in this house? Get out!"

"Where is my wife?"

"She is in the other room...through that door over there."

Edging warily around his boss, the handyman moved toward the door Carson had indicated. Once he stepped quickly inside the now empty classroom, the door closed behind him with a satisfying "click" that told Carson he wouldn't need to worry about him for awhile. Pushing button #1 on the console again, he confirmed that Manuel was inside, but...now Greta was back!

What the...!

Carson stared at the monitor, dumbfounded, and wondered if he was hallucinating. One minute Janet and Greta were in the classroom with Janet's friend, and a second later they were gone. Now Greta was back, and weeping uncontrollably in the arms of her husband. Well, the only way these two would get out would be if someone opened the door from the courtyard – again – allowing them an opportunity to leave. That must not happen.

Now he had to find Janet and her friend, who were apparently in the courtyard. He feared his attempt to shock some sense into Janet might have been too late. He angrily pushed the camera button #2 again and again, but the monitor continued to show nothing but blue screen. He hated to open the door into the courtyard without knowing what was on the other side.

No telling what they were up to.

110

I could scarcely believe my eyes. The crane operator, who had gestured at me to "stay right there" – an unnecessary directive, as far as I was concerned – had disappeared. It was beginning to get dark. Were they going to leave me up here all night?

The other men who had been gathered on the ground seemed to have scattered, but even those who were still down in the yard seemed oblivious to the fact that a grown man was standing on the roof, embracing the chimney. It seemed as though hours had gone by, but I suppose it was less than ten minutes. One's sense of time gets corrupted during a panic attack.

Then, without warning, the crane operator was back, climbing into his cab. After he yelled something to a couple of guys on the ground, they climbed up onto the overturned cement truck and, after the operator gave some slack in the cable, disengaged an enormous hook at the end. The hook then began ascending back into the top of the boom, even as the boom began moving toward me.

Oh, no he's not! He is not going to expect me to crawl out onto this steel ladder coming my way! I...am...not...letting...go...of...this...chimney!

Just as quickly as the boom had started toward me, it abruptly stopped – as though it had changed its mind. I saw the crane operator shout something to one of the men standing on the ground who then climbed up into the cab, trading places with the previous operator.

The original crane operator made a large circling motion with his hand, and the big hook began to descend to the ground.

I watched, transfixed, as the guy on the ground grabbed the cable and hook and wrapped them around his chest under his armpits. With some effort, he managed to clasp the hook to the cable itself, forming a sort of loop in which he now stood. To my horror, he nodded at the man who had taken his place in the cab, and the cable, the hook and the man began to rise into the air.

He isn't coming up here, is he? Is he nuts?

As soon as he was hovering at about the same height I was standing, the big boom slowly began its trajectory toward me and the chimney. I could now see the guy's face, and he was grinning from ear to ear, like he was on a carnival ride. I realized I'd been holding my breath – *What if he falls? What if he slips?* – and finally took a big gulp of air, just as his feet touched down on the steep surface of the roof about five feet from where I was immobilized.

"I don't suppose you'd take my hand, would you?" he said to me. He was middle-aged, maybe late 50's, trim, clean shaven, with salt-n-pepper hair a bit long over the ears. He had a kindly face, the kind you want to respond favorably to.

"No fuckin' way," I said.

I grimaced. Apparently that word was back in my vocabulary. Sir would not be pleased.

"Fine, then," he said calmly, as though he were talking to a potential jumper on the Golden Gate Bridge. "I'll just stay here and keep you company." With that, he slipped out of his self-made harness and sat down on the slate shingles. The cable he had just released remained suspended right where he'd left it. Using his hands to propel himself, he quickly scooted on his butt over to the chimney and, after securing his footing, pulled himself upright until his face was a just inches from mine.

"How ya' doin'?" he asked, a big smile on his face.

I was close to tears. But, simultaneously, my fear seemed to be subsiding. I didn't loosen my grip on the chimney, but I felt my muscles began to relax somewhat.

"Where did you go?" I managed.

"Whadaya mean?"

"You disappeared down there," I said, pointing with my head toward the ground. "Where did you go?"

"Oh, I went into the house to see if the owner was there and to see if he had any tall ladders we could use to come get you. All the doors to the house were wide open, but nobody seemed to be inside. I noticed that the electrical breaker box was wide open with all the switches cut off, so I turned 'em on so I could see what was going on. Then," he added, "I looked around the kitchen and living room and yelled for help, but since nobody came, I went back out to the crane and decided to come get you myself. I couldn't have been gone for more than three minutes."

"You turned the electricity back on?" was all I managed to say.

111

"Mark!"

It was Janet's voice, coming from below. I cautiously peeked around the corner of the chimney and saw her and Troy standing against the far wall of the courtyard, presumably so they could see above the roof line. Janet had no sooner finished shouting my name than Troy started shouting it as well. I could hear panic in their voices. "Mark! Mark! Mark!" I absentmindedly wondered what had become of Greta. She had lowered herself down first; where did she go?

The crane operator couldn't see around me, but he heard the commotion and could see where I was looking.

"What's going on?" he asked.

"My friends are down there. They're in trouble."

Just saying those words seemed to trigger something in me. As quickly as the acrophobia had hit me twenty minutes ago, now it was gone. The sense of panic which had anchored me to that spot now dissipated and returned my wits and motor abilities to my own control.

"We need to help them," I said.

The crane guy clearly wasn't expecting such a quick mental turnaround in the nut job he'd come to rescue. One moment I had been frozen in place, barely able to whisper; next I was proposing that we rescue somebody else. He looked skeptical and maybe just a little bit miffed.

I didn't care. I needed to help my friends. I could hear the fear in Janet's voice when she shouted my name, and it was just the jolt I needed to recover. I peeked around the chimney again, this time allowing myself to edge toward the downward side. My right foot slipped a few inches and I tensed up, but I continued on. I spotted the coiled yellow rope at the edge of the roof and followed it with my eyes up to where it was tied around the chimney. I glanced down at my feet and saw the knot Troy had quickly tied before rappelling down the roof and over the edge. Reaching down, I grabbed the rope and began quickly reeling it in, toward us. I sensed that my rescuer was watching me closely. Glancing across the yard at the crane, I could see that the new operator was taking in the scene as well.

"Listen," I said, as I continued to pull in the rope, "do you suppose you could get your colleague to swing that cable into the courtyard there?"

"Maybe, but why would I want to do that?"

I stopped and looked directly at him. "Because those people down there are trapped and they're in serious danger."

Just saying those words aloud seemed to open my eyes to what was really going on. For the first time in the five years since I had been released, I realized I'd been enamored with my kidnapper as though he'd been my savior, but now I realized he was a dangerous psychopath.

True, he had saved me from a life of alcohol and drugs. True, he had given me new vision and confidence. But at what price? He tortured me, for chrissakes. When I didn't perform the way he wanted me to, he shocked the shit out of me, or doused me in ice water, or starved me. Those are not "teaching" methods. I didn't sign up for that kind of abuse. Hell, I didn't sign up for anything. I was just sleeping on a park bench, minding my own business, when this sick fucker kidnapped me and tried to make me over into his own image.

These new thoughts enraged and emboldened me. Here I'd been worshipping "Sir" when I should have been trying to stop him – stop him from doing to others what he'd done to me. Maybe if I'd reported what he did to me earlier, he would have been apprehended by now. Maybe Janet wouldn't have ended up being one of his victims.

I had to face the facts. Not only was he a sadistic kidnapper; for all I knew, he could be a murderer. He must be stopped.

The guy who had come to rescue me now looked like he wanted to run from me. "What's wrong with you, buddy? You look like your head is about to fly off."

"Nothing. I'm fine. Sorry. But I need you to help me get those people over that wall down there, quickly. Trust me: they really are in serious danger." I realized I didn't even know this guy's name. "By the way, I'm Mark, I said, nodding my head in his direction, but I didn't offer my hand. What's your name?"

"Brett."

"Brett. OK, Brett. First, thanks a lot for coming up here. Now, will you help me help those two down there? I'm going to lower myself to the edge of the roof so I can provide some direction while maintaining eye-contact with the guy in the cab." At this point I noticed the crane was moving erratically all over the place, barely missing one of the chimneys. Clearly, this guy wasn't a fully trained operator. Brett obviously needed to return to his post. "Do you think that will work, Brett?" Not waiting for an answer, I continued: "In fact, why don't you have your guy in the crane take you back over the wall so you can take back the controls. Then, if you can swing the hook back over here, we can airlift them out of here one at a time."

"I suppose I can do that," he said, straining to look around me into the courtyard below. "But why don't we just go through the house? There must be an entrance to that courtyard."

"Oh, there is," I said. "But inside the house is where the danger is."

He didn't respond, but I could see that he still thought I was nuts.

I had the other end of the rope in my hand now, and quickly wrapped it around my waist a couple of times before tying as secure a knot as I knew how to tie. Brett, meanwhile, had begun signaling the operator in the cab to once again extend the boom back to pick him up. The sense of urgency I now felt made me want to get down to the edge of the roof as fast as possible so I could see what was going on in the courtyard. Bracing myself and taking up all the slack in the rope, which was still tied around the chimney, I started my descent down the steep slope.

As I fed the rope out while quickly stepping backwards, I briefly reflected on the fact that only moments earlier I had been anchored -- for life, I thought -- to that chimney, and now I was walking around the roof like a mountain goat. Sir was right: it is amazing what a guy can do when he makes up his mind to do it.

112

Troy's perfectly thrown rock did just what he intended: it tore the under-eave camera from its mount, so it was no longer transmitting a picture to the control room. It was, however, transmitting sound, and Carson listened attentively as two voices – Janet and her friend Troy – shouted, repeatedly, "Mark! Mark!" That could only mean the author was within their line of vision, presumably on the roof. Was he about to descend into the courtyard? *Good. That's just where I want everybody.* His mind was whirring. *Maybe I can salvage this unfortunate situation yet. It shouldn't be too difficult to convince the authorities that the two rescuers had left the premises. Or, perhaps he would tell them they were so distressed they decided to stay in his guest rooms and preferred not to be disturbed. Then, during the night I will dispose of them and their vehicle.*

As he continued to watch Greta and Manuel on monitor #1, he marveled at the fact that she had all but escaped – at least to the courtyard – and then voluntarily re-incarcerated herself. *She really is crazy.*

Obviously he hadn't shocked her as the lights went out, but no matter: there would be plenty of time for that – and her husband could come along for the ride.

He could always take care of her – and Manuel – later. *Better be careful, though. You don't want to fill the pool with bodies; there won't be any room for water.*

Why hadn't he installed a locking mechanism on both sides of that damn door into the courtyard? *Who knew that people would be dropping out of the sky!*

More shouting. In addition to the two voices he'd heard a moment ago, he could now hear Mark's voice, as clear and recognizable as it had been during his three months as a student in the School of Life.

But now there was a fourth voice. *Jesus. How many people are out there? My poor tulips.* A man seemed to be yelling "wrap it around your face!" *What are they doing? Do they have masks? Are they getting ready to make an assault on the control room?* That they wouldn't be able to do, he was sure of that. All the doors – except the one into the classroom – were well-fortified and could be opened only with a recognizable palm print.

"Wrap it around your face!" the fifth voice shouted again.

Wrap what around your face? Or, is he even saying face? Face? Or was it waist? Waist! That's it! Wrap it around your waist! They must be using a rope to get over the wall.

Carson reached for the power switch controlling voltage to the uninsulated wire atop the exterior wall of the courtyard. *Well, this ought to slow you down.*

113

Once I "manned-up," as Troy called it, I made good use of my perch at the lower edge of the eave to supervise the airlift of Janet and Troy up and out of the enclosed courtyard. Seeing Janet dangling from the end of that cable was worth the price of admission. It reminded me of those pictures you sometimes see on the news of helicopter rescues of people stranded on their roofs after a particularly devastating flood, or cows being airlifted from frozen fields following a big blizzard – but I doubted she would appreciate that particular analogy.

Before Troy was about to go over the wall, I shouted down to ask where Greta was. "I'm not sure," Troy shouted back. "She came flying out the door, but a couple of seconds later she crawled back in. But, we better get some help before we go through the house to find her." I nodded, since I knew the courtyard had only one point of access – through the classroom – and I certainly didn't advocate going in there unless you planned to stay for a long time.

I was worried that Sir would burst out into the courtyard at any time and...well, I'm not sure what. I can't imagine him as a killer, but at least now I know he's crazy.

But what could he do to us? There wasn't any electricity outside, as far as I knew, and he certainly couldn't drench us with hot or cold water, so...?

I finally stopped worrying about it as I ordered Troy to secure the steel cable around his waist. I was about to signal the crane operator to pull him up when I heard a small pop and saw a spark at the far end of the courtyard wall, where it looked like a wire came out of the house. I followed the path of the wire visually, from my position directly across the courtyard, and could see now that it was an electric wire which appeared to be bare copper. The wire came out of an outlet on the house wall and snaked along the top surface of the wall. It had to be Sir's way of preventing his students from escaping the so-called playground, and I shuddered as I considered the implications. I never thought about escaping when I was at recess out there, but who knows about some of the others. What if Janet had tried to escape? Judging from the kick-ass, mind-altering jolts I received just for saying the wrong thing, who knew what voltage level the escape wire carried?

Just as I was processing this thought, I noticed that Troy was waiting to be lifted into the air. He looked at me expectantly. I glanced at the crane operator, who was also looking at me as though wondering what the hell was taking so long. I held the guy's eyes as I shouted, "Hey Troy! Make *sure* your feet don't touch the electric wire on top of the wall when you clear it!"

The crane operator couldn't hear me of course, so I had to communicate with him using hand signals. With Janet, I had simply circled my thumb and forefinger when she was ready to be lifted, and the guy pulled her up into the air and over the wall. Now that the fence had come to life, as it were, I didn't want to take any chances. I flattened out my hand and turned it upward and, still holding the operator's eyes, began an upward motion to indicate that he should raise Troy up into the air. I must have looked like an orchestra conductor telling the string session he wanted more volume. But it worked. Troy went up, up, way up, clearing the wall by at least twenty feet before I gave the circle "OK," so the crane operator knew he could swing him sideways and lower him to the ground.

I was still on the roof, and the only one left on the wrong side of that exterior wall, other than Greta and she was apparently back in the house. I could see that Brett had now re-entered the crane cab and was once again back at the controls. He began swinging the big boom toward me. It was, at the same time, telescoping out, extending its long arm across the courtyard to the edge of the roof where I was sitting. All I needed to do was grab it, wrap the cable around my waist as I'd instructed the others to do, and in less than two minutes I would be free, rejoining my friends on the other side of the wall.

So, why didn't I grab it?

114

"Hey, Troy! Make *sure* your feet don't touch the electric wire on top of the wall when you clear it!" As soon as Carson heard those shouted instructions, he knew he had been right. They *were* escaping over the wall, and it could only be with the assistance of that big crane. The stakes had just gotten higher. As long as Mark and his friends were his hostages, he had leverage to negotiate his own surrender – or, if he played his cards right, his escape. But if they all escaped, he would have no cards to play.

He wasn't ready to give up. At least not yet. There were still too many people out there who needed his help: homeless people who had given up hope. Drug addicts, alcoholics, and all the other losers who needed direction – firm guidance which he alone seemed prepared to provide. He'd been too successful and seen too many of his students turn their lives around. It had happened time and again. He couldn't stop now!

Look at Mark Boston. He may be his nemesis now, but it wasn't always the case. Mark didn't even want to leave the school, and for good reason. The kid had been totally washed up – at only twenty years old, for heaven's sake! He was an alcoholic and a drug addict. There was no way he would have made it to his 21st birthday if Carson hadn't rescued him.

Yes, look at him....

While he'd been self-talking, Carson had moved into his study and slowly drew open the top center drawer. There, at the back, behind notepads, pens, pencils and paper clips he found what he wanted.

Checking the chamber to see that the Browning Hi-Power was loaded, he raised it to his own head.

He held it there for a moment, thinking.

And then...*No. I'm not giving up yet. This is not over.*

Slowly, he lowered it and stood up. Carrying it in front of him, he re-entered the control room. Placing the gun in his left hand, he flattened his right palm against the palm pad and heard the immediate click releasing the door into the courtyard. He returned the gun to his right hand and pushed the door open, not knowing what he would find.

115

Janet and Troy stood, embracing, as they waited for Mark to join them from the other side of the wall. The crane operator had moved the boom into place and seemed poised waiting for the signal to lift him over.

Troy could tell by the look on the crane operator's face that something was wrong. From his perch in the cab, he was the only one who could see what was happening on the roof, because the high exterior wall of the courtyard effectively blocked the line of sight.

Troy did a quick assessment of the situation. He could run to the far side of the yard, beyond the unfinished swimming pool, where he would probably have a better sight line to see what was going on. Or he could go into the house and try to break through doors, but Mark had told him the place was like a fortress. No, it would be far quicker to just run over to the crane and climb up to the cab so he could see whatever the crane operator was watching so intently.

"Be right back," he said, dropping his arm from around Janet's shoulders. He took off at a run.

116

When I heard the door open below me, I knew it would be Sir, coming to find me, but I no longer wanted to see him. In little over an hour I had gone from seeing him as my savior, worthy of my undying gratitude, to seeing him for what he was: a sadistic, controlling megalomaniac.

I watched him enter the courtyard from my vantage point on his own rooftop. Seeing him from above made him look smaller and more vulnerable than he did earlier, standing in the side yard next to the construction site. But he was carrying a gun, which seemed oddly out of character with the Sir I had known, and I had to wonder what he would do when he finally saw me.

It didn't take long.

Almost as quickly as he cleared the doorway he turned and looked up right at me.

"I think you'd better come down, Mark. We need to talk." He lowered the gun to his side, although I could see his finger was still on the trigger.

I nodded, even though I knew it was foolish on my part to descend from the roof, which was my only means of quick escape. If I used the yellow rope to pull myself up the slope of the roof, there was a chance that I could reach the chimney and hide behind it before he would be able to aim and fire. Once I got to the peak of the roof I could easily use the lightning rod cable to scramble down the other side before he would be able to get through the house and out the door. Maybe by that time my friends would be able to help me.

Even though he had lowered his weapon, I made a show of raising my hands like I was surrendering to someone. The crane operator was still expecting me to attach myself to the steel cable that dangled only a few feet in front of me, and I wondered what he would make of seeing my arms in the air, like a teller in a bank robbery. Would he say something to the others? Would they come to my rescue?

It worked. As I sat there with my hands in the air, the operator's eyes widened. He motioned to Troy who, within seconds, clambered up into the cab.

"That won't be necessary, Mark. I'm not going to hurt you," Sir said. Then, almost as an afterthought, he added, "I need your help."

You need help all right. But it's not the kind of help I can give you.

I nodded and slowly lowered my hands. Then, surprised at my own agility, I stood and, tightening the slack in the rope, did a tight pirouette and jumped off the roof. My feet swung under the eave and made contact with the wall below. From there, I gradually eased the rope through my hands as I walked backward down the wall.

When my feet touched the brick walkway below me, I untied the rope from around my waist and dropped it to the ground. Looking up, I could see that the boom of the crane was slowly retracting. I turned to face Sir and saw that he was once again aiming his gun directly at me.

Uh oh.

117

Deputy Gary Briggs couldn't get the cop from Denver out of his mind. What must it be like to have your girlfriend disappear off the face of the earth without a trace? He'd thought of little else since he first read about the mystery, and he couldn't believe he'd actually gotten to meet the guy right here in Summit County.

After he watched the Denver cop and his friend re-enter the traffic on 285 – right behind a cement truck – he radioed his buddy Art, who was stationed five miles ahead. It was a gambit they had perfected – positioning their cars about five miles apart to make sure nobody got through their low-tech speed trap. Usually, Art simply caught the lead-footed drivers Gary had missed, but once in awhile he would get to issue a second speeding citation to a driver who had just gotten one five minutes earlier. It was mind-boggling how many people speeded up once the cop they'd just seen was no longer visible in their rear view mirror. It wasn't unusual for the two men to grab a beer after their shifts ended and compare notes on how many doubles they'd nailed that day.

Gary was in the process of bringing Art up to speed on the day's events when the latter interrupted to say, "I got a visual, Gare. Here they come now. They haven't slowed down much, that's for sure."

"Who could blame him?" Briggs responded. "Give him a pass, why don't ya." Then, realizing he might be able to provide some assistance after all, he added, "But, uh, you might want to keep an eye out for that cement truck in front of him. Seems to be slowing him down unnecessarily. 'Spose he has an expired registration...or something?"

Art got the message. He knew he was to get the cement truck out of the way.

"Got it. Will do." With that, he switched on the light bar on top of the cruiser and peeled out. Even as Troy's Camaro started to pull over, Art passed him, giving the Denver cop a half-salute as he sped by. Troy returned the salute and watched as he signaled the cement truck over onto the shoulder about half a mile ahead, pulling in close behind him. Troy smiled. The locals were clearing the way for him.

Less than an hour later, the two deputies met at the Dew Drop Inn – a frequent occurrence when their shifts ended. Art could see that his pal was upset.

"Poor bastard," Art said, after Gary brought him up to speed. "I feel for him. I really do."

Downing the last of his beer, Gary said, "Me, too. In fact, I think I'm gonna head down the road a bit and see where he ended up." Then, seeing the startled look on his pal's face, he said, "Don't worry; I'll take my own vehicle. Chances are I won't even spot him. But, if I do, I'll see if I can lend him a hand."

118

"Let's go to my study, Mark," Sir said, tipping his head back to indicate the courtyard door. "I don't think you've ever seen my study."

I didn't budge. Instead, I looked him right in the eye and said, "Should I have my hands up? Are you going to kill me? Because if you are, why don't you just do it out here. But don't forget, Sir, you've already kidnapped one cop, and she and her boyfriend cop aren't going to just drive back to Denver."

"Kidnapped one cop? I've never kidnapped a cop," he said.

"Sure you have. Janet's a cop, and you can bet she's plenty pissed to have been enrolled in your little school against her wishes. Think about it," I added, driving home the point, "I'll bet you know cops take a dim view of anyone who places one of their own in harm's way."

"Do tell," he said, in that posh way of speaking I used to admire. "There's only one thing wrong with that, Mark. I didn't know she was a law enforcement officer; I thought she was a homeless person who was down on her luck or on drugs or something. In fact, she told me she had run away and had been forced into a life of prostitution." Jerking the gun slightly to indicate that I should move ahead, he smiled weakly and said,

"Nevertheless, I'd like you to come with me to my study. And, no, I have no intention of killing you – remember, I have quite an investment in you."

At this point, I figured I didn't have a choice. I went through the door into a small hallway and through another open door into an elaborate control room of some sort – full of illuminated buttons and switches positioned beneath one large television monitor showing an image, and several others which seemed to be switched off.

As I walked by, I looked at the monitor and saw the housekeeper and her husband, both of them sitting on the edge of the steel bed and looking terrified.

"New students, Sir?"

"Not exactly," he said. "I'm afraid Greta and Manuel are having, shall we say, a time out. They disobeyed my instructions, and now they must face the consequences."

"See, that's what I mean, Sir," I said as I took a seat on a small sofa against the wall of his study. I continued to talk as I looked around, taking in the display of luxury all around me. "You're not really helping people if they don't want to be helped. You're...you're..."

"I'm *what*, Mark?" he said impatiently.

"You're forcing them to change against their will," I said quietly. I knew it was a weak accusation, and I sounded meek to boot, which I didn't like. Trying to sound a bit more sure of myself, I added, "You can't force people to change; they'll just go back to the way they were before you tried to make them over."

"Oh? And has that been your experience?"

"Well, no, but I'd be surprised if I'm not the exception."

He laughed derisively. "Oh, really? What an ego you have, Mark. And what, may I ask, makes you so special?"

I was glad I was saved from having to answer because, quite honestly, I don't know what I would have said.

What makes me so special? *Now there's a question.*

119

Art decided at the last minute that his buddy shouldn't have to go looking for the Denver cop on his own. Climbing into Briggs's pickup, the two men threw their duffle bags into the truck bed behind them.

Forty-five minutes earlier they'd both turned in their day books at the Sheriff's office before continuing on to the locker room to change out of their uniforms. Each man double-checked the safety on his weapon before stowing it in its holster, and then into their respective duffle bags. They left the building carrying department-issued radios, which they were permitted to take home.

"Dew Drop," Gary said as he headed out the door.

"Right. Three minutes," Art responded.

Now, accurate as always, both men pulled into spaces next to each other at the Dew Drop Inn exactly three minutes later.

As they pulled out of the parking lot and onto Highway 285, Art said "Think my car will be all right?"

"Sure," Gary said. "What the hell could happen to it? Besides, we probably won't be that long."

120

"Do you know," Carson said, "that my system is the only social experiment of its type that has achieved useful results in the past two hundred years?" We were seated in his study, me on a small, overstuffed sofa with a magnificent view of the side yard – now lighted dramatically by a combination of strategically placed landscape lighting and huge light poles aimed at the overturned cement truck in the unfinished pool. Even though the sky was now black, I knew Mt. Princeton loomed in the background. Gazing past my own reflection in the window of the study, I was able to imagine what Sir meant when he told me one morning that "Princeton looks particularly beautiful today." I almost smiled at the memory – and the fact that the private investigator I'd hired – Kinsey – had traveled to every village and burg with the name Princeton, including the New Jersey school itself. I made a mental note that I should call her as soon as I had the chance to tell her I no longer need her services. She wouldn't be bothered, I knew that. She's the busiest P.I. in the country as far as I can tell.

Sir was still talking, but he seemed bothered by the fact that I was staring out the window and picked up a small remote control on his desk, aimed it at the window and watched as the heavy drapes moved into the closed position. He'd put the gun down on top of his desk, a beautiful antique that must have set him back a few bucks. The barrel was now aimed away from me, so under the circumstances I was as relaxed as anyone could be. At one point he paused and reached for the phone before he caught himself. He smiled wryly and said, "Oh, I forgot. I guess we can't ask Greta to bring us some tea."

Greta! That's her name! In the brief time we'd been seated I'd already forgotten the housekeeper's name, mixing her up in my mind with her sister, Mrs. Rosencranz. The resemblance was jarring. Now if I could just remember that her name was Greta, I wouldn't have to keep referring to her as "the housekeeper," or, "Mrs. Rosencranz' sister."

But now Greta and her husband were trapped in the classroom, and I knew I had to get them out before Sir shocked the shit out of them – if he hadn't already. I'd seen the whole place crawling with people, including the cops and emergency personnel attending to the accident, so how did he possibly think he could get by with kidnapping two more people?

As I tried to imagine how this would end, I sat listening to him as though he made sense, which he certainly did not.

"As I was saying, Mark, most social programs make it easy for the participants to drop out – and many do. By holding our students here – temporarily, of course – even if it is against their will, we have a chance to do the intense work required to quickly rid them of their addictions and teach them how to cope with the temptations the world has to offer."

"That may be true, Sir, but I doubt that your housekeeper and her husband have any addictions that need your attention. How do you justify holding them?" I was stalling, but he didn't seem to notice. All I could think about now was getting those two out of the classroom – and Sir into custody. I knew Troy and Janet would have called in by now, so every law enforcement agency in the state would soon descend on this place. I was no longer scared – unless Sir decided to do something with that gun.

121

Summit County Deputy Sheriff's deputies Art Tomlinson and Gary Briggs were about thirty minutes out of Salida, well out of their own jurisdiction, when they became aware that something big was going on. Both their portable radios crackled to life at the same time, advising them that any and all officers in the vicinity of U.S. 285 and U.S. Highway 50 should report to the estate of a Mr. Carson Kirkpatrick, followed by the GPS coordinates. Both men looked at each other, puzzled. "Isn't that the guy who is supposed to be one of the richest men in the world?" Gary asked.

"That's what I heard," Art responded. "Did you know he lived up here?"

"No, actually...but there's a lot I don't know."

"I'll say!"

Gary Briggs smiled at that because he knew that was a dig and a reference to his buddy's coming out story a year earlier.

Less than twenty minutes later, the pickup pulled up to the imposing wall of the Kirkpatrick estate. The double gates were already open, and several vehicles were parked up and down the lane leading to the driveway. The two deputies drove past the entrance and parked on the side of the road in the first space they found. As soon as Gary killed the ignition, they retrieved their weapons from their duffle bags, and each man stuck his inside the back waistband of his jeans. Grabbing their radios, they moved toward the open gates where a uniformed officer from nearby Salida had been posted to keep out passers-by.

"Sorry, gentlemen, we're in a lock-down here," the cop said.

They flashed their Summit County badges. "We just came to help out," Gary said.

"Gotcha," the cop said, eyeing their badges with a nod. Stepping aside, he said, "C'mon in guys. Make yourselves at home. My boss is the guy down there shooting off his mouth," he said, pointing. "Why don't you see what he's organizing."

The two joined the Chief of the Salida Police Department, who was standing near the back of the big crane, and had been joined by a half-dozen officers from nearby jurisdictions. Art and Gary stood at the back of the group and listened to the little speech the Chief was making.

"The thing we gotta remember, fellas, is that we don't know a lot about this guy, except what we've all read in the papers – that's he's rich and a recluse, and all that other bullshit. What we don't know is, if he's armed – and we don't know if he plans to put up a fight. We've had no communication with him whatsoever, but two of his former hostages have indicated that he is unstable. One of them, as you know, is Detective Janet Gardner who, along with one of her fellow officers, managed to escape." Gesturing, he said, "The two of them are standing over there."

Continuing, he said, "It also appears that he is holding at least one other hostage, his housekeeper." Pausing for effect, he added, "And there may be more."

"Now, as most of you know we don't have a regulation SWAT team up here, but a few of you have had basic training in SWAT operations so, based on the intelligence we've received, we are going to see if we can handle this right now on our own. The boys from Denver are also on their way up here and should be here within the hour, so if we get any indication that we should delay our efforts until they arrive, we will do so."

Briggs spoke up: "Summit County Deputy Gary Briggs, here Captain. My fellow deputy Art Tomlinson and I are here to see if we can be of some help."

"Thank you and welcome, gentlemen..." the captain responded.

"Thanks, Captain. We arrived a few minutes ago, so we may have missed something. May we ask what kind of operation you're planning, sir?"

"Well, Briggs, that's what we're trying to figure out. We already have access to the residence, but apparently there are several quadrants inside that have restricted access due to a high-tech security system involving biometric palm readers. To the best of our knowledge, there is only one exterior window accessing those secure parts of the house, which we understand to be in Kirkpatrick's personal study. I've just sent one of my officers to see if he can get a visual through that window."

As if on cue, an officer rounded the corner at a jog, running over to his boss. He lowered his voice and addressed the chief confidentially. When he finished, the chief turned to the small group assembled before him to announce that "The suspect has been spotted through the window and appears to be conversing with the hostage. A firearm has been spotted on the desk."

"Sorry, Chief," Gary said. "You just said 'the hostage,' but I thought you said a moment ago that there could be others."

"That is correct. Thank you, Briggs. Initially, we only knew for certain that there was one hostage – who was himself held here against his will at one time but who somehow managed to escape. We've been told it is a book author by the name of Mark Boston. He's quite famous."

His final comment made him sound like a starstruck fan and didn't pass unnoticed. A few members of the group sniggered, and the Chief allowed himself a small smile, as though he understood the absurdity of what he had just said. Pressing on, he added, "But now the housekeeper and her husband have gone missing, so until we know for sure where they are, we must assume that they also may be inside."

His little speech finished, the Chief began moving around the circle, pointing to each officer in turn, as he barked "You!" before indicating where each one was to go and what he or she was to do. When he got to the new arrivals, who were complete strangers, his tone softened slightly. "And why don't the two of you station yourself at the front door of the residence to control access."

The men nodded, but as they approached the porch, Gary couldn't maintain his silence any longer. "Can you believe this? Goddam *door duty!*" Just what we drove all the way out here to do: guard the goddam door!"

"Calm down, you hot head," Art responded. "He just said we should control access. I'd say all we need to do is go inside and lock the door behind us. That ought to control it, don't you think?"

122

I felt like I was in school again. The School of Life, that is. The lessons I was now hearing were just like the ones I'd heard over and over again the first time I'd been here. The sole difference now was that I could see Sir in the flesh, rather than an animated character on a monitor in his so-called classroom.

Thinking of the classroom reminded me of the couple who were still locked in the classroom. And I still hadn't thought of a way to get them out.

"You see, Mark," Sir was saying, "personal freedom has come at a great cost to modern civilization. Back when society subscribed to certain standards of behavior that everyone was expected to follow, or else, it was a much more pleasant world in which to live."

"Oh?" I said, not really paying attention to what he was saying. I needed to get out of there. I needed to get that couple out of there.

"That's right. There may have been less personal freedom, but it actually made daily living much more civilized. People had good manners back then. People placed their napkins on their laps. People wrote thank you notes. People said 'please' and 'thank you.' And, perhaps most notably, people spoke proper English."

"I'm not sure putting my napkin in my lap has made the world a much better place," I offered sarcastically. I could see he didn't appreciate that comment, but after a piercing look, he apparently decided to ignore it and continue on.

"My guiding principal, as you know, is that if people will simply adhere to a set of rules on which we all agree, we can eliminate all of society's ills." Pregnant pause. "But no," Sir said, shaking his head sadly, "people today care only for themselves. They insist on getting their own way, no matter what the cost. 'Do what feels good and others be damned!'" he said derisively.

I couldn't stand it anymore. "You can't be serious: 'We can eliminate *all* of society's 'ills'? Let me get this straight, Sir. You're saying that all we have to do is enforce good manners, and we'll have no more divorce? No more broken families? You're saying that all we must do is be more polite, and that will take care of the problem of battered and abused children, school drop-outs, unemployment, sickness, and disease?" I was fairly shouting now, my sarcasm palpable.

I was unprepared for his answer. "Precisely," he said with a perfectly straight face.

"You must be fucking kidding me," I said. He flinched at the word fucking, but there was no button he could push to shock me, so I was able to continue.

"Fine. So, let me ask you something, Sir. You have impeccable manners and you are unfailingly polite. So, may I ask you a favor?"

"Of course, Mark."

"May I have that gun, please? It's making me nervous." I said it as casually as I might say, "Please pass the salt and pepper." But I knew what the answer would be.

I watched him intently and waited. He realized that in light of everything he'd just said, he had no choice but to honor my very polite request. If nothing else, he knew that his own philosophy required a civilized end to the stand-off he'd created.

"Very well," he said, extending the gun in my direction. "I will honor your respectful request, but I must make a request in return: that you not turn it onto me."

123

I was dumbfounded. Fleetingly, I found myself wondering if maybe he was on to something. If every criminal and nut job merely did as they were requested, there would be far fewer hostages and murders, that's for sure.

Taking the gun, I did the only thing I could do: I turned it on him. "Sorry, Sir, no can do. I guess this kind of refutes your theory, doesn't it?"

I could tell he wasn't expecting this response.

"Now Mark..." he began, as though talking to a misbehaving child.

I cut him off, but I hope he appreciated the fact that I did so politely. Trying to maintain a civil tone – he'd taught me well – I quietly said, "Thank you. Now, if you will just come with me, let's go allow your new students their freedom..."

He rose without comment and turned toward the door through which we had entered. I saw the couple on the monitor, sitting just as they were when I first passed through the control room, cowering on the steel bed and looking like two frightened children.

"Mr. and Mrs. Martinez?" he said after flipping a switch on a microphone projecting out of the panel. "You are free to go now." But even as he spoke those words, I saw him nonchalantly reach for a large red button. I knew instinctively that it wasn't the lock release on the door. In that instant I knew – I'm not sure how – that I had been controlled by that very button, and the correction it doled out had been measured in volts. There was no way I was going to let this man harm these sweet people for doing nothing more than cleaning his fucking house.

So, just as he started to push it, I did the only thing I could have done. I tried to kill him. I aimed at his heart and pulled the trigger. Having never shot a gun in my life, I suppose I shouldn't be surprised that I hit his hand instead. He screamed, blood flew everywhere, and less than a second later, the lights went out, once again plunging us into darkness.

124

After that, things happened so quickly I almost lost track. I knew Sir was still standing less than three feet from me, but I couldn't see a thing. He screamed when I shot him and, if I'm not mistaken, he also yelled "fuck!" Then, he was silent. I could hear other noises, but I wasn't sure where they were coming from.

It seemed like forever, but it was probably only a minute or two before I heard the unmistakable sound of a doorway opening behind me, in Sir's study. "Stay right where you are!" a male voice shouted. It wasn't Troy but someone equally businesslike.

"Don't worry, man," I said, and then added, "I'm Mark Boston and I've just shot the owner of this house." It promptly occurred to me that if I'd murdered Sir, I had just admitted to it. It's weird what goes through your mind in moments of stress.

About the same time I heard a door opening from the other end of the room we were in, which I knew from walking through it earlier was the hallway outside the classroom.

"Hello?" a man's voice said, and I knew from the Spanish accent that it must be the housekeeper's husband.

"Mr. Martinez?" I said. "Mrs. Martinez?"
"Ja...?"

Just stay where you are, please, until they get the lights back on." I wondered how they had managed to walk out of the classroom when I knew Sir hadn't actually pushed any buttons on the control panel. I then realized the security system must de-activate when there is a power loss. Foolishly, I wondered if the same thing happened at a regular prison.

Again, it's weird the stuff you think about in moments of stress.

We needed light. It was creeping me out to be standing here in the dark, knowing Sir was only a few feet from me, probably bleeding to death – or worse.

"Hey, Mr. Martinez!" I said.

"*Si?*"

"Please turn around and feel around on the wall to see if there is a door going outdoors. If you can open it, we can get some light in here."

"*Si.*"

I waited and listened as I heard him feeling his way along the wall. Finally I heard the click of a door lock and the room was filled with a soft light. I realized the sun had gone down by now, so it was getting dark outside. I could see the handyman's figure in the doorway, his wife at his side. I noticed they were looking in horror at the body of their boss, sprawled on the floor between us. Behind me I heard the same businesslike voice say, "I think you can put that gun down now, sir. Why don't you put it on the floor and slide it toward me?" I did as I was told and a figure slowly moved toward me from what had previously been total darkness. A moment later he spoke into a walkie-talkie: "Briggs! It's all good. I'm toward the back of the house. I've got a guy on the floor with a gunshot wound, so let's get the paramedics back here. Oh, prop open the doors and then see if you can get the goddamned lights back on!"

"Will do," was the only response I heard.

A few minutes later the lights went back on and I could see the guy clearly. He was holding a gun aimed at *me*. Turning, I saw the housekeeper and her husband, looking completely ashen. Mrs. Martinez appeared to be propping herself up in the open doorway to the courtyard. Between us, on the floor in a pool of blood, was Sir.

I wondered if it was over.

Epilogue

Sir wasn't dead, in spite of the fact that anybody who saw him in that pool of blood would have guessed he was riddled with bullet holes. Troy still gives me shit about that, but I always remind him that it was the first time I'd ever fired a gun – and, besides, I tell him, "If I ever really wanted to kill anyone, you'll be first."

Sir was taken away, handcuffed to a gurney. The photos made front page news all over the world, although when I looked at the pictures later I decided it didn't look anything like him. Troy and Janet agreed and we wondered if anyone who saw the real man would identify him from the photos taken at the scene.

My own photo accompanied many of the stories, and my book sales soared.

I don't suppose anybody will be surprised that he got off with little more than a hand slap – although it would have to be on his left hand because I had in fact hit an artery in his right hand and it eventually was amputated. He probably didn't know how lucky he was: I'd aimed as his heart. Unbelievably, some time later Carson's attorneys filed a ten-million dollar civil lawsuit against me. Troy says it was just a ploy to intimidate me, and I'm ashamed to say it might have worked, but we never had to find out: the judge immediately dismissed it as "without merit."

I continue to marvel at how the rich seem to live by a different set of rules. As far as I know, Sir never spent even one night in jail. He had a 24-hour police guard at the hospital, of course, but that hardly counts as jail time. The day he was released he was taken directly to Denver where a battery of high-priced attorneys had pre-arranged his release pending trial. Bail was set at a couple of million dollars, which was probably chump change to him.

A lot of people were pissed that he was allowed to get out on bail, since he was charged with kidnapping, but that's what I mean about the rich getting different treatment than the rest of us. At the trial -- by a judge and not a jury, at his request, his attorneys – and there were lots of them – argued successfully that nobody was taken across state lines and nobody was killed or seriously injured and that "Mr. Kirkpatrick was just 'eccentric,' and only trying to help the less fortunate reconstruct their lives...blah, blah, blah." I'm not alone in wondering if the judge was dirty; that somehow Carson paid for his own freedom.

Much was made out of the fact that nobody was "seriously injured," except Carson, of course. I've always wondered about that, though. I am absolutely convinced that he had every intention of killing Greta and Manuel – and probably would have, by electrocution – if I hadn't stopped him. So, I think he was capable of it, but since the people he kidnapped were apparently homeless they couldn't connect him to any missing persons, especially since no "student records" were ever found, including mine.

Janet said she had seen my photograph, along with several others, on the wall behind Sir when she got a glimpse of him on the monitor, and about a dozen frames were located, but they were empty. The photos themselves were never located. I decided he had time to shred them before flushing the remains down the toilet of the bathroom next to his study.

Everybody feels sure there were other victims, but there's no way to prove it. I mentioned in court that he talked a lot about a guy named Harry, whom he described as his only failure, whatever that means. I'd love to talk to the guy, just to see if he's alive, if nothing else.

After the many delays Sir's attorneys were able to conjure up, the trial took place almost five years to the day after we freed Janet. Under intense questioning by Sir's legal team, Janet admitted that she was never physically or sexually abused and that he actually presented her with various gifts during her "incarceration."

The attorneys were hardest on me – observing correctly, as much as I hate to admit it – that a "normal" person who had been kidnapped and released might have mentioned it to the authorities along the way. I'm sure the jury was left with the impression that I was a bit flakey and certainly not harmed by what had happened to me. No argument there. They painted Sir as a well-intentioned, if somewhat "eccentric" do-gooder who had simply made "errors in judgement."

In the end, Sir was acquitted of the kidnapping charges, which created quite an outcry in the media, but it soon died down when everybody involved in the matter – including Sir, of course – refused to be interviewed.

Janet is fine, although she and Troy have gone their separate ways. I'm still friends with both of them, although I don't talk to either one about the other. Janet left the police force, and Troy has gotten his act together in terms of the pot smoking and actually seems a little more "alert."

Mr. and Mrs. Martinez filed a wrongful termination suit against Carson Kirkpatrick which was settled out of court. The settlement was sealed, but I heard it was around five mil. No wonder they packed up, moved to east Denver and opened a B&B. Apparently Mrs. Rosencranz and Mrs. Martinez see or talk to each other every day. When they go out in public, everybody says they look like twins, which pleases them.

The two sheriff's deputies from Summit County received commendations for initiative and valor which were well deserved. Troy and I were impressed when we found out they came to help us even though they were off-duty.

The last I heard, Sir had closed up the big mountain estate and moved back to the family home in Connecticut. One of the reporters asked at the end of his trial if he would be selling his Colorado home and all he said was, "Never." But I saw in a supermarket rag not long ago that he was building a big walled compound on the outskirts of Palm Springs, California.

Read a preview of the sequel to Makeovers, "Anything Will Help" on page 493.

Acknowledgments

I am forever indebted to Bradley Snyder for his invaluable editing skills and unconditional support.

Special thanks to our dear friends and neighbors, Geoff and Hellen Simpson who read every draft and offered helpful written suggestions.

My writing group was instructive and supportive, and I could tell they spent a great deal of time on the book because of all the red ink. I accepted every one of their suggestions, so a special thank you to Stella, Sally and Richard.

Our friend Annette Gilbert was kind enough to read my "final final" draft -- and found 31 changes that needed to be made. Next time she gets the first draft. Thanks, Annette.

The first "edition" of this book was printed on June 28, 2011. One of our dear friends and neighbors, Tom Keating, very kindly purchased a copy through Amazon. Some time later, he returned that copy with at least a hundred typos circled! I was mortified, of course, and the copy you hold in your hand -- error free, I hope -- is a direct result of his crack proofreading skills. Needless to say, I will never publish another book without his final check. Thank you, Tom. (And to the hundreds of you who purchased the earlier, error-ridden copies, my sincere apologies. Look at it this way: you own a collector's edition!)

So many other friends and family members have also encouraged my writing through the years, and I am grateful for their love and support. I have a terrific group of friends in Houston, Denver and Palm Springs who have been after me for years to "get busy!" Well, you know who you are, and I hope you're happy!

Finally, the names of my kids are omitted here on purpose because, as loving and supportive as they have always been, they may not be entirely pleased with my first effort and I don't want to embarrass them. The next book will be for them....

**Advance preview of the sequel to *Makeovers*,
Anything Will Help
Publication: early 2012**

Something in the eyes of the guy just ten inches from her darkened window wasn't quite right. He didn't have that vacant, drugged out look that most street beggars had. His eyes were bright and alive, like somebody was actually home on the other side.

She looked at the homemade cardboard sign he held up for her to see, like a kindergartner who had just made a picture for his teacher. She knew he couldn't see her -- unless he moved to the front of the car and looked through the windshield. It is illegal in California to have your front windshield completely darkened, the guy at the car place had told her, something about the cops needing to be able to see who's in the car. But she knew all about that, since she used to be a cop herself.

They all have a sign, don't they? Funny how they all look similar: hand-lettered in crude block letters, all ending with "God bless." Was there a special rack at OfficeMax? She could imagine the dividers: For Rent, For Sale, Help Wanted, and...Street Begging.

Her ex-boyfriend once said, "they need one that says 'I'm insane. God bless.'"

Now that would be truth in advertising, she agreed. They had both laughed uneasily at this lack of sensitivity, but she knew he didn't mean it. He was a cop at the time, too, and she knew how cops all tried to bluff their way through emotions like fear, anger, and even the sympathy any normal person would feel for the mentally ill. Mocking it kept it from getting to you.

She looked at the light, which appeared to be stuck on red. *C'mon! Let's get this show on the road!*

Annoyed, she realized the guy with the sign was still standing there. She allowed herself to read the words: "Anything will help. God bless."

Without taking her eyes from the guy and his sign, she felt for her purse on the passenger seat next to her. Finding it, she pulled it onto her lap and opened it quickly. Extracting a hundred dollar bill, she snapped the bag closed, made sure the traffic in front of her still wasn't working, and turned back to the closed window. She pushed the button twice in rapid succession which kept the window from automatically sliding all the way down. A mere crack appeared at the top of the door frame. She slid the bill out the window, retaining only one end by her fingertips. The guy looked startled, then ecstatic, as he pulled the bill into his hand. She pushed the button to return the window to it's original position. She barely noticed that he smiled broadly and mouthed the words "Thank you."

She had done her good deed for the day.

To request notification when "Anything Will Help" is ready for sale, please send an e-mail to rex@rexjohn.com

Author's note...

This is my first foray into the ever-changing world of publishing -- and what a ride it's been! Thank you for taking a chance on me, a new author.

I hope you liked "Makeovers," and if you did, I hope you will tell your friends. Today, the success of a new author depends almost entirely on word of mouth. Any kind words you pass on about my book will be greatly appreciated!

Rex John

Made in the USA
Charleston, SC
08 March 2012